THE
THOMA$
PROTOCOL

THE MONEY

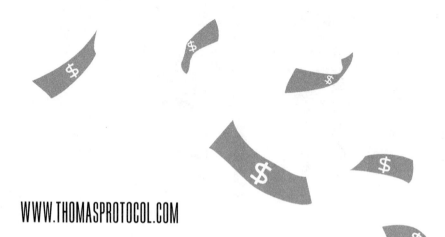

WWW.THOMASPROTOCOL.COM

◆ FriesenPress

Suite 300 - 990 Fort St
Victoria, BC, V8V 3K2
Canada

www.friesenpress.com

ISBN
978-1-5255-3386-0 (Hardcover)
978-1-5255-3387-7 (Paperback)
978-1-5255-3388-4 (eBook)

1. FICTION GENERAL

2. FICTION, ACTION & ADVENTURE

3. FICTION, ESPIONAGE

Distributed to the trade by The Ingram Book Company

Derek & Judy

THE THOMA$

PROTOCOL

THE MONEY

KEVIN McINTYRE

Kevin

CHAPTER 1

APRIL 16, ZURICH

Not bad, I thought. A nice British Airways flight from Vancouver to London Heathrow, and a quick change to Zurich. Business class all the way for a total of fourteen hours. Got a decent night's sleep, some tasty food, and a couple of pleasant drinks. I was tired, but running on a bit of adrenaline. This trip was all about solving a mystery regarding an inheritance. My inheritance to be exact, although I still had no idea how much it was, or really, who it was from.

I walked through the airport to the luggage area where the exits always were. I just had a carry-on bag, so I kept walking right out the secure-area door. Immediately outside the door in the arrivals lounge was a man in a black suit holding a sign for Stephen Thomas.

"Hi, that's me," I said, and pointed to the sign. "Stephen Thomas." I reached out my hand to shake his.

"Very good, sir, welcome to Zurich. I am Andrew Sutherland. If you will just follow me, please." Done shaking my hand, he took my bag and rolled it quickly along. I had a bit of trouble keeping up. This man had a swift stride. We exited the airport and walked over to a black Range Rover sitting in a special parking zone.

Pressing a key fob, he unlocked and then opened the right rear passenger door, motioning me inside. Once I was settled, he closed and locked my door. Then he raised the rear luggage-compartment door, put my bag inside, and climbed into the driver's seat.

"Sir, there is a cup of tea for you in that thermal mug in the cup holder, and a couple of newspapers for you on the other seat. Enjoy your ride. I will have you to the bank shortly."

With that, I knew the conversation was over. I knew he wasn't Swiss, because he had a pleasant prep-school English accent. *If his job is driving a car-service vehicle in Zurich, he must have been a poor student,* I thought to myself, but he seemed nice, and that's all that counted with me. I always liked nice people.

I took a sip of the tea. It had just the right amount of milk and sugar. "The Thomas formula," a friend of mine called it. We both knew black tea was better for us, but two sugars and milk just made it better all around.

I didn't feel like reading a newspaper. Reading in the car, or on a plane, always made me a bit queasy. I decided to just sit back and enjoy the sights on the ride into town from the Zurich Airport—or Flughafen Zürich if you were a local. My driver exited the airport property onto Highway 1 to Zurich.

"Excuse me, but how far is it to the bank?"

"Mr. Thomas, it's only about twelve kilometres, but with slower traffic in the city centre, it will take us a little over twenty minutes to arrive."

As the car rolled along, I thought about the past few days. Things like this didn't happen to guys like me. Since selling my successful insurance brokerage firm at age 52, my life was not exactly filled with business meetings. My business had been worth several million dollars, and selling it had been like winning a lottery for me. When you grow up in a comfortable middle-class or maybe even upper-middle-class background, you don't really change your lifestyle much even when you suddenly have money. I lived a pretty normal life, and since retiring it was even more uneventful. While I had three homes and I move around among them, beyond that I was just living a comfortable life. With places in Victoria and Vancouver, and a winter home in Arizona, life was very good as far as I was concerned, and I always considered myself to be a lucky guy.

A few days earlier, a lawyer had stopped by my home, asked to speak with me about an inheritance, and then told me that he needed me to fly to Zurich for a meeting in the next few days. He explained the importance and the urgency of the matter, and handed me a thick envelope. It all seemed pretty strange.

I had opened the envelope and pulled out thirty pages of various documents. The first was a letter from a Swiss bank, advising me that I was to receive an inheritance and inviting me to come to Zurich to meet with Herr Wilhelm Altermatt. There was no copy of the will and no amount stated other than a reference to it being "substantial." Although they assured me that I was who they were seeking, I was asked to bring some proof of my identity. They preferred my passport, driver's license, birth certificate, my latest tax return, social insurance card, property tax notice, and my Trusted Traveller or Nexus Card.

Another page gave me a contact number to call to arrange an airline ticket. They advised that they would pay all travel costs, including business-class return airfare, two nights hotel stay at some place called the Dolder Grand Hotel, and any incidental costs I might incur. A car and driver would meet me at the airport and drive me to the bank. They specifically stated a flight and airline they preferred I take, and that I should arrive in four days on the date they indicated.

I had to admit this seemed like a scam, but if it was one, it was damn professional. One of the benefits of early retirement was that I didn't have any plans over the next several weeks, so there was no reason not to avail myself of the free trip. After several calls with my personal lawyer, asking him to check it out and make sure it was all legitimate, I felt more comfortable that this was not a scam. He convinced me I should go, so I called the number for the travel agent listed in the envelope, and the arrangements were made.

I continued to watch the scenery as we whisked down the highway. It didn't take long before we were exiting onto congested streets, with very long lines of cars and very long names, like Stampfenbachstrasse and Beethovenstrasse. Seeing the name Beethovenstrasse, my brain made the musical connection and I found myself humming *"da da da duuum"* from Beethoven's Fifth Symphony, of which pretty much everyone knew the first four beats.

Soon we pulled over in front of a very old and stately building. The letters GCBS were emblazoned over the fifth-floor windows, and a more discreet brass sign, about a metre across, was mounted at ground level. The building appeared to be sandstone, and had first-floor windows nestled into large archways, each at least two storeys high. Each of the floors above held large tall windows, each fronted by a Juliette balcony. There were columns built into the façade and gargoyles on the roof. Not quite a gothic design, but it displayed certain elements of it. More of a palazzo style. It was built to be imposing and impressive, and to instil confidence and permanence in the minds of its clients. It was beautiful.

The driver got out and darted around the car to open my door, which I tried to open myself, only to find that I was unable to open it from the inside. He must have had the child locks on.

Seems about right, I smiled to myself.

I heard an electronic beep and the door opened, with the driver holding the handle and motioning me outside.

"I'll just grab my bag..."

"We will take care of it, Mr. Thomas. We will be waiting here until you are done your meeting, and then we'll escort you to your hotel. Please, let me escort you inside."

"Who is 'we'?"

"Oh … Mr. Thomas, I just meant me and our company … The 'royal we,' so to speak, sir."

"I am sure I can find my way to my hotel—"

"No sir, it's all arranged. We are here and at your service."

I followed him up to the huge, ornate brass and glass doors, and walked inside. The interior was much like the exterior: grand. Its ceiling was at least thirty feet high and hung with chandeliers alongside modern recessed lighting. There were deep, heavily carved mouldings, marble floors, and lots of brass wall sconces and fittings. While dimly lit, it was incredibly impressive. Everything seemed to be from a different era until your eyes settled on the technology in the room: sleek computer monitors, security cameras, and phones that appeared to be from outer space. What a contradiction.

"Wow," I heard myself murmuring.

My driver led me to a massive reception desk, where a lovely woman of about forty was waiting and smiling warmly. Before I could say a word, she greeted me.

"You must be Mr. Thomas. Welcome to our bank. Herr Altermatt is expecting you. Please give me just one moment." She spoke with a beautiful accent. Clear, crisp, professional, and oozing kindness. She had also used the proper Swiss German "Herr" when referencing her boss. She pressed a button on her phone, and then spoke softly into her headset, "Hello sir, Mr. Thomas has arrived to see you." She paused for a moment, listening, and then nodded. "Yes, Herr Altermatt."

Almost instantly, a well-dressed young man of about thirty appeared and introduced himself. One of those young executives, he was wearing a very slim-fitting suit, tailored shirt, and narrow shoes. His light brown hair was trimmed very short on the sides and combed very smartly on top. He was European trim and fit, with the benefit of youth. His smile was dazzling as he offered a slight nod and bow, then reached for my hand.

"Mr. Thomas, I am Jacob Van Vloten. If you would be kind enough to follow me, I will take you to Herr Altermatt's office."

Leaving my driver at the reception desk, I followed Jacob toward a set of three elevators located at the back of the bank. He walked a half step ahead of me and to my right, with his hands behind his back, turning his upper body slightly in my direction, so I would be sure to see his approving smile and his interested eyebrow-raises in response to any comments I should make. Van Vloten initiated small talk, inquiring about my flight, if I had ever been to Zurich before, the weather in Vancouver this time of year, if the ride from the airport had been satisfactory... the usual chitchat of strangers. He was quite charming.

We walked into the smallish, wood-panelled elevator, and Jacob pressed the fifth-floor button. As we rose slowly in the creaking old elevator, I inquired about meeting Mr. Altermatt and asked what he was like, knowing that young Jacob would struggle to find an answer that landed somewhere between fawning and truthful.

"Oh, Herr Altermatt has led this bank for nearly forty years. He is one of the two or three most important bankers in Zurich. He is also a very good man. In fact, well... he is also my grandfather." Jacob smiled apologetically and shrugged his shoulders just a little bit.

I smiled back at him and laughed.

"And," he continued, "if that's not enough, Mr. Thomas, my mother is Ursula Van Vloten, senior vice president of the bank. She loves this place and works harder than anyone to build it and ensure its success. She works very hard."

I nodded approvingly.

Well handled, I thought.

Odd to see that nepotism was so alive and well in Switzerland, but good that Jacob seemed to be working his way up the ladder.

"This is a beautiful old building," I commented. "How old is it?"

"It took five years to build and was completed in 1889. It is lovely, but I confess I am more of a modern-architecture fan myself." Jacob smiled at me.

The doors slid open on the fifth floor, and we walked about fifty feet down a hallway to an archway blocked by thick security glass. Using a key card, Jacob buzzed us through the doors and into an outer-office waiting area with several support-staff members present. Clearly this was the executive suite, with clearly marked office doors for the various important types who worked here. The support team seemed equally male and female. It might be an old bank, but it appeared inclusive and progressive. That pleased me.

A door to my left opened and out strode a man who introduced himself as Wilhelm Altermatt and welcomed me to the bank. We walked the length of his office, and I was shown to a chair across from his desk. Three male assistants in the room were quickly introduced. Like many people you meet too quickly, I immediately forgot their names, and in my head dubbed them assistants one, two, and three.

"Mr. Thomas, before we begin, we asked you to bring along some identification documents. May I see those first before we begin our talks? Jeffrey, please bring Mr. Thomas some tea."

I reached into my brown satchel briefcase and pulled out a file folder with various documents. I added my passport from my jacket pocket, and handed them all over to assistant number two, whose name later turned out to be Noah, to pass along to the elegantly dressed older man.

Jeffrey, assistant number one, carried over a tea tray with a teapot, a matching cream and sugar set, and a bone china teacup, and set it on the table next to me. He poured a rich brown cup of tea, then added milk and the right amount of sugar. He placed the teapot on a sideboard and quickly moved into position behind Altermatt, who was seated at his desk.

These guys do their homework, I thought. *Tea in the car, tea here. Prepared just the way I like it.*

Herr Altermatt, the president and managing director of the General Commercial Bank of Switzerland (the GCBS), studied the documents closely while his assistants looked over his shoulder. Over six feet tall, with a full head of white hair, Altermatt was likely carrying more than two hundred pounds on his large frame, but he carried it with authority and dignity. His hair was slicked back, and he wore dark-rimmed glasses. His dark suit, white shirt, and blue tie appeared to be almost his personal uniform. He probably dressed like that every day.

After studying my passport, Altermatt handed it over his shoulder without looking back. The third assistant scrutinized the document carefully with his squinted eyes, while holding his eyeglasses up on his forehead. Pulling out a black light, he double-checked it. The four of them looked at each other, and eyes all around grew in size as nods were exchanged.

I'd sat quietly as the documents were passed around between the four men, quite unsure of why I was really there. I knew it was sup-posed to about an inheritance, but I was not aware of having any Swiss relatives (or even any European relatives) who might have left me a sum of money, large or small. This seemed like the royal treat-ment for a Canadian boy like me. Yet here I sat, rather confused, in one of two large, heavy, leather wingback chairs, across the desk from four seemingly important men, while drinking a perfect cup of tea.

To relax, I crossed my legs in the casual way I often do, and then realized that might appear rude or lazy in this country. I quickly uncrossed them and sat up straight, trying to seem like a good guy.

Having just gotten off a plane, I felt unkempt and a bit sloppy compared to these tightly tailored men. I had not shaved in nearly twenty-four hours, but had washed up, brushed my teeth, and combed my hair on the plane. There was a shower in the first-class section, but I was in business class. I had to admit to doing an eye roll when I saw people heading to the shower on the plane. I wondered just how much of a princess you had to be to need to shower on a plane.

As they continued to study my papers, I cast my eyes around the room. The office I was in was huge, at least twenty feet wide and fifty or sixty feet long. Altermatt's desk was massive, ancient, and carved, with leather inserts on the surface. Behind the desk was a huge fireplace, with a mantel stretching the full sixteen feet to the high ceiling. The walls were all covered in square panels of some dark woodwork, and adorned with what appeared to be museum-grade masterpieces. The ceilings were coffered and three huge crystal chandeliers hung down, sending sparkles of light all over the room. At the far end of the huge space was a formal sitting area with two sofas, four deep armchairs, and a coffee table with a fantastic jade statue arching toward the ceiling. *It looks like a porpoise from here*, I thought, but wasn't entirely sure. There were various other objects and awards decorating the office, some likely of great value.

There was another fireplace at that end of the room. *It must have been cold in here a hundred and thirty years ago.* In between the desk area and the seating area was a meeting table with seats for eight people. This was a power office, but one built for power a long time ago. It had clearly been kept nearly intact in its original elegance, except for the modern computers, phone systems, and ergonomic desk chairs, which really did not fit the aura of the room. Clearly Herr Altermatt had a bad back, a big job, an interesting history, and likely a massive ego.

I wondered when Altermatt was going to get down to business. I am financially comfortable, as my mother would have described it. At least on paper, I'm worth about seven million dollars. Like most people's net worth, mine was mainly tied up in real estate and other investments, and I lived comfortably on the growth and dividends. Whatever this inheritance amount was, I didn't need it, but I figured it would be good fun money, and a nice way to top up my investment accounts.

I cleared my throat. The four of them looked across the huge desk at me.

"Herr … uh, Mr. Altermatt, how do I properly address you?"

He smiled back. "By all means, Mr. Thomas, call me Mr. Altermatt. 'Herr' is the word we use here in place of 'Mister.'"

"Mr. Altermatt then. I am not really sure what I am doing here, but this is all very interesting. I am hoping we can wrap this up, and perhaps before I head home, I can do a little sightseeing. How do we arrange to transfer whatever amount of money this involves to my bank?"

"Transfer? Oh, I am not sure you understand, Mr. Thomas. We have a sizeable portfolio, which has been designated to your control. It was designated by lineage, rather than by name, to the second son of the first son of Moses Thomas, if still alive in the year 2018. Your grandfather was Moses Thomas, and his first son was Maurice Thomas, and you, of course, are the second son of Maurice Thomas. You have an older brother and two older sisters, correct?"

I nodded.

"In 1918, a Mr. Wilbur Thomas deposited a sum of money into our hands, and we were instructed to invest and care for this money for one hundred years. He wanted us to strive for an annual rate of return of at least three percent, and he knew it would turn into a great deal of money. We made some very wise decisions some years, and

probably some very lucky decisions in other years. A few times it performed in the thirty percent range, while the odd year we did have a
loss. Still, with it compounding over the century, well … it has grown
enormously. We managed to average just over fourteen percent. We
foresaw the technology boom and got in early with IBM, Microsoft,
Apple, Dell, Amazon, Intel, and others. We invested in oil stocks
and properties around the world. We invested in things we knew
would be needed by a growing population: food production, energy,
real estate, transportation, weapons and armaments. You are now a
shareholder in many of the world's best publicly traded companies."

Really? I thought, and then shrugged mentally. *There's probably ten
shares in each company.*

CHAPTER 2

Two blocks away on a rooftop, a sniper was getting into position. Dressed as an electrician, he had earlier erected a small white tent over a rooftop heating unit and appeared to be working on it. He had draped the sides of the tent as well, leaving only about a one-foot section open, which had a clear view of the bank's entrance. No one in nearby buildings took any notice. Instead of tools, he was assembling a long-range sniper rifle with a silencer muzzle. It would not eliminate all noise, but would dampen the sound and make it harder to spot the location of the shooter. He had killed targets from thirty-six hundred yards. This target would be less than five hundred.

"This will be a piece of cake," he mumbled aloud to himself.

The kill order had been placed about three weeks earlier, with the exact go order to follow. His final go order had been placed on short notice, only three days earlier, which is when he received notification from the party that hired him that all the travel arrangements for the target had been confirmed though a New York travel agent and that the target would be in Zurich.

From his vantage point, he had a clear line of sight over the Paradeplatz and right into the main entrance of the bank. He mounted the rifle on a tripod and used the scope like a set of binoculars to watch the entrance. It was estimated that the meeting would be less than an hour, and that the subject would exit the building and get into the car with the driver who had brought him from the airport. The vehicle remained parked and waiting, and the driver was still inside the bank. This area was not open to normal traffic, so it was very unusual to see three more black Range Rovers wheel up and get in line with the original one. One pulled in front of the parked one, and the other two lined up behind it.

Four Range Rovers, all in a row. To the shooter, it kind of sounded like a nursery rhyme.

He remained keenly aware of his surroundings, but stayed focused on the crosshairs of his gun scope… trained on the front door of the bank.

CHAPTER 3

"Well, this is all very interesting, Mr. Altermatt, but perhaps you can tell me how much money this is. Enough to buy us all a few drinks and dinner?" I joked.

"Mr. Thomas, I am glad you are already seated. It seems that near the end of the First World War, Wilbur Thomas deposited a very substantial sum of money into our bank."

"Yes, you have already made that clear." I confess I was growing frustrated and probably sounded a bit arrogant at the moment.

I was growing excited but tried to seem calm and businesslike. Perhaps I had underestimated. Inside my head I was doing the math, and realized that, even with minimal growth of whatever classified in 1918 as a "substantial" deposit, it would likely have grown to be worth several million dollars today. This was getting more interesting by the minute. Visions of a Rolls Royce popped into my head. So gaudy, but perfect. I would never buy such a silly car, but I did drool over them once in a while.

"Mr. Thomas, there is an envelope, sealed one hundred years ago, for you to read first. Sorry for the apparent theatrics, but we are following the instructions prescribed a very long time ago by your great uncle."

All right, I thought. *I'll continue to play along with the melodrama.*

I am pretty sure I did an eye roll, but then felt guilty for doing it. The man was only doing his job.

A very yellowed envelope of a thick, beautiful paper stock was placed on a silver tray and brought around the desk by assistant number two, Noah, who bowed slightly to lower the tray to my level. With a grand flourish, Altermatt's third assistant handed me a gold letter opener, handle first.

I took the opener and slit open the flap of the envelope. This was a fascinating moment, and certainly one that my favourite fictional character, Sherlock Holmes, would have loved. My brain scrolled though words in my head and arrived at *The Mystery of the Swiss Letter* as the title Sir Arthur Conan Doyle might have chosen for this crazy situation. I had read every one of his books, and smirked at my internal joke.

I pulled out the ancient letter and held it with the reverence it deserved. No one had seen this letter for over a hundred years. I slipped on my reading glasses. The paper was crisp but delicate from age, and I did not want to damage it. The letter alone was pretty cool. It was written with a fountain pen, clearly by a person with a rough-hewn handwriting style, but the somewhat faded ink was clear and the message properly written. I studied the look and feel of it, the rough edges of the paper, the fold lines, and even the smell. My thumb and index finger rubbed the paper to gauge its feel.

It read:

Dear Great Nephew,

You are the second son of the first son of Moses Thomas, so you are my great nephew. Moses was my brother, and I always admired him as a man of hard work and honesty. I know that his offspring will be men of good stock, and that you must be a man of integrity. I cannot say that this money came easily, nor did it come completely honestly, but as soon as I had it, I knew that I could not keep it. I thought perhaps, if left for a while, it could lose its dirty stench and do some good one day.

I have a set of rules for you to follow:

1. I trust you to use your judgement however you see fit.
2. Take 10 percent of the money for yourself to live a life I would only have dreamed of.
3. Use the balance to do good works for others. Apply a simple protocol to every expenditure: Will this make the world a better place?

It will make me happy, whether I ended up in heaven or down below, to know that my deeds finally did some good.

Go now, and make the world a better place. I am hoping that this money might grow to be worth much more by the time you receive it. I know this is a big responsibility, but if you are a Thomas, I know you are the man for the job.

Sincerely,
Wilbur Thomas,
April 17, 1918

I looked up from the letter, quite excited, but also feeling the weight of the moment. I had never even heard of Wilbur Thomas. I never knew anyone related to my grandfather. He had died when I was a very small boy. This all seemed insane ...

The four men looked at me with anticipation, desperately wanting to know what the letter said. I demurred, folded it, slid it back into the envelope, and slipped it into my left inside suit-jacket pocket. That part about "nor did it come completely honestly" made me cautious.

"Well, gentlemen, how much money are we talking about? Seems I have some hundred-year-old instructions to complete. And this sounds like it might be a lot of fun."

"The amount is significant," Altermatt said, almost stammering.

"Fair enough. How much, Mr. Altermatt? Could we please stop with all the mystery?"

"Of course, Mr. Thomas, I have the number right here. I want you to know that we are here for you, to hold the funds, manage them, and anything we need to do to assist you. My team is your team, and we are at your disposal."

Oh ... my ... God, I slowly uttered inside my head. *Get on with it, man! This is getting silly.*

My weariness from travel and anticipation was setting in. I was losing both my patience and my usual pleasant disposition. *Let me take this money, at whatever amount the old guy dreamed it would grow into, and make a few donations already! Holy shit, these Swiss love their fucking banking ... Cut the drama already, and let's get on with it.*

With a very subtle wave of a finger and an approving nod from Mr. Altermatt, his assistant Noah moved around the desk, carrying the silver tray again with yet another small envelope on it. This envelope was unsealed. He bowed to me slightly as I lifted the envelope from the tray and slipped out the card inside.

Oh ... my ... God ... indeed. That was a very large number. Fourteen digits long. I read it three times, counting the digits back to make sure I was correct.

My eyes flicked upward and met Altermatt's. He smiled his most obsequious smile yet. My heart was pounding, and due to the rushing blood, I was not sure I could hear anymore.

I felt weak as I reached with a trembling hand to have a sip of tea, wishing for the first time that it was something stronger.

Now at least, I understood all the fuss.

CHAPTER 4

"This dollar figure is real, Mr. Altermatt? It can't possibly be ..."

"Yes, it certainly can be, and it most assuredly is. I am sure you can imagine that it is not sitting in cash in our bank. It is invested in literally thousands of stocks, bonds, and funds all over the world, as well as commercial real estate, mortgages, and other financial instruments.

"Well, of course ... No, it wouldn't be sitting in cash."

"Mr. Thomas, it is important to realize the destruction and havoc that the sudden liquidation of such massive assets could do. We need a measured, cautious approach. If we dumped stocks or bonds too quickly, we could cause serious damage to the markets, to individual companies and organizations, and even to certain economies."

It was a good lesson for me, and I would try to remember it.

Altermatt continued. "Now, we have made provisions for you. We knew that once you were aware that this was now your responsibility, you would have certain immediate needs, especially in terms of security issues and personal protection."

My mind was reeling. Once people knew about this, my life was probably in immediate danger. If I could rely on the movies I had watched about the superrich, I needed my lawyer (probably a few actually), a security team, and a secure way to get out of this building and back home to Vancouver. Once there, I would be safe and able to get my head screwed on straight and figure out my next steps. This was inconceivable. I wasn't sure I even wanted any of this.

"Mr. Altermatt, what if I don't want this money. I assume I can refuse it?"

Altermatt looked utterly stunned. One of his assistants audibly gasped. Altermatt began to stutter and stammer his disbelief, voicing a few barely intelligible syllables before taking a deep breath and gathering himself.

"Mr. Thomas," he said, after a few moments, "I suppose that, if you did not want it, we would have to go on to the next named recipient."

"May I ask who that is?"

"I normally wouldn't say, but in this case … if you were unavailable, or deceased, the entire amount was to go to the United States Treasury for the benefit of the United States military. It was specified to be used for the purchase of weapons to deter future wars."

"Oh brother, helping veterans would be great, but not military stockpiling. Okay, carry on. I'll do it."

They all looked visibly relieved, and Altermatt quickly nodded and continued his speech. "Mr. Thomas, to provide you with personal security, and I do hope you will approve, we have arranged some things on your behalf, for the next several weeks and onward. Outside this office is a twelve-man security team. They are all former British Special Forces and work for a security firm that is owned, well … by you now. They will take you to your hotel, where we have arranged an appropriately secure suite for you and your new team. There is a plane, a brand-new extended-range private jet, I forget the model, outfitted and staffed for your travel needs, and there are four armoured Range Rover SUVs to accommodate your travel in the city. We have been preparing for this day for the past ten years."

My mind was spinning, and he could see I was dumbfounded.

"If I may suggest, take this evening, get a good night's sleep at your hotel, and return here in the morning, at which time we will take care of the details. There are forms and some other documents for you to sign. We have arranged for caviar, the finest champagne, and a lobster dinner for you tonight in your suite to celebrate and enjoy. You will need some time to take all this in, but we are here to help you move into this incredible next phase of your life. Shall we see you tomorrow morning, at say ten o'clock?"

In a rare moment for me, I was relatively speechless, but also excited and scared. My personal safety, with this kind of wealth, was my initial concern. I confess I felt nervous and my stomach was churning.

"Who knows about all this? Who knows I am here? How can we keep this quiet for a few weeks?"

"Mr. Thomas, we work in the utmost confidentiality at all times with all our clients. Your security detail know you are a man of wealth, but not the amount in question. They believe you are a successful Canadian businessman here to collect an inheritance, and that we have engaged them for you because there have been concerns for your safety. That is all they know at this point. They are here to, uh … well, 'babysit' you … until we tell them they are done. I hope that meets with your approval."

"Thank you, Mr. Altermatt. You have no idea what this all feels like. It seems as though you have thought of everything. I look forward to working with you and your bank for years to come."

A genuine smile spread across the rather serious face of Altermatt, and he appeared comforted by my words. His assistants all smiled at each other and at me.

"By the way, Mr. Thomas, at your instruction, we will move an initial amount into your Canadian accounts, so that you can take care of all your immediate needs and begin the changes. We have prepared a wire transfer in the amount of ten billion American dollars. When you are ready, it will appear in your account within twenty-four hours and arrive in sums of about one billion a day for the next ten business days."

"This is crazy…absolutely insane…" I looked at Altermatt, and he again smiled knowingly and actually chuckled a little.

"Mr. Thomas, trust me, this is going to be an amazing new chapter in your life. Now, go enjoy some champagne, relax, and try to get some rest. You must be exhausted from your travel. Let me introduce you to the head of your security detail."

Altermatt rose from behind his desk and came over to me. As I stood, he reached out to shake my hand warmly, gripping my forearm with his left hand. He smiled and nodded reassuringly. I have to admit, he had a way of making it seem that everything would be okay.

As he turned toward his office door, it opened and a square-jawed man of about forty entered. He was dressed in a black business suit, white shirt, and black tie. Formal, fit, and powerful, he looked oddly familiar, even in my current stupor. Quick introductions were made, and I realized this was the same man who had picked me up at the airport: Andrew Sutherland. He spoke into his sleeve and three more men appeared. Two moved behind me while he and the other man stood on either side of me. My name was spoken softly and the lead security man gestured toward the door. We exited the office, heading through the bank toward the elevators, down to the main floor, and finally toward the front door. The guards all looked alike: same suits, same businesslike haircuts, all about six feet tall, and all appearing physically ripped.

It seemed like a few heads turned at this unusual sight walking through the bank, and I felt a bit like a prize racehorse being strutted out onto the racetrack, or maybe a prisoner being escorted off to jail. I wasn't sure yet which image seemed more appropriate.

My four security agents stopped in the middle of the bank, and motioned me to come with them. We made a ninety-degree turn and headed for a side door that was normally locked tight and sealed. An elderly bank guard had just unlocked it and held the door open for me, while the five of us stood and waited in the alcove.

More security men were just inside the main bank doors at the other end of the bank, from which I had originally entered. My understanding later was that four others were stationed outside that front entrance, and by this point, had settled into the driver's seats of all their vehicles. The security "act" now began. One of the four remaining guards in the bank removed his jacket, so he was in a white shirt and tie. He and the remaining guards exited with the three of them pretending to be guarding the fourth, whose shirt and tie made him stand out from the others. They were all busily scanning their surroundings, looking for threats. None were apparent.

Once they had loaded their "protectee" into the back of the third vehicle, the Range Rovers moved forward in unison and pulled tight against the side of the bank building, leaving about three feet of space, at which point my four bodyguards and I immediately exited by the side door, and were quickly inside the vehicles. The men stayed very close to me. They closed the heavy car door as soon as I was seated, and it immediately locked. Then the men "moved out," getting into their cars and into position.

In my Range Rover, a driver was in the front seat and the lead security man, Andrew, climbed into the front passenger seat. All twelve men were now in the four vehicles. A few commands were spoken into sleeves, and less than seven seconds later, we were moving. We roared away from Paradeplatz, where the bank was located, and turned onto Bahnhofstrasse.

Jesus. Next, I will be exiting through kitchens and service entrances. Hey, isn't that how Bobby Kennedy got shot?

A little chill ran down my spine.

CHAPTER 5

Back on the rooftop inside the repair tent, the sniper had repacked his gear and was about to leave. He never had a clean shot. The bodyguards had stayed too close. Sure, he could have unleashed a bloodbath and taken out a few people, but in the melee that would have ensued, the target would likely have escaped and then would be alerted to impending danger.

He was pretty sure that the guy in the white shirt was not his target anyway. They probably stuffed the actual guy into the car when they stopped next to the bank building, which was out of his line of sight. They would have other kill opportunities. But he knew it needed to happen soon.

The tent folded down quickly, and he abandoned it behind the ventilation system. It was more important to clear the area quickly than to worry about a stupid tent.

Once he was back in his electrical-service truck, he drove several blocks away and then pulled over. He called a special secure line and tapped in a code.

"Report?"

"Negative."

The line went dead.

CHAPTER 6

"Andrew, where are you taking me anyway?"

"Mr. Thomas, we are taking you to the Dolder Grand Hotel. It is the best hotel in Zurich, sir. It is located on Adlisberg Hill about two hundred metres higher than the city centre, so the views are spectacular. It is just a few kilometres away. We will have you there soon, Mr. Thomas."

"This rig is armoured, isn't it?" I could tell by the thick window glass and the resultant smaller window frames that were needed to accommodate it. I had thought the windows seemed strange when he picked me up at the airport, but it just had not registered to me at the time.

I got no response from the front seat.

"Andrew, would it be too much to ask you to call me 'Steve'?"

"Thank you, Mr. Thomas, that's very kind of you, but we will be calling you 'Mr. Thomas' or 'sir.'" And then, with a slight turn of his head toward the rear seat and a smirk on his face, he said, "That's just how we roll, sir!" The driver's reaction showed that he enjoyed his little joke too.

We all chuckled slightly, my laughter more from nerves than anything else. I was glad to see a little humanity in him, but realized that Andrew was keeping his distance for professional reasons, and I had to respect him for that.

I kept quiet in the backseat after that. There was some traffic to contend with and the drivers did an amazing job of keeping the vehicles never more than ten feet apart. No one seemed too concerned that our four-SUV convoy ran a few lights in order to stay together. A few horns were blown, but beyond that, the Swiss drivers seemed calm and considerate. I didn't realize until later that each SUV had blue and red lights flashing under the front grill, and the rear car had similar lights flashing in the rear window. To the public, I'm sure this appeared to be some sort of head of state motorcade or something. This was getting wilder by the minute.

As the Dolder Grand Hotel came into view, it became clear that the original section of the hotel was probably older than the bank building I had just left. Turned out it was built in 1899. Later, I read the brochure in the room, and it said it had a hundred and seventy-three rooms, conference facilities, restaurants, a bar, and a spa. *Cool place*, I thought. *Probably haunted.* It was a like a Camelot-style castle with a modern addition wrapped around it. Very cool.

As we wheeled up to the front portico of the hotel, the motorcade positioned itself so that my vehicle door was directly in front of the entrance.

Andrew turned around. "Now, Mr. Thomas, we will wait a few seconds. The security team will exit their vehicles and take up their posts. Then I will exit the vehicle, open your door, and escort you inside. Please follow my lead and instructions. Oh, and it looks like the hotel manager has come to say hello."

One of the guards motioned the manger to go back inside the hotel. He looked offended but did as instructed.

"Okay, let's go."

The men were in position. The four drivers stayed in their seats, four of the men entered the hotel lobby, and the remaining four, including Andrew, stood near my door. Andrew opened my door, and I stepped out of the vehicle and stood there a bit awkwardly, but for just a second. Andrew motioned me forward and closed the door.

The motorcade stayed in place to provide a physical barrier. After we had entered the building, the motorcade slowly rolled away to a secure parking area.

Walking up a couple of steps and into the lobby, with one man on either side of me and two behind, I felt like a bit of an imposter. This felt like some kind of a game or act.

Seriously Stephen, I asked myself, *what the hell are you doing here?*

CHAPTER 7

We were barely inside the lobby when a grand voice boomed a welcome. The manager reached for my hand and began to shake it vigorously.

"Mr. Thomas, welcome to the Dolder Grand Hotel. I am Urs Hurlimann. Mr. Altermatt from the bank tells me you are his best client and to do whatever it takes to make sure you are comfortable. Your suite is ready for you. May I show you upstairs?"

I looked at Andrew, and he nodded subtly.

Putting on my best confident-and-in-control act, I nodded calmly. "Thank you, Mr. Hurlimann, I am looking forward to some dinner and some rest."

Four security men remained in the lobby. Two had gone ahead to secure the room, and the other four were with me and Mr. Hurlimann.

How odd this all felt, kept echoing through my head, and yet… I was elated somehow too. I was awash in emotions. What the hell was going on? My emotions were up and then down, excited and then scared. I reached up and touched my fifty-five-year-old face, confirming my suspicion that a huge grin was foolishly splashed across it. Inside my head, I breathed, *Fuuuck meeeeee.*

Well, I thought, *I always dreamed of being president of the United States when I was a kid; this almost seems like what I imagined.* The US presidency was a bit of a tough goal for a Canadian to achieve, but honestly, I'd just wanted the motorcade, the mansion, the helicopter, and Air Force One. The rest seemed like a lot of work.

At this point, I was not surprised when we arrived at the royal suite. I mean, really… where else would I have stayed, right? In the past, the closest I'd come to the royal suite was a room with Royale brand toilet paper. Unless I was on an expense account, I had always been pretty cheap with hotels, before I sold my business. Afterwards, though I'd tried to book the presidential suite at two different hotels, each time they turned out to be booked. Simple bad luck really.

It reminded me of that old joke where the customer arrives at his hotel to find they are completely booked. There are no rooms available. The man says to the desk clerk, "So, you are telling me if the president of the United States walked in here right now, you wouldn't have a room for him?" The clerk thinks for a moment and replies, "Well, if it was the president, I guess we would have a room for him." To this, the man replies, "Great! The president isn't coming, so I'll take *his* room."

Mr. Hurlimann opened the door and walked in ahead of me, then turned as though welcoming me to his home. Two security men came from inside the unit to greet us. They looked at Andrew and said quickly and firmly, "All secure, sir." Hurlimann guided me from room to room. The suite had a lovely living room with very modern furniture and sleek lines, two normal bedrooms with their own baths, and a master suite with a huge bed and a sumptuous bath. There was also a small kitchen and bar area, fully stocked with drinks and treats, a dining room, and an office area. There was a knock at the door, and a butler entered with a cart carrying a bucket of ice with champagne, an iced dish with what looked like beluga caviar, with all the trimmings, and a charcuterie plate with meats, cheeses, olives, and berries.

Mr. Hurlimann turned to me one last time before leaving. "With your agreement, Mr. Thomas, we will be bringing up some incredible Atlantic lobster for your dinner at seven. We have secured some one-pound lobster tails, and they are sweet and succulent. If there is anything you need, my direct number is on a card next to every phone. Please, call me."

"Thank you for everything, Mr. Hurlimann; you have been too kind. Everything is perfect, and dinner sounds like it will be perfect too. One small favour … could you please provide my security detail with anything they need as well, in terms of rooms, food, and so on?"

"It is already taken care of, sir."

I looked over at Andrew, and he smiled and nodded in approval. As the door closed behind Hurlimann, Andrew said, "I like the way you roll too, sir."

We both laughed. It was a good stress relief.

CHAPTER 8

"Now, Mr. Thomas," Andrew said, "I need about five minutes of your time to brief you on procedures while you are here. Would right now be alright?"

"Sure, let's sit down at that dining table and chat. Besides, that's where they put the food and champagne."

Andrew nodded and joined me there. "First of all, I am told that you have had quite a day. I hope you will forgive Mr. Altermatt; he did not want to alarm you with all this security. My team and I do not risk our lives without knowing who and why we are protecting someone, so I was brought into the circle of trust in terms of what is happening to you. I know that you were advised of a massive inheritance today, and precautions are being taken. No one gets this kind of security treatment unless it was a massive amount, so on that basis, my men and I will assume there are either existing threats or possible threats emanating from the existence of that money.

"We will be stationed as follows: Four men will remain with and protect the vehicles; four men will be in the lobby; and there will be four men who will remain inside this suite with you, rotating sleeping shifts in the two extra bedrooms. There will be two men outside your front door in the hallway. There will be a further twelve men stationed throughout the hotel and occupying the rooms on either side of this suite."

I had been counting as he spoke and now butted in. "That is twenty-seven men including you, Andrew. That's a lot of people. Should I be frightened?"

"No, not at all, sir. Anyone who has an issue with you should be frightened." He smiled when he said that. "You will have your dinner in the suite tonight, as well as breakfast tomorrow. There will be a guard in the kitchen watching the food preparation. You can feel comfortable eating anything prepared for you." He pointed to what had already been delivered to the room. "We have already been on duty, watching the preparation of all this.

"Sleep when you like, and in the morning, we will wake you at eight-thirty. At nine thirty-five, we will leave here and return to the bank. I have been told that your meeting should last about two hours, and then you will be free for the balance of the day, during which time I have arranged for you to be looked after in this suite by a masseur." Andrew smiled again. "You are getting pampered tomorrow. Then the plan is that, at seven o'clock, Mr. Altermatt will come here and join you for a quiet dinner in your dining room.

"At nine thirty p.m., we will be taking you to the airport for your trip home. We expect to be wheels up at eleven o'clock."

"I thought I was staying here for two nights and leaving on the eighteenth."

Andrew was firm and very polite. "That's what we wanted people to think. You will be home safe in Vancouver before you were even supposed to leave Zurich. I am sorry, but you will be leaving tomorrow night, boarding a private aircraft for a direct flight back to Vancouver. The pilot and crew are all former British military. They will get you home, and are all, in fact, employed by you now. My team have international credentials, every one of them is single, and we all work for you. We are employed by Guardian Security, and so are the pilots and crew, and even though you may not know this yet, you own Guardian Security. We love our work, and we are very good at it. We have never lost a client. Ever!"

Good to know.

CHAPTER 9

Andrew remained sitting at the table after we had finished our security chat.

The two envelopes were still in my jacket pocket. I reached in and fished out the smaller of the two, slid out the paper with the amount of the inheritance, looked at it, and slid it back in.

I smiled and shook my head. *Oh my God. Crazy shit… A little over twenty-seven trillion dollars. How is this remotely possible? And it's in US dollars to boot. I wonder if I should show it to Andrew.*

I pondered this for a moment, looking at the man. Finally, I took a deep breath and decided to dive in.

"Andrew, I need someone to talk to right now, and you're it. This all seems impossible, but yes, I am to receive a massive inheritance … of inconceivable proportions. My job will be to give ninety percent of it away. In fact, I have already decided it will be closer to ninety-nine percent.

"I am supposed to 'make the world a better place' with these funds. I'm not sure how exactly, but it is going to feel incredible doing it. I would very much like to have you along for the ride. I will want the best of the best in security, and I will be very generous, I can assure you. What do your team members make per year?"

"Guardian pays well, about a hundred thousand BPS a year, or about one hundred forty thousand US."

"Well, I think double that for my detail is appropriate, and three times for you. I need a loyal and motivated team to help me do nothing but good work and to keep me safe."

Andrew's hand extended quickly to seal the deal. We shook and both smiled. I liked this guy, but wished I had his courage and steel.

"I know already that my life will never be the same after tomorrow's meeting. In the next few days, we will sort out a business plan and working structure for going forward, but let's assume for now that you are head of security operations, and all that entails."

Andrew nodded in agreement.

"I hope to keep all this under wraps for a few weeks, so we can get security and other processes in place, and form a corporate structure to begin donating funds, although I have no idea to whom or to where. I haven't had much time to think yet, but those are the immediate ideas I've come up with.

"Andrew, I think you should know the amount, and I know I can trust you to say nothing about it for now." I looked at him, and he nodded so effortlessly that I knew it could have gone unsaid. I was glad.

I slid the card in its envelope across the table. "Soon, we will probably hold a press conference, and then the world will turn upside down." Andrew looked me straight in the eyes as he reached for the card, frowning slightly in confusion at how serious I was being.

He pulled back the flap and then peered inside at the number. "What the fuck…" he said in a breathy tone, slouching in his chair for just a moment and then quickly straightening and looking at me.

"Oh, I am sorry, sir, excuse me."

I laughed. "'What the fuck' is just about right, Andrew. Just about right. Weirdest fucking thing I could have ever imagined. You want a drink?"

"Absolutely not, sir! But I will stay with you and chat if you like, while you enjoy yourself. I think we are safe for this evening."

I got up, went to the small kitchen, and came back with a can of Coke for Andrew, and poured some champagne for myself. He gratefully accepted. The rest of the food was already on the dining table, and I began to enjoy it. I'd never had beluga caviar. Tasted a lot like fish eggs, and I'm sorry to say, it just wasn't that good. I chuckled. Andrew had a couple of bites, but his face said his lips were fibbing when he said he liked it.

I checked again with Andrew that his men were looked after, in terms of their care and feeding. He confirmed it was all in hand. He smiled. "Not our first rodeo, sir."

"You have a lot of rodeos in the UK, do you?"

He grinned at me.

I had to say, the champagne was excellent. It was a bottle of Dom Pérignon P2 Brut Rose, 1995. I looked it up on my iPad—$800 a bottle. So, it was tasty, but let's be realistic, not $800 tasty. I tried not to waste any though. The most I had ever spent on champagne at the store was $170. I prefer a brand called Tsarina, which runs about one hundred dollars a bottle. I guess I just don't have the taste buds of the superrich yet.

My biggest personal dream, which I'd assumed would go unfulfilled forever, was to simply ride in a private jet. Now it looked like I was going to own one. What an upgrade! I wondered if it was a Gulfstream G650. I confess to nearly having an airplane obsession, and had read all about them. They were just so pretty.

"So, Andrew, this private plane … have you seen it?"

"Gorgeous and unreal, sir. I have never seen anything like it. It's a Boeing 787 Dreamliner BBJ, and it is configured for private use. I have a team on board guarding it, sir."

I'm sure my eyes bulged out of my head. "Holy shit! A Dreamliner? Oh my God!" I slapped my hand on the table, incredulous at the news.

"Yup, it sure is, sir. It has a private stateroom in the midsection with a bedroom, a private washroom, and a private sitting room. There is a great, full kitchen galley, nice, cushy seating areas, and lots of room for your security team just behind your stateroom. Tables and couches … the sort of things one normally finds in private jets, seating an additional twenty-four more people. So, all in, I think there is seating for sixty-two in there, plus the flight deck and crew seating. There are five washrooms, a shower, and crew sleeping quarters up above. There will be plenty of room for everyone. You, sir, will be travelling in style."

"A shower, huh?" I shook my head and laughed. I guess, if I didn't have to line up to use it, the darn thing would probably be great.

"Sorry, Andrew, what's your last name again?"

"It's Sutherland, sir."

"And out of respect for you and your men, what do I call you?"

"Well, sir, Andrew works just fine, and besides, I prefer it."

"I know how you feel. I am not used to constantly being called 'sir' or 'mister.'"

"For us, we need that emotional separation. My team will never be so relaxed in their speech with you, because it leads to being relaxed in their roles and that *cannot* happen. Just like in the military, there is a rank and order, and we are all trained in it and respond to it. My men will treat you like a four-star general, in terms of their respect and deference to you, and that is the way we want it to be, sir. You can call my men by their first or last names, once you learn them, or simply call them 'agent.' They will not be offended."

"Oh my God, Andrew …" I sighed and shook my head. "What an insane day. I woke up on a plane, wandered through an airport, had a meeting, and suddenly require two dozen personal security guards and a private jet. I hope I can sleep tonight."

"You know what I hope, sir? I hope you *can* make the world a better place, and I am honoured to help you facilitate that process any way I can. No one likes guarding some shitbag, sleezeball, or corrupt government official just for a paycheck. When we get to do this for passion, along with the money … well, that's the dream job."

He smiled and began to apologize for swearing again. I waved him off with my hand and a don't-worry-about-it look. "I am not so pure, Andrew; colourful language in private is the least of my worries. So … you picked me up at the airport and you did so all alone, but then an hour later, I left the bank with a huge security detail."

"You only thought I was alone. The other three cars were all there, but you had no reason to look for them. We knew that pretty much no one would know who you were when you arrived, and so there would be a very limited risk, but just in case, my men were following you from the moment you boarded your plane."

"Boarded?"

"Boarded. Actually, even before that. Remember, we have *never* lost a client. That's why everyone was so specific about the flights and travel days. We needed to be sure we were on the same flight. I had four men flying with you. The pod in front of you, behind you, and across the aisle from you were all my men. Oh, and your cab to the airport? One of ours too. And you probably didn't notice, but we had two other cabs following yours."

"You said there were four of your men on the plane; where was the fourth?"

"Sadly, for him, he was in the very rear of economy, so he could keep an eye on the whole passenger cabin."

"Fuck … You guys are good. I never noticed a thing, but I guess that's the whole idea."

"Yes, sir. Ideally with security, unless we *want* to be seen, we want you to be able to live your life and move about normally, with us relatively invisible, seamless, and innocuous. For example, leaving the bank and arriving here, we wanted to show a presence to ward off anyone. This hotel hosts many heads of state and important people, so this is not really unusual here. Even less so in Geneva."

The doorbell to the suite rang, and Andrew stood up. One of his men moved to answer the door. It was the butler with the dinner that had been promised. He spread it out on the table with a flourish and was ushered out. I was embarrassed we had not tipped him, but was told by Andrew that it was all looked after.

Shellfish is probably my favourite meal, and this was shell-fish extraordinaire. The meat from two huge lobster tails probably totalled about a pound and a half of meat, and it was waiting for a tasting. There were sauces and butter for dipping and dunking. I confess to eating most of it. Any rumours of me eating all of it are purely … well … speculation. I was stuffed, though, and very tired. It was only eight fifteen, but with jet lag and such, I was done. It was time for bed.

Andrew escorted me to my room, double-checked his men's work and that the windows were locked, and said good night. I stripped off my clothes, tossed them on a chair, and wandered into the bathroom. My shaving kit was laid out on the counter. I suddenly remembered my suitcase, which I had not seen since we left the airport. I went back into the bedroom and found it in the closet, and saw that my clothes were hung and pressed. This was definitely a full-service hotel. While looking in the mirror, brushing my teeth, I saw the early wrinkles of a fifty-five-year-old man, with salt-and-pepper hair and a few too many extra pounds.

On the inside, I felt like I had not aged mentally after thirty-five. I smiled at myself, embarrassed by my physique, and committed (for about the 912th time) to do better. Over the years, I had joined several gyms, each time committing to doing better. Twice, I had paid for a year in advance, and never gone. Not even once. I joked with friends: "People kept telling me that if I joined a gym I would lose weight and get fit. So, I joined. Then they said I actually had to show up and work out. And I said, 'You never told me I had to show up! You just said I had to join!'" It always got a laugh, but the pounds remained.

I crawled into bed and was soon ensconced in the thick mattress and gorgeous linens. I closed my eyes and began to count slowly back from one hundred. It was my self-hypnosis sleep technique I used when I had too much on my mind. One count on each deep breath. I think I got to ninety-three before I was out.

CHAPTER 10

My bedroom door burst open. There were loud voices and footsteps. I had no idea where I was. Lights were turned on. I was blinded, and covered my face with my hand, trying to look through my fingers and see who was in my room.

"Mr. Thomas!"

"Jesus Christ! What the hell is going on?" They had scared the shit out of me and woken me up at the same time. I was incoherent and sleepy and almost yelling.

"There has been a perimeter security breach; a truck ran the security checkpoint at the entrance to the hotel and crashed into a couple of cars."

This was being said while two agents were hauling me out of bed, and quickly walking me into the bathroom, which was windowless and therefore more secure. Two of them stayed with me while others were all over the suite. It was then I noticed the weapons that were drawn and held close. After that, I noticed I was naked. Mortified, I grabbed a robe from the back of the door and covered up.

I laughed nervously, "I don't want you guys to go blind." They didn't laugh, or even acknowledge the comment. They were listening intently to their earpieces.

My heart was pounding a bit too quickly and a bit too loudly for my comfort.

"False alarm. Stand down. False alarm," the agents calmly said, in unison.

Calmly for *them* maybe.

I was allowed to go back to bed, except there was no damn way I could sleep now. *Give me a break!*

Andrew tapped on the bedroom door and entered.

"Nice way to wake up, Andrew. Holy shit, I thought I was done for."

"I am so sorry, Mr. Thomas, but we refuse to take chances. You are safe, which is all that matters. The situation was domestic in nature. The man who ran the night gate is an estranged spouse of one of the staff here. I will station two men inside your bedroom, if that might help you sleep."

"What time is it anyway?

"It's 4:17 a.m., sir."

I sat up in bed and reached for the TV remote. There was no point in pretending I would go back to sleep. I turned on CNN International and reached for my phone to check messages and emails.

"Andrew, if you can sleep, by all means. I will just lie here until about six and then get up. There's no way I'll get back to sleep."

"Sorry again, sir."

"Don't be sorry, I clearly have a huge learning curve ahead of me. Thank you, Andrew."

"Thank you, sir." With that, he withdrew from the room.

After I had checked messages, I googled an annuity program to try and figure out how someone could amass so much money in just a hundred years. It wasn't as hard as I thought. Working the calculations backwards, and at the average rate of return of 14 percent that Altermatt had stated, Wilbur had likely deposited something in the order of $50 million in 1918. I have no idea where the hell Wilbur had gotten $50 million in 1918 though.

For perspective, I knew from various books that, in that period, the Rockefellers were worth about $1.2 billion, and the DuPont family was worth about $50 million. This was serious money in those days. I would need to figure out where this money came from … or maybe it was better not to know. There was much to consider, but it was the First World War after all, and who knew just where and how money was moved around, earned, skimmed, or stolen in those days.

And now my job was to use it to make the world a better place. Just imagine …

CHAPTER II

The butler opened the front door for Jacob when he arrived at his grandfather's home, and escorted him to the dining room where Herr Altermatt was having a cup of coffee and reading the newspaper.

Wilhelm Altermatt smiled broadly and welcomed Jacob, who bent over and kissed his seated grandfather on the cheek before sitting down to a very early breakfast in the dining room. The housekeeper brought in their plates, loaded down with melon, eggs, toast, smoked salmon, granola, and yogurt. Fresh coffee was poured, and the delicious aroma filled the room. They made small talk while they ate.

Altermatt, relatively speaking, lived like a king. He was blessed. A big house, four servants, and a car and driver. He had spent his whole working life making other people money and building wealth, and he was a near genius at it.

"Jacob, I am glad you could join me this morning, but I confess, I am surprised you could get up this early," Altermatt said, as he took a last bite of his eggs.

Van Vloten squirmed a little in his chair, never quite knowing if he was being teased or insulted, or if his opa was serious. Jacob was a genuinely nice and decent young man, striving hard to please his grandfather. Dealing with his own overbearing mother, Jacob had learned the skills he needed to please other people and walk a fine line around strong personalities.

"Well, Opa, they have this app on mobile phones now called an 'alarm,' and it rings to wake you up. It's quite an advancement." Jacob raised his eyebrows at his grandfather and smiled at him.

Altermatt laughed. Jacob had nailed it. His grandfather was only playfully teasing his millennial grandson.

With the eating portion of the meal now over, Altermatt turned to business and the real reason for the breakfast meeting.

"Jacob, I have your first major assignment to give you, and I wanted to sound you out on it. Today I will be passing along overall control of the Thomas portfolio to Stephen Thomas. My hope is that the bank retains the operations of the account, and frankly, due to its size, I can barely imagine any other alternative. Thomas seemed to give us his nod of support yesterday. The management fee we charge on the account is only a tiny fraction of one percent per year, but this results in fees of about seven billion dollars annually. As this account diminishes, through distribution to charities and other projects, we will see those fees diminish. It will be catastrophic for the bank's bottom line, our stock price, and dividends for our shareholders."

"How can I help?"

"Well, I would like to suggest today that we insert you into Mr. Thomas's life as his personal executive assistant. That you be seconded to him and the organization that we have created for him, and become absolutely indispensable to him. It is imperative that he remains pleased with our services. You need to cater to his every wish, demand, or need, and do so using your impeccable manners, grace, and charm. You are a well-bred young man, and this is a challenge befitting a future president of our bank."

Jacob beamed. He couldn't help it. Pride might be one of the seven deadly sins, but at that moment, he could not have been more proud. Pleasing his grandfather was one thing, but the opportunity to actually impress him was almost his life's calling.

Jacob slipped into work mode. "Herr Altermatt, I accept your challenge and will do my utmost to serve you and the bank, by doing my utmost to serve Mr. Thomas."

Now there was a grin on the proud grandfather's face. He stood up, and when Jacob followed suit, he embraced his impossibly thin and well tailored grandson and young protégé. They began to walk toward the front door while still talking.

"Opa, does my mother know about this new assignment? She might be displeased for me to be so far away."

"Jacob, your mother has been displeased with everything since your father left her, and I suspect she will continue to be until she dies. It disappoints me to say this, but she has been difficult ever since she was a child ... and with the loss of your father, well ... it hasn't helped. She certainly knows how to get things done, though."

Jacob knew his grandfather could not be more accurate. His mother could be horribly bitchy when the mood struck her, but she could also be a caring mother and an elegant professional. She had been through a lot, and he was glad she had her work. It certainly seemed to make her happier than he had ever been able to.

"Opa, I am going to avoid telling her about my new assignment until I have left the country. I am not sure I can stand the drama. You know what she will be like. You and I will both be in trouble. I can see her when I come back the next time."

"Good boy. That is probably the right idea. She'll get over it. She always does. Be at the office by nine thirty at the latest. You should pack a large bag. You can simply buy whatever else you need. Unlimited expenses. I expect you will be leaving for Vancouver late tonight, and that you will be gone for an initial period of at least a couple of weeks, followed by extended periods in Canada."

For Jacob, this was too fast, but he had no choice. He would leave this breakfast meeting and race back to his apartment to say goodbye to his boyfriend. It might be a while before he would see the man—whom one day soon he hoped to marry—again.

Altermatt called after Jacob as he walked out the front door, "Say hi to Zachary for me, and tell him I am sorry to be sending you away. We will make sure you get to see each other as often as possible."

Altermatt knew how happy the boys were together, and hoped they would both be able to wait for each other as Jacob took on this new role. Zachary was good for Jacob and kept him focused and grounded. Jacob's troubles had completely subsided since Zachary came into his life.

CHAPTER 12

I had watched enough TV news and enough CNN for a while. It was six a.m. now, and I was ready to get up. I slipped on my robe and popped out into the living room. One of the agents stood up and greeted me. "Good morning, Mr. Thomas."

"Good morning! Would I be out of line asking you to order some breakfast for me, or us, or for whoever wants to eat with me? Bacon and eggs, and some tea and orange juice?"

"No problem, sir. If it's alright with you, I could order breakfast for all the agents stationed in the room with us now. Would that be okay?"

"Sure, we'll make it a party. I'll hit the shower now. Tell them seven o'clock is fine. No hurry. Thank you, and uh ... forgive me for not knowing your name ..."

"Sir, my name is Joe Mortlock."

"Great, Joe, and who is the other agent on duty now?"

"Dan Myers."

"Thanks Joe, I will get all these names down in time. Thanks for being patient with me."

"Oh, no worries, sir, we understand the tremendous stress you're under. Enjoy your shower. I will take care of breakfast."

Man, this is a nice shower. Great water pressure. When I was a kid, I had a boss who joked with me that before you moved into any house or apartment you should be able to have a shower. "If the water pressure sucks, move on!"

Old Hurlimann had nailed the whole soaps and towels thing. Everything was perfect. I had a good shave, combed my hair, dressed in black slacks, black shoes, a white open-neck button-down dress shirt, cuff links, and a cashmere Glen Plaid two-button blazer. I looked like a somewhat tubby country squire. I really needed to lose twenty-five pounds.

As I was slipping on my shoes, there was a rap on my bedroom door. Without waiting, Andrew walked in.

"Morning, sir. You are looking well today. Did you manage to get back to sleep?"

"Well, not really, but I had slept about eight hours before you guys burst in here and gave me a heart attack, so I guess I'm good. We only have one meeting today, and I can sleep more on the plane. I hope it's okay, but I had Joe order us all breakfast. Probably against regulations, but we have to eat, and I will enjoy the company."

"Really nice of you, and I think with the building fully secured the way it is, we should be fine."

"Andrew, let's not mention this incident from last night to Altermatt, okay? Unless you are required to report it to him, I would rather just avoid the whole drama."

"Mr. Thomas, as of last night, I work for you. No issue at all. We will keep it to ourselves. He may find out from someone at the hotel, but we will just indicate you were safe at all times, and that the matter did not involve you. We will only say that though, if pressed on it."

"Any chance we can go for a bit of a walk around the grounds after breakfast? Not a hike … just to get some fresh air? I confess I am feeling pretty cooped up in here."

"It's our job to make that happen for you. Give me a few minutes, and I will have the team sort out the logistics for you to take a twenty-minute walk, post breakfast. Fair enough, sir?"

"Thanks, Andrew. God, I appreciate that." The doorbell rang. It was our breakfast being delivered.

This was a bit more of a presentation than I expected. A chef had arrived, along with a butler. The chef prepared individual plates of eggs and accompaniments for each of us. It was a great breakfast, with some good banter and a few laughs with the agents.

Deep down though, while I was starting to enjoy the novelty of all this, I still wondered what the fuck I was doing here. *Talk about a fish out of water!*

The walk was not quite a romantic walk in the rain ... or whatever. Here is how it went: We left the suite, and I had four agents with me in the elevator. We descended to the lobby, and went through the convention area and out to the back of the hotel property to wander around on some pathways and through some gardens. I had two agents about fifty feet ahead, two agents about twenty-five feet ahead, two more agents six feet behind me, two more twenty-five feet behind me, and another four walking along the flanks some distance away.

Anytime anyone approached us on the path, the two agents behind me came up alongside me, single file to form a barricade between me and the approaching person. Needless to say, most people gave us a wide berth. After about ten minutes, I suggested we head back and the whole process reversed itself. In my head I was thinking, *Great walk, so relaxing, oh brother ... what a joke. Next time, the treadmill.*

I imagined that, if I wanted to hit the gym, they would have it sealed off, kicking everyone else out. Who was I kidding? I didn't want to go to the gym anyway. I was starting to find, though, that there was this strange sense of entitlement that was beginning to settle in, as though this was somehow normal. And it was already normal for the agents. They were used to taking privileges on behalf of their charges, but for a normal person used to standing in line and holding doors for other people, this was going to take some getting used to. I hoped I would never lose my humility. It was the very essence of being Canadian.

As I walked along in some frustration, I thought about how I could create so much good with the money I was about the receive, and that I wanted to always appreciate this special gift. I knew it should always be a humbling thing, passing it along and sharing it with others, actually "living the culture" of making the world a better place. I scolded myself in advance: *Don't let this stuff get away from you. Keep it real, stay humble, be caring, demonstrate compassion, give people a hand up, not a hand out. Teach a man to fish, don't give him fish ... or whatever the hell that saying is.* I needed to remember all that stuff ... all those good life lessons found on the back of pamphlets or online memes. I hoped their simplicity could be turned into reality.

We were back in the hotel and soon back in my room. We still had an hour to kill before we needed to leave for the bank. We watched CNN again, while I tried to focus on anything other than the money, and all this newfound commotion in my life.

I knew that today's meeting with Altermatt would be ... interesting.

CHAPTER 13

"What the fuck do you mean you're leaving? You can't be serious?" Jacob had arrived home and had given Zachary the news, and it had not gone well.

Zachary appeared devastated. His eyes had welled up with tears. He hugged Jacob hard and did not want to let go. In fact, he wouldn't let go for several minutes. Jacob began to squirm to get free. He had to get to work.

The two had shared a large flat in the gay-friendly Aldtstadt area just across the River Limmat from the financial district. They were a great couple. Jacob, a fairly uptight perfectionist, was held his whole life to the highest standards, which always seemed just out of reach, and Zachary was a deep-thinking, brooding, schoolteacher with a whimsical streak that ran counter to the rest of his character. Spontaneous, he was the one to whisk Jacob away for a weekend in Paris, or an unplanned picnic in the park, always designed to show Jacob the simple beauty of life that he normally missed.

Finally, Zachary released Jacob. "Tell me why? Why you and why now? Your mother is sending you away to break us up, isn't she?"

"Zachary, she doesn't even know about this yet. It was my grandfather's idea."

"So, he is trying to break us up then?"

"God no! He loves you; he really does. Please, let's not make this about him."

"It's always about him or her. They control everything and every-one. It needs to stop. You have a life. We have a life. I love you. I love you so much! This just isn't fair."

"Zachary, I have no idea if this assignment will even work out. Why don't we plan for me to be gone for ten days? I will insist on coming home for some time off, and we will see if I need to go back. Or … maybe we can both go?"

Zachary looked hopeful. He would follow Jacob anywhere. "Both go? Do you think that's possible?"

"I have no idea, but I'll know more in a couple of weeks. Please, forgive me, but this might just be my big career break. I need to do this."

"Yeah, okay … and I need to get to school. I assume you will be gone when I get home? I love you. No matter what, I love you. Please, Jacob, come home soon, and call me every day, okay?"

Zachary took Jacob's face in his hands and tenderly kissed his boyfriend goodbye, and then, with tears in his eyes, he grabbed his backpack, went outside, and jumped on his Vespa for his ride to work. He had tears in his eyes the whole way and could barely see. He knew he was a good guy, and he felt he deserved more. What he really deserved was a husband.

Jacob packed a big bag and took a last look around the flat, not knowing when he would be back. Finally, he waved goodbye to his apartment and lugged his bag down to the car that was waiting to take him to the bank. Step one, accomplished.

CHAPTER 14

Andrew closed the door to the Range Rover, and we were ready to roll. *What a fucking production.* I was beginning to realize that I might never drive a car again. Life was about trade-offs, I guessed. Still, I liked cars and enjoyed driving them. I had been a BMW man since my late thirties when I could finally afford one. I currently owned a BMW sedan and a Mercedes convertible. I knew I would miss driving and likely would just get rid of them.

The ride to the bank was easy and uneventful. The motorcade rolled up in front of the bank, and we went inside. I was starting to feel like I was playing the role of a king or a mobster or something. "Me and my men" walked in with great authority. The security team fell back in groups of two until we reached the reception desk, where four agents remained with me and would accompany me upstairs today. Jacob was waiting for us with a big smile.

"Good morning, Herr Thomas, I mean Mr. Thomas; so good to see you again. Please, follow me."

"Morning, Jacob, it's a beautiful day today. How is your grandfather this morning?"

Jacob looked a bit pained and embarrassed by the grandfather reference in front of the four agents. "He is fine, sir, and is anxious to see you. It is an exciting day for everyone here at the bank, and I imagine a life-altering day for you, sir."

I nodded and smiled in response.

With that, we quietly rode up to the fifth floor, strode down the hall, and were immediately shown into Altermatt's office. Andrew and lead-agent Joe came into the office and positioned themselves at the door. The other two agents stayed outside.

Altermatt was gregarious in his greetings this day. Hands were shaken, greetings extended to everyone in the room, tea poured, and seats taken.

There were large stacks of papers on the meeting table, and by large stacks, I mean about twelve piles, each about twelve inches thick.

Altermatt began. "Well, Mr. Thomas, today is April 17, 2018. It is exactly one hundred years since Wilbur Thomas deposited fifty million dollars into this bank, and we began our mission. It has grown nearly every day since then, and today stands at about twenty-seven trillion dollars."

No one in the room had heard the numbers said out loud before. There were quiet murmurs and exchanged glances.

"It is incredible how much can be achieved simply by time, excellent management, and quality investments. Those papers over there require your signature to take care of a great deal of title transfers and such. Today, I only need one signature to transfer the control of the master account into your name and fulfill the terms of the instructions. The rest of those papers over there you will need legal advice on. There was an ironclad legal undertaking signed when the money was deposited, so that there could be no legal challenge in the future, so effectively… we will be done once we sign it over to you today. I will have my staff pack up those documents and have them delivered to your plane before departure.

"Today, Mr. Thomas, you become the richest man in the history of the world. Congratulations. May I ask you… have you given any thought as to what comes next?"

"I've hardly thought of anything else, as I'm sure you can imagine. The letter you gave me from Wilbur had some instructions. Using my own judgement, I am to keep ten percent and use the rest to make the world a better place. While thinking about all this last night, I decided that I would use ninety-nine percent of it on good works, and only keep one percent, which still leaves me as the richest man in the world, but perhaps not in the history of the world. Either way, it is not exactly a financial struggle.

"I will need some time to set up a structure to utilize all of this wealth. We will work slowly and deliberately, and continue to work with you, Mr. Altermatt, seeking your financial management, advice, and counsel."

Clearly pleased, Altermatt nearly gushed, "You can count on me, Mr. Thomas. In fact, to help you get started, we have taken the liberty of putting a skeleton corporate structure together for you. I will speak more of that in a few minutes. There are so many details to discuss."

"Mr. Altermatt, may we start with a simple first step? Can you please call me 'Steve'?"

Altermatt smiled, rose from his seat, and came around to my chair. "Steve." He shook my hand. "Please call me 'Wilhelm.'"

His assistants looked shocked. No one called him that. Not ever! Everyone in the bank called him "Herr Altermatt." Their reaction made us laugh.

Sitting back down, I said to Wilhelm, "Now, my first concern is security and safety, and keeping all this commotion confidential for a couple of weeks. I assume you can assist me with that?"

He nodded. "Let me advise you what we have done so far, Steve. First, security. Andrew, back there by the door, is your head of security. In fact, as he may have told you, you own his security firm one hundred percent. There are seventeen thousand employees in that firm, which operates worldwide. Andrew and his team are in the elite division. Through the security company, we commissioned a fleet of armoured vehicles for your use in Vancouver. Perhaps you have heard of Guardian Security? Well, that's yours now. You also own the aircraft we mentioned yesterday, and there are more aircraft on order.

"Aircraft have a long waiting period between the order date and delivery window, and usually have lots of delays. We, therefore, pre-ordered three duplicate Boeing 787s, four Gulfstream G650s, and four 737Max BBJ jets. These aircraft will all be used by you and your team for travel and to service your projects worldwide. There are also a dozen cargo jets, which can handle logistics and move vehicles, and most importantly, allow you to deliver food, medicine, or equipment anywhere in the world. Oh, and as well, there are two helicopters. We might have over-anticipated on some of these, but it was all through holding companies you now own. So, your security and travel needs have been met.

"You will need secure, permanent accommodations, and we have engaged Sotheby's Luxury Real Estate agents to search the world for properties you can enjoy that have either a secure compound or a very secure building that is large enough for your needs. They have located four possible properties in greater Vancouver for you to view with Andrew and his risk-management team."

My head was spinning at all of this. It was overwhelming. "Outstanding work, Wilhelm! Thank you."

"Thank you, Mr.… uh, Steve. Now, Andrew has determined that your current properties will simply not be suitable from a security standpoint, nor can they be made secure. To protect you properly and comfortably in the interim, we have rented a floor in the Fairmont Pacific Rim Hotel for your use, effective immediately. They are very familiar with extremely wealthy clients and world dignitaries. They have been informed of your imminent arrival. You also now own a luxury 330-foot yacht that is moored in the Vancouver harbour.

"We have also secured for you a fifteen-year lease on office space in the Bentall 8 Tower. It was leased about a year ago, and is now staffed, equipped, and operational. A legal team is in place, as well as personal assistants, a management team, and an administration staff. There are currently about two hundred employees working there. It is top drawer, right across the board. We hired you the best people. That is the skeleton corporate structure I mentioned. Your CEO, or general manager as you may prefer to call him, is a man named Jack Dickinson. He is excited to meet you."

Suddenly something hit me, and I was confused. "Wilhelm, how could you have possibly known I would need any of this?"

Wilhelm smiled and reddened slightly. "You were not the only one to get an instruction letter from Wilbur. Ours was to be opened ten years before yours, in preparation for this day. He could not have dreamed of the amounts involved here, so we had to extrapolate his desires and instructions, but effectively, our letter said that your mission was to make the world a better place, and our job was to be prepared to help you, and to make sure some good people would pitch in. He was probably expecting a couple of helpers. The reality, however, is a little more along the lines of what we have prepared. The only variable was you!

"We were advised who the beneficiaries of the account were from the time the account was opened. We began monitoring your grandfather, and then your father from when he was born, and then you, staying well back in the shadows, but making sure you were safe. We stepped in and helped you when you got in a bit of trouble as a young man. You might recall that near brush with the law that went away. Well, that was us. We needed you to be alive and well when this day arrived."

I sat there silently. Stunned. Shocked, really. I felt like I was on *Fantasy Island* or something, or that my guardian angel had just introduced himself. This was fucked up. Basically, I had been followed and monitored my whole life, and I now knew my dad had been as well.

After a long pause, I said, "Where is this paper I need to sign? Let's get this done."

Jeffrey, Altermatt's assistant, came over from the corner where he was standing with a black leather folder. He opened it, and there was a two-page document, which was already signed by Altermatt on behalf of the bank. It was an account transfer of control and ownership statement. I read it carefully. Effectively it gave me control of the master account, and power of attorney over every holding within the account. It listed a value calculated on December 31, 2016, at slightly less than the figure I was aware of now.

While I am no lawyer, this seemed a very standard document. "Looks like I will need a witness. Andrew! Come here, please."

I signed the form in two places, and Andrew signed in one place as indicated. Jeffrey then stamped and notarized the document, explaining he was both a notary public and a lawyer. Andrew smiled and shook my hand.

"Well done, sir. Congratulations."

Everyone stood and shook hands with me. Altermatt surprised everyone when he took hold of both my shoulders, pulled me toward him, and hugged me. He had tears in his eyes.

My God. Really?

As Herr Altermatt released me, he said, "You have no idea how long I have waited for this day. My life's work and mission are complete. Now we move on to the next phase, and I am very excited for you, and for us all."

Who knew Altermatt was warm and had a soul? I had to admit I was impressed, and found myself warming to the old guy. Maybe Jacob was right.

"Now Steve, we are done for today. We have already started the initial transfer as promised. You might want to check your bank balance. I have to say that your bank was rather excited by the deposit. I have just one more favour and service to offer you that I hope you will accept, as a courtesy to me."

"And what would that be, Wilhelm? You have already done so much."

"You are about to embark on one of the most exciting adventures anyone has ever undertaken. It is important that we are available to you at all times, and I want you to have the best possible attention. My grandson, Jacob, has asked to be seconded to your organization, initially for a year, to act as the bank's representative within your organization, as well as to act as a personal executive assistant to you."

I am sure I made a slight face at this point.

"Before you say anything," Altermatt said, "let me assure you he has a business degree in finance from Oxford, is brilliant with technology, and is exceedingly well mannered, as well as a natural helper. Would you please allow him to join you? He will learn so much, and offer so much."

I looked over at Jacob, who looked uncomfortable as his grandfather spoke so highly of him.

"Can I speak to you alone for a moment, Jacob?" I asked.

Everyone looked awkward, and then Altermatt looked at his assistants and motioned them toward the door.

"We will leave you to talk."

Andrew and Joe remained in the room and looked for some direction. I simply nodded and motioned for them to hold their positions.

"Jacob, grab a chair." I motioned to the seat next to mine. "I feel like I am being offered a human being as a gift, and it feels weird. How do you feel about this?"

"I think it is an amazing opportunity, especially knowing what you plan to do with the money. I mean … could anything truly be more worthwhile or rewarding?"

"Jacob, do you have a boyfriend or a partner?"

Jacob looked surprised.

"Jacob, I have a number of gay friends. I knew within the first five seconds of meeting you. Does the old man know?"

"Absolutely, and he is entirely supportive. He has been amazing, actually. And as for me, yes, my boyfriend, Zachary, and I live together. We hope to marry in a year or so. To be completely candid, he is not too happy about me leaving."

"What about if he comes along too? I am sure we can find some work for him, regardless of what his skills are. Would that work? You both come for a year, and together we can all do some good work. What do you say?"

Jacob beamed a massive electric grin. "I hear we leave tonight, sir? Can I make a quick call?"

"Yes to both, Jacob. Tell Zachary to quit his job today and pack a bag. You boys can come back in a couple of weeks and clean up loose ends."

Jacob reached for my hand and gave it a firm and grateful shake, and then jumped up, whipped out his phone, and dashed to the corner of the room. I nodded to Andrew, and he opened the door and asked the others to come back in.

We would be leaving for the hotel shortly.

CHAPTER 15

I could hear one side of Jacob's conversation.

"Zachary, it's me. This is all very sudden, but quit your job, get home, and pack your bags for two weeks. We are going on this adventure together ... Yes, we will come back in a couple of weeks to tidy up loose ends. For now, we have to go tonight ... Yes, seriously. He will hire you too ... I have no idea, but it will be more than you make now ... No, of course not. He's not that kind of man ... Trust me ... You will have to be extra spontaneous this time ... Okay, I will call you with more instructions later ... I love you too."

Jacob turned, caught my attention, and gave me a subtle thumbs-up and a big smile. His grandfather, who had re-entered the room, looked over at him, and Jacob smiled and nodded to him as well.

Now that we had all reassembled in the room, the assistant named Noah headed straight for a cabinet near the entrance. He opened a door, revealing a set of crystal glasses and some very expensive-looking bottles of liquor. He poured two glasses of Louis XIII Cognac and brought them over on a tray. In the meantime, Altermatt had been thanking me for agreeing to take Jacob, and was even more happy when he heard that Zachary would be coming along as well. We clinked glasses and toasted the magnificent future that lay ahead for all of us.

"Steve, you are all prepared to go now. I imagine we will be speaking every day for the next while, if not for years to come. Is there anything else I can do for you today?"

"You can walk me to my car. I can always use an extra decoy." He looked very startled, and then I laughed and waved him off so he knew I was kidding. He actually laughed pretty hard then. I decided he was a pretty good guy.

I turned to Andrew. "Are we ready to go?"

"We are, sir."

CHAPTER 16

I was starting to get used to the rhythm of the security detail. Basically, I just needed to walk in the middle of the group and follow Andrew's lead, keep moving, and move at a good pace. When they open a door, walk through, and when they open a car door, get in or out as the case may be. Don't distract the agents while we were moving. And most importantly, let them do their job, especially since they were risking their lives to protect mine.

Once the car was underway, I asked a question of Andrew and the driver:

"So, gentlemen, since I have apparently been under surveillance for most of my life, I assume that you were briefed on every terrible thing I have ever done."

Andrew squirmed a bit. "In order to begin preparations, this team was assigned to your file exactly six months ago. I am unaware of what went on in your past. Nor do I care. We judge on character, and that's all. Welcome to 2018. I am glad we live in a modern world, sir."

"Well, Andrew, just so you know, that so-called incident with police happened when I was a kid. I was attacked by a creepy drunk guy in a bar, and ended up kicking him in the balls and slugging the drunk in the face to subdue him. Then the cops somehow decided to haul me off to the police station, threatening to charge me with assault. Seems they charge the last man standing. A lawyer showed up within thirty minutes of me arriving at the station, claimed to be a public defender, and had me out the door in five minutes, with nothing further said about the matter.

"I guess Altermatt and his predecessors had to have been following me closely. Later in life, I needed a criminal record check a couple of times, and was always concerned something might show up. Now I realize they made it disappear."

I admit, I felt creeped out, but there was nothing I could do about it now. It just felt like an invasion of my privacy, which was something I no longer had in any case. I sat silently for a while.

"You are pretty quiet back there, sir. Is there anything about our schedule today you would like to review?"

I recounted what I knew. "Back to the hotel, some lunch, and a massage, followed by dinner with Herr Altermatt. The only thing I don't know is when we leave for the airport."

"We will leave about nine thirty p.m. We are to depart the airport at about eleven o'clock. It's about half an hour to the private gate at the airport, but I thought you would want a bit of time to explore the jet and feel comfortable before we depart. Is that all okay, sir?"

"Sounds good, Andrew. Thanks." Suddenly I was exhausted. I needed a nap. I closed my eyes, and fell into that odd state between sleep and wakefulness. Soon we were at the hotel, and my door was being opened.

"Same protocol as yesterday, sir."

I was glad when we arrived at the room. There was a massage table set up in the bedroom, and a masseur was finishing drawing a warm bath for me. Thick terry-cloth sheets covered the table, and there was a warm blanket ready to cover me up. Towels were placed next to the tub, and a glass of wine was ready too.

Two agents had been left in the room all day, so we knew everything was okay. The masseur, Lars (Yes, "Lars"… for real) suggested

I have a fifteen-minute bath, and he would knock to let me know when to hop on the table.

"Thanks, Lars." I tossed my clothes on the bed, used the washroom, and slipped into the warm water. Naturally, it was the perfect temperature. I risked falling asleep and drowning as the richest man in the world, so I turned on the news in the bathroom, had some wine, and relaxed. It wasn't long before there was a gentle tap on the door.

It was Lars. "Sir, I will wait in the living area while you towel off and get on the table. Just call for me when you are ready."

I got out of the water and was on the table in a couple of minutes. I told Lars I only wanted a relaxation massage, gentle and not therapeutic. When they dig too deep, they release toxins, and it can be very painful unless you drink a ton of water to clear the toxins away. Lars was great. He was done in about an hour, and I felt rubbery with relaxation.

I flipped on the TV, and sadly, CNN International was announcing the death of Barbara Bush, the former First Lady of the United States, at the age of ninety-two. I sat on the foot of the bed and watched the pundits heaping praise on a woman who many saw as the nation's grandmother. I never knew her, of course, but strangely I felt like I did. Odd how between the media and the internet we are so connected that these people seem to be a real part of our lives.

I flipped channels, and Andrea Mitchell on MSNBC called her a "grande dame" in the old-fashioned sense of the words, and a "handsome woman." Others spoke about her compassion for people suffering with AIDS and how she had gone with a film crew to a hospital, holding and hugging AIDS babies. She also hugged a man dying from AIDS, and this was back in the day when no one was quite convinced that you couldn't catch it from simple contact. She had spent years committed to literacy and other charities. She was a fine woman. I felt a sense of loss and knew I would feel so again when her husband passed away. Without his beloved wife, I felt that would be sooner rather than later.

The other big news of the day was that, prior to a planned summit meeting, the new and yet-to-be confirmed US Secretary of State, Mike Pompeo, had made a secret trip to North Korea for direct talks with North Korean President Kim Jong Un. It was a big day in the news, to be sure.

CHAPTER 17

In preparation for this evening's dinner with Altermatt, the dining table was set for three people, with several layers of china, three types of wine glasses, enough cutlery to conduct a surgical procedure, fresh flowers, and flameless candles. There was soft music playing, and the lights had been dimmed slightly. Three hotel staff were in the small kitchen, finishing the presentation of various dishes that had been brought up to the suite.

The third chair was for Jacob. I had requested his presence at dinner, because I felt it was important to have him see his grandfather before departing, and I also wanted to make part of the celebration about him, instead of everything being all about me. I think they were both pleased by this. They arrived exactly fifteen minutes before dinner was served at seven o'clock.

We enjoyed a lovely champagne with our green salad, a white wine with our soup, and a red wine with the main course, which was rack of lamb. The meal was nouvelle cuisine, with small portions for both the wine and the food. Then we had a small dessert plate, followed by some cheese and port, and then tea or coffee. If I kept this up, I was convinced I would be six hundred pounds by the end of the year.

At precisely 9:20 p.m., Andrew gave us the ten-minute warning. Altermatt said his goodbyes and hugged his grandson. I am pretty sure I saw him wipe away a tear. I realized I had not packed yet, but Andrew advised that it was all taken care of.

"Sir, all you have to do is slip on your jacket and get in the car."

"You guys really are the best." I turned to Jacob. "Well, young man, we have some travelling to do, so let's get to the plane. Where is uh ... was it Zachary?"

"He is meeting us there, sir."

Oh great, another one calling me, sir. Just what I need.

"Jacob, let's lay some basic groundwork now." I immediately had his attention, and he looked like he expected to be scolded or disciplined for some serious infraction.

"I really don't like being called 'sir' or 'Mr. Thomas.' I never have. So, in private, please call me 'Steve.' If we are around some big shots and it seems like you should be more formal, do what you think is right, okay? And I would appreciate it if you would advise everyone we come into contact with that this is what I prefer. That includes advising our staff and teammates, okay? Don't bother with the security agents, though. That's one battle I'm not going to win. So ... this is your first directive as my executive assistant. Tough job, huh?"

Jacob smiled, and looked relieved. "Yes, sir ... I mean, Steve. Understood. Please don't get mad if I mess that up a few times."

At 9:28 p.m., Andrew got our attention again. "Gentlemen, we are ready to go."

Jacob was advised by Andrew that he should walk ahead of the men who were in front of me so that they could provide maximum coverage to me. He was to climb into the vehicle first, then slip across the seat to sit behind the driver, and do so quickly. He was not to delay my entry into the vehicle, or enter from the other side, which would open the interior of the vehicle to danger.

Not surprisingly, he nodded and followed directions flawlessly.

CHAPTER 18

The sniper had arrived in the early afternoon and had ridden a motorcycle into the hills just above and to the east of the Dolder Grand Hotel. He'd squirrelled his way into some bushes on the edge of the property and was effectively invisible to passers-by. Then he had waited. At nine p.m., the motorcade was moved into position under the large roof of the portico in front of the main entrance. He waited some more. At 9:28, there was movement as men took up positions that formed a human wall to protect their employer.

At nine thirty, a variety of men exited the hotel. A very slim young man in a suit exited first and quickly climbed into the backseat of one of the SUVs. Then a group of men marched smartly from the building and never slowed down while moving Thomas into the back of the vehicle as well.

While the sniper was in position and had a bead on the target, there were people too close and moving too swiftly to guarantee results. Again. He had been hoping for a short stop at the vehicle, or a pause on the stairs to look around. Nothing. These bodyguards were good. Out of the building and into the car fast. He had to smile.

They would get him with the backup plan; he was absolutely sure of that. Plan A and B had failed, but plan C was a sure thing. There was no way this guy was getting out of Switzerland alive. He would wait until the vehicles had left the area before crawling out of the bushes and walking back to his motorcycle.

He could make a call, however, so he called the secure line again. When it was answered, a single question was posed: "Report?"

"Negative."

The line went dead.

CHAPTER 19

Jacob and I managed to follow all the security rules and were soon on our way to the airport and through the "private aircraft" gate. I absolutely love planes, so for me, this was really getting exciting. Then it came into view, off in the distance: a gorgeous, brand-new Boeing 787 Dreamliner BBJ.

For anyone who has ever flown regularly in economy, you know how awful it can be. If you fly in business class or first class, you may enjoy the perks, but if you travel often enough, you know how horrible air travel is no matter how nice they make it. Convenient maybe, but generally uncomfortable and boring.

The gold standard for air travel is a private jet. We have all seen the pictures. There's a few comfortable seats, maybe a couch, maybe a bed … no waiting, no lines, no hassles, and better food.

The private jet I had fantasized about was a G650 by Gulfstream. My biggest desire was just to take a tour of one at an air show, and I was pretty sure that would never happen. They seat about twenty people and are an outstanding aircraft, with beautiful lines.

Now, here I was, with a private Boeing 787. In a normal configuration, these could seat up to three hundred people. They are wide bodied, have a stunning design, and a very modern cockpit and instrumentation. They are an awesome aircraft. They are known for being extremely quiet and having excellent fuel economy. I was as excited as a kid arriving at Disneyland, and I was a bit embarrassed by that, so I was trying to seem at least a little bit cool. It was a struggle, I assure you.

Altermatt could keep the money. Just give me this plane, and I would be happy. Fully outfitted, these planes cost about $400 million.

We rolled right up to the stairway of the plane. The exterior was gorgeous, and had a stylish blue-and-white paint scheme. The agents were positioned outside around the plane, providing perimeter security. I was so excited that I was ready to bound out of the car and run up the stairs. My damn door was locked. *Fuck!* Andrew turned to chat.

"Slight variation on entry procedure, sir. The five of us will go up the stairs at very close quarters. This offers you maximum protection. Jacob, you can follow up a few paces behind."

Four men had formed up outside my door. Andrew released the lock, and I stepped outside. It was less weird than explained, and we just walked up the stairs quickly, in tight formation.

My grin that night was so wide it could break a window. We entered the aircraft, and it was awesome. Let me give you a visual tour:

At the very front of the plane was the cockpit. No shock there, but it also had space for a communications officer to run all the communication systems on the aircraft, which included satellite telephones, internet, and streaming television. Just behind and above the cockpit, in the ceiling effectively, was a crew rest area with seating and two beds. The headroom was only about five feet up there, but very comfortable once you were seated or lying down. In the cabin, just behind the cockpit, was a galley area, and behind that was a large, comfortable salon with a sofa for four, plus four big single seats, and another two seats sharing a small table. In the next section back was a first aid station and a sort of entry hall area, with a coat closet and such.

Then the plane got really good. A hallway ran down the starboard side of the plane, while on the port side was a private stateroom, with a sofa, easy chair, coffee table, and television. It had an adjoining bathroom with a full shower, and a bedroom with a queen-size bed. The next section back had another comfortable living area with a couple of sofas and more easy chairs (think luxury business-class seats) and a table and chairs for dining. Behind that were two small staterooms with convertible sofa beds. At the rear was an economy-seating section with seating for thirty-two, so you had a place to put extra people. At the very rear of the plane was a large galley area, and access to the flight attendants' rest area, which was up above as well. This crew rest area had sleeping spaces for four crew. There were four general-use washrooms on board plus the private washroom in the master stateroom. It was all spread over twenty-four hundred square feet of luxury flying accommodation.

It was a stunning design, with swirl-patterned carpets, white leather-covered seating, dark woodwork and furnishings, and nickel-plated trims. The walls were a lovely warm cream colour.

The pilot had led me through the plane, pointing out features and fittings. It was gorgeous. The onboard kitchen was shockingly well equipped. It offered wine storage and fresh food storage in addition to prepackaged foods. Amazing.

The plane had two pilots and two first officers for this long flight. Four flight attendants would work in shifts, and we also had a chef and a communications officer.

Oh, and on that massive plane, in addition to the security detail, there were only three passengers: me, Jacob, and Zachary, who had just arrived.

Jacob and Zachary hugged and were obviously delighted to be together on this adventure.

"Steve, please let me introduce you to Zachary Norguard."

I shook Zachary's hand, and enjoyed his firm handshake.

"Zachary, I am Steve Thomas. Please, call me 'Steve.' Welcome aboard my plane," I still couldn't believe I was saying these words, "and thanks for coming along for this wild adventure we're all about to take together. You two make a handsome couple."

"Thanks, Steve, I am barely sure why I am here, but I hear I have a job with you, and I get to stay with Jacob, so my world is complete. Are we on the clock tonight or off the clock?"

"Well first, let's all just relax and enjoy the ride. Second, your sweatpants and hoodie kind of made me think you're dressed for sleeping, so I think we will have to assume you are off the clock. We will figure everything out over the next few days. Let's just assume your job roles will sort themselves out over time, but I will need some help doing all sorts of random tasks, both important and menial, so just help me where you can, okay?"

Both Zachary and Jacob nodded.

Andrew and I quickly sorted out that the agents would use the thirty-two-seat area at the rear of the aircraft, and could utilize the rear living room area. They would have a very comfortable space. I suggested that Jacob and Zachary could use one of the small state-rooms, and that Andrew take the other. We would all need our rest. I did not hesitate to declare the large private stateroom as mine, and I likely had a dumb grin as I did so.

"There will be no coin flipping for the large stateroom tonight. It's a curse, but it's mine!"

The boys and I would hang out in the forward living room area in the meantime.

Like Jacob, Zachary was about thirty, close to six feet tall, with a handsome face and friendly eyes. Instead of having to dress smartly every day like Jacob, Zach was more casual. He had a very short-trimmed beard, and his dark brown hair was a bit shaggier. At rest, his face always seemed to wear a slight smile, which made him instantly likeable. While Zachary got tanned in the sunshine on his Vespa, Jacob had the pale skin of a man who worked in an office.

I was looking forward to spending time with them. "Why don't we all sit down in the main salon area up front, get some drinks, and get to know one another better. Then we can all get some rest later. Hey, Andrew, can we leave early, or will that mess things up for you?"

"We are ready now, actually. Forty-five minutes early. I will ask the pilot."

The pilot confirmed with the tower, and found there was a clear window for an early departure. The main cabin door was sealed, and within three minutes, the plane was taxiing toward the runway. Once positioned at the end of the runway and cleared for takeoff, it only took thirty-five seconds for the Dreamliner to lift off and climb up and out of Flughafen Zürich.

CHAPTER 20

Standing thirty-five hundred yards away from the airport, a man swore. The man in charge of plan C was not happy.

He had been held up in a traffic jam caused by an accident and had arrived with only an hour to prepare. He would have preferred two. He'd trained his binoculars on the 787, verifying its position on the tarmac in the private-aircraft area, then began to unload and unpack the SAM (surface-to-air missile) from the rear of his SUV. It was dark outside, and he was well hidden in a stand of trees to the northwest of the runway's end.

The SAM was a shoulder-mounted model, but he had a special apparatus he could attach to the roof of his SUV for better stability. He had it all set up, and in accordance with his instructions, was ready to send a permanent goodbye message to Stephen Thomas as his plane departed at eleven p.m. From where he was positioned, he would aim directly at the belly of the plane as it rose to about fifteen hundred feet. The heat-seeking guidance system would take over from there. It would be spectacular. The aircraft would likely explode upon impact with the SAM, and crash into some nearby farmland. With about twenty minutes to spare, he had his gear all set to go.

He picked up his binoculars again to watch and track the plane.

"What the fuck…? Where the fuck…?" He spun the binoculars around, looking for the plane on the tarmac, the apron, the runway… Gone. *FUCK!* He slammed his fist repeatedly into the roof of his SUV as he stood on the back bumper. He had missed his chance.

This was unacceptable. His employers had insisted that Thomas not be allowed to leave Zurich alive. The hit team had failed completely.

Three strikes and they were out. His colleagues back in North America would need to take it from here.

He couldn't believe that this son of a bitch had eluded them three times already. He called the number on his secure mobile phone. It was answered by an automatic system. He pressed in the security numbers and waited.

"Report?"

"Negative."

Just before the line went dead, he heard a voice growl, "FUCK!"

CHAPTER 21

The power of this aircraft was amazing, especially since it was so light from being virtually empty. The two massive Rolls Royce jet engines produced intense thrust, and the plane took off and went into a steep climb in order to clear air traffic in the vicinity. The climb from runway 34 to five thousand feet was swift, followed by the pilot powering back to respect noise rules in the area. He climbed more slowly and quietly to ten thousand feet and then throttled up the engines again and climbed to thirty-nine thousand feet for the ride home.

Being as the Dreamliner was one of the quietest aircraft flying today, it was easy to have conversations while in flight.

Our two flight attendants for the early part of the flight were Jessica and Becky. Talented and charming, they were also former military. They were employees of Guardian Security, as were the pilots and crew. They very kindly brought us cocktails. A sidecar for me, a glass of single-malt scotch for Zachary, and a Heineken for Jacob.

Jacob and Zachary were nice guys. Both were well mannered, and very nicely balanced in their handling of each other. Both laughed easily and could take being teased with grace. I am bad for teasing people, but I only do it for fun, never to be mean.

These two were comfortable in their relationship and in their gayness. Switzerland did not allow gay marriage, but had full legal rights for same-sex relationships, and their society was pretty relaxed about it. They loved the fact that Canada had allowed gay marriages since 2005.

They asked me about my life, and if I had a wife or partner. I told them I had been with a fantastic woman for ten years, during my thirties, but on my own since I was forty. She had developed cancer and died a slow, painful death. It was brutal to watch, and left me feeling so helpless that I struggled with the notion of being with anyone else. I had always been independent, and decided that if I couldn't be with her, I preferred to be alone. Call it devoted or selfish, I was never sure. I knew I was selfish at times, but I did enjoy sharing my good fortune with others.

I sometimes wasn't an easy friend. I found that I tended to challenge people intellectually, and while well intentioned, I often accidentally intimidated people. Years before, I had been told by a friend that I had a certain "presence." I understood what he meant. I had the ability to be commanding when I wanted to be, but I was always generous with my friends, so long as they were good friends who cared about me as well.

And even though I had been a fish out of water these last few days, I was normally very comfortable being in charge or in control. I had always been a pretty decent leader. My philosophy started from the premise that I would never ask someone to do something that I would not do myself.

Not surprisingly for young gay men, both Jacob and Zachary were into fitness. Jacob ran or cycled almost daily, which explained his pencil-thin physique. Zach was more of a gym bunny and worked out more with weights and less with cardio. He was fit and buff, but not extremely so. He looked the way I had always wanted to look, but I was never able to have my desire for physical perfection overwhelm my enjoyment of food and drink. Okay, maybe I was just lazy when it came to fitness. Okay, not maybe. There you go. The truth.

Becky had made the sofas down into beds in the two smaller staterooms just aft of mine. She let me know that my stateroom was ready any time I needed it, and that the bed had been turned down. It was about midnight, after a long and pretty stressful day, and we were all ready for some sleep. Plus, that massage several hours ago had made me both a bit sore and a bit weak.

My drink was long gone, and the glow had settled in nicely. A good sidecar was a triple, and that one had definitely been a good one. I said good night to the boys, and headed to my stateroom.

Forgive me for droning on, but I was so happy to be in this room. I kept thinking, *dream come true*, because there was no other way to describe the feeling. I took off my clothes, and went to hang them in the small closet. Inside were the rest of my clothes, cleaned and pressed. My empty suitcase was on the floor of the closet. I poked my head into the bathroom, and my shaving kit was there. I brushed my teeth, washed my face, and climbed into bed.

Even in an aircraft as quiet as this one, the engines still make noise, a sort of constant hum. The queen-size bed felt exactly like my bed at home, and the pillows were feather, which is my preference. Again, these guys had done their homework. They probably broke into my place to see what I had. It oddly made me laugh and shake my head. Then I turned onto my side, closed my eyes, and found myself hypnotized by the humming. I had no trouble sleeping this night. I was asleep faster than normal.

It would be good to be back in beautiful, casual, laid-back Vancouver.

CHAPTER 22

A three-man hit squad had arrived in Vancouver from just west of Larkman, Wyoming. Upon arrival, they met up with five more locals. The mission was the elimination of Stephen Thomas. They had been given detailed instructions, and the local team had scoped out the sniper locations.

Although the hit team was unaware of the reason for this elimination, their client needed to make sure Thomas died tonight. Before he had a chance to reveal to a wider circle what he was now the custodian of… they wanted him dead.

After the first two attempts at a selective kill had failed, and the third attempt that would have taken out the aircraft, passengers, and crew had failed as well, there were now "no restrictions." Kill as many people as you have to, but he must die. Those were their instructions. There were only two roads in and out of the airport property. Both would be covered by snipers. The vehicles would be disabled first by sniper fire, and then would be destroyed by RPGs, also known as rocket-propelled grenades. The standard Cadillac SUVs generally used by Guardian Security would be a piece of cake.

Four men were assigned to each team. They arrived in black-ops vans, and then positioned themselves for the best sight lines on buildings or structures. The driver would handle communications, while the other three acted as snipers. Two snipers would position themselves pointing into the oncoming vehicles and the other would shoot more from the side. The ideal tactic would be to take out the first vehicle and the last vehicle, trapping everyone between them, and then using the RPGs for cleanup and total destruction. No one would survive. They guaranteed it.

Unlike in Dealey Plaza where JFK was shot, there was no grassy knoll, but there would be a hail of firepower similar to a war zone, certainly nothing that Vancouver had ever seen before.

Guardian Security had sent in a six-car motorcade, and it was waiting about five hundred yards from the terminal buildings in a holding area. Once the 787 had touched down, the cars would roll out onto the tarmac, led by an airport pilot car with a flashing yellow light. The car would guide them safely to the plane while avoiding any safety issues for other aircraft taxiing around the tarmac.

The kill teams had now settled into their positions and were ready to aim and fire.

The Guardian Security teams were also in place. The aircraft was about an hour out.

CHAPTER 23

Is that bacon I smell? My eyes opened, and it took my brain a few seconds to remember where I was. I had slept like a log and barely moved. I looked at my watch. It was seven fifteen a.m. Zurich time.

I switched my watch to pacific standard time, and saw that it was ten fifteen p.m. the day before. Hmm, it was exactly the same time now as when we left Zurich. Who said time travel was impossible? We would be landing in about an hour or so.

I decided a quick shower was in order. Yeah, the same stupid airplane showers I was making fun of only two days before. I brushed my teeth, had a quick shave, and a fast shower. It wasn't bad either. It wasn't as good as my shower at home, but it was better than the shower in the boat I'd once owned. Then I put on my comfy travel clothes: a pair of polyester track pants and a golf shirt, socks, and sneakers.

Jacob and Zachary were already up and having breakfast. Bacon! Our flight attendants brought me some breakfast, with juice and tea, and we were advised that we should eat fairly hurriedly because in about thirty-five minutes, we would begin our descent.

The boys told me they'd each slept about five hours. Jacob was dressed in his suit, ready for work, while Zachary looked a bit more like me, comfortable.

Andrew joined us to discuss our landing procedures.

He filled us in on the six-car motorcade and the fact that we'd be met at the plane and driven downtown to the hotel. The trip would take about twenty-five minutes. He knew the motorcade would get broken up at traffic lights, so I was not to be shocked as the vehicles did a bit of a "driving ballet" or conducted a vehicular shell game, so that no one would really know who was in which vehicle, in case we were being followed or watched.

"When we are disembarking the aircraft, please just do as I say, when I say it, no questions, okay?"

Everyone nodded, wondering what the hell that meant.

I glanced over at Zachary. "This stuff seems a bit crazy, eh? Basically no one knows who I am or what any of this is about, so I can't imagine a security threat... but better safe than sorry, I guess." Little did I know then that there had already been three attempts on my life.

Zachary told us he had come to Vancouver for the 2010 Winter Olympics, and loved the city. He was excited to be back.

"Were you here to see the Olympics, or were you competing?" I asked.

"I would have competed, but there was no category for Olympic fashion." He grinned. "I am very good at fashion events."

"I can tell by the sweatpants and hoodie."

"Yeah, but you have to admit, it's a great hoodie."

This Zachary was a character. I liked him.

The pilot announced our descent, and the big plane began to glide smoothly downward. There are always a few rattles in every plane as it slows and bounces through the cloud cover, but this was very minimal. It was pouring rain and dark in Vancouver. Absolutely pouring rain. Welcome home.

We touched down, heading west on runway 26L. The plane landed softly and slowed with the reverse thrusters in action. The pilot taxied the aircraft over to an area normally used in winter months for de-icing, and pulled to a stop.

This part of the airport was viewable from certain parts of the terminal, but not visible from the exit roadways leading away from the airport grounds.

Two helicopters landed nearby just behind the aircraft. A small white car with a flashing yellow light was leading the motorcade up to the plane.

Looking out the windows, I saw six matching black Cadillac Escalades, with blacked-out windows, rolling up in unison.

Andrew gathered Jacob, Zachary, and me together and quietly told us some final instructions. We immediately descended the stairs as a tight group of fifteen, including the security detail.

Everyone fanned out, getting into their respective vehicles. The motorcade sat for about two minutes and then signalled the pilot car that they were ready. The motorcade began moving, following the little white car with the flashing lights, and being sure not to exceed the listed tarmac speed of fifty kilometres per hour.

It was quite a production seeing the cars rolling across the tarmac in formation, stopping for the odd aircraft that had the right of way as they headed to the secure exit gate.

With all the starts and stops and airport procedures, it took about ten minutes to get to the exits. The motorcade swung east onto North Service Road, and then turned right onto Aviation Avenue, stopping at the light, and waiting to turn left onto Grant McConachie Way, which was the main exit road from the airport.

The light turned green and all six vehicles turned left. As a single unit, they increased their speed and headed east again, heading toward an overpass.

The snipers were prepared, focused on the driver and the windshield of the lead SUV. The first high-powered shot pierced and shattered the windshield of the vehicle, injuring the driver and causing him to react involuntarily with a hard pull to the right. The Escalade rolled onto its driver's side. Sparks flew from the metal grinding against pavement until the vehicle skidded to a stop, blocking most of the two lanes heading east.

CHAPTER 24

I was looking forward to this ride, and it was a nice surprise.

The rotors had been engaged, and within a couple of minutes, the two helicopters had lifted into flight. Aboard mine were Andrew, myself, and two agents, Joe and Dan.

Jacob and Zachary were in the other helicopter with one other agent.

We were onboard two Augusta Westland AW109E helicopters. The same one the queen uses, I was told, so they must be okay.

"Sir, the cars were a false-flag security measure," Andrew explained via the headset, now that we were underway. "It might be overkill, but we wanted to test out our systems, and I thought you might enjoy the helicopter ride. The city is gorgeous at night, even in the rain."

Andrew had had some last minute instructions for us, just as we were about to descend the aircraft stairs and get in the back seat of the cars. The cars were in a line, visible from the airport. Mostly hidden on the other side of the line of cars, and blocked by various large service vehicles, were the two helicopters. We were supposed to get into the car, close the door, slide across the seat, and exit the other side, and then run to the helicopters and get in. The motorcade would block the view of the helicopters from the airport, and then it would pull away as though we were inside. In the helicopters, we would give the motorcade a little while to move off about a thousand feet, and then the choppers would lift off and head in the opposite direction. Rather than heading toward the city, we would initially head west, out over the ocean.

"The motorcade will head down to the hotel taking the long way, and by the time they arrive, we will have landed where we will be staying for the next while."

I looked at Andrew. "We're not going to the hotel?" I'd assumed we were helicoptering to the hotel.

He shook his head no. No further information was offered. Guess it was a secret. *I might as well sit back and enjoy the ride.*

The two aircraft headed west out over the ocean, banking right around the tip of the west side of Vancouver. We then flew north over English Bay, right over the downtown business core of the city, out over the harbour of Burrard Inlet. We had been in the air less than ten minutes.

As I looked at the city from the air at night, I was impressed by its natural beauty, even in the rain. Greater Vancouver was made up of the city of Vancouver and several other municipalities and smaller cities. Collectively, there were about three million people in the region. Bordered to the west by the Pacific Ocean, and to the north by the Pacific Range of the Coast Mountains, the rest of the area was a massive river delta, formed over thousands of years and still sliced up by rivers and streams. The delta land was great for agriculture, but was increasingly covered by cities and towns. It was technically a rain forest area, and got more than its fair share of moisture, but on a sunny clear day, it was a magical place. A modern skyline, set against the backdrop of the ocean and the mountains, helped push Vancouver to the top of the list of the world's most beautiful cities. Common on anyone's list were San Francisco, Sydney, Zurich, and Vancouver. Any day of the week, one of those four cities could be on top. It felt good to be back home. No matter where and when I travelled, I always felt safe when I was back in Canada.

Back at the airport, the motorcade had taken its time to give *us* time to get a head start. But they were on the road now.

Suddenly, Andrew was reacting to something in his ear. He started barking orders into his radio, and then realized that he had a more essential priority. Me. His local counterpart was in charge of the motorcade diversion. He would have to handle his own situation with his team. Andrew came on the radio system in the chopper, and now we all heard him as he spoke to the pilot.

"Motorcade is under attack. Motorcade is under attack. Fastest possible speed and route to our destination. MOVE! MOVE! MOVE!"

Now I was scared. "Andrew, what the fuck is going on?"

"Sir, the motorcade is being fired on, taking heavy fire. We have to get you to safety. Let me do my work now, please, sir."

Yeah, great, sure, do your work. Now I was scared shitless. What the fuck had I gotten involved with? *Jesus Christ … Holy fuck!*

We were at about twelve hundred feet, and already moving pretty fast. My stomach got woozy as the helicopter dropped down to about five hundred feet and flew at top speed. We flew over the middle of the Ironworkers Memorial Bridge, and then the Second Narrows Rail Bridge, and then zoomed down even lower to about a hundred feet above the water, flying more like a military attack plane, following the inlet until we turned north again into Indian Arm and flew at top speed all the way to the end of the fjord. The moonlight had broken through the clouds and was shimmering on the water. A large yacht was anchored in the bay, and the front and rear-landing pads were flooded with light.

One helicopter landed on the helipad on the foredeck of the yacht, while mine landed on a small helipad on the stern. The boat had about four or five decks and was three hundred and thirty feet long. This was the yacht Altermatt said I owned. Unreal. I was met by several other agents and was pretty much grabbed and hurried inside to the safety of the yacht's main salon. The blinds had been drawn for added security.

Although we could not see them in the dark, I learned later that there were three thirty-six-foot, inflatable, hard-bottomed boats with two big outboard engines on the back of each. They were gunboats, each with a deck-mounted fully automatic-machine gun and had four heavily armed men. They were drifting, idling their engines to stay in position, each about five hundred feet off the sides of the yacht, providing a triangle of security.

There were probably six men on deck, armed with automatic weapons, and half a dozen agents inside the yacht as well. No one expected the need for this amount of security, but Andrew had orchestrated this as a drill tonight, and in the end, it was lucky he had. Everyone was intently listening to their earpieces for any signs of trouble or further instructions.

Andrew was on the radio again. He could not raise anyone on the motorcade detail. Then, he was on his cell phone, trying to get information. The news could not be good.

CHAPTER 25

As the first Escalade flipped onto its side, the five SUVs following it were in chaos. A hail of gunfire rained down on the vehicles, seemingly coming from all directions, although it was actually only three.

There was a covered, elevated foot bridge for commuters to use to walk across the divided roadway, and two snipers were lying on the roof about a hundred feet apart, each having a wide-angle view of the road. The third sniper was behind a concrete barrier at ground level.

These were professional shooters, and they spared no ammunition.

The two agents in the first vehicle had been killed almost immediately.

The second car slammed into the first, while the four behind scattered right and left and attempted to keep moving forward. Tires were shot out, front grills and windshields shattered, and engine blocks were damaged.

This was not actually an armoured motorcade. It didn't need to be. It was just a diversionary tactic, with no real threat expected. This was mostly a training exercise.

Trapped in the second vehicle, the driver took a bullet right between the eyes. His seat-mate managed to open his door and roll to safety, only to be run over by the following car. He died minutes later.

The third vehicle managed to run the line, though the windshield was shattered and the car riddled with bullets. The sniper positioned on the roof of the overpass to the left spun around and took out the fuel tank as the vehicle attempted to speed away. The vehicle burst into flames when the tank exploded, killing both men inside.

The fourth, fifth, and sixth cars all managed to stop, and used their vehicles as shields, returning fire, but only for a short while. Then the unthinkable happened. The rocket-propelled grenades were launched. The man behind the concrete barricade aimed and fired, and repeated the action five times. There were massive explosions. Death was everywhere, and of the six cars that had carried twelve men, only one man was left alive—barely.

In black gear, and wearing helmets and visors, the snipers now ran toward the vehicles, looking to see if their target was dead. They couldn't find him.

They found the one live agent, lying in a pool of blood.

"Where is Thomas?"

"Safe. Fuck y—" A bullet ended his sentence, splitting his skull in two.

The men ran to their black-ops van, where the driver had the door open. They piled inside and roared away. Total time of attack: two minutes, seventeen seconds. Six vehicles destroyed. Twelve men dead, and not a single injury on their side. They would be back across the border within the hour. They didn't drive far before they reached two pre-positioned getaway cars. While the local black-ops van driver headed to a red Chevrolet, the other three men jumped into a white minivan and were soon onto the freeway heading toward the Canada-US border. After a few miles, they exited the freeway and took city and rural roads until they were in the Township of Langley on Zero Avenue.

The border along the rural road they were on was defended by nothing more than a shallow ditch. A road and homes lined the Canadian side, with open farmland on the American side. They turned the van into a driveway on the Canadian side, and quickly cut the engine, abandoning the vehicle right there. No one was awakened, nor did anyone even notice them getting out and running as fast as they could, jumping the ditch and dashing through the farmer's soggy field. Another vehicle was waiting for them on the other side, and they were soon safely on their way home. They would be in Wyoming in about sixteen hours.

The other kill team who had joined them were local mercenary types in Canada. The airport exit they had been covering was not used by the motorcade, so they had simply scrubbed their mission and quietly faded into the woodwork.

Back at the scene of the massacre, sirens wailed, lights flashed, and traffic was backed up all the way to the airport. Happy travellers returning from vacation wondered what all the commotion was about… and what was burning.

Police cars, fire trucks, ambulances, and even media helicopters were on the scene within minutes.

Of the original twelve agents who had flown in from Zurich on the Dreamliner, four were dead. Four more had stayed with the aircraft to protect it, and the other four were in the helicopters, but eight local agents had been lost.

Once back in the US, the kill-team leader called the special number and punched in his security code.

"Report?"

"Negative."

"AGAIN?"

The line went dead.

CHAPTER 26

Andrew was on his radio and his phone. He could not raise a single man from the motorcade by radio, including the senior man who was his local counterpart.

The agents remaining on the plane were instructed to hunker down and go to SECPRO 1: Protect the aircraft, the crew, and themselves at all costs.

I didn't drink much, but right now, I thought I needed one, so I wandered over to the bar in the yacht and started rummaging around in the drawers that held the liquor bottles. A female member of the yacht's crew offered to help. I found a suitable bottle of scotch, she got us glasses, and I poured several, handing one to each of the boys, and one to Andrew. I didn't even like scotch, but tonight, I decided I did.

"Anyone else need a drink?" The rest of the agents refrained. Andrew took his glass and drank about an ounce. He made that face you make when your throat burns a little and then the glow takes over.

Andrew filled us in on what he knew. The TV was on, and media reports were filling in the blanks.

"Andrew, this is just about the worst night of my life. I can only imagine how you must feel. Oh, my God. People have died tonight because of me."

"NO, SIR! They died tonight because of me! ME, sir. We were underprepared and did not properly assess the risks. No one should have died tonight, and it could have been you. We have never ever lost a client, and we still haven't, but tonight is not a proud night. Good men … good men have died. My God …"

I was angry. "This shit pisses me off! I don't know who the fuck is behind all this, but God dammit, they will not fucking win this!"

I reached out, put a hand on Andrew's shoulder, and started to speak in a firm voice, making sure everyone could hear me clearly.

"Listen up, everybody … I want to propose a toast to the fallen agents. I'm not sure what the hell is going on right now, but I am just fucking angry. Someone wants to kill me to prevent us from doing some good in the world. I didn't ask for this, but it is my mission now, and I'm going to finish it. We will be careful. We will take precautions, but we will be brave. And we will work together and change this world for the better, whether the world likes it or not! And we will NEVER forget the men who gave their lives tonight to make our mission possible."

Andrew slowly stood up and raised his glass. Zachary rose to his feet. Jacob joined in. We solemnly clinked glasses. We were committed to succeeding.

"Fucking right, sir," Andrew said quietly but appreciatively. "Fucking right."

CHAPTER 27

Just north of Iron Bay, and south of the former Wigwam Inn, dawn was breaking in the safe, quiet bay in which the yacht was anchored. We had been up all night, but we had slept on the plane earlier. And anyway, who the hell could have slept after what had happened?

Today was our last day in the shadows.

A long-dead US Supreme Court Justice, Louis Brandeis, once said: "Publicity is justly commended as a remedy for social and industrial diseases. Sunlight is said to be the best of disinfectants; electric light the most efficient policeman."

He was right. The public needed to know what was going on, and fast. The sooner this went public, the sooner we would be safe. I had come to the conclusion, right or wrong, that some rogue government agency, likely in either Russia or the USA, was trying to get these funds through whatever means necessary. From a confidential informant to the Swiss government's counter-espionage organization, we had heard during the night about the three other attempts on my life that had failed.

"Jacob, let's get to work. Get hold of our new office, and find out if we have a communications department, and lots of lawyers. I am going to clean up, we are going to get in that helicopter, fly to the office building, land on the fucking roof like we are Batman or something, and get this party started. Andrew, we need that building secured. Can you check?"

"Already done, sir. It is a fortress."

"Yeah. Not convinced. Check again."

Andrew was mildly offended, but given the circumstances of the last few hours, he knew I was right.

"Yes, sir."

"And Andrew, we are leaving here in fifteen minutes. Get your men ready at both ends."

As I was shaving, Jacob came into my stateroom. "Steve, there is a full communications team. A man named Mark Crombie is the communications director. What should I tell him?"

"Tell him we need a press conference at noon today, and that we want everybody they can get to be there, either in person or by satellite feed. I need CNN, BBC, Fox, NBC, ABC, MSNBC, CBS, Global, CBC, CTV, and on and on. Tell them this will be the biggest story in the last hundred years, and it involves trillions of dollars and espionage. Tell him we are not kidding."

I was about as clean as I was going to get for a guy wearing track pants and a golf shirt. I had no other clothes yet. Then it dawned on me, and I opened a closet in the stateroom and smiled. There were pants, shirts, shoes, jackets, and everything else I would need, all in my size.

These guys are good...

I selected dark tan slacks, a medium-blue blazer, a blue button-down Oxford shirt, brown shoes, a brown belt, and a tan pocket square. All set to face the world.

The engines in the helicopter were warming up.

I came out of my stateroom and everyone looked at me. I looked down to see if my fly was open or something and realized it was the new clothes.

"Yes, I do look good ... and I am a rich guy now, so you have to tell me that even when it's not true."

They all laughed a little. I was glad that they could see I was kidding, and not some self-absorbed moron. There would be plenty of time to be self-absorbed, and I could certainly be a moron, but today I needed to be at my absolute personal best.

CHAPTER 28

The helicopter had room for six passengers, plus the pilots. Aboard were Jacob, Andrew, Joe, Dan, me, and there was still a seat for Zachary. He was very happy he wasn't being left behind.

The rotor blades whirred faster and faster. The pilot carefully lifted the helicopter off the pad and let it hover about two feet above the pad for a few seconds, and then pulled us backward and upward at the same time, spinning us around, tilting the nose downward and quickly gaining speed as we raced forward down the centre of Indian Arm. He banked right at Deep Cove and flew over a residential area and the Upper Levels Highway before aiming directly at the downtown's highest building. He was going the fastest, most-direct route today. Last night was more stealth oriented. Today, we wanted to make a big showing.

We landed on the rooftop helipad of the forty-five-storey building at the corner of Dunsmuir and Burrard, Bentall 8, the eighth-tallest building in the city, at 552 Burrard Street.

Our security detail was waiting on the roof as we landed. They were armed and had their weapons out; men were scanning nearby buildings for snipers.

I was tired of scurrying. I walked at normal speed to the door, entered, and went down a flight of stairs to the forty-fifth floor. I heard the helicopter lift off, and assumed it was heading back to the yacht, but was later told it was just flying to a nearby heliport for refueling.

The Thomas Protocol occupied the top five floors of the building. I was escorted to a large, gorgeous office on the forty-fifth floor, with sweeping northward and westward views of the ocean, the city, and the mountains. The nameplate on the door read "Stephen Thomas." A large modern desk was in the corner, and gorgeous Impressionist paintings hung on the walls. There was a comfortable sofa and sitting area for about a dozen people, and a large worktable for projects or displays, or so I supposed. A couple of potted plants and a few art pieces sat on cabinets.

Through an adjoining doorway, I could see a massive boardroom with seats for thirty, with all of the latest tech and communications equipment.

For my security detail, I had Joe and Dan in the office. Andrew located a small office with his name on the door right next to my office, just off the executive outer office area, and Jacob was shown to a small office next to Andrew's. We all had work to do. I sat down, and my new communications manager, Mark Crombie, came in and introduced himself. He informed me that he was fully aware of all the financial matters, as Altermatt had called to inform him, and that he knew about the events of the previous evening. He'd had all the media outlets alerted, and they would be here for a noon press conference.

"We've had several requests for interviews," Crombie said, "so I have set up a number of them for this afternoon."

"Look, this is all new to me, but I need someone big … and serious. Who can we get here who has a worldwide reputation? Get me Jeff Tapper from CNN. Let's just do one big one and let them all use it."

"How about Everett Copper? He's in town for an economic forum."

"Perfect. Get him here for two p.m. We'll meet with him and even do the interview live if they want."

Crombie clearly thought that was a bad idea, but he agreed, and left the room.

I began to write my own press conference speech. I needed this to be true, in my own words, and showing my real feelings. When I was done, I edited it a bit, and ran it past Zachary. He was an English teacher after all, so I figured he must know something about this stuff. He proved to be very helpful.

A few miles away in East Vancouver, in an old Italian-run café, was Jack Dickinson, CEO of the Thomas Protocol, who should have been at work hours ago. He hadn't even met Stephen Thomas yet, and knew he was supposed to support him through his initial meetings and press conference.

Instead, he was sitting with a cappuccino in front of him, while a heavyset and poorly dressed man, seemingly straight out of mafia central casting, sat across from him. The man, who did not offer his name, was explaining to Jack how he could make him a very rich man.

Jack gave the man his undivided attention.

CHAPTER 29

At 12:02 p.m., I entered the packed boardroom. Mark Crombie gave a few details concerning my name and proper spelling and such, and advised that my written biography could be picked up at the end of the session or accessed online. When he saw me enter, he quickly introduced me.

"Ladies and gentlemen, Mr. Stephen Thomas." Then he moved over, off to one side and out of camera shot, but remained behind me and to my right. Jacob, Zachary, and Andrew stood along the wall to my left.

I stood at the microphones and began to speak:

"Just a few days ago, I was approached and asked to travel to Zurich to accept an inheritance. It turned out to be from a great-uncle I never knew. He deposited the sum of fifty million dollars into a Swiss bank one hundred years ago, intending it to grow and be used in the future. He left me a letter that told me to keep ten percent of the total balance for myself and use the rest to 'make the world a better place.'

"Today, that money has grown to about twenty-seven trillion dollars ... Yes, you heard right: twenty-seven *trillion*.

"I plan to keep less than one percent and will donate more than ninety-nine percent of these funds to causes around the world, and will do so as quickly as possible, hopefully over the next ten years. It is very early days, so we need some time to develop all of our strategies."

The reporters were pulling eye rolls and not quite believing this story. One started to pack up his gear.

"At the end of this press conference, our lawyers will provide you with any technical information you require and show you proof of the fund's value from the Commercial General Bank of Switzerland. As you can imagine, these funds are not in cash, but in stocks and bonds and mortgages and so forth, but there is in fact about one point five trillion dollars in ready cash. The transfers have started for my personal portion. In the last two days, two billion dollars has been transferred into my accounts, and we will show you that as well.

"I know this sounds crazy, but it is real. And if it seems crazy to you, imagine how I feel."

"Rich," someone mumbled, and there were some laughs.

"The other thing that seems crazy is that I have been threatened, and my life has been in danger ever since learning of these funds. Three attempts on my life were planned while in Zurich. They all failed. Last night, the shooting and explosions near the airport were an attempt on my life, which likely would have succeeded if my security chief had not planted the motorcade as a decoy, flying me out by helicopter instead. Last night, while doing their jobs to protect me, twelve security agents were killed. It was a horrific day, but it only serves to stress the fact that there are forces either trying to get these funds for themselves, or trying to prevent me from doing the good work for which these funds were intended. There are people in this world who do not want to see other people have their lives improved.

"The men who died are heroes. We will honour their service with good works in their names and care for their families forever.

"As former US Supreme Court Justice Brandeis once said, 'Sunlight is said to be the best of disinfectants.' I believe that only through transparency and openness can I hope to lead a reasonably normal life, and it is my hope that the world will want me to succeed in completing my great-uncle's dream to use this money for good.

"There is every reason to believe that people in every country of the world can, and will, benefit from this money in some way or another. But for that to succeed, we must understand that there are also forces of evil that must be defeated. Maybe we can kill them with kindness.

"The entire amount is legally mine now to distribute. Killing me will not result in the funds reverting to the organization that was to receive these funds in the case of my premature death: The United States Treasury... or more specifically, the United States military, where the money was earmarked to be spent solely on weapons. One hundred years ago that might have seemed like a good idea, but it does not seem so today.

"With that in mind, I want to announce my first two financial commitments:

"Canada is the country of my birth, and my home. As such, to the Government of Canada, I commit to donating, within twelve months, a sum equal to the entire national debt of Canada, which is about one point seven trillion dollars. There are a couple of conditions:

"Interest on the national debt costs about forty cents of every tax dollar collected. With the debt gone, I will ask the government to reduce taxes on everyone by the equivalent of twenty-five cents on the dollar. This will mean Canada will have no debt and a rich population. Canadians can build a country for the ages, and will be a role model to the world.

"I will also request that the government pass a law that, in future, they will not borrow funds to run the government on debt, except in the case of a national emergency. I will leave it to them to decide what constitutes a national emergency. My hope is that the people of this country will hold future governments accountable for keeping that promise.

"My other major financial commitment is to set aside one trillion dollars to assist military veterans in all the democratic nations of the world. We will build hospitals, build housing, pay for surgeries, and help with pensions. We need to support and celebrate brave men and women who have fought for freedom.

"Think about the enormity of this amount of money... twenty-seven thousand *billion* dollars... twenty-seven million *million* dollars... If we just split it between every man, woman, and child on the planet, everyone would get thirty-six hundred dollars. How would you use yours to make the world a better place? I will need ideas, and help and support. Come with me, work with me, and let's truly do some good... together.

"I will take your questions now."

There was a collective shouting of questions. Mark Crombie stepped in and began to create some order. I let him select questioners.

Question one: "Let's start with last night. Twelve people died, vehicles and property were destroyed, traffic was snarled for hours, and you fled the scene. Will you be arrested by the RCMP?"

Answer: "First, let me say that the Royal Canadian Mounted Police knew about my arrival and arranged permission for the motorcade to drive on airport property out to my plane. So, they were aware that a motorcade was... uh... well... motorcading. I was not actually at the scene of the explosion. We were far away in a helicopter when we first heard about the attack."

Question two: "Will you be meeting with the police?"

Answer: "Absolutely. We will do everything we can to assist them in tracking down the killers and bringing them to justice."

Question three: "Where is this letter and can we have a copy?"

Answer: "The letter is personal, and I plan for it to stay that way."

Question four: "Where did you stay last night?"

Answer: "I won't answer that."

Question five: "There are more security people in this building than I have ever encountered. How many bodyguards do you have, and how did you arrange for an office and security and staff like this so quickly?"

Answer: "Why they are here must seem obvious. I won't say how many there are, and as for the speed of arrangements, the bank in Switzerland had been working for several years to set certain processes and facilities in place, so that when they approached me, there would be a seamless and safe transition for me to begin my work. Obviously that safety has been challenged, but I am here, alive, and not willing to be stopped in my mission."

Question six: "Who was this relative of yours, and where did the money come from?"

Answer: "I have to say I have never heard of the relative, and have no idea where the original funds came from. He must have been a successful man in his day who stayed below the radar. We will investigate that ourselves, and announce those findings when we have them. At this point, I truly do not know, and for now, will keep his name private."

They pressed more on the name and the money. Eventually, they realized I had no idea beyond a name... about which I eventually caved.

"Okay, his name was Wilbur Thomas. Beyond that I have no information."

"Was that so hard?" one of the reporters sarcastically mumbled.

Then we got into questions about the money. How would I spend it, in which countries, in large or small donations, or would we buy companies and invest it? On and on they went. Many questions I could not answer. Some I refused to answer, and some I could, but sounded vague. I wished I was better prepared. Finally, I realized we were no longer accomplishing anything, and knew I needed to wrap things up.

"Ladies and gentlemen, in the coming days and weeks, we will begin to make announcements, ask for input, and seek advice and suggestions. We want lots of ideas. And no idea is too big or too small to merit consideration. The only criteria is what I call 'The Thomas Protocol,' which simply asks of any expenditure, 'Will this make the world a better place?' It's pretty simple.

"So, in my mind that can mean many things. It could mean building water plants to make sure everyone has clean drinking water, or curing diseases through increased research. Maybe it's helping to improve our existing and future environment, while figuring out ways to clean up our current damaged environment. Perhaps it's building schools in poor countries and educating the uneducated, or hospitals and healing the sick. Maybe it's all of those things …

"Imagine … just imagine what *you* would do … and when you come up with something," I smiled, "tell me, and let's do it! Thank you all very much."

Crombie stepped to the mike and answered a few routine questions to flesh out the story. Mostly they were about me.

I felt better. We had announced. I was either bathed in a bright disinfecting sunlight now and freed from pursuit, or I had just shone a beacon on myself as a target. I was pretty sure it was a bit of both, but I was not going to be scared. That part, I was sure of.

CHAPTER 30

Back in my office, I asked everyone to leave me alone for a few minutes.

I sat in my desk chair, leaned on the desk, and held my head in my hands. The adrenaline I had been running on was gone, and I felt completely exhausted. I was also hungry. I stuck my head out the door and about twenty sets of eyes looked at me.

I smiled. "Andrew, is there some way I can get something to eat?" Andrew introduced me to Paige, a very helpful office assistant.

"Paige, I am starving; do we have a coffee room here, or a cafeteria somewhere in this building?"

"Sure, Mr. Thomas, what would you like to eat? There is a food court in the lower lobby."

"A sandwich would be good, just ham and cheese, and a little mayo. No mustard or anything else on the sandwich. A Pepsi, and maybe a couple of cookies. Oh, and white bread. Yes ... I already know it isn't healthy. And Paige, thank you for doing this. Seems I can't just run down there myself anymore."

"No problem, give me ten minutes, sir."

She headed for the door, and Andrew signalled Dan to go with her to make sure the food was prepared safely.

"Where is Mike? I mean Mark? Can you ask him to join me in here? Jacob, you too."

Jacob came in immediately and stood near my desk. I sat down, leaned back in my chair, and exhaled.

A tap on the door announced Mark Crombie, who immediately entered.

"Mark, is Everett Copper on track for two p.m.?"

"Yes. The CNN team are already setting up their gear in the boardroom for a one-on-one. Everett will be here in about twenty minutes. Shall I bring him in for a pre-chat when he arrives?"

"Yes Mark, please do. Jacob, I would like you to make sure that CNN has access to anything they need from the bank to verify or prove our statements. I don't want there to be any doubt that we are telling the truth, so please get on the phone to the GCBS and handle that, okay?"

"It's evening in Zurich Steve, but I will do what I can."

"Good point. Okay, I'll leave it with you to handle."

Another tap on the door and Paige entered, holding a plastic tray with my sandwich, a Styrofoam bowl of chicken soup, a can of Pepsi, and a glass of ice.

"They were out of cookies, so I got you some soup."

"Paige, you are an angel. You have no idea how delicious this looks to me today. Thank you so much."

Paige beamed, and quickly turned and left the office. She was a gem. I could tell right away. She probably had great parents.

Quickly, I plowed my way through the food and washed it all down with the Pepsi. *Nectar of the Gods!* I laughed. So unhealthy, but damn tasty.

CHAPTER 31

Everett Copper was shorter than I thought he would be, but every bit the handsome anchorman he was on TV. Slim, fit, well-dressed, and personable. He was the son of Emmett Copper, one of the original titans of evening television.

I spoke first, as he was ushered into my office by Mark Crombie. "Mr. Copper, thank you so much for coming and helping me tell my story. Although I feel like I have known you for years, it's a pleasure to meet you in person. Call me a fan, because I am one. Your reporting from Tahrir Square in Egypt was remarkable."

Copper smiled. "Wow, you either have a good memory, or are very well briefed."

I took my finger and tapped the side of my head as though to indicate "there's a good memory in this noggin."

He continued. "Mark has briefed me on your situation. I know it's early days for you, but it looks like your story will be unfolding in the years ahead. Perhaps we can check in regularly to see the progress you're making, especially if all this is about charity and public service. We don't get a whole lot of good news stories these days."

I waved him to a seat, and Mark sat down next to him.

"Everett, can we get you anything to drink?" He asked for water and Jacob brought him a cold bottle and a glass. He drank from the bottle.

"Look, Mr. Thomas, we will do about a thirty-minute interview, and then we will edit that down to something like five minutes at most. If you want to come on my show live at some point, we will do that too, but today will be recorded. We will broadcast it later tonight. We edit on the fly, and will have it ready within about an hour of when we're done filming. We might even make the six o'clock news block in New York.

I nodded. "Let's get started."

We walked into the boardroom, and I sat down. A makeup artist brushed a little makeup onto my face to remove sheen, and a sound man wired a lavaliere microphone onto my blazer. They were ready in five minutes.

Everett settled into a seat across from me. They were using two cameras, one focused on him and the other on me. Everett would add in the introduction points later, so now he could move straight into questions:

"As I understand it, six days ago you were approached by a man who let you know you were about to receive a massive inheritance. Tell us about that meeting."

"A lawyer with a major law firm came to my home to verify my identity, and to let me know there was an inheritance in Zurich with my name on it. There was no indication of who it was from, or how much it was. It was big enough though, that the bank was willing to fly me, at their expense, to Zurich to meet with them. It didn't seem like there was much to lose, so I decided to go."

"Just like that? You got on a plane and flew to Switzerland?" Everett asked.

"Well, the lawyer had a few documents to leave with me. I ran them past my own lawyer, and it all appeared to be legitimate, and of course ... it was."

"So, what happened when you arrived in Zurich?"

"A man picked me up at the airport, and I was taken to the GCBS bank, to meet with the bank president, and that is when the story got interesting."

"What did he have to tell you?"

"He danced around the story for a while, and seemed mysterious, but apparently he was following some orderly process of his own. They verified my identity again, very carefully, but perhaps that was just as a formality, because I think they already knew who I was. Eventually, he told me that I was the sole benefactor of an inheritance left for me one hundred years ago. A great-uncle I had never met, or known about, left this sum of money to be given to a grandson of his brother, a hundred years in the future."

"You have other family members I assume, Mr. Thomas?"

"Yes, my parents are deceased, but I have a brother and two sisters."

"So, just out of curiosity, how did this great-uncle pick you over your brother as some future grandson to receive all these funds?"

"His instructions were that the funds go to the younger brother, probably assuming that there was a better chance the younger brother would still be alive a hundred years out. My brother is a really good man, but he's also a shy man who would hate the public attention this role will require, so it's probably just as well. Who knows though, perhaps all my family will be able to join in and help with this monumental task.

"Either way, my family has nothing to worry about. I will be very generous financially, and take care of all of them out of my share."

It occurred to me, at that point, that in all the rush of the past couple of days, I hadn't even told my family about any of this yet. I realized that when this interview was done, I had some calls to make. Each of them would be very wealthy in short order.

Everett pondered for a second before continuing. "So, *who* would want to kill you, and *why* would anyone want to kill you?"

I shrugged. "Keep in mind, it has only been about forty-eight hours since all this happened, so there hasn't been a lot of time to consider everything, but it's apparent from the bank's preparations that they knew there would be risks for me personally. You see, if I had been killed before the transfer of the account was completed, others could have stepped forward to try and claim the funds. Since these funds are now in my name, and the information is public, I can assure the United States military, the CIA, or anyone else who *might* have been interested, that they are now out of the running. Whoever was behind the attempts on my life has absolutely nothing to gain now, so hopefully I will be left alone."

Copper was frowning now. "You suspect the US military and the CIA were trying to kill you?"

"No." I took a deep breath to gather my thoughts. "I'm not saying that. I just know that someone did try to kill me, on multiple occasions. And some facts are hard to overlook. As I said at the press conference, the United States military was the secondary beneficiary. As such, if I was out of the picture before taking ownership of the fund, it would all be theirs. That is not an accusation, as I truly have no idea who was behind the attacks. It is simply the reality of the inheritance arrangement.

"Either way, the word is out now, and their window of opportunity has closed. The money is mine now, and will be used as I see fit." I leaned forward a bit in my chair. "Let me be perfectly clear... whether I am alive or dead, this money *will* be used the way my great-uncle intended: to make the world a better place."

CHAPTER 32

The CNN interview was pared down to three and a half minutes. Everett's introduction was as follows:

In Vancouver today, I met with a man who has just found out that he inherited enough money to make him the richest man in the history of the world... and following a protocol that requires him to use the funds to "make the world a better place," he plans to give away ninety-nine percent of it.

Is he a new political force who will bend world governments to his will through financial means? Will he convince communities or countries to meet his own view of goodness in order to get their share? Does he want to be a king or a potentate, the next tyrant, or someone more in the vein of the Dalai Lama, a man of true altruism? Time will tell. Here is our interview:

It was a disaster. Oh my God. But at least the word was out, and it was out worldwide.

CHAPTER 33
LARKMAN, WYOMING

The clandestine hit squads, which were part of an underground mercenary-for-hire service, with members around the world, had failed in their mission.

A fucking retired businessman from Canada, of all places, had eluded them.

Once a week, these agents were all required to call a special number, key in their access code, and hear a recorded message with instructions. Most of them were not involved in missions from week to week, so these were routine check-in messages.

This time, when they called, they each heard the same cryptic message:

"Stand down. Repeat. Stand down. Operation Zurich aborted. Operation Zurich aborted."

CHAPTER 34

"The prime minister is on the phone, sir."

"The prime minister?" I asked.

"Yes, sir, you know … of Canada. Martin Turner."

"Oh, my goodness. Wow." I picked up the phone. "Prime Minister, how good of you to call."

"Good morning, Mr. Thomas. I received a full report this morning about the events at the Vancouver airport two days ago. My God, how are you and your people holding up? This is so tragic."

"Prime Minister, it was horrific, and such a terrible loss. I feel responsible, even though technically I had nothing to do with it. We are doing our best to move forward and do some good work."

"Well, Mr. Thomas, please extend my deepest sympathies to your team. On other business, I saw your press conference, and I have to say I was astounded, delighted, and … to be perfectly honest, I could not believe what you want to do for Canada. Were you serious?"

"Yes, sir, I certainly am. I believe this is the best country in the world, but it has struggled to get ahead at times, and I have always thought … imagine how rich this country would be if people paid less taxes, and if the country had no debt. We would become an economic powerhouse."

"I could not agree more, uh … may I call you 'Steve'?"

I smiled. "Please do."

"Steve, we should meet and put a letter of understanding in place. I briefly met with my cabinet this morning. They are excited, but are concerned about strings being attached. We just can't let it seem that a non-elected person is forcing decisions on our democratic government. How about I fly to Vancouver and come see you."

"No, Prime Minister, you are a far more important man than me. I need to come to you. I need to make my offer in person, and I would like to have the pleasure of meeting with your cabinet to offer assurances. Do you think there is any chance we could make this an all-party decision? Could you arrange a meeting with the leaders of the five parties, so we can truly come together as a group and do this thing for Canada together? I would really like that."

"Hmmm… Well, fewer political points for me, but way better for the country. Let's do it. How about Saturday? We can meet at my residence for lunch with the other leaders, and then have a press conference outside."

I agreed to all the terms and ideas.

"Steve, I want to offer some further assistance. I am going to ask the RCMP to provide you some added security for a while, and that they accompany you to Ottawa. After the incident the other night, it seems essential."

"Oh my God, you have no idea how much we would appreciate that, but I must insist that it be temporary, for say thirty days, just until we can get everything sorted out, and I'll reimburse the government for all costs. That should help with any political problems that could cause you."

"Fantastic, Steve. My staff will connect with your people, and sort out all the details. See you on Saturday."

We both hung up. I had four people in my office eavesdropping.

"Okay, folks… *now* this is getting fun!"

CHAPTER 35

The yacht had become home base. The coast guard agreed to declare the last mile of Indian Arm as a "no-go zone" to all boat traffic. They put two smaller coast guard boats into the area to enforce the order. There were no roads into the area on either side of the fjord. The hills were very steep, though it was normally accessible by hikers, boaters, and aircraft. Our three patrol boats kept the closure area secure, and the RCMP provided two police boats as well. I travelled to work by helicopter each day. What a way to go!

The yacht was not brand new. It had been purchased from a major shipping company on the West Coast. Originally built in 1999 in Everett Washington, it had been completely refitted in 2010 by the brilliant Oregon Group's design and construction team, and an additional thirty feet was added to her length. The yacht was powered by two diesel engines, each producing 6600 horsepower, and having a range of over 6500 nautical miles. Spread over five decks, there was 25,000 square feet of space, housing fifteen guest suites, and accommodations for the crew of twenty-one. Known as the *Alissa IV*, her name would soon change to *Protocol MY IV*, which stood for Protocol Motor Yacht IV.

Until we felt secure in another location, I would be flying to and from work, and living aboard the yacht, for several weeks. Andrew was busy working with Sotheby's to find a secure home base for me. I assigned Zachary to tag along with him to learn about our security needs, as well as to offer some thoughts. He seemed to have good taste and a nice way about him, and I was growing to value his opinions.

We were still paying to reserve the floor at the Fairmont, but Andrew felt the yacht was more secure at the moment.

Jacob stuck to my side, attending every meeting, dealing with any large or small needs I might have, and attending to bank issues. He was amazing. Altermatt would be proud, and I told him so in one of our daily calls to discuss liquidation requirements to fund future projects.

We had all managed to get some sleep over the past few days. Our security was increased and there were no further attacks. We were told by the RCMP that "chatter" (whatever that was) was almost non-existent. Apparently, that meant we were pretty safe.

We had been inundated with calls and requests for meetings. There were thousands of great ideas and a few swindle attempts, but we were doing our best to keep up. We brought the whole staff team together for some brainstorming. While relying on many of the younger teammates for ideas, we had concentrated some of our initial focus toward water purification and water provision in poorer nations. Food and medical initiatives were also high on the list. We considered creating our own Doctors Without Borders type of program where we would pay highly trained doctors for their temporary work in far-flung places. We would look at desalinization plants to create pure water, and ways to provide solar-power systems that could be dropped anywhere and quickly put into use. The group would continue to edit and refine these items and would make a presentation to me in a few days.

It was Friday today, and I needed to get to Ottawa for lunch tomorrow. Andrew and my detail were ready to go. Our RCMP contingent was also ready. Working in conjunction, it made for easy transport. We motored to the airport from the office. We had two police cruisers in front with lights flashing, six motorcycle cops leapfrogging intersections for our three armoured SUVs, and were followed by two more police vehicles.

Leapfrogging was where the motorcycles would race ahead to the next intersection and block the cross traffic temporarily. The first few intersections would be blocked, and in a leapfrogging motion, they rotated like a giant tornado lightly touching down at intersections, so we never had to stop for a traffic light. I was pretty sure other drivers were pissed at us, but this was the RCMP's idea, not ours, and we were grateful for it.

The Dreamliner, now named Protocol 1, was gleaming as we approached her. The team and crew had her provisioned and cleaned. The RCMP had made sure that a bomb squad and dog team had sniffed everything out. With no issues and no problems, we were cleared for departure. Paige had been assigned for this trip to act as my personal assistant, meaning she was in charge of everything from putting away clothes and helping with wardrobe in Ottawa to attending to calls and alerting me to any business matters. She was a special kid and a fast learner, and I was glad to give her this exposure and experience. She would be running an empire one day; you could just tell. She ate up the challenges, big or small, and positively glowed when given praise.

Flying at thirty-seven thousand feet, it was about a five-hour flight. We were wheels up at two p.m., and with the three-hour time difference, we would be in Ottawa at about ten p.m. local time. We had decided that I would stay on the plane for the night. The airport grounds were just about the most secure place in the city. The security team would reduce to just Andrew, Joe, and Dan inside the plane, and the local RCMP would secure the plane at ground level. The rest of our detail, plus Paige and Jacob, would stay at the airport hotel, where they would likely sleep better and clean up easier in the morning. We had the shower on the aircraft, so I could share it in the morning with the other guys. Including the crew sleeping quarters, everyone had a bed. One flight attendant and the chef stayed on board to care for us.

It was quite an ordeal to transport an entourage of staff people, attendants, crew, and security. I wondered if it would get any easier, or if it would just feel easier because we would get better at it over time.

I had a drink before bed, and lowered the blinds in my stateroom to block out the blinking lights of the RCMP police vehicles stationed around the aircraft for the night. As I lay in bed, I knew tomorrow would be a monumental day, meeting with the prime minister.

CHAPTER 36

Saturday morning started on board the plane, at seven, as the staff returned from their hotels to begin our day. Onboard, we had a coffee meeting scheduled for nine-thirty with eight senior members of Cabinet, excluding the prime minister, who we would be seeing at lunch. They came across the tarmac in a small airport-shuttle bus.

They were obviously impressed and envious when they boarded the plane. Politicians travel a great deal, and in most cases, it's by scheduled airlines. Sometimes it is by a small private government jet. Only the prime minister had the full use of a "head of state aircraft." The RCMP actually made the decision about which aircraft he would be using based on security needs, but it was most often the Polaris CC-150, which is a military version of the Airbus 310. It was comfortable inside, but spartan. They all wanted a tour of this Dreamliner beast before we sat down to chat. We moved to the forward salon area, which had seating for ten. Andrew, Jacob, and Paige stood off to one side, while the eight ministers took their seats. I sat in one of the single seats opposite the four-seater sofa. The flight attendants brought around coffee, tea, and lattes.

"Well, thank you so much for coming this morning. It is very exciting to have you aboard 'Protocol 1.'" (I air-quoted 'Protocol 1,' hoping to get a smirk, which it did.)

"I am sure you have a bunch of questions for me, so fire away."

Given his role, the minister of finance seemed to be the leader of the group.

"We understand you have offered to pay off the national debt. Let me start by saying that... that is incredible! To cut to the chase, though, what's the catch? How many strings are really attached? After all, we are talking about one point seven trillion dollars."

I responded carefully. "Let me be as clear as I can. This is a gift, pure and simple, to the people of Canada and to their future. There are no 'strings,' but there are a couple of *requests* which I hope you will voluntarily adopt.

"About forty percent of taxes collected goes to pay the interest of the debt. If I pay off the debt, then you can afford to reduce taxes, and I would suggest something like this. Of the forty percent currently used for interest payments, reduce taxes by enough to take away twenty-five percent of that and keep the other fifteen percent to bulk up reserves and invest in the future.

"You will have no debt, taxpayers will keep more of their money, and the economy will roar with activity.

"My second request is the passing of a law to hold your own feet to the fire, and that law would simply say, uh... Jacob, what is that language we worked on?"

Jacob was holding a pad, and said, "Something simple like, 'The Government of Canada commits to no future deficit financing, except in the case of a national emergency. The Government of Canada will, from time to time, define what constitutes a national emergency.'"

"Thank you, Jacob."

The minister of national revenue spoke up, and she did not look happy. "No offence, Mr. Thomas, but isn't this a case of the super wealthy elite telling the masses how to run their country? I mean, who are you to tell us what to do?"

Everyone squirmed uncomfortably in their seats. I stared at her with a smile on my face and let the silence linger. Just for fun. In business, I had always hated bullies and assholes, and had been involved in enough political lobbying that I knew how to play the power game too. When she finally squirmed in her chair from the uncomfortable silence, the timing was right.

"Well, first, I have been superrich for about a week. Second, with a one-point-seven-trillion-dollar debt, it would be hard to convince anyone that you are doing a great job of running the country now, so yes … maybe someone does need to tell you how to run *our* country."

There was dead silence, and then I continued, "But look, I am a nobody. I have no right to tell you what to do. I am speaking as a citizen and simply offering you a suggestion to consider. If I have made this too onerous, I completely understand …. and if you prefer, I am prepared to withdraw the offer. I certainly don't want to cause any problems for the country that I love.

"My preference would be that the government keep it simple. Put out a press release like, uh … Jacob, what is that other language we worked on?"

Jacob cleared his throat. "The government is pleased to announce that, after careful consideration with all parties in the House of Commons, and in order to enhance our country for the benefit all Canadians, we shall pass a law that states that the Government of Canada commits to no future deficit financing except in the case of a national emergency. The Government of Canada will, from time to time, define what constitutes a national emergency. We will lower income taxes on citizens and businesses by an amount equivalent to five-eighths of the taxes currently collected to pay the interest on the national debt. This should mean a general tax cut for all in the range of twenty-five percent."

I took over again. "Thanks again, Jacob. Here is the thing... call me stupid, but once I pay off the debt, you can repeal this law and do whatever the hell you want. You are not held to anything, but I believe that, unless there is a genuine national emergency, most citizens will hold you to that bargain. That will be good for Canada, for government, and for our democracy.

"Oh, and one more thing, I want the all-party vote to be unanimous." Now they all mumbled, knowing that would be nearly impossible.

"Create your own language, and come back with a different plan if you like. The strings attached to this are tiny threads that you can cut anytime you want. And really, how is this not a win for everyone? Ask yourself this: Is this Thomas guy getting anything out of this? Nope. Not a thing.

"But more importantly, will this help make the world a better place? As a proud Canadian, I can think of nothing better for the world than a strong, prosperous, united, growing, and thriving Canada.

"Oh," and I looked at the minister of national revenue, who was still eyeing me suspiciously, "I was only kidding about it being unanimous, but let's try to make it close. It would be good for the country, but I won't be offended if you personally vote against it. I am sure your constituents will reward you at the next election for your bravery."

She finally smiled at me. "Mr. Thomas, you are a very good arm twister. You will have my vote, but I had to be skeptical."

"Yes, you did," I responded very quickly. "And good for you, and thank you in advance for letting me make this gift to our nation. We are all counting on each of you to make the world a better place every day. I admire each of you. I thank you for your service, and thank you for coming today." With that, I stood up, signalling that the meeting was over.

They wanted to take a couple of pictures of the meeting, which Jacob obliged, taking them with various cell phones. When he was done, I escorted them to the aircraft door, shaking hands with each before they left and boarded their bus.

I looked at Andrew. "I think I might have been an ass back there. Was I an ass?"

In a playful tone I had not heard from Andrew before, he said, "Yes, sir, if you insist on me saying so, you were definitely an ass, but that was fun to watch. I am not sure they have ever been spoken to quite so directly."

I smiled at Andrew and laughed a little, and then turned back to the main salon.

"Okay, Andrew, Jacob … what's next?"

CHAPTER 37

"We have the luncheon at the prime minister's residence at noon. They asked us to have the motorcade to the residence by eleven forty-five, and they will be giving us a police escort, but no leapfrogging today. Ottawa is a heavily secured city, so they feel confident about our safety."

"Okay, Andrew, sounds good. When do we need to leave?"

"We would like to be rolling at eleven fifteen, so you have about thirty minutes before we leave."

"Perfect, I need to use the washroom, and check some personal emails."

I headed to my suite and into the bathroom. To be perfectly honest, I was nervous. I had never met the young prime minister, but I had voted for him in the last election. I swung between Conservative and Liberal governments, depending on the state of the economy and what economic or social philosophies were needed at any given moment.

Turner was an interesting guy. I had initially assessed him as a lightweight. He went to university and became an engineer in Vancouver. His family was from Montreal. His father had been prime minister of Canada for eleven years, with three straight majorities. He was loved by some, admired by many, and hated by a few, but such is the life of a politician.

As a kid, I remember it was almost a requirement to "hate Turner" if you were from the west. At that time, from the Manitoba-Ontario border to the West Coast, the Liberals held only eleven seats in the entire western side of the country.

History was kinder after Turner senior retired. It became evident that we had been led by a truly deep thinker, and an intellectual of his day. Brilliant, combative, and whimsical, even if you disagreed with his politics, he was a magnificent creation in many ways.

Martin Turner had stepped out of his father's shadow, giving an emotional eulogy at his father's funeral, and was instantly in the national spotlight. It was not long before his name was on the list of many as a future leader of Canada. To his credit, he took the long route. He ran as a member of parliament and won. He served wherever needed, and kept a low profile to learn his job. After a couple of failed elections that the Liberal party lost while led by far more experienced men, the party turned to young Turner as the next great hope. He was now the leader for the next generation.

While Turner was serving as leader of the third largest party in parliament, and out of town on business, his home was entered by an intruder. A photograph of a handgun and pictures of his children were left on the kitchen table in order to frighten him. The intruder left, and Mrs. Turner found the photos the following morning, causing obvious panic and fear for the family's safety.

In Canada, where security is normally not a huge deal, the leader of the third party had no personal protection. He was on his own. He rushed back from his trip to be with his wife and family. Until the intruder was caught, local police stepped in to protect the family.

I remember, at the time, being amazed by the lack of reaction by Prime Minister Winston Mathers.

At the time, I recall chatting with friends and saying that Mathers had a chance to look magnanimous and instead looked cruel. If I was him, I would have come out and said to the press: "With Mr. Turner's house being broken into and a threatening message left, we feel it is prudent to provide the leaders of all the parties with temporary protection until the intruder is caught and this case is solved. Therefore, the RCMP will be providing protection to the Turner family until this is over."

Instead, Mathers did nothing. Oh, and Mathers' security detail? A hundred and twenty people. Turner's? Zero.

I voted Liberal because of that level of unkindness.

Turner went on to win the next election in a surprise upset, leaping from third party status to first place with a majority government. He selected his Cabinet, and populated it with an equal number of men and women. He embraced all races and religions, straight and gay, men and women, young and old.

And now, a few years later, I would be joining him and his lovely wife, Melissa, for lunch at his residence.

CHAPTER 38

Jacob found me sitting and looking at my iPhone.

"Steve, the motorcade is ready. What do you want me to do at this lunch?"

"Just be your charming self and be deferential to our hosts. They are the leaders of the five parties in parliament, and they will each feel very important. We told them that my executive assistant would be joining us for lunch, so they are expecting you."

We headed for the door of the aircraft and actually walked down the stairs in a normal fashion. Andrew was loosening his tight grip on security.

We had three cars of our own. Plus the RCMP had four, so the seven vehicles moved off in unison and soon we were nearing the prime minister's residence.

"This is not the most impressive home in Ottawa, Jacob, but it looks stately. The US ambassador's residence is actually one of the finest estates in the city, along with the Vatican's embassy."

"Have you been to each of them?"

"Nope, but I went on a tour once and then saw photographs. I am just a normal guy, remember? At least until a week or so ago."

The prime minister's residence, known as 24 Sussex Drive, came into view on the left. The gates were open, but there were construction vehicles all over the place, and construction dumpsters and such. That was when I remembered that the house was being totally gutted and renovated. It had fallen into disrepair over the years and needed about $10 million of upgrades to make it new again.

Turner was staying in a smaller government home, normally occupied by the principal secretary to the governor general of Canada. The governor general was Canada's official head of state and the queen's representative in Canada. It was predominantly a ceremonial position.

The motorcade was led through the gates of Rideau Hall and driven down a long driveway to the stately home of the governor general.

"Oh my gosh, this is way grander than I had expected. I had no idea we were coming here!"

There was even a red carpet. As we pulled up, the governor general was standing there to greet us. I confess I found it embarrassing to be treated so grandly.

We were greeted graciously and led into the grand mansion. Jacob followed a few steps behind, and only Andrew and Dan came along for security. The entire property was well secured, so there were few worries. As we entered the dining room, we were greeted by the other party leaders. Security remained in the hall while the rest of us went inside and the doors were closed.

The room was stunning, overlooking a lovely garden area.

In addition to Turner, the four other party leaders were Brian Stanfield, leader of the Conservative Party; Daljit Sandu, leader of the New Democratic Party; April Weaver, leader of the Green Party; and Adele Chabot, leader of the Bloc Québécois.

Each were charming in their own right, and fighters for their causes.

We all found our seats, which had small paper name plates, and sat down. Governor General Janice Lebot sat at the head of the table. I was seated in the middle on one side of the table, and the prime minister was directly across from me. He had Jacob on his left and Adele on his right. I had April to my left and Brian Stanfield to my right. Daljit sat at the other end of the table.

The governor general spoke, welcoming everyone to Rideau Hall, for what she hoped would be a monumental day for Canada. She was a former fighter pilot who had flown missions over Afghanistan, a fascinating résumé to be sure. She reminded us that her role was apolitical, so she would stay for lunch, and then leave us to our work.

That set the stage for a very social lunch. Considering the five leaders were adversaries, they got along very well in this setting. It was good to see people who could disagree, but not be disagreeable.

Lunch was spectacular, and another step along my path to also becoming the fattest man in the world.

Now that we were finished lunch, the governor general suggested we move to the sitting room next door, and said that she would leave us now. She took the time to say goodbye to everyone, offered a few hugs, and then left us to our business. I think I was smitten.

CHAPTER 39

We were all seated, had our coffee or tea, and were ready to get down to business.

Turner spoke first. "Steve, you have made an incredible offer to Canada. Can you tell us more about what you have in mind? And then we would like to ask some questions."

"Of course, Prime Minister. Look, I am sure you all know the story so far about this ton of money dropped on me by a distant relative."

There were smiles at my casual verbal approach.

"As a citizen of this country, I always thought about how rich the country would be if only it had no debt. Instead of always paying for yesteryear, we could live for today and save for tomorrow. So, when all this happened, I knew I could make that wish come true.

"You probably have heard that I have a couple of basic requests. Jacob, perhaps you can read that document we prepared and shared with the senior Cabinet this morning."

Jacob cleared his throat, just as he had done this morning. "The government is pleased to announce, after careful consideration with all parties in the House of Commons, that in order to enhance a country to benefit all Canadians, we shall pass a law that states that the government of Canada commits to no future deficit financing, except in the case of a national emergency. The government of Canada will, from time to time, define what constitutes a national emergency. We will lower income taxes on citizens and businesses by an amount equivalent to five-eighths of the taxes currently collected to pay the interest on the national debt. This should mean a general tax cut for all in the range of twenty-five percent."

I took over again. "And, as I said this morning, you can call me stupid, but once I pay off the debt, you can repeal this law and do whatever you want. You are not held to anything. But I believe that Canadians will hold you to that deal unless there is a genuine national emergency. And all of this will be good for Canada, for our government, and for our democracy."

I let that settle for a moment and then continued. "So, let's think about this politically. The Conservatives win by letting me pay off the debt to make Canada more prosperous and reduce taxes for businesses. The NDP voters win because average Canadians will get a big tax cut and keep more of their money. The Green Party wins because, with no debt, there is money left for government to focus more on the environment. The Bloc Québécois wins because a richer Canada can do more for Quebec. And the Liberals win because their next budget will be balanced, with no national debt.

"So, let me ask you, is there a downside to this agreement, even with my small, temporary strings attached?"

Turner spoke first. "On behalf of all of us, let me say thank you for this tremendous offer. I am sure we all agree on that." Heads nodded as they all affirmed the comment.

On specific issues, Stanfield spoke up first. "My party preaches fiscal responsibility. This helps us achieve that. My only concern is that there should be a sunset clause on the deficit-financing aspect. I say that because I think it would be good to have that debate, say every five years, and re-up the provision to remind Canadians of what this is. We can vote in parliament to keep fiscal responsibility front and centre."

Daljit, the newest leader, was next. "I would rather we paid off part of the debt and use this windfall to create more benefits for Canadians now."

April looked at me directly and asked, "Steve why don't you just use it to solve global warming? Governments will just waste the money and create new debt in time. Spending it directly will do the world better."

The leader of the Bloc felt the deal was possibly acceptable as offered. She didn't want to endorse anything that might make Canada look too good, though. After all, her party wanted Quebec to separate from Canada.

Turner said, "I love the flexibility it would give our nation, and we all know it will deliver long-term prosperity for our country. What other nation has this opportunity?"

It was my turn again. "So, do you think we can get unanimous support? There may be the odd naysayer, but could we get an all-party resolution and have everyone approve it? I would like you all to get credit for this. This should not be a political win for Prime Minister Turner. It should be a win for all Canadians."

A few people mumbled that, realistically, nothing ever passes unanimously.

"Okay, so here is my deal," I said, cutting to the chase. "You have seven days to arrive at an all-party agreement. Then we will pay the funds within thirty days. Next, you will have the tax legislation and anti-deficit financing legislation passed within those thirty days, contingent on receipt of the funds. Do it together and share the credit."

Stanfield asked, "And what happens if we don't meet the timeline?"

"I move on to the next project. Fast but fair, right? Don't delay. This is about as easy as it gets. Let's make the world a better place!" I stood up. "Thank you all so much for lunch. I appreciate you taking the time to meet with me today, and I am grateful to you for considering this offer. I hope you will take the deal. It may just be the greatest moment for Canada, ever."

I nodded to Jacob, who got to his feet. "Now, we need to get going."

Handshakes and a few hugs later, and we were outside, climbing into the motorcade. We left early and skipped the press conference.

CHAPTER 40

The five leaders stared at each other.

April Weaver, the Green Party leader, noted for her colourful language, said. "Holy fuck, you guys, this is amazing. Going forward, imagine the financial position this puts us in. In a decade, this country will be one of the richest per capita in the world!"

Stanfield asked, "Does anyone see a downside to this? The guy has made this so easy for us. The strings he has attached have no real force. Everybody wins in my view."

No one disagreed.

Turner, trying to be magnanimous, said, "So, how about each of us go back to our caucuses, explain the deal, and meet again in forty-eight hours. Then we can introduce an all-party motion, get unanimous consent, if that is the decision, and then I would suggest that the five of us hold a joint press conference, and announce this to Canadians."

Daljit added, "The public would kill us if we refused!"

They all rose, smiled at each other, shook hands, and headed outside to meet the reporters who had gathered. Four leaders spoke with great conviction about the benefits to Canada and the desire for an all-party resolution.

The leader of the Parti Québécois confirmed she was supportive, but also said that she had some serious reservations.

They were all political opponents of one another, but were rarely separated very far on the major issues. They knew they had to make this work.

CHAPTER 41

It was good to be back on the plane. It wasn't long before we were taxiing to the runway and leaving Ottawa behind. We were heading back to Vancouver, and would be staying on the yacht again. Tomorrow was supposed to be house-hunting day.

There really were no existing properties that would meet our needs anywhere close to the downtown area, or even within twenty minutes of it. To acquire the needed space, we would likely be in the outlying areas, and that didn't really appeal to me. The little condo I always kept in the city was only a bit more than seven hundred square feet, but it was within a twenty-minute walk of nearly anything a person would want to do.

Zachary had the list narrowed to three possibilities that he felt would work for me. He had taken on the house-hunting challenge with gusto, and had been wearing down the realtors for the last few days, but he had another concept he wanted to discuss.

I decided to have some quiet time and headed to my suite. I lay down on the couch to watch some TV, and then figured I might as well have a nap, since we would be in the air for five hours.

Our flight attendant checked that I didn't need anything and then left me alone.

We arrived in Vancouver at four thirty p.m. local time. Zachary, who had not accompanied us on this trip, had come along with the motorcade to meet us, and was waiting in my car.

"I have an amazing idea of how we can accomplish two things with one effort."

"What's that?" I asked.

"Well, we have a few homes for you to look at, and I am sure that one of them will work for you temporarily, but long-term, I have a better idea. You need a spectacular property, something on the ocean, with great views, in an amazing neighbourhood. I have found a parcel of land that would work perfectly, especially if we bought the neighbouring two properties as well. There is only one problem with it: It is currently a city park!"

I laughed. "There is no way the city of Vancouver is going to let me buy a park to build a house on. How do you plan to convince them?"

"Simple. Money! Pick a number, any number, take it to the mayor, and tell him that you will make a colossal donation, which he and the city can use to buy and build parkland and recreational services throughout the city, improve roads and infrastructure, build lower-income rental apartments, public transit, day care centres, feed the homeless, whatever they want. The entire annual budget of the city is about one point five billion dollars. Imagine if they had fifty billion dollars dropped into their laps. Then tell them that the park you want will revert to the city upon your death. That's the plan!"

He looked at me with the eyes of a very enthusiastic schoolteacher who had never made a business deal in his life.

I smiled at him, and then smiled some more. It was a crazy idea. It might just be crazy enough to work.

"Let's drive by this park and have a look. I actually love this idea. The amount of good that donation could do for the people of this city would be amazing!"

Zach had already told the security team about the park, and they knew the way. It wasn't long before we were sliding along Point Grey Road and pulled up in front of Volunteer Park.

The view was truly amazing. If we were to acquire the two properties to the east, it would be an extraordinary parcel of land. Andrew felt it could be fully fenced, gated, and secured reasonably easily, and would be about a fifteen-minute drive to the airport, and a ten-minute drive to the office. Combined with the neighbouring lots, it was about three or four acres, measuring about two hundred feet from the road to the ocean, and about eight hundred feet along the waterfront.

Zach was beaming as we walked the property, took in the views, and smelled the salt air. He was looking for some reaction, and he was getting one, because I was struggling to wipe the smile off my face.

"If we could get this, it would be a piece of heaven. My only concern is that this city has a serious dedication to parks and parkland, and there will be a battle to try and buy any of it. The other alternative is to just buy a strip of existing homes along this street and do the same thing. We could do that for under a hundred million. Let's meet with the mayor and see what he thinks. You and Jacob set up a meeting with him, but don't talk any specifics. Just tell him I need an hour of his time."

Not surprisingly, the next day (a Sunday yet), the mayor had cleared his schedule and was available to meet at two p.m. Since city hall was closed on Sundays, we arranged to pick him up at the Helijet Terminal in the harbour and fly him to the yacht.

As the helicopter came into view, people scurried to get ready for his arrival. Jacob and Zach were in suits and ties, and so was I. It was the mayor, after all. He showed up in slacks and a golf shirt and wind breaker. He was a handsome guy, who looked pretty good in anything.

In such a small landing area, the pilot made sure the passengers stayed seated until the rotors had come to a complete stop. Once they had, Mayor Robinson and his assistant hopped out, and I went outside along with Andrew and a couple of security men to greet him.

I walked forward with an outstretched hand and shook his. "Welcome aboard, Mr. Mayor; thank you so much for joining us today."

"Thanks for having me. Please, call me 'Craig.'"

Finally, another first name guy. I liked him already.

Craig and I had never met. He was a hardworking mayor who cared about people, but sometimes made it tough to do business because of his social and environmental positions. This would be an interesting meeting.

A steward came forward and offered the mayor a glass of champagne. I showed us to some seats in the main salon, and promised the mayor a full tour if he wanted one when we were done.

"Steve, I understand you were in Ottawa yesterday. How did your meeting go?"

"It is interesting how hard it is to give away money, Craig. I am already learning. My new role in life may be more difficult than the fun I anticipated it being, but nonetheless, it will be rewarding."

We made a bit of small talk, and then I asked if we could speak about some business.

"Of course. I was fairly sure I was asked to come and see you about something other than just a fine glass of champagne."

I raised one eyebrow and responded, "Never discount a fine glass of champagne." We both smirked. "Now, here is what I want to talk to you about. I want to live in Vancouver, and to do so, I need to find a plot of land that can accommodate my home and security needs. I need about three to five acres. So, here is what my team is thinking: I can go and buy several adjoining properties, tear down the existing homes, merge them into one, build what I need, and when I am done with the place, sell it for a pretty penny, or I could look at another more generous idea, involving a donation to the city."

"Well, that has a nice ring to it indeed!"

"So, here is our better idea: We've found a small parcel of land the city owns that would work perfectly for us, especially if we can buy the two places next door. The only problem is that the plot of land is currently a park."

"A park? The city doesn't sell parkland, Steve."

"Oh, I appreciate that, so here is the idea. I won't buy it. You will grant me a lifetime lease on the land for the total sum of one dollar. In exchange for that, I will donate fifty billion dollars to the city of Vancouver to be used to revitalize existing parks, acquire new parks, improve public transit, build low-cost rental apartments, rebuild infrastructure, help the homeless, build day care centres, and anything else the city wants to do with it.

"In thirty-five years, or when I die, whichever comes *second*, as I am enough of a target as it is, the property reverts to the city along with all the improvements on it. We can agree now to either leave the buildings, destroy them, or return the property to parkland. We will also turn over the two lots next door that we hope to acquire. I am fifty-five, so this is probably a thirty-five-year deal at the very most. You will have more money than any city in Canada, and all the advantages every city can only dream of. And you, sir, will be a hero for negotiating such a tremendously one-sided deal in favour of the city."

"Which park?"

"Volunteer Park on Point Grey Road."

"You have good taste. I live close by."

"If you agree, my only other request is that you will handle all of our permits and inspections on a total priority basis. We don't want special treatment; we want to obey all the rules and laws, but we need to build this as fast as possible, and that requires city hall to clear the decks and make us a priority. If that entails additional costs to the city, we will pay those costs too.

"And I need an answer in seven days. Every day we delay is a danger to my life. Can you make that happen, Mr. Mayor?"

"What if we need longer?"

"Vancouver is my first choice, but we have a plan A, B, and C in the works, in surrounding municipalities. You get first crack, sir, and in the interests of the city… please, do your best to make it work. It would be fantastic."

"Then I had better get to work. Is there anything else I need to know, any other terms, conditions, or items?"

Robinson's assistant was madly making notes.

"None, Craig, it is as simple as that. I get the park, rezoning, and speedy assistance from city hall. I give it all back when I die, or soon thereafter, and the city gets fifty billion dollars. Oh, and that other one dollar for the lease too." I playfully winked.

"Got it. We have a council meeting tomorrow. I will present this in camera and have a preliminary answer for you tomorrow. There is a legal process for us to follow. I will see how fast we can make this work. I will call you tomorrow night. Wow, this is incredible. Thank you, Steve."

"Have a safe flight, Mr. Mayor."

He climbed aboard the chopper, the rotors started, and in three minutes they had lifted off. We waved from the yacht windows and hoped he could make it happen. It would be crazy, and sad for the city if he couldn't.

CHAPTER 42

The council meeting was called early. The mayor's assistant had been on the phone late into the evening, convincing all the councillors to be at city hall by nine a.m.

They held the meeting in the boardroom off the mayor's office, which sat about twelve people. The mayor pitched the idea. There were muffled exclamations (like "holy shit") around the table.

Everyone smiled at each other as the mayor began to suggest some of the things that could be accomplished with that much money.

"So, he wants a waterfront park, huh?" Councillor Jackson asked. "We are actually going to give this guy a gorgeous little park right on the ocean, located on one of the nicest streets in the city?"

"Well first, it's not that gorgeous. It is a piece of land, with a lawn, a few trees, and nothing else but a great view. And no, we are not giving or selling it to him," the mayor corrected him. "We are leasing him the park for thirty-five years for an outrageous amount of money."

"Well, I want you all to know I will be voting against this, regardless what the deal is. I won't give up one square foot of parkland, no matter how much money he offered."

"I'm with Jackson. It goes against my values. The superrich can't just demand the best piece of land and have it given to them by the city," Councillor Chen added.

The mayor couldn't believe what he was hearing. "This is a chance for us to do more good with more money, in a shorter period of time, than could have ever been hoped for. We could eliminate property taxes for a generation if we wanted to. The possibilities are endless. What do the rest of you think?"

One by one, they asked questions, and gave their vote. Three more said they couldn't support it under any conditions. The other five were on board, and with the mayor's vote, they would have a majority. It was pretty clear that two of the naysayers were planning to run for mayor, and the other three were strong supporters of one of them.

The mayor called for a ten-minute recess and retired to his office. He called Jacob's line, who handed Steve his mobile phone.

"Steve, we are sitting at six to five, so it looks like we can get this passed, and expedite a decision for you on this by Friday."

"Six to five? Seriously? Who was dumb enough to be in the five? Unbelievable. I confess I am shocked, Craig. Remember when I said how hard it is to give money away?"

"I'm pretty shocked too, Steve."

"Well... I think we will withdraw our request, and move on to Plan B. I don't like putting you or the city in such a difficult position. It just wouldn't be fair to anyone."

"What?"

"I am just imagining local politicians picketing the job site, protesting the use of the park by me, and it all just becoming a giant gong show. With unanimous support or very strong support, it would not have been a big deal, but now... I have to say I am really shocked. I thought you had more support on your council, but hey, this is how democracy works, and I'm fine with that."

"But, Steve—"

"Thanks for calling, Mr. Mayor. And please tell your fellow councillors that we appreciate their consideration. Oh, and be sure to let them know that, in my interview with the local media in a couple of minutes, I'll let them know that we appreciated your consideration, but that we could not work an acceptable deal with Vancouver's council. I will be sure to say that you were a strong supporter.

"By the way, do you have the direct line for the mayor of Surrey? I need to move on to plan B. Well, never mind. It's all good. Thanks again, Mr. Mayor, I truly appreciate your support."

Before the mayor could say goodbye, Steve had hung up.

The mayor walked back into the boardroom. Even the naysayers were chatting about all the initiatives they would like to see built or developed with this enormous windfall.

Jackson looked at the mayor with a big smile and asked, "So, when do we get the fifty billion?"

The mayor raised his voice a bit. "We don't! He didn't want to be the subject of a giant political shitstorm by a feuding council barely able to pass the greatest gift in history, so he asked me to thank you all very much for your consideration of the idea. He has moved on to his plan B. Surrey, of all places. Jesus fucking Christ, have we blown it or what? And worse yet, he is having a press conference this afternoon, as we speak." The mayor flipped on the television.

CHAPTER 43

Steve stepped to the microphone in the board-room of his offices and addressed the gathered press. He had specifically invited only the local press to this briefing.

"Hi, all … thank you for coming. I have called this press conference to inform you that I made a request to the city of Vancouver to demonstrate my commitment to this city. I met with the mayor, who was very helpful, and asked him to discuss the matter with his council.

"What we were seeking was to make a massive donation to the city of Vancouver to be used for lower-income housing, feeding the homeless, improving public transit, building day care centres, improving infrastructure, buying up land and creating more parks, and anything else they wanted to spend the money on. We believed that this would make Vancouver the greatest city in our country, and most certainly, the richest.

"In exchange for the donation, we asked for a thirty-five-year lease on a two-point-nine-acre parcel of land that is currently used as a park, and for the city to use every possible way to expedite the building process of a new home for me on that site. At the end of the lease, the property would revert back to the city. Everyone would be a winner.

"Unfortunately, in a straw poll of councillors, the decision was only six to five in favour. From my perspective, this would have led to the property becoming a political football instead of the home and personal sanctuary I was hoping to build. I don't want controversy; I want security and comfort.

"I fully understand and appreciate the consideration the councillors gave the issue, and respect their position. We will now move on to our plan B. Thanks again to the mayor, who was very helpful and supportive. I will take your questions now."

"How much money was the city going to get?"

"Fifty billion dollars."

"Billion?"

"Yes. Next question."

"Five city councillors turned down fifty billion dollars to lease a two-point-nine-acre park? Was it part of Stanley Park?"

Stanley Park is a jewel of the city. There is no way it would be sold or leased or used, even for a trillion dollars.

"No, it was for Volunteer Park on Point Grey Road. It's a two-point-nine-acre parcel on the ocean. Hey, I have no hard feelings. I fully appreciate that they want to protect parkland."

None of the reporters had even heard of Volunteer Park.

Another reporter dove in. "So, let me get this straight, they advised you that they would approve it, but they didn't have a big enough margin of approval to please you? So, after approving it by a one-vote margin, you are walking away? That sounds pretty arrogant, doesn't it?"

"You can judge that better than me. The budget of the city of Vancouver is one point five billion dollars a year, and I offered a gift of fifty billion dollars. Imagine what that could have done for this amazing city. The fact that fifty percent of the council would vote against it tells me that my request must have been unreasonable. I think that taxpayers will appreciate that the city council was looking out for them ... and that is fine. That is what democracy is all about."

A shouted question: "Who was against it?"

"No idea. You will have to ask the mayor."

Back at city hall, several councillors and the mayor were gathered around a television, watching the press conference live. Every one of them knew the voters would politically annihilate them. Their careers would be over. Thomas had boxed them in, and done so rather brilliantly for a political novice.

The mayor spoke up. "Our regular council meeting starts in seven minutes. I suggest we get in that room, and that one of you brings this up under a point of order, asks for debate on it immediately, and that we publicly vote on it and approve it *unanimously*. We have to fix this."

Seventy-four minutes later, the motion to approve the lease of Volunteer Park for one dollar for thirty-five years was approved unanimously, in exchange for the donation to city coffers of $50 billion—an approval reached in record time. Every hurdle was dealt with and the paperwork would all be concluded within twenty-four hours.

The mayor called a thirty-minute recess. The councillors followed him to his office, and stood around as he made a call to Jacob.

"Hello, Mr. Mayor, this is Jacob. What can I do for you, sir?"

"Hi, Jacob, is Steve available?"

"At the moment, sir, he is on his phone. We are actually en route to a meeting in Surrey. Can you hold one moment, sir?" Forty-five seconds later, Steve took the call.

"Sorry to keep you holding, Craig. What can I do for you?"

"Steve, you said we had seven days to get this deal done. I hope you are a man of your word."

"I believe I am."

"We got the deal done, unanimously. Politicians are way less courageous in public. The park is yours, the zoning will be done tomorrow, and the paperwork will be finished by Thursday. I am hoping you will just say 'done' and we can get this finalized, so you can make your contribution to the city."

"Listen closely, Mr. Mayor. 'DONE.' The money will be in the city's account on Friday by five p.m. I will have Jacob call your office tomorrow for the routing numbers."

The mayor ended his call, which had been on speaker phone. The councillors high-fived each other and shook hands. They had taken it to the precipice and almost made a massive error by being arrogant and playing politics, but let's face it, they thought Thomas had been pretty arrogant too. He had pushed them, but they knew they had agreed to something that would truly benefit their citizens for generations to come, and they would have the opportunity to make the world a better place in the process.

"Well, look at us. We put politics aside and did the right thing for the people," the mayor said. "If we aren't careful, this might catch on!"

They all laughed, except Jackson.

But he's a fucking asshole anyway, thought the mayor.

CHAPTER 44

In Northern Wyoming, about six miles west of Larkman, overlooking Rolands Reservoir, there was an unusual site, though it had been well hidden. Buried twelve feet underground was a doomsday bunker. A series of ten-by-twenty-four-by-seven-foot-high steel modules were connected together like an anthill. A massive hole had been excavated, the modules installed, the soil put back, and vegetation replanted. The rabbit's warren totalled 3360 square feet of space in fourteen modules.

There were camouflaged air shafts. The power lines were buried. And there was a parking area surrounded by an earthen berm with a frame of camouflage netting overhead to mask the vehicles. An obscure, clandestine branch of the US Government had funded the facility.

This small facility was a secret outpost, utilized by an outfit of self-professed patriots, former military, and military wannabes, who wanted to serve their country and arrive in glory one day. Much like foreign terrorists, these domestic terrorists were available for hire. They could be contacted through the dark web by various government agencies looking for some "off the books" assistance. The group had performed work for the highest bidder, but it was mostly routed through the CIA in the US, or MI6 in the United Kingdom. They had also executed a couple of jobs for CSIS, Canada's fledgling spy agency. While the nineteen men of this organization considered themselves patriots, in any courtroom in the world, they were simply murderers and terrorists.

Module One held the entrance area, storage for coats, boots, gear, and a washroom. The next two modules were all weapons storage and maintenance areas. Modules Four and Five formed an office and planning area, followed by a living room and entertainment areas in the next two modules. These were followed by Module Eight for food and provisions, Kitchen-Module Nine, and Dining-Module Ten. The last four modules were sleeping barracks, washrooms, and shower facilities.

Buried nearby was a generator module, which was nearly sound-proof when operated. There was also a five-thousand-gallon water storage tank, which was fed water pumped from the nearby reservoir.

This facility could be entirely self-sustained for nineteen men for up to sixty days, without running out of food or provisions. They might well kill each other before sixty days were up, but if they had to "go to ground," they could. The property surrounding the area was signed with "no trespassing" and "violators will be shot" postings. The rolling hills made the whole place invisible from the nearby dirt roads, but it could be noticed from the air. In this part of Wyoming, people kept to themselves. A series of holding companies held the title to the land, but nobody cared as long as the $1407.12 in taxes were paid each year.

A hundred and fifty-one people occupied the little town of Larkman, at an elevation of forty-three hundred feet. The density of the population was about ten people per square mile. The county was even fewer. There was plenty of room to get lost.

The Crow people called the place *'Awaasúuachiikaxiia'*, or 'house that leans', because the original saloon in Larkman had a roof that had one side longer than the other. Larkman was the kind of place where poor people worked hard and minded their own business.

There were six men in the bunker who were beginning to prepare for a mission. Planning was every bit as essential as deployment and execution. They would do better next time. They had been told to stand down by their employer, but also to "stay ready." There would be a call soon.

CHAPTER 45

The motorcade kept heading to Surrey City Hall, but the nature of the meeting was about to change. Jacob and I were delighted with the outcome of the Vancouver situation, but sorry we had to push so hard. I believe that average people, when shown the right path, will usually take it, and even if pushed, will thank you for the push. Making a mistake never satisfies anyone.

At city hall, the mayor was waiting in her office. Andrew and the security team surrounded Jacob and me, and led us through the building. Three men remained with the three vehicles, and six men accompanied us. While Jacob and I were shown inside the mayor's office, the agents stationed themselves as discreetly as six men in suits and sunglasses, with bulges under their arms, could possibly do. Andrew came in with us, surveyed the scene, and then removed himself to the outer office.

Mayor Darby was charming. She had been mayor for three years, and a councillor for nine years before that. She was mayor of a diverse community with a large Indo-Canadian population, rich with cultural traditions. Surrey had been mostly a rural and farming community up until fifty years ago, but was now both a bedroom community of Vancouver and a growing city in its own right.

She showed me around her office, and we looked at some photographs on her walls, and a model of a new town centre area that was currently being built. She showed us to seats at a small boardroom table, and we got down to business.

"Well, Mr. Thomas, you have certainly had an interesting couple of weeks. I admit I am thrilled to meet you, glad you are here, and very curious to see what I can do to help you in your work."

"Very nicely stated, Mayor Darby, and thank you for being such a gracious host. I am here to discuss ways that I can help you make Surrey a better place.

"If you have chatted with any of your political friends, you will see that I am making large donations for great causes that will make the world a little bit better. To make sure those funds are put to best use, I attach a few strings, but they are very minor, I can assure you, and they are only intended to ensure success. So please, tell me, what are the biggest issues facing Surrey?"

"Well, Mr. Thomas, there are a number of things, some of which are municipal in nature and others that are better served by different levels of government. Personally, I think that educational opportunities are the most important long-term benefits we can provide. As well, we need more sports facilities, parks, skating rinks, and the like. Low-income housing is a huge issue in the greater Vancouver region. Public transit is always a priority, and it would be nice to celebrate our cultural mosaic more. I also think that drugs and crime are becoming an increasing issue as we grow. If you could help us with one of those areas, it would be awesome."

"Wow, those are big-ticket and forward-thinking ideas. I like them ... and we will do them."

"Them?"

"Them. As in all of them."

The mayor gasped, and actually lost her composure. She got choked up, and before catching herself, sobbed briefly. That impressed me. She was a tough, capable, competent mayor, who had a warm heart.

I continued. "I am thinking that a new university would be a fantastic thing to fund. How does 'Darby University at Surrey' sound to you?"

The mayor's mouth hung open. "Are you seriously ... for real?" she asked slowly, looking from me to Jacob and back again several times.

"As real as I'm sitting here." I smiled. "We want to move very quickly to donate these funds, so I will add the following strings for you: First, you agree that the city will manage the funds. Second, you will complete every project within five years. Third, you will not name anything after me. And fourth, you will pass whatever you need to pass in the next thirty days to have your council agree to accept the funds to take on these projects. Jacob, any sense of the cost of these things?"

Jacob was totally thrown. He had no idea of construction costs in Canada. I was really just teasing him, and was unfortunately making him feel awkward. As Jacob looked at me quizzically, I gave him a very light little punch in the shoulder, as if to say "just kidding, man." Relieved, he laughed a bit.

I let him off the hook and continued. "Madam Mayor, I imagine a great university will cost a lot of money. Let's start out with a five-billion-dollar endowment for the construction, staffing, and operations. I may contribute more later. For all the other ideas, I think that another five billion should do the trick. And if you have more good ideas, let me know. This is how, together, we make the world a better place.

"Jacob will need the city's routing numbers. Once you have passed things through council, call him and we will have the funds in your account within forty-eight hours. I am delighted to have met you, Mayor."

I shook her hand energetically, and as I rose I added, "I am glad you can help me make our world a bit better, in this case, one mind at a time!"

CHAPTER 46

"Jacob, please let Andrew know we are ready to leave."

"Right away, sir." I looked at Jacob and smiled. Jacob had decided that calling me "sir" in the mayor's office was more appropriate. Probably right. Smart young man.

As we exited the office, the security team had come to attention and was back in formation. At our usual full stride, the group exited the building and piled into the SUVs for the ride back into the city. Traffic was not expected to be light at this time of day. Andrew had taken care of that though. The vehicles drove to a nearby hospital and pulled into the parking lot. The chopper had been circling the area, and now came in for a quick landing on their helipad.

Andrew turned around in the front seat of the SUV. "Sir, I'm afraid you are going to get your hair messed up. We will be leaving the rotors running at low speed."

The chopper touched down. Andrew, Jacob, and I, as well as one extra man from each of the other two SUVs, darted to the helicopter. We were in the air within sixty seconds and headed back to the yacht. Flying at about fifteen hundred feet, the chopper zipped along at one hundred knots over central Surrey, the Fraser River, Coquitlam, and then dropped down toward the ocean and over the Port Moody area of Burrard Inlet. We stayed about three hundred feet above the water and passed the sulphur yards and the nearby power substation, then turned right up Indian Arm and flew low and fast to the yacht.

"Man, I need a cup of tea," I said, and immediately saw Andrew speak into his sleeve. One would likely be waiting for me on board. I smiled. I confess that I liked this part of my new life.

As we entered the main salon, a steward brought over a small tray. "Earl Grey, sir?"

"Thanks, just what I needed. How did you know?" He just smiled back at me and winked.

Jacob's phone rang, and as he reached for it, I gave him an "I'm not here" hand wave.

"Hello, Jacob speaking ... Prime Minister's office? Yes, just let me see if Mr. Thomas can take the call."

I rolled my eyes and reluctantly signalled for him to bring me the phone with yet another subtle wave of my hand. I seemed to have learned a lot of different waves.

"Steve Thomas here ... Yes, I will hold." I did, but not for long. "Hello, Prime Minister! Nice of you to call. Uh huh ... uh huh ... Really? Wow, that's crazy. People have odd motivations at times for sure. I understand fully, and that will not be a problem. Keep me posted, sir. Have a good night."

I turned to Jacob, and to Zachary, who had joined Jacob on the couch. Andrew was also in the salon.

"Seems that the Green Party, with one whole seat, is voting unanimously in favour. So, that's good! The Conservative party has one vote against, the Liberal Party and the NDP are unanimously in favour, but the Bloc Québécois is unanimously opposed. Apparently, they felt it was demeaning to the nation to have a superrich person bailing out the country. So, the vote in parliament tomorrow should be almost unanimous with about ten votes against. I can live with that, but I have an idea.

"Jacob, I want you to call the office and get hold of Mark Crombie. Have his communications team call the prime minister's office and find out the names of each person they expect to vote no. Then, have our people contact those folks directly to let them know that we fully appreciate their positions and respect their votes, and to that end, will make sure that none of the funds that we donate across the nation will be spent in their ridings. Let them know we just committed over sixty billion dollars to two cities in this province, and we intend to do more across the country. Then tomorrow, we shall see just how committed they are to their 'principles.' Never forget the old saying: 'Never look a gift horse in the mouth.'"

Jacob, who had grown up in Zurich, of course looked quizzically at me.

"Uh, let me explain. In the olden days, if you were buying a horse, you always looked in their mouth to see if their teeth were okay. So, the adage is basically to say that, if someone is giving you a free goddamn horse, just take it! Say 'thank you' and shut the fuck up! We are paying off the national debt for fuck's sake. What is there to say no to? Give me a break!"

Jacob got on his phone, and soon the communications team was working their magic.

CHAPTER 47

"Andrew, are we in for the night now? I sure hope so."

"Yes, sir, you have the whole night free." Andrew smiled. It was already past nine.

"Okay, grab something to drink, grab a chair, and let's have a chat."

Once Andrew had settled into a chair with a tall glass of iced tea, I began.

"I have noticed a lessening of security and a more comfortable process the last couple of days. And I have to say, I appreciate it, but with the attacks and everything … what's going on? Do I need to be worried, or should I just go on about my life?"

"Sir, the best thing you can do is to live your life, and let us fill in the gaps and make everything happen for you. We'll do so in as secure a manner as we can without it becoming stifling. You do need to listen to us, and if we bark orders, it is only because of imminent danger. So far, you have been a natural, and easy to work with."

"Have you heard anything from the authorities on the airport attack?"

"Yes, sir, there were two hit teams there, one at each exit. These were discovered on security camera recordings after the fact. The crew that did the shooting took off to the east, changed vehicles, and ditched that vehicle near the US border, likely running on foot across the border to another waiting vehicle. No one could track them after that.

"We don't know if they were part of a government body, a kidnap team, a private hit team, or why they were trying to kill or scare you. It would seem pretty obvious that, with the US Government being the secondary beneficiary of the Wilbur Thomas money, they would be much richer today if they could have eliminated you. They have certainly eliminated people for less. You were right about going public. Once you took control and let the world know the money was yours to distribute, the US was done in."

I sipped my drink and nodded for him to keep going.

"CSIS has been monitoring chatter along with US Homeland Security and the NSA, and there was a lot of chatter from the moment you were visited by that lawyer at your home to verify your identity. From that moment, the chatter ratcheted up, but has mostly vanished since the press conference. I think you have dodged a bullet, sir, and I will make sure the dodging continues."

"Thanks for the update, Andrew, and for all the work of your team. We will make sure that the deceased agents' families are all financially looked after, and we have already taken care of their funeral costs. That whole thing was brutal and gut wrenching. I can't imagine how you and your team could even continue."

"We are professionals, sir, and they were not the first deaths we have encountered. The military training really helps in a situation like that, but it also explains why we try to stay disciplined and formal. And why I stick with calling you 'sir,' sir."

"Understood. Andrew, in two days we need to head to Washington, DC. I asked the team at the office today to make arrangements for travel. I want to move forward with the money for the veterans. The US has carried the load for a lot of wars and battles, and lost a lot of men to injury and death. They are first on my list. I want to meet with the Veterans Affairs secretary and see how we can help. And if they are unwilling to let us help, I have another idea that I think could be even better."

Andrew simply nodded. "I have been informed of the plans, sir. We will be ready."

Jacob and Zach excused themselves and headed to bed.

I nodded after them. "I think I'll follow suit. Get some sleep, Andrew. I am wiped. A long, but very good day. Thanks for your work today. Oh, and I want to spend all day tomorrow at the office. I need to get a handle on the team, and what we're all doing there. This mission is going to start moving very quickly."

Andrew smiled. He liked his protectee. He just needed to keep him alive.

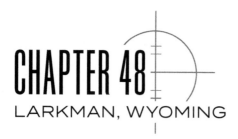

CHAPTER 48
LARKMAN, WYOMING

The call was brief: "Check web. Target loaded. Be prepared to act within fourteen days. Await final go order."

The line went dead. A six-second call.

The communications officer had transcribed the call. He walked from the office area to the dining hall and handed it to the man they all called "the colonel."

The colonel read the message and took a bite of his toast. A big bite. The bite of a thuggish, ill-mannered man, stuffing more into his mouth than reasonable. He brushed his hands together to knock off the crumbs, and took the last swig of his coffee. Then he stood to gain everyone's attention.

"Men, we are to be ready in five days, but I want to be on the ground and ready in four. Our target has been loaded on the web and approved. We are just waiting for the go order."

The communications officer backed up the colonel with an approving nod, confirming to the men the message they had received.

One of their simple codes was in the prep days. For example, fourteen days actually meant you should take the one and the four and add them together to get five days, thirty-six days would be nine days, and so on. If they were being monitored, they would have the job completed before any authorities thought they were even close to deploying.

The colonel spoke again to the communications officer. "Once you've checked the web and gotten the details, bring them to me immediately."

The communications officer nodded. Then he thought to himself, *What the hell else did he think I would have done with them? The colonel is such a fucking jackass, but he sure as shit knows his job.*

He signed onto the web, and then entered a series of commands and codes to access the dark web. Uploaded as advised was a single webpage with a photo of their target, and some location details. The rest was up to them.

He handed a file to the colonel, who opened it, glanced at it, and tossed it on the table.

"Fuck, I hate these international jobs. We have failed to terminate a target for this client more than once. We had damn well better be able to report a success on this one, or we may be out of business. We'll get it done, right?"

The communications officer nodded. "Sure will, Colonel."

The colonel sat down again, and under his breath, muttered the slang military refrain for "let's get ready."

"Lock and load, boys," he drawled. "Lock and load."

CHAPTER 49

The office was bustling this morning as we arrived. People all over the world knew what we were up to and were sending in meeting requests, project ideas, gifts, invitations, and flowers. It went on and on. There were also several marriage proposals. Just what I needed...

The Thomas Protocol Global Initiatives, as the office was now known, was already too small, but we would make do just fine. In the rare moments I had previously spent in the offices, I had already met the CEO, a man who had run large organizations before.

Jack Dickinson was very likeable and easy to underestimate. He was about five foot nine, with medium brown hair, and a slender build. At age fifty, he looked thirty-eight and had only a couple of grey hairs. He had a commanding exterior, but an easy laugh. These hid the ruthless business skills he had learned working in government and publicly traded companies.

With Jack as the CEO of my organization, I declared myself the chairman and chief philanthropist. His office was next to mine, because we would be spending lots of time together. My job would entail being the public face of the organization and meeting with donation prospects. His job, along with the rest of the staff, was to make it all happen. My job was the easy part, no doubt.

With the three-hour time difference to Ottawa, the morning debate in parliament had already concluded and a vote would take place immediately after the lunch recess, at two p.m. their time.

Calls had been made to each person who had indicated they would vote against the proposal.

In politics, one of the easy ways to stand your ground is to vote against something that is easily going to pass without your support. So, let's say there is a project to build a new highway in your region. You can vote for it in committee and preliminary rounds to make sure it moves ahead. When it is obvious it will pass the final vote, you can vote against it, knowing it will still sail through. The advantage of this approach is that if the project is wildly successful, you can indicate how you were a strong supporter of it "right from the beginning." And if it fails miserably, you can say, "I supported it in the early stages, but had some serious concerns about it failing just like this, so I voted against it." Either way, you can play the matter to your favour.

The members of the Bloc Québécois were supporters of an independent Quebec. They did not want to do anything that would be good for Canada, only things that would be good for Quebec. A debt-free Canada would be such a rich country that Quebec's voters would never want to separate from it, so accepting our donation went against their stated goals. They needed to create an environment where they could convince their fellow Quebecers that Canada was a bad deal, and that Quebec should secede.

I had learned this technique at the hands of a local city councillor in the municipality of Coquitlam, where I had grown up. Old Lou Suskind, later nicknamed Lucky Lou, was a master at this technique, and a friend of mine. He was always on all sides of every issue.

I was pretty sure this was the ploy being played by the people voting against the deal I offered to the party leaders. I was not prepared to let them have it both ways. Although no one knew it yet, I planned to give a donation of $50 million to each member of parliament's riding, or district, to be used to make their area better. I would NOT give any money to the ridings who voted no.

With 338 seats in parliament, this would cost about $17 billion. Chump change in my world now.

So, we tipped off the naysayers about what we were planning, and made it abundantly clear that, in line with their voting preference, their riding would be excluded from these donations. We advised them that we respected their position and would not want to embarrass them with having to accept or reject further funds designed to help make the lives of their constituents better.

The reactions to the calls were mostly stunned silence.

We had the parliamentary channel turned on in my office and watched the vote live. Every single vote in favour. *What a shock.* I laughed. The Bloc members leaped up to vote yes, with almost more gusto than anyone else. How cute. It was sad too though, and certainly left me feeling jaded about the tactics we'd had to employ.

On the bright side, they had done the right thing, for themselves, for the country, and for their constituents. There were no losers in this whatsoever, and perhaps they had learned a lesson about what they could accomplish by working together.

Moving forward, Canada would be a role model to the world for fiscal responsibility. Hopefully it would also increase its reputation as a generous and kind nation.

In my view, those outcomes alone qualified as having met the test of the Thomas Protocol.

Well done, Canada.

CHAPTER 50

It was wheels up at 8:12 a.m. on Wednesday, as the team headed to Washington, DC to meet with the undersecretary of Veterans Affairs.

Aboard Protocol 1 was the usual security contingent. Jack Dickinson had joined us, and we brought along Paige from the office, Jacob and Zachary, and Mark Crombie from communications. There was a handful of support staff as well.

The newcomers were enthralled with the aircraft, and all were given tours by the flight attendants. It was a lot of fun to be able to share this bird with everyone.

We spent time reviewing the strategy that the team at the office had put together. It was a reasonable approach. We planned to offer the US Government $300 billion to be used in three ways:

First, $100 billion, divided into lump sum settlements, would go to all currently living disabled vets. Anyone currently on a disability pension or awaiting adjudication of their claim would be eligible.

The plan would have three tiers of payments:

1. To veterans with over 70 percent disability, the lump sum of $40,000.
2. To veterans with over 40 percent disability, the lump sum of $25,000.
3. To veterans with under 40 percent disability, the lump sum of $17,500.

There were 3.8 million disabled vets in the USA with 1.1 million of them having over a 70 percent rating. 1.3 million were over 40 percent disabled, and 1.5 million were under 40 percent.

The second $100 billion was designated for the building, outfitting, and funding of fifty new veterans' hospitals.

The third $100 billion would be to build seventeen hundred veterans' retirement or low-income apartment buildings, which would house up to 335,000 vets.

The "strings" were that, for these funds to be paid out, the government had to agree not to simply reduce their own expenditures in lieu of these new funds, or reduce their commitments to their own VA hospitals. They also needed to show that they had a method to distribute the lump sum payments within forty-five days. We wanted to get the help out, fast.

Jack and I took part of the six-hour flight to get better acquainted. I was impressed by Jack, but he often seemed awkward or uncomfortable around me, almost the way a dog looks when it's guilty of something. Like he always had his guard up with me. Maybe it was my just sense of humour. I know that some people had a hard time figuring out what to make of it. I don't know. By the end of the flight though, I finally felt I knew him a bit better.

Jack was married to a woman of German descent, lived in North Vancouver, and had two daughters. One was in university, and one about to head to university. They also had a golden retriever. Nice family folks for sure.

I asked Jack how he had been hired. He said it had been a bit strange, and that he had wondered if he was being hired by some shadow organization. I guess he kind of was! He was told that the firm was to be a philanthropic organization and would be funded soon from a truly massive inheritance. He was provided few other details other than that the amount was in the multiple billions. He would not have believed anyone if they had told him it was in the trillions, because that would have been absurd. Who knew?

Jack had put together a workforce, prepared some target recipients for funding, built the communications and legal team, and put an accounting and management structure in place. He also hired people who would travel the world seeking out opportunities where we could help. All he knew on timing was that it would all fall into place by the end of April. He was hired in the fall of 2017 and given six months to get everything operational. He had done an amazing job.

"So, who interviewed and hired you?" I asked.

He pointed through the glass door to Jacob, and could see by my shocked look that I'd had no idea.

"Jacob? Seriously?"

Jack nodded and smiled. "Pretty much. And the final interview was with Herr Altermatt from the GCBS Bank via a video link."

"Okay, that makes a bit more sense." I got up and slid open the door of my private suite and asked Jacob, who was standing nearby, to join us.

"Jacob! I want you to come with me, please."

He was in the middle of laughing with Paige about some joke, and looked startled by my tone. When he looked at me, I was waggling my finger in a "come here" motion.

"Yes, sir." He immediately followed me back into my suite.

"Jacob, please sit down."

Jacob looked concerned. He was a pleaser and was very uncomfortable if he thought he had displeased me, or anyone else for that matter.

"How can I help you, sir?"

"Well, first, it's Steve, and second, Jack here tells me that it was you who hired this son of a bitch to run this organization. You didn't think to tell me?" I was struggling to not smile or laugh...

"Well, uh, Steve, uh … it was ultimately my grandfather who made the final decision. I was involved in seeking out quality candidates and handling the first two rounds of interviews. Um, have … have I done something wrong?"

Jack and I were both glaring at him. And then we couldn't hold it in any longer and both cracked up laughing.

Jacob appeared confused, looking at each of us in turn, trying to figure out what the hell was going on.

"Jacob, I'm sorry, we are just teasing you." I sighed. "Okay, I feel mean now. That wasn't my plan. You did a fine job. Jack is great. I was just shocked to find out that you put a lot of this together. I have not given you enough credit, and I'm not sure I realized or appreciated the depths of your talents and capabilities."

"Thanks, Steve." Jacob blushed a bit and lowered his head.

"Look, you have been very kindly acting as my executive assistant. Is that job big enough for you, or would you prefer to take on other responsibilities?"

Jacob held up both hands, with his palms facing me, and shook them from side to side, "No, no, I want to keep doing exactly what I am doing. I love to assist and be in the thick of things without being the one in charge. I am not that good at managing others, but I love supporting those who are doing something important, and being part of the team. Please, I hope I can keep doing what I am doing for years to come. We are already doing some great things."

Jack looked at Jacob and said very softly and sincerely, "I want to thank you, Jacob. I am really happy to be here. I am sure you had a number of choices, so again … thanks. And if you get tired of Steve … well, there will be a place for you somewhere else in the organization. I can already tell that Steve is going to be very hard to work for."

Now we all laughed. He was right, to a point. I was a perfectionist, but I was also a good guy … or at least I liked to think so. In my past business life, my key staff had always been very loyal, and became like family to me. But I could be a better boss. I knew that, in this new role, I had to be a better delegator, and had to set a very high example of integrity for all my team to watch and model.

"Jacob, stay and chat with us if you like, or if you prefer the other gang out there..."

"Thanks, Steve, but after your cruel joke I will get back to Paige and Zachary." He said this while glaring at me in playful retaliation, and as he left, broke into his usual big, happy grin.

"Jack, just so we are clear, I see you running the show, and me being like some sort of queen bee that flits in when needed to make a deal, shake the right hands, or apply the right pressure. I will be the figurehead and the face of the organization for now, and you can be the majordomo. Does that seem about right to you?"

"It's exactly right," he said, seeming to like the sound of that. "I will make sure you have everything provided for you, from housing, security, transportation, and your executive support team. They will all be top-quality people, and will all report to me with the exception of Andrew, Jacob, Zachary, and Paige. That way you can be free to focus on giving away money, while we look after the business."

I nodded, satisfied with the arrangement. "And Jack, I will want to have a weekly meeting with you, probably for about an hour, to be updated on projects, finances, travel, and any other items you feel I need to know."

"Done." Jack shook my hand. "If you don't mind, I have to make a few calls." With that, Jack retired to one of the two smaller staterooms and got to work.

For at least a moment, I was all alone. I exhaled. It felt good. Things were falling into place and everything was running more smoothly.

Soon, we would be landing in Washington.

CHAPTER 51

Our beautiful, big bird glided in to Ronald Reagan Washington National Airport. We landed on runway 1, heading north, at four thirty eastern time.

We had to get special permission to land at Washington National. This was a very busy terminal in the nation's capital and not a place where private aircraft typically land, but due to the size of our aircraft, and who we were, we were accommodated.

After landing, the aircraft taxied about two miles back to the southwest corner of the airport property, and we were directed to park the plane in an open area near the Southwest Airlines Terminal. It was also a stone's throw away from a security gate through which the motorcade could access the plane. Very handy!

The motorcade pulled up to the plane. Four black SUVs and a stretch limo. I preferred the SUV to be honest, but this would be fine for today. Guardian Security had sorted out the vehicles, and some additional local bodyguards. We had eight on board the plane, and there were eight more locals.

Thank God they had been very clear about where to meet the undersecretary. There were actually ten different VA office locations in Washington. We would probably never have figured it out.

We walked into the office and had to clear security, which could have been a bit of a challenge with twelve armed bodyguards accompanying me. Luckily, we had been pre-cleared and so were waved through. Andrew was at work again and had everything arranged.

The undersecretary was Bob Wallace, who had actually been serving as the acting secretary for the past few weeks, since President Tripplehorn had fired Wallace's predecessor, David Shumpka.

He greeted us warmly for our five p.m. meeting. He had been briefed in advance of our arrival.

"Mr. Thomas, I understand that you want to make a substantial contribution to our veterans. What did you have in mind?"

I explained the three areas where we thought we could help, and how we saw it working.

"Mr. Secretary, do you have a database that can sort your disabled vets by their disability percentages, so that the lump sums can be paid out quickly?"

"We do. In fact, that would be the easiest part. The other two areas are a cause for some concern, though. Building new hospitals is great, but the ongoing operating costs can be a killer. Ultimately, bricks and mortar are not the only solution, and I doubt this administration would want to take on the added and ongoing management and operating expenses."

"I imagine the disabled vets' retirement homes are similarly problematic?"

"I would think so. We would need to get some views from the White House, but those views can change almost hourly these days, though you didn't hear that from me."

We discussed the matter in depth for quite some time, and then I moved on to plan B.

"Okay, Mr. Secretary, we will change our offer. We will pass along the one hundred billion dollars for the lump sum payments to the vets, and will add an additional ten dollars per person to cover admin costs. So … we will deposit one hundred billion, thirty-eight million dollars into the account you designate.

"I will withdraw the offer for the other two hundred billion dollars, but *will* deliver those programs in a different manner. Thank you so much for your time. Jack Dickinson will be in touch to sort out the final details, and please be sure we are very honoured to help, and extremely grateful for the opportunity to assist your veterans in a small way."

The secretary looked devastated that the amount had shrunk by two-thirds, but he did not ask what we planned. He was just grateful for the money they were going to receive.

There was a crush of reporters waiting on the steps of the Veterans Administration, just as Mark Crombie had arranged. I stepped up to speak.

"Well, this is a nice surprise to find you all here today. Thank you for coming. We are delighted to report that the acting secretary of the VA has agreed to take our one-hundred-billion-dollar contribution and divide it amongst three point eight million disabled vets. Cheques will range between seventeen thousand five hundred dollars and forty thousand dollars, depending on a vet's level of disability.

"We were hoping to provide an additional two hundred billion dollars to build veterans hospitals and veterans housing, but the administration felt these might be better provided through other means. So, let me announce today that our fallback plan is to meet with the Mayo Clinic and most of the major private hospitals throughout the United States, and to purchase up to one hundred billion dollars of medical services for vets. This will alleviate backlogs in the current VA hospitals and will also support the private sector. The veterans should end up getting better access to treatment all around.

"We will also meet with a major operator of specialty housing in the US. In preliminary talks, they have agreed to build and manage seventeen hundred apartment buildings, each having two hundred suites in them to house up to three hundred and thirty-five thousand retired or low-income veterans.

"Veterans in the US, Canada, and other democratic nations worldwide who have fought for freedom deserve our respect, and they certainly have mine. We will need some time, but we will get this done, and will be making their world a better place, one veteran at a time, both here and in other countries as well.

"To those veterans out there... this is the way that the Thomas Protocol says, 'thank you for your service.'"

I took a few questions, and then we had to leave.

"Thanks, everyone, but we have a plane to catch."

In the end, this was so much better than giving money to the government to run programs for veterans. The department had proven for years that it was relatively incompetent at delivering medical services. We would get these guys the best treatment available. It was a shame that government had not done it already.

Back in the car, we were all pretty proud of ourselves. We hit the threshold of the aircraft and everyone felt exhausted. We were wheels up at 7:10 p.m. eastern time. Once the plane was airborne, we sat down and had dinner together, and then I headed for a nap while others found seats in which to recline and relax. A few others decided to watch a movie, and Jack went to his room to be alone and continue his work. We had so much to do, but we would just take it one day at a time. Even Andrew seemed more relaxed. I hoped that was a good sign.

CHAPTER 52

Back in Larkman, the men were ready early. In the morning, they would be departing for the kill location, and would have some time to prepare so as to be ready to make the hit on day five.

They had been to the city before, so it would be familiar territory. They were using six men this time. They would be flying instead of driving. Weapons had been arranged at the other end for them—borders and planes don't mix well for carrying heavy firepower.

For the moment, they were trying very hard to stay calm and get some sleep. They would fly to their destination on three different aircraft, with two men on each so they didn't attract attention. They would sit separately and would not speak to each other from the time they left the bunker until their arrival at the rendezvous point.

They would leave Larkman in three vehicles in the morning, at thirty-minute intervals starting at four thirty a.m. At that hour, they would leave the area completely unseen. Four of them would fly from Billings Logan International Airport in Montana, about a two-hour drive from the bunker, while the other two would drive three hours south to the Casper Natrona County Airport. They would all make their way to Seattle, and then fly the final leg from there.

For now, it was time to rest, chill, and sleep.

CHAPTER 53

The media coverage of our veterans' plan was fantastic. Veterans' groups, the NRA, members of Congress, and various talking heads were all unable to find fault with the plan, other than that it could always be more.

There was some negative press, asking why the president was not involved, and had not even met with me. Tripplehorn was taking flack for it, but in fact, he was not guilty of anything this time. Honestly, we had never even thought to include him or drop by for a photo op. Our goal was for people to know what we had donated to, and what we hoped to achieve, but we really didn't seek any credit beyond that. I am quite sure, in hindsight, that had we approached the White House, President Tripplehorn would have somehow managed to either take credit for our work, or denigrate us in some way. He seemed to be a master at both.

Others said the government should have been doing the same thing a long time ago, but were thrilled with this massive step forward.

Veterans were complimentary, glad their disabled buddies were finally catching a break, and happy that soon no veteran would ever have to be homeless again.

Governor Blundell of California suggested that states and communities who had the ability to donate land should do so, so perhaps the money could be stretched to do even more good. He was ready to give some state land and sell other parcels to get projects underway.

Mayors of major cities commented positively, and wondered what other initiatives they could partner on with the Thomas Protocol.

The world was starting to take us seriously. It had only been two weeks since the meeting in Zurich. We had dodged bullets—literally—gone public, and had done a couple of fast first initiatives to get the word out. The process of making the world a better place was underway.

The plane arrived back in Vancouver, and the team headed out. The chopper was waiting at the airport to take six of us back to the yacht, while the rest made their own way to their respective homes.

While airborne, just after liftoff, Jacob spoke into his headset, allowing all six of us to hear him.

"Steve, are you doing okay? You have been really quiet for the last while."

"Yeah, I'm fine," I answered. "I'm just pondering the last couple of weeks, and I can't believe what we have already done … and what is already underway. It is pretty damn monumental. Kind of blows my mind."

After we landed on the yacht, we all stretched and yawned and realized how long our day had been. It was ten twenty p.m. Pacific daylight time, and we were all pretty tuckered out.

Jacob headed for the bar and got a European beer for himself, a scotch for Zach, and a Grand Marnier for me. We all sat down in the main salon. Andrew, Joe, and Dan were off duty and had headed to their cabins. We had two other guards in the room with us and the usual contingent out on deck and in the surrounding waters.

I turned to Jacob and Zach. "Guys, once we have the house built, I really hope you will consider living at the compound going forward. We will make sure you have your own self-contained suite, so please, give that some thought."

"No thought needed by us," Zach said. "We would love that. This is such an exciting ride we are on. Who knows in time, but given our current roles for the next few years, it's just the natural place to be."

Jacob smiled and nodded his approval.

For me, it was kind of like having a couple of sons, which was very sweet, especially since I had never married or had kids of my own. The more I got to know them, the more I saw what fine men they were. They had good hearts too. They really reached out to make every day easier for me, which with all the stress was a very comfortable feeling.

"You guys need a few nights off. Vancouver has a vibrant gay community and some terrific casual restaurants. You need to get off this boat, experience the city, and blow off some steam."

"Maybe this weekend. We could grab a hotel in the city."

"We are already paying for a hotel, so just stay there! I am hoping all us can get off this boat and into the city soon. I will speak to Andrew in the morning and see if he thinks we can move into the hotel soon. Jacob, how are things going with the bank?"

"Steve, we held five percent of the account in cash, so there was already one point five trillion dollars sitting in cash when you took ownership of the fund. Since then, we have liquidated a variety of other instruments to increase that amount to three point five trillion in cash. So, everything you have committed to so far is covered, and there is still nearly one point five trillion in ready cash left."

I smiled at Jacob. "I need to call your grandfather in the morning and thank him for all his work. He and the bank deserve about ninety-nine percent of the credit for everything we have done. In fact, we should be saying some of that publicly at our press conferences.

"Well, boys ... By the way, does it bother you when I call you 'boys'?"

"Not at all," they both said at once and smiled.

"Good; I mean it affectionately. Anyway, boys, I am heading to bed. Before I do, I want to ask you both a favour. Please, reign me in if I get going too fast in one direction, or if I start to forget what a humbling experience this is. I want to be seen as a good guy, and for my great-uncle's gift to be seen as positive. I think I may have been pretty arrogant with the mayor of Vancouver and the councillors, pushing them around a bit. I really don't want to be that guy, so if I start acting like an ass, tell me I am being an ass. There is probably no one else who would tell me that now, so ... I am serious, okay?"

"Be happy to call you an ass ... sir." Jacob grinned coyly. Throwing in the 'sir' thing made it even funnier.

I laughed, got up from my seat, and headed toward my cabin. "Alright, good night, guys."

As I lay in bed, thinking about my new life, I realized I was feeling cooped up living on the isolated yacht. I wanted to lie in the sun for a while. *I wonder...*

Before heading to bed, Jacob called his grandfather and filled him in on the events of the last few days.

Altermatt said that he wished he were a younger man and could have been more involved in the adventure of a lifetime. As he always did when ending a phone call with his grandson, he said, "I love you, Jacob, and I'm proud of you too. Goodbye."

Jacob ended the call, smiled warmly as he thought of his amazingly supportive opa, and headed to his stateroom.

CHAPTER 54

I had no significant meetings planned for the next three days, and it was now Wednesday. I had an idea.

I called for Andrew and Jacob.

"Good morning, guys. Andrew, I want to take a relaxing break for a few days at my home in Arizona. It's spontaneous, so we should be safe there. No one will expect us. Easy! You work out the security, and Jacob, you take care of the flight details. Let's leave mid-morning. See if you can make it work."

Even before I had finished speaking, they had both grabbed their cell phones and started making calls. Jacob had the pilot on the line, who confirmed the aircraft was fuelled and ready. He would just need to file a flight plan, check on landing permission, and get the crew and food to the plane. He needed at least two and a half hours, but thought he could make it. In future, he pointed out, twenty-four hours would be appreciated.

Andrew called the Guardian Security office in Phoenix. They would drop everything and have secure transport ready to move out on command. Although I was unaware of it, they were already guarding the house full time. They would take care of provisions for the residence and would have everything ready. They had also arranged for two house stewards to cook, serve, and tidy whenever I used the home. These were actually fully trained security people who had some added talents. They were both former military, and had worked in the hospitality industry as well. They were perfect for the role.

Within ten minutes, both Andrew and Jacob had reported all systems go. It was six forty-five a.m. now, and we would be wheels up by about nine fifteen, which would put us into Phoenix by noon, and to the house by twelve thirty, in time for lunch.

I was very happy now. I loved my place in Phoenix. So comfortable. The house was a nice, normal place that I'd gotten for a steal in 2010, after the market crashed in 2008. It was twenty-eight hundred square feet, with a pool, an outdoor fireplace, a putting green, four bedrooms, three baths, and an office. I entertained there a lot, loving to cook and have a good time. I had always been able to relax there, from the moment my feet hit the entrance hall.

"Andrew, do we need much security there? Just a couple of guys should be fine, eh?"

Andrew looked at me and smirked. "Sir, the property has been secured twenty-four-seven since your first meeting in Zurich on April seventeenth. Everything is in order, and you will be able to fully relax. We have a local security team, so it will just be Dan and Joe and me on the flight, followed by the full detail on the ground."

I hadn't spoken to my neighbours in Phoenix since the news of my inheritance. What must they be thinking, with a bunch of guards around the house, and likely a couple of SUVs parked out front twenty-four hours a day? My neighbours razzed the hell out of me already for being a rich Canadian (at least from their perspective), and that was before the inheritance. Well, I was just going to have to make sure nothing changed. I had a good friendship with the couple next door, Dick and Rosie, and wanted to keep it.

With Dick, our favourite pastimes were arguing about politics, and searching greater Phoenix for the perfect chocolate malt. We thought we had found it at the Sonic Drive-In. Then much to our chagrin, Sonic stopped selling malts! Oh, the humanity!

Then Dick and Rosie had driven over to Los Angeles one time for family reasons, and ended up at a place called Ruby's Diner. There they enjoyed (what they described as) the best malt ever. We were going to try and find a Ruby's in Phoenix on my next trip.

The flight to Phoenix was uneventful, and our pilot had arranged to land at the Phoenix-Mesa Gateway Airport. Located in East Mesa, it was a former military base now used as an airport for Allegiant Airlines, the odd flight from other airlines, some military aircraft, and some private aircraft. Embraer Executive Jet Services operated from there as well.

We came in from the southeast, landing on runway 30C and taxiing to a berth located on a large, unused area right in front of the Phoenix-Mesa Gateway Airport Offices, instead of near the passenger terminal.

As we came to a complete stop, an exit stairway was rolled up to the door, and the motorcade moved in to the base of the stairs.

I was looking out the window, and there were a few other people gathered around the base of the stairs. I raised the issue with Andrew, who spoke into his sleeve and reported back that it was the governor of Arizona, the mayor of Phoenix, and the mayor of Mesa. There were a couple of photographers and a local news camera crew setting up as well.

My heart sank. It would be lovely to meet these people, but I just wanted to be a nobody and enjoy a couple of quiet days at the house, like old times.

Rather than descending the steps like some visiting dignitary, I suggested we invite the three of them aboard, and then all leave together.

I welcomed and shook hands with Governor Doug Lindsay, Mayor Greg Stapley of Phoenix, and Mayor John Gilbert.

"Nice to have you aboard, but how the heck did you folks even know I was coming to town? I was just trying to sneak in and enjoy a few quiet days at my house here."

"We have our ways, Mr. Thomas. We heard from a reporter who called and knew you were on the way; he had a tip from someone locally when your pilot got landing permission prior to your departure. We are sorry to intrude, but we just wanted to welcome you to the area."

I knew that wasn't true, but what were they going to say? Let's be honest, this visit was about money.

"Thanks for that, but I am just here for a few days of rest. One thing I do hope is that all of you can help us with our veterans' initiatives."

"Great initiative for sure, and we are ready to help," Mayor Gilbert added. "You can imagine we might have a few other ideas too."

"Gentlemen, you may have noticed that I have started with my favourites. I took great care of my country and my city. Arizona is my next favourite place. In time, over say the next month or two, we will reach out to you and see what we can do for Arizona specifically. Now, fellows... I don't want to be rude, but I really want to get to my place. It's really kind of you to say hello, and if you will leave your contact info with Jacob here, we will reach out to you in the next few days and schedule meetings where we can talk about ideas we could help with or partner on."

They were all smiles. We agreed to take some photos with them, and then we all headed to the door. At the foot of the steps, we shook hands, the photographers on the ground took their pictures, and the news team tried to ask a few questions.

"MR. THOMAS! MR. THOMAS! Are you here to make a big announcement today?"

I stepped forward, asked the reporter her name, introduced myself, and shook her hand. She was disarmed by the charm offensive.

"Today, I am just here for a few days of rest and relaxation. The governor and the mayors were here to say hello and to let me know they have a few ideas they would like to discuss. We have promised to chat in the next few months, but for today, I just want to sit on my patio and enjoy the warm sunshine. Jacob will take your card, and we will give you an interview when we come back next time, okay? Thank you for coming; thank you, everyone!"

And with that, we jumped into our three-car motorcade and headed to the exit. As we went through the gate, two motorcycle cops swept into formation in front of our lead car, and two cruisers fell in line behind us.

"Oh my God… this is crazy. Life really has changed." I could already tell that my little sanctuary in Phoenix was never going to be the same. I was embarrassed. The police escort led us onto Highway 202, and then Highway 60. Not surprisingly, we were at the house in record time.

CHAPTER 55

The kill teams from Larkman, Wyoming, had all arrived at their designated airports and got out without much delay. Within three hours, they would all have boarded flights to their mission's destination.

The rides had been mostly uneventful, except where the speed limit changed as they entered the outer city limits of Billings, and one of the guys had been pulled over for speeding. The officer checked his licence, and noticing the veteran's plate on the car, gave his fellow former military a break.

"Which branch of the service?" the officer asked.

"Marines."

"Hoo-rah. It's your lucky day. Let's just call this a warning. Keep it down to five over the max, okay? Take it easy, boys, and thank you for your service."

As they pulled back onto the highway, the passenger, the colonel, commented, "That was close. Last thing we need is a record of our movements."

The other vehicles got to their destinations with no issues.

As each truck found a spot in their respective parking lots, the passenger would get out and head into the airport. Then, ten minutes later, the driver would do the same. They were now in their "no communication" mode. They didn't even know each other… until they regrouped at their final destination.

CHAPTER 56

Back in Zurich, Wilhelm Altermatt was struggling a bit. As usual, his day at the office was ending late. He was having a hard time liquidating parts of the portfolio to raise cash. This wasn't because it was difficult, or there were a lack of buyers. It was because it tortured him inside to sell off great assets. And it killed him even more to reduce the bank's fee-income every time he reduced the size of the Thomas portfolio. It had taken a hundred years to build, and Steve Thomas had already committed nearly two trillion dollars of the funds in just a couple of weeks. Altermatt had hoped it would take decades to spend all the money.

Still, given the alternatives of having Thomas blowing the money on good charitable projects, or the US government spending it on weapons systems, he knew where his loyalties were. After all, he lived in Switzerland, a traditionally neutral country.

At least Thomas was genuine, decent, and honest. Being a Swiss banker did not always afford one the luxury of only dealing with honourable people, and as a result, Altermatt had met more than his share of slimy people. In fact, the slimiest might have been the resident intelligence officer for the US Embassy in Geneva, who had paid Altermatt a visit about thirty days earlier. The CIA had picked up communications over recent weeks and months and knew about the Thomas money, and they had learned that they were the second beneficiary of the will. What they didn't know was who number one was, and they applied terrific pressure on Altermatt to talk, but he resisted, as any good Swiss banker would do. He increased his own personal security from none to one bodyguard. He was glad when Thomas had gone public. That took the heat off. He had not heard from the Americans since.

He spoke to his grandson almost every day. Clearly, Jacob was loving his work. Zachary was happy too, and they were thrilled to be on a great adventure. Together, Altermatt and Jacob liaised on needed funds, transfers, financial reports, and information, making sure the bank was doing everything they could to support Thomas.

Altermatt had hoped Jacob would take over the bank one day. He was bright—super bright to be clear—well educated, and had learned the business well. It would likely never happen though, because Jacob had a scar on his résumé. As a young man, Jacob had succumbed to pressure and had gotten into some personal trouble with drugs. He had been clean now for nine years, and Zach had been a tremendous support. Dealing with university, a domineering set of parents and a demanding grandfather, the challenges of being gay, looking for love, and all the other pressures of youth, he had lost control. He fell in with a party crowd and spiralled downward for a few months.

Rehab treatment and the love of his grandfather had brought him back. Jacob also had tremendous personal fortitude, as does anyone who faces and overcomes addiction challenges. Of course, it was questionable whether he was actually addicted or just voluntarily partying. In the end, his recovery was swift, and he returned to being the fine, well-mannered young man everyone expected him to be. Living up to expectations was never fun or easy, but he had done it, and all of that was part of what made him a pleaser. He needed positive reinforcement, a bit of praise, and to know he was valued. In such an environment, he flourished. By all accounts, the last couple of weeks with Thomas were exactly what the boy needed.

Altermatt was proud, and while he wouldn't admit it, he missed his grandson terribly.

Wilhelm Altermatt was seventy-two years old. Two years before the summer of love swept through America, he had married his school sweetheart. He was nineteen in 1965, and was much more a product of the fifties than the sixties. He came from a very conservative family. He and Lydelle had two children in short order, one of whom was Jacob's mother, Ursula, born in 1966.

Their son, Henry, was born in 1968. He had been a challenge. He was difficult to control, and by the age of eleven had been sent off to a strict boarding school to find the discipline he needed. It didn't work. He was kicked out at fifteen, and ran away for a year. When he came home in 1984, he was a lost soul. They arranged a job for him in a local grocery outlet. He stayed there his whole working life, prior to dying of a massive heart attack at age forty-eight, while moving some large boxes in the store. Wilhelm blamed himself and felt like a failure as a father.

His wife, Lydelle, was a tremendous woman. As she aged, she maintained an elegance and a grace rarely seen anymore. To the day she died, Wilhelm had felt a twinge of joy in his stomach every time he saw her walk into a room. He loved her completely and never, ever, looked at another woman.

She had died of breast cancer when she was sixty-four, and he had been alone ever since. He grew very close to Jacob in this period. Jacob's parents were no longer together, and he and Altermatt needed each other. Yes, he adored the boy, and missed him tremendously.

He would speak to Jacob tomorrow, and also to Steve. His practice had been to call Jacob at the end of the day in Zurich, which was the start of the day in Vancouver.

He was still struggling to call Thomas "Steve," but he was doing his best. He shook his head and smiled to himself about the man's informality. He certainly was a likeable enough fellow.

CHAPTER 57

My normally quiet little middle-class neighbour-hood in Phoenix was now officially a circus. The only thing missing was the midway. My street ended in a cul-de-sac, with nine houses in total, four on my side of the street and five on the other. This was snowbird heaven, with five of the nine owners on the street being from elsewhere. Three owners were Canadian, and two other homes were owned by Americans from Minnesota, who spent their winters in Arizona. The other four owners included three working couples and one retired couple. The end of the street where it joined a busier street was blocked by two police cars. One backed out of the way, and our three SUVs turned the corner onto my street and backed into my driveway, which conveniently could hold three cars. The two motorcycle cops stopped at the entrance to the street, as did the two cruisers.

I jumped out of my SUV, and told Dan and Joe to follow me. I walked down the street, past a couple of houses to the police pres-ence, and sauntered over to the two cops on the motorcycles. The other officers started to exit their cars and stood nearby.

"Gentlemen, thank you so much for the escort. You are too kind. I have great respect for the police, and I really appreciate your efforts today."

They all came forward to introduce themselves, and I spent a few minutes chatting, talking about this crazy inheritance, and what a weird life I suddenly had.

"I thought I was grateful when you guys showed up here for a false alarm one time, but this service is over the top. So, guys, let me ask you a question ... Is there some equipment or effort I could help you with that would make your jobs easier and safer?"

Comments came fast and furious and from different voices: fewer guns on the street, less criminals, more Kevlar, more police officers, better-mannered young people, and some specialized kinds of equipment for their county.

One mentioned a new speedboat, and everyone laughed, knowing he meant that one for himself.

"Jacob, did you get all that?"

"Yes, sir."

"Scratch out the speedboat."

The cops all laughed.

"We will see what we can do, fellas. And thanks again; I hope we are not causing you too much trouble."

The police were all smiles as I walked back up the street, and I could hear mumbled phrases, like "good guy" coming from their chatter.

Back at the house, I walked in to find my usually quiet space filled with too many people. Zachary had picked a bedroom for himself and Jacob, and declared it theirs by tossing their luggage on the bed. The two stewards would apparently be live-in help, so they would take the other two guest rooms.

I motioned Andrew to follow me into the master bedroom, and closed the door.

"Andrew, this isn't really what I had in mind. This is like an armed camp. We have the road blocked off, the house is already full of people, there is security everywhere ... I was hoping for something low-key."

Andrew gave me a "don't be an asshole" look. "Now, sir, here is how this will work. The road will stay blocked. We have spoken to every neighbour, and they know they now live on the most secure street in all of Phoenix. The local police will be sent home now that we are all here. There are eight outside guards, basically two at each corner of the property. There are two stationed on the roof as well, where we built a small platform behind that decorative raised section.

"We will have two of the SUVs block the street with four men there. The cul-de-sac will have two more SUVs with four men. Those are to keep a watch on the open desert. We have also rented two of your neighbours' empty homes for barracks and logistics. It's all been taken care of. You can just wander around in your bathrobe and pretend you are here relaxing all on your own."

Andrew was greeted by perhaps the biggest eye roll in history, and when he saw it, he laughed out loud.

"Listen, sir, it wasn't too many days ago we were at SECPRO 1. We are now at SECPRO 3, so you can relax. I suspect in a month or so it will be SECPRO 4, but you will never be at SECPRO 5 for the rest of your life, so you have to adapt to all this."

"What the hell are you talking about? I have no idea what any of that means."

Andrew tried to smile as he taught his apparently dumb student. "SECPRO is short for 'security protocol.' For us, we define the various levels as follows: SECPRO 5 is the lowest level of readiness. Security is here but very relaxed. Think almost no security. SECPRO 4 has an increased intelligence watch with strengthened security measures. SECPRO 3 has increased force readiness and basically means we are ready to engaged if and when danger presents itself. SECPRO 2 is our maximum level of defensive readiness. And SECPRO 1 is where we are at maximum defensive and offensive readiness, where we shoot first and ask questions later.

"So again, we are operating at SECPRO 3, a serious level of security, and we will be for some time, sir. That is simply because, at present, there are too many unknowns. So, just let us do our job, and try to relax and enjoy yourself."

"Thanks, Andrew. Don't get me wrong, I appreciate everything, but fuck… these changes are hard to take. It's one thing when we are in working mode. I foolishly didn't expect anything like this here, but please, let's not irritate the neighbours."

"No worries, sir, we're on it."

"I want to visit with the guy next door. How do we get him here?"

"How would you usually get him here?" Andrew asked.

I picked up the phone and called next door. Dick answered, and when he heard my voice, he boomed, "JESUS CHRIST! You sure as HELL know how to make an entrance, bud!"

I asked him to come over, and within a couple of minutes, Dick was being frog-marched inside, with a man on each arm. He didn't look too happy.

The guard looked at Andrew and spoke. "We know he was invited over, sir, but he was armed. He voluntarily disarmed."

I was horrified. "Please let him go, gentlemen; he's fine. Dick, how are you?" I shook his hand and Dick looked around at all the commotion in the house.

"Holy shit, these guys don't mess around. I forgot I had my little gun in my pocket. You know I always carry it."

"Hey, my fault. Totally my fault, I should have warned you." I apologized like a good Canadian: repeatedly.

We sat down and chatted, and I filled him in on what the heck had been going on these last couple of weeks. He was wide-eyed and incredulous, especially about the attempts on my life. In the past, he and I had argued about gun control and had some great debates. There was no middle ground, and we both had extreme views.

He waved his hand in the direction of my security people and said, "Guess you aren't against guns now." He smiled an argument-winning grin.

"Actually, Dick, I have never been worried about guns. It's the bullets that scare the hell out of me."

He laughed, and I continued. "Now, more important than all of this, is that you and I are still on a mission to discover the best malt in all of Phoenix. So, how would you feel about a rather well-secured drive to an ice-cream place?"

His eyes lit up. Riding with all these security guys was like a dream come true for him.

"In the armoured SUV? With these guys? When?"

"Now. And I will pay. Seems I have come into some money." I turned to Andrew. "Sorry, but we want to go for ice cream. Let's keep it simple. No cops. Just the motorcade, okay?"

"Yes, sir, if you say so."

Keeping it simple still meant three armoured vehicles, Dick and me, and eight security men.

We pulled up to the local ice-cream place, and ordered at the drive-through… in a motorcade. The kid taking the order almost fainted. "One strawberry and one chocolate malt, please."

I tipped the kid fifty dollars, and we ate in the SUV while driving back to my place.

Dick, who was seventy-seven years old and a lifelong tough guy, looked at me a bit sympathetically. "Things are never going to be the same, are they?"

"I am afraid not, Dick, and I can already tell that I'll need to sell the house. I still want a place here, but I will need something a lot larger, with a secured compound and a lot more space to house staff and security. Life is getting pretty strange, but this is an amazing opportunity to do something good, and I am going to do my best."

Dick nodded, and looked at me a bit strangely. "I saw what you are doing for the veterans. Got to say … I am totally impressed. Our government should have done more."

"I think we can almost never do enough for those guys, and I am really proud that we can help. We will look for other veteran-related opportunities to help with too. Have you got any other ideas of things we should look at?"

"Yeah, give the money to build that wall on the southern border."

"Not with my money, but good luck with that." We both laughed. "But I will look at helping to improve education and employment opportunities in Mexico for Mexicans. If those are successful, it should help slow the flow of immigrants to the states. We will not spend this money to build prisons or to put people in jail, though. I need every dollar to be spent to create some good."

Dick knew the wall was a long shot, but he enjoyed trying to get my goat. Usually he succeeded.

We pulled back into the driveway at my house, and I turned to the security guys and said, "Please give him back his gun and escort him safely home."

"Thanks, bud!"

"Have a good night, Dick."

I would miss our bull sessions, as it was unlikely I would see him much anymore.

CHAPTER 58

I was awake at six a.m., and walked from my room to the kitchen to make a cup of tea. Warm, sunny mornings were my favourite time of day, and I loved sitting outside by the pool, reading the news on my iPad and enjoying the morning silence. The birds, the pool pump, and the occasional car passing nearby with someone on their way to work were normally the only sounds.

It was a little different this morning. Mostly because there were four security guards in my backyard. I waved good morning to them, sat in my usual chair, and tried to pretend I was alone. It was not quite the same...

I got up and went inside and put the coffee pot on. Ten minutes later, I returned with four cups and waved the agents over. One at a time, they each came over, got what they wanted, and then returned to their post before the next one moved. *Man, these dudes take this seriously.* While it was all a bit too much, I knew I was only alive because of them. And since twelve guys had died, I knew I was probably not a primo assignment for them, either.

Coffee was literally the least I could do.

Back in my chair again, enjoying the morning warmth, the door opened and a tired-looking Zach came out in a robe and bare feet.

"Morning, Steve, may I join you?"

I waved him to the chair opposite me, but when he saw the coffee, he ran back inside for a mug and then rejoined me outside.

"What a gorgeous morning."

"And Zach, it is like this nearly every single day. Some days warmer and some days cooler, but April and May are just spectacular months."

"Steve, I am not sure if you want to work at all while we are here, but on a personal matter, I have three sets of blueprints for you to look at as a starting point for the new house, and then the architects will take it from there. We also looked at those three places as temporary housing until the new house is built. Was there one of those that caught your eye?"

"Let's look at the blueprints after breakfast, and as far as other houses in Vancouver go, let's just stay at the hotel. I mean, it solves all of our room needs, has restaurants and bars and room service, it's right downtown, and it is not like we have a money problem."

"Okay, I will let the realtors know, and let the hotel know we will be occupying our floor as early as next week."

More people were starting to move around inside. I could hear voices. *Fuck… Well, I enjoyed the quiet for at least twenty minutes…*

Jacob appeared with a towel and in his swimsuit. "I'm going to take a morning dip!" With that, he jumped into the pool, swam the length under water, and came up wiping the water from his hair and face. "The water is great, Zach, come on in!"

Zach looked at me, cocked his head to one side with a grin that said "I could do worse," and trotted inside to get changed. Soon the two of them were swimming, talking, laughing, and horsing around a bit. Water tended to shave a few years off a person's maturity, and they were no exception. At the moment, in the water, they were a couple of twelve-year-old kids messing around. It was fun to watch.

I finished my tea and was heading inside when Zachary asked if there was a gym nearby. I told him where it was and that he was welcome to go.

Inside, the two stewards, who I found out were named Greg and Linda, were going to set the table on the patio for breakfast. Not sure why, but I have always loved eating outdoors. Even when you just make yourself a sandwich and take it outside, it feels luxurious. Maybe growing up in Vancouver, where there are perhaps sixty days a year with mornings warm enough to do so, made it always seem like a treat.

Yeah, I thought, *this house is now way too small.*

At twenty-eight hundred square feet, it was perfect for me and guests, but not for an entourage that would always continue to grow. We already had eighteen local guards plus my three, plus Zach and Jacob, plus the stewards and myself. Twenty-seven people. Nice.

I asked if I had time for a shower, and was told breakfast would be ready in thirty minutes. Plenty of time. I was done in twenty, and back outside in shorts and a polo shirt, barefoot. *Heaven...*

I got on the phone and called my local realtor friend.

"Patti, Steve Thomas. Looks like I have a house to sell and a much bigger house to buy. Can you help me out?" *Like she would actually say no?* We chatted for a while, catching up and chatting about market conditions. Of course, she had heard about what was going on in my world. She and her hubby were a really nice couple. Good folks indeed. She said my current home was worth about four hundred and fifty thousand dollars. It was a nice normal home. The new place would cost...well, who knows?

"Yeah, there's no issue there. I doubt I can go house hunting with you, so I need you to pull together a few ideas. Let's make it easy. Bring me the four most expensive properties for sale in greater Phoenix. We can look them over here, and I will send a couple of my people out with you for an inspection. That shouldn't take you long, should it? Can we do this later this morning?... Eleven is perfect! See you then."

Breakfast was delightful. They had made us thick-cut bacon, eggs, toast, sliced melon, blueberries and strawberries, and juice. Six-hundred pounds was staring back at me from the plate. So, I ate the eggs and the fruit and a half slice of bacon, and skipped the toast. *Good boy.*

After the dishes had been cleared away, I asked Zach to fetch the architectural drawings. He brought them outside, along with a T-shirt for Jacob, and donned one himself.

We spread the first plans out, and I had a look, then the second and third. The third one had some extra sketches done by the architects to incorporate some specific needs for me.

"Anything catch your eye, Steve?"

"Yes, this third one is really good." It was two storeys, with a low-profile flat roof, which would be good for the neighbourhood sight lines, and massive. They recommended sustainable materials wherever possible. And their concept would build three buildings on the property, with a covered walkway between them for inclement weather.

At the eastern end of the property, which was a shallower lot from front to back, we would have a building holding living accommodations for household staff and security. It was about eighty feet deep and fifty feet wide. With two storeys, it was eight thousand square feet, and would have twelve private, six hundred-square-foot, one-bedroom, self-contained apartments.

At the other end of the property, positioned the same way, would be a building a hundred feet deep and fifty feet wide. Also two storeys, it would span ten thousand square feet. The lower floor would house security offices, a gym, a recreation area, an indoor sauna, a hot tub, a game room, and a TV/entertainment area. These areas could be available for anyone in the compound to use. The upper floor would hold three one-thousand-square-foot apartments for our senior team, and a fourteen-hundred-square-foot apartment for Jacob and Zachary, overlooking the ocean.

The main building was twenty-one thousand square feet. The rooms were all large. The building was about a hundred and fifty feet long and seventy feet deep. The long side faced the ocean with floor to ceiling windows. The entire ocean side of the house was bulletproof glass. Underneath the house would be underground parking. The main floor would house a massive living room, four thousand square feet in size, which could accommodate parties. There would be two dining rooms. One would hold up to forty people at five round tables. The smaller "family dining room" would accommodate up to ten. There were two kitchens. One would be a gorgeous family-style kitchen, while the second was a professional restaurant-style kitchen, to be used for events and catering. The catering kitchen was about fifteen feet by twenty-five, which was big enough to meet our needs, but small enough not to be ridiculous. The main floor also had a theatre room for twenty-four, a bar/lounge area, a wine cellar, a library/study, and a spacious home office with an ocean view for me, a small boardroom, an outer office, and private staff offices for up to six people. This floor plan was ideal, because at some point, I hoped I would work from home and Jack would run the office downtown without me. It also showed four normal household washrooms on the main floor, plus two commercial-style washrooms, one for men and one for women, with multiple stalls in each. No waiting at parties.

Upstairs in the centre section, overlooking the ocean, was a centrally located family TV room. On one end of the house was my suite, which had a sitting area, bedroom, massive closet, and a huge bathroom. The master suite was fifteen hundred square feet. The rest of the upstairs was a series of guest bedrooms, each with their own bath. Eleven bedrooms in total, including the master. There was also a set of stairs leading to a roof deck about two thousand square feet in size. And a rooftop helipad!

The outside space was sketched out roughly. If you imagine a sheet of legal-size paper turned sideways, that was roughly the shape of the property. There is eight hundred feet of oceanfront at the top of the page, the road runs all along the bottom, and neighbouring homes are on either end. The property was about two hundred feet deep from road to ocean.

On the paper, in the lower left corner, was a tennis court. Behind that, running toward the ocean, was the building with apartments, offices, and game rooms. On the far right side of the paper was the twelve-suite building for staff accommodations, again running from the front of the property to the ocean. And between those buildings, running lengthwise on the property and situated well back by the ocean, was the main house. The gated driveway entered from the lower right side, and there was a circular, teardrop-shaped driveway near the ramp down to the underground parking. There would be surface parking for up to twenty vehicles, and underground parking for up to twenty-eight vehicles. On the ocean side of the property would be a swimming pool, whirlpool, and plenty of outdoor seating, some covered and some open.

"Zachary, this place is a dream come true. I am almost ashamed to admit it, but I have no suggestions for changes. It is perfect. I will want to discuss finishes, colours, and furnishings, but I am going to leave this in your hands to bring along. Get it built. Fast."

Three hours later, Patti arrived with some ideas for the Phoenix property, and the choices were pretty cool.

She had two choices that met our needs. Both were approximately twenty-two thousand square feet. One was glitzier than the other, but not in a way I liked. The other one was a house I had driven by many times. It sat on the top of a bluff. Ten bedrooms, fourteen baths, and tons of space. There was also an indoor basketball court, which because of its height, could easily be turned into a two-storey space with offices and guest rooms for the staff and security.

The asking price was $9,995,000. I told Patti to call the other realtor and make a full price offer, plus another million to include all the furniture and contents. Basically, take your clothes and personal belongings, and get out.

They got back within the hour, and said they would leave their one-million-dollar art collection for an additional five hundred thousand. We told them yes, if they vacated within seven days. In the meantime, we would drive over to view the art and do a walk-though, but either way, the deal was firm. We would close, all in cash, in seven days.

We looked at the property on Google Earth. There was a single street ending in a cul-de-sac. The winding road had the potential for extra homes, which we could build if we decided we wanted or needed to do so. We instructed Patti to buy all the lots still not built on, and to buy the one other house that sat right at the entrance to the road up to the house, regardless of what it cost. If we acquired that, we wouldn't need to convert the basketball court; we could use the extra house for staff and offices, and it would enable us to secure the entire street. Andrew was all over it, and approved. We could fence the land, install gates, and it would be easy to secure. Since it sat on a bluff, the entire property could be guarded from the roof. Oh, and there was room for a helipad. Yes, another helipad.

I used to drive by that house and muse that it looked like a huge Tuscan winery or something. I would always point it out to friends when I gave them tours of the area. No one could believe it was just a single house, because it was so big. But now, holy shit, it was mine. *Wow. This is incredible.*

I called the next-door neighbour. "Hey, Dick, leave the gun at home and pop over, okay? … Okay, see you in five." I hung up.

"Andrew, can you make sure he is let in?"

Andrew smirked, spoke into his sleeve, and I am pretty sure I heard him instruct them to "let the redneck in."

I looked at him and gave him a stern expression. He laughed a little and shrugged. Humanity was leaking out of him. I appreciated the sense of humour.

Dick was, in fact, a bit of a redneck. I described him to my friends as a "God-fearing, gun-toting, conservative redneck." But that belied the fact that he was also a gentle soul. Tough guy, yes, but he had a good heart. On the day I originally moved into my place, he had knocked at the door and introduced himself as Dick, "But most people just call me 'Asshole.'"

I had replied, "Well, Dick… that is going to be a problem, with both of us having the same name." We were instant friends.

Dick arrived and I took him out to the patio. "Listen, you know that massive house down the road, on the bluff, that we looked at that time?"

He nodded.

"I just bought it. I was wondering if you and Rosie would mind being my eyes and ears on the ground there and looking after the place. I don't need you to work on it or clean it, just be there when needed, keep it running, bark a few orders now and again, and have it ready when I arrive. We would put you on the payroll, at say a hundred thousand a year? It would be really helpful to me if you could do it."

"Holy shit, man! I know you're a generous guy, but that's nuts! Are you serious?"

"Yup, completely serious."

He seemed almost speechless, but that didn't last long. "Well, you know I have to talk to my wife and that she'll make the decision. After all, she only gives me an annual renewal of our marriage each year as long as I fall in line." He was kidding, but serious about Rosie needing to approve of it.

I laughed. "Oh, I know. Look, since she is out of town, you just ask her in a couple of days when she gets home, and let me know. We get possession in seven days, and once we do, I need someone there to oversee a variety of changes and improvements. I think you're the man for the job, and anyway, you know how I like to do nice things for good people? This is one of those times!"

Dick was in a bit of shock, as he headed out the door, almost stumbling down the driveway and laughing and pointing back at the door, while saying to the guards, "Crazy-as-shit Canadian inside there."

He was a good guy.

By the end of the day, Patti had checked on the extra plots of land, and there were seven lots on the street. All had been bought by a contractor who had been sitting on them for years, waiting for a stronger real-estate market. He had paid $2.8 million for the bunch. After a bit of back and forth, we bought them for $6 million. The extra house was owned by absentee owners in Cleveland. They hardly used the place and had been thinking of selling anyway. The house had a market value of about $1.8 million. We offered them $2.5 million, fully furnished, for a seven-day close and they took it. When we asked about their personal belongings, they told us, "Just throw away what you don't want." Seemed they never kept anything particularly personal there. We told them we would box up anything we thought was personal and ship it to them. The guy remembered he had a really good set of golf clubs in the garage, and we said we would ship those to him too.

"Andrew, how big is the Guardian Security office here in Phoenix?"

"It's a good size, sir. We have about four hundred employees here and handle administration work for the various services throughout the state. We might need to expand somewhat just to meet your personal needs, but that's fine. It's what we do."

Perfect. Andrew would get a hold of the head guy and have him assign someone to undertake the security issues, and to look after all the initial administration work of getting all the services transferred into my name and all that sort of stuff. He could handle fencing the property, installing gates and electronic access, cameras, guard huts … whatever was needed. I would have Jack Dickinson sort out the rest of the paperwork, and asked Jacob to call Jack to take care of it.

Zach said he would work with the security guys to pick out a stylish fence. Back home in Canada, people build wooden fences, or maybe put in chain-link fences. In Arizona, due to the heat, wooden fences would just dry up and fall apart, so the normal fencing was a six-foot concrete block wall. We would do stone posts and wrought-iron sections instead. This would allow better visibility and be slightly harder to climb over. There would also be a main access gate and a secondary way out in case of emergency. I didn't need to worry about that stuff, but found it pretty interesting listening to Andrew describe how everything would work quite easily with this particular property.

We had steaks that night on the barbecue, and sat outside by the gas fireplace until nearly eleven, chatting and laughing. It was really a good chance to get to know one another a lot better.

When I asked Zachary why he seemed so at ease with the security people and stewards and such, he told us quite a story.

"Steve, I guess you wouldn't have known, but I was raised in a pretty wealthy family in Geneva. My great-great-grandfather was involved as a key advisor in the creation of the United Nations, and also had been in banking and politics his entire life. He only had one son, and my grandfather only had one son, and strangely enough, I am the only son of my parents. No daughters anywhere down the line. As a result, we all lived in the same huge home in Geneva, and I grew up with servants and chauffeurs and private schools. Life was great until I was eighteen. I assumed I was going join the family business and become a banker one day. Just as I was getting ready to head off to university in England, word got back to my parents that I had been seen hanging out at a gay film festival. Some friends of my parents, who were pretty eclectic people and were there themselves, spotted me, and spoke to my parents.

"So, I guess, as the story goes, these people—Ken and Monique were their names—came to the house for dinner one night. They were very liberal minded and had no issues, but during dinner, Monique said to my mom, 'Is Zachary gay? We attended a film festival event the other night and saw him there with a number of gay people.'

"So, I guess my mother just about had a heart attack and looked at my father, and the two of them were horrified and embarrassed. They were very Catholic and didn't approve. When I got home that evening, they confronted me, one thing led to another, and I was asked to leave the house and never come back."

I looked at Zachary and was horrified for the poor man. I noticed Jacob was holding his hand for support.

"My God, Zach, that's awful. What the hell is wrong with some parents? I am so sorry."

"Actually, Steve, it worked out for the best in some ways. I couldn't afford to attend that fancy British university I was destined to go to, but had enough money to go to a lesser university in Zurich. I never wanted to be a banker anyway. I always wanted to be a teacher, so I got my education and my certification, and then one night at a club, I met Jacob. None of that would have happened if my parents had not first rejected me and then ejected me that night."

These young men were remarkably strong. I was impressed.

"Zach, do you ever see your parents? Has it been resolved at all?"

"My mother calls me on my birthday every year. I think she has to sneak the call. My father, to this day, cannot understand how a 'man like him' could have produced a gay child. He thinks it makes him seem deficient somehow. Sad. I miss them both. It's been hard."

Jacob spoke up, "People make choices in life. You don't choose to be gay, regardless of what the crazy people think. I mean, why would anyone 'decide' to have a life that is so much harder, and that in many countries could even be a death sentence? Sometimes when we travel, we face discrimination. The younger Swiss people are great, though. Times are changing."

I looked at them both. "Thanks for sharing that, guys, I really mean it. That's very personal and I am glad to know the story. I hope that one day your dad can get past his prejudice and recognize the fine man you are. He will truly regret his actions one day, and he is needlessly making both his and your life harder. It's sad that certain ideas can overwhelm love. Very sad."

Zach drank the last of the scotch in his glass and announced that it was past his bedtime. We all agreed. We turned off the outdoor fireplace and headed inside for the night, leaving the guards standing in the shadows of the backyard to work the night shift for us.

CHAPTER 59

The Larkman kill team had arrived. They had their weapons, had selected their positions, and would not fail this time.

The go command had been received and confirmed.

Three men were on three nearby rooftops with sniper rifles, and planned to fire in synchronized fashion.

The three other men were on foot. If the snipers succeeded, they would melt into the crowds. If the snipers failed, they would simply walk up to the target and blow him away with a double tap to the head. They were positioned near a coffee shop, a nearby bench, and next to a fountain.

A black Mercedes sedan rolled up. The elegant, well-dressed man exited the vehicle, and straightened his jacket as he stood at the vehicle door. He reached in and picked up his briefcase, said goodbye to his driver, and turned to head into the building.

The sniper rifles had silencers but still made a loud "woof" sort of sound. Almost simultaneously, one bullet entered the right side of his skull, another hit him dead centre in the heart, and a third landed in his mid-section. His body was literally thrown to the ground in a heap of torn and exploding flesh. Blood poured from a massive hole in his skull and from his gut wound. His heart had stopped instantly and was no longer pumping blood, but it still oozed from his body.

There were screams and shouts, and people scattered everywhere. One bank guard, and then another, ran from inside the building to help the man on the ground.

Even through the mess, the blood, and the human destruction, the guards recognized the hair, the suit, and the briefcase.

The snipers ditched their weapons and exited the rooftops immediately. The three ground-level hit men melted away, and three minutes and two blocks later, everyone was in a van heading south from the area.

Back on the busy Zurich Street, in front of his beloved bank, Wilhelm Altermatt lay dead.

The colonel called the special number, and keyed in his special code.

A voice queried, "Report?"

"Target eliminated."

There was a muffled noise. The line went dead.

CHAPTER 60

There was a rap at the door to my bedroom, followed by the door being opened and the lights turning on. I was sort of half awake. It was around three in the morning, and as I gained focus, I could see four agents standing in my room.

I covered my eyes with my hand to filter the glare from the light.

"What's going on, guys?" I was startled, but not too concerned for some reason.

Andrew spoke up. "We have had a call from Zurich, and we have some sad news, sir."

"What? What's going on?"

"Sir, Mr. Altermatt was gunned down and killed on the street in front of the bank a few hours ago. He was killed instantly."

"Oh my God! Jesus Christ… What the hell happened?" I sat up in bed and waited for an answer.

"Police are investigating. All we know at this point is that he was shot three times by a sniper or snipers, and died instantly. We are going stay close to you for a while, sir. We have more security on their way here at this moment, and the local police are also securing the area around the house. At this point, we don't know if this is an unrelated matter, a coincidence, or part of a coordinated attack. We are not about to take any chances."

I slipped out of bed and pulled on my robe.

"Let's go out into the family room. Has Jacob been advised?"

"Not yet, sir."

"Then … let me tell him."

I walked down the hall and turned down the guest-wing hallway, which held three guest rooms and a couple of bathrooms.

I knocked on their door, then quietly opened it up and whispered their names. Zach and Jacob roused, and were a bit shocked to see me standing in their doorway. They sat up in bed and wiped their eyes, asking what I wanted.

I walked a few steps and sat on the end of the bed. They moved their feet to give me some room.

"Jacob, I have some very sad news. We just heard that your grandfather has died. I am so sorry."

Jacob sank into Zachary's arms.

"Heart attack? He had a bad heart …"

"Jacob, it's far worse. He was shot and killed in front of the bank this morning. He didn't suffer. They said he died instantly, not that that helps much. I am so sorry, Jacob."

"Oh my God … Poor Opa. I need to get back to Zurich. I need to call my mother."

"Jacob, you do whatever you need to do, and we will be here to support you in every way we can."

I turned to Andrew, who was standing in the doorway. "We are going to need to speak to our pilot. We need to get out of here and fly to Zurich as soon as he can be ready. Can you arrange it?"

With a simple, "Yes, sir," Andrew left the room to take care of details.

Jacob was sobbing quietly into Zach's shoulder, and then in a moment, it was over. He sat up in bed, pulled his legs up toward his chest, wrapped his hands around his knees, and rocked himself forward and backward a bit.

"I will leave you two alone," I said softly as I closed the bedroom door. "We will let you know when we hear more."

Back in the kitchen, Andrew was finishing a call.

"Well?"

"Sir, for the first time, I just lied to you in front of the boys."

"What do you mean?"

"Sir, there is no way we are taking you to Zurich immediately following a murder of a close associate. We are going to hunker down here for a few days, let the smoke clear, and then decide what to do."

"Andrew, we have to get Jacob back to Zurich."

"Sir, Jacob is not really my concern. Your safety is."

"Well, Jacob is my concern, and we are either flying there today on the jet, or we are flying there commercially."

Andrew pleaded with his eyes. "Sir—"

"Andrew, please, it's important. Wilhelm put me in charge of Jacob, and I feel a deep responsibility for him and his welfare, and this is one of those moments when I will do whatever it takes."

His shoulders drooped for a moment, before he straightened once again. "Alright, sir, it is against my better judgement, but we will be wheels up at noon. It will put us in there at about seven a.m. local time tomorrow."

I went back and tapped on the bedroom door and asked permission to go back in. I told Jacob that we would all be flying to Zurich and leaving at noon. He was very grateful, and said so.

"Have you called your mother?"

"I have. She is devastated. Sobbing really loudly on the phone. She wants me to come home."

"Is your dad with her?"

"No, my dad isn't with her. I guess I never told you this, but my parents are separated. They have been for a long time, nine years to be exact."

I nodded my understanding. "We will have you home in time for breakfast. You two feel free to rest. It's not even four yet. We will probably not leave the house until after ten. Is there anything else I can do for you, Jacob?"

He shook his head and gave me a grateful but sad half smile. He had been so close to his grandfather. This was going to be very hard for him.

CHAPTER 61

The Larkman Six, as they were playfully calling themselves on this mission, were now out of Switzerland and into Germany. They had made the three-and-a-half-hour road trip to Munich slightly quicker than planned. Once in Munich, they split up to go their separate ways. They each had the documents they needed to travel, credit cards in fake names, and cash. They carried no weapons and nothing to make them suspicious.

They would rendezvous back in Larkman to debrief in seven days, taking their time getting there. The slower, the less suspicious. Different travel, different days, different routes, different airlines.

Mission accomplished. Now to get home.

CHAPTER 62

The Boeing 787 roared down the runway at Phoenix-Mesa Gateway Airport and lifted into the sky, turning and banking steeply to the east to stay clear of the traffic from Sky Harbor (PHX), the main airport. The pilot was cleared for a steep ascent, and we were up and over the Superstition Mountains in no time. We were at our full cruising altitude of forty-one thousand feet shortly before we reached the New Mexico border.

The three of us were all sitting in the forward salon. Andrew had a twenty-four-man security detail in the rear of the aircraft, taking no chances, and was finalizing all the details for our arrival.

"Boys," I said to Jacob and Zachary, "I would like you to take my cabin for the flight over. I will be just fine in one of the smaller staterooms."

While Zachary began to protest, Jacob looked at me and tears welled up in his eyes.

"Thank you, Steve, you really are very kind. Thank you so much."

I smiled back. The steward brought us some drinks. With raised glasses, we toasted Altermatt, and Jacob told stories about his grandfather, alternating between laughing and choking up.

We had some more drinks. And then a couple more.

I said good night and headed to the smaller stateroom, crawling into bed. I hoped the boys slept well. They would need their strength far more than I would.

We descended into Flughafen Zürich and parked the jet in the same spot it had been in a few weeks before. Our six-SUV motorcade was waiting, as were four police cruisers. We needed a lot of vehicles for the number of security men we had. Four agents stayed with the aircraft, and the rest of us headed to the home of Jacob's mother, Ursula Van Vloten.

We arrived at a stately row house located in a wealthy neighbourhood. It was narrow, but four storeys high. As the motorcade rolled up, blocking the street, and men poured out of our vehicles, Andrew and the senior men went inside the house to make sure it was safe and that we were not walking into a trap. All was clear. Jacob's mother came outside, embraced her son for a long time, then turned and took him by the arm and led us all inside the house.

I am not sure I had ever felt more awkward, and frankly I felt somewhat responsible. It just seemed that all of this violence had erupted since my inheritance had come my way. I mean, we didn't know why Altermatt had been gunned down, but it didn't take a rocket scientist to do the math.

Ursula was lovely. A striking woman, around fifty years old, she had porcelain skin and dark blonde hair done up in a ponytail. Jacob's mom was at least partly responsible for his good looks. You could see parts of her face in his, and in the way he carried himself.

"Ursula, I am so pleased to meet you, but so sorry for the circumstances of our meeting. We got Jacob home as soon as we could."

"Oh, Steve, thank you so much. I need my son right now. Thank you for bringing him home. No one could believe that anyone would want to kill my father. Such a good man, and he loved us all so much."

Jacob excused himself and his mother from the rest of us, and took her into an adjoining room. They hugged some more and shared a few tears. Zach stayed with me, and when I motioned for him to join them, he shook his head.

"No, they need some family time. Let's leave them be. Come to the kitchen and let's make tea for everyone."

We headed to the kitchen. Zach had been coming here for many years, and knew where to find everything. We boiled some water, made tea, and took cups to Jacob and Ursula. She was very happy when she saw it, and pleased by the simple, considerate act.

I went and found Andrew and suggested it might be wise, just in case, to provide Ursula some security for a while. He got on it and arranged for her to have a couple of agents around the clock for the next three months.

I decided to excuse myself and let the three of them sort out family details, including making funeral arrangements. While it might be some time before the body was released, they still had to make plans.

"Jacob, may I see you for just a moment? Ursula, please forgive me, but I just need your son for a moment."

Jacob came with me and we went back to the kitchen.

"Listen, Jacob, your mother needs you for a while. I know you were only assigned to me temporarily, but I want you working full time with me, side by side. You and Zach have been amazing, so I need you to think about two things, given what has happened: First, give some thought to leaving the bank entirely and joining me permanently; and second, if your answer is 'yes,' then just let me know when you are ready to return to work. I don't need an answer now, but I just wanted you to know."

"Steve, I would like to be here for my mother until the funeral is over and then maybe a couple more days. She has a housekeeper who is off today, so she is not normally alone, but this will be a big transition. As for working with you permanently, Zach would kill me if I said no. We really feel like we have found our calling, so just give me a bit of time. I will be fine, so Zach can head back with you sooner, while I stay on here for a short while."

"That's great news, staying on with the team I mean, and I'm sure you won't regret it. I know I won't. Okay, get back to your mom. Until you both can return to Vancouver, Zach should stay with you. I'll see you later. I am going to go to the hotel, but you can let me know if you need anything."

I said goodbye to Zach and Ursula and headed outside with Andrew, who hustled me into one of the vehicles.

We headed out to the Dolder Grand Hotel. Mr. Hurlimann had been pleased to take my call, and made the same suite available for me and the security team again. He expressed his deep sorrow over the loss of Mr. Altermatt. They had both been members of the Rotary Club of Zurich, which was the very first Rotary Club in Switzerland, started in 1924. It had a long and storied history of service to its community, and he and Wilhelm had played key roles in their most active years. They had also served on the board of the Chamber of Commerce together. They were old and dear friends.

Security was tighter than normal, for obvious reasons, but I had started to give up on concerns or fear for my own safety. I followed the team's lead, but moved with confidence. Lars was available for a thirty-minute rubdown before bed, and I slept very well that night.

CHAPTER 63

There was little need for an autopsy of Wilhelm's body. It was obvious from the shots through the heart and head what had killed him. It only took forty-eight hours before all the necessary samples and DNA were taken and his body was released to the family. Ursula ordered it cremated immediately. She did not want anyone to see her father in that condition.

A memorial was scheduled for two days later. I decided to stay on in Zurich to attend it and be of support to Jacob and Zach, and also to offer whatever comfort I could to Ursula. I also wrote Ursula a cheque for twenty-five thousand dollars to help defray the costs. She smiled, tore it up, and told me she was just fine. I found her to be a classy lady.

The Fraumünster Church was the site of the funeral. The church was famous for having five stained-glass windows that had been created by artist Marc Chagall. The church was located only two blocks from the bank and was one of the most famous churches in Zurich.

The building was packed. I had a seat of honour next to Jacob. He and Zachary were flanking Ursula, with each holding one of her hands.

Everyone attended, from the mayor to the prime minister, as well as all the local community and business leaders, plus a huge retinue of people from the arts community. The Zurich Boys' Choir sang, and to my surprise, the key eulogy was delivered by none other than Jacob Van Vloten.

When it was Jacob's turn, he walked up to the podium positioned near the high altar.

"Good morning. Herr Wilhelm Altermatt was known by many names. He was father, husband, uncle, grandfather, and son. To others he was the boss, a friend, an advisor, and a leader. To more, he was an anonymous contributor and a charitable man, a major supporter of the arts and community events. He was so proud of his bank, his city, his country, and of the many Swiss traditions he celebrated. He especially loved the opera, the ballet, and live theatre. He was in many ways a refined and dignified man from a different era. A man of grace and sophistication.

"To me, he was both my grandfather and my boss. He was also a fan and a supporter of whatever exploits I undertook. He was the smartest person I have ever known, the kindest grandfather, and when my grandmother was alive, the fiercest promoter of his love for her.

"My grandfather was born in 1946, one year after the end of the war in Europe. A war that destroyed so much, killed so many, and accomplished so little. Lives were lost, treasures were looted, families were ripped apart, and nations were destroyed. As a result, he was born a builder. Someone who would help remake Europe in a manner befitting its history, and help it rise from the ashes of the monstrous atrocities it had just endured.

"As the world now knows, he spent the last forty years of his life managing the Thomas Protocol Fund, and recently turned it over to its beneficiary. It was his life's work. He knew that, one day, the fund he built would change the world for the better. He was proud to have accomplished so much, but also sad that his journey was at an end.

He knew that cultivating this fund would continue his life's work, constructing not just a better Europe, but a better world.

"I am so proud to have joined the Thomas Protocol to assist in delivering to the world something that took a hundred years to prepare, and to carry on my grandfather's work at the same time. There is so much I have to do, and I will do much of it in my grand-father's memory.

"Opa, if you are listening, I am standing on your shoulders as I carry on your work. I will make sure that your life's work makes a difference. May you always know that our family loves you, and will miss you every day. You were a man among men, and we can all aspire to your goodness. Sleep well, until we see you again."

With that, Jacob silently walked back to his seat. You could have heard a pin drop. I reached over and patted him on the knee. His head dropped slightly, and he wiped away a tear.

CHAPTER 64

Without any fanfare, I left the church. Paige had flown in for the funeral, and joined me outside. We walked about a block with my security team in a tight formation, got into the motorcade, and headed directly to the airport. We had been in Zurich longer than planned, and it was time to go home. The plane was warming up as we arrived. The team boarded the plane, the door closed, and the stairs were pulled away. We were cleared to taxi, and then for takeoff. We were in the air twelve minutes after arriving at the airport. It felt good to be heading back to Canada.

We left Jacob and Zach behind. In fact, I didn't even tell them we were leaving. We had Paige send them a text saying we would check in with them in a week to see if they knew when they would be ready to rejoin the team, wherever we might be in the world by then.

Before heading to my cabin, I sat with Paige and chatted for about an hour on the flight. She was twenty-three, a graduate of the Simon Fraser University's business program, and while attending school, had worked for the Fairmont Hotel chain. It was there she learned her terrific service skills and efficient, client-focused manner. Paige grew up in Burnaby BC, in the Capitol Hill area. Her parents lived in an older home they had bought from her grandmother. The area had amazing views over Vancouver and the harbour, and had become a very popular area for the up and coming. She told me she was single, but seeing a young guy. His name was Angus, and they had met in her last year of university.

"What does Angus do?"

"He works in the tech industry, for Microsoft in their offices in Pacific Centre. Don't ask me what he does, because I don't really understand it, so let's just say it's in program design."

"Wedding bells in the future?"

"Not sure. We are not engaged, and we don't live together. My mother would kill me if we did." She grinned, "You don't see a ring on this finger yet, so who knows. I am not really sure I am ready, anyway. How do you know if you're really in love?"

"Oh my gosh, Paige, don't ask me. To be perfectly honest, I have loved my parents, my dog, and one incredible woman. Defining love is so hard. I am not sure how to explain love, or even if you can. That magic has mostly eluded me."

"Yeah, I am not sure either. I miss Angus when I am away from him, but hey, I miss my own bed, and my best girlfriends too." She laughed.

"Give it time, Paige. I think love reveals itself when you least expect it. I know for me, I met Sophie through some friends at a dinner party. When I shook her hand that first time, it was electric. I didn't want the night to end. I wanted to sit near her. I couldn't stop looking at her. I sort of melted. We dated for about a year and then lived together for nine more. She died of cancer shortly after my fortieth birthday. When we were together, there was no place else I wanted to be, and there was no one else I wanted to be with. I was crushed when our time together ended. I still haven't recovered from that bout of love. Ever since, I have convinced myself that being on my own is where I belong. I'm not sure I'll ever get a second chance at that kind of love, but I'm fine with that."

"I am so sorry to hear that she died, but how lucky that you found each other."

I nodded my agreement. "And then, there is the other thing you have to watch out for. Paige, I can't count how many couples I have seen through the years who are married and have a family, but can't stand to be in the same room, and would clearly be better off if they were not together. What a sad way to spend your life. And the funny part is, it's usually those friends who tell me they really wish I would find someone again, so I could be as happy as they are!"

Paige and I both laughed.

"Makes me wonder if they are my friends or enemies!"

Paige smiled a very thoughtful smile. "I will give it time, and hopefully the right one will come along."

"Good for you. And with that, Paige, I am going to head to my stateroom and unwind for the next while."

I watched a little TV by myself, and then laid down on the bed and thought about Sophie. It would have been incredible to have taken this new journey together. I drifted off, lying on top of the blankets. In a few hours, the steward knocked to let me know that dinner would be served in thirty minutes. I freshened up in the washroom, and wandered back to the main salon.

Dinner felt strange without the boys. I invited Andrew, Joe, and Dan to join me and Paige. Dinner was salmon, salad, roast potatoes, and various cookies for dessert.

A few hours later, the lights of Vancouver came into view, and we gently touched down. Shockingly, it was not raining. The helicopter whisked me to the yacht for the night. It had been decided that tomorrow we would be moving into the hotel.

Back at the yacht, and forgetting the time difference, I called Jacob to see how things were going. After accidentally waking them up, Jacob put me on his speaker phone so both he and Zach could talk, and they told me the latest developments. Shortly after the funeral service, the bank's chairman advised Jacob that his mother, Ursula, would be the next president of the bank, continuing the long tradition of an Altermatt at the helm of the GCBS.

The announcement had stabilized the bank's stock price. In her professional life, Ursula was an extremely well-regarded, tough, and popular leader in Swiss banking circles. She would be one of the first females to lead a major bank, and deservedly so. It was great to think of this talented woman breaking through the glass ceiling.

Jacob indicated that once his mother went back to work, in a couple of days, he and Zach would be coming home. Zach suggested they would take the time to help Ursula, as well as tidy up loose ends at their old flat. They also had to pack their belongings to ship to Vancouver.

I told him not to bother "shipping" belongings. One of our new aircraft had been delivered, and I would send it to pick them up. They would be the first to use the new 737-Max BBJ. Much smaller than the Dreamliner, it was still one hell of a jet for two people! It was similarly outfitted as the larger aircraft, but had been equipped with six smaller sleeping cabins for our team to use when travelling around the world seeking projects. At least that was the plan for it when it was ordered.

The boys were delighted to get to use the new plane, and were profuse in their thanks. The plane had a substantial cargo area, so as long as they boxed things up, it could all be loaded in for transport.

I told them to take care of themselves, to stay in touch, and that they should contact Paige with their travel details.

I had to admit that I felt greedy taking these two away from Zurich. Somehow, I knew that family was a hell of a lot more important than working for me, but they insisted on getting back at it. Death comes along in everyone's life, and I know that in my own case, I had taken only a couple of days off when my mother died, and the same when my dad died. My grandparents had all died when I was a child, so I had no experience in that department.

Jack Dickinson had emailed that he had some new proposals sorted out for us to look at supporting. He would be waiting for me in the office in the morning, but for now, it was time to get some sleep.

CHAPTER 65

In Larkman, the first of the six arrived at the bunker. He was home a couple of days early. It had just worked out that way. Having them all arrive on alternate days was probably a good thing anyway.

He had racked up the miles pretty well. He had travelled by train to Berlin, then flown to Athens, and on to Cairo. From there he flew to Singapore, then to Hawaii, and finally landed in Seattle. His last flight was back to Bozeman. Since he had been a passenger on the drive to Bozeman a week before, a different truck was stationed at the airport for his use to drive back to the bunker.

Within a couple of days everyone should be back. They had completed their mission and the funds would have already (or soon would be) paid into their master account for dispersal to each of them. He was proud of his performance in the hit. He had been the one to fire the shot straight through the heart. The old guy had nearly exploded as the shots riddled his body. He cringed a bit as he remembered the moment, but this was his job now.

The team would likely debrief, disband, and then go home for a couple of months and act like normal citizens until their next assignment. They liked to keep some distance between jobs so that their absences from their normal lives did not raise red flags.

He wondered which of his colleagues would get back next.

CHAPTER 66

100 YEARS AGO, MARCH 1918, BERLIN

The war was turning against the Germans. Their leader, Kaiser Wilhelm II, had been in power in Germany since he ascended to the throne in 1888. He ruled until nearly the end of the war, abdicating his throne in November of 1918, when he fled to the Netherlands. He died there in the town of Doorn, in 1941.

Strange as it may seem, he was the eldest grandchild of Queen Victoria, but was locked in battle with his royal cousins in the United Kingdom.

He was a belligerent man. When Archduke Franz Ferdinand and his wife were assassinated in Sarajevo by factions of the Black Hand, it set off a chain of events that culminated in the First World War. Not surprisingly, the Kaiser supported the Austro-Hungarian Empire because they were a major ally and natural friend.

His leading generals, Paul von Hindenburg and Erich Ludendorff, dictated policy during the First World War with little regard for the civilian government, and for that matter, barely listened to the Kaiser.

Kaiser Wilhelm II was considered a very ineffective wartime leader, and while they showed early success and daring, his generals now began to show evidence of failure. Contemplating the loss of the war, and of his throne, the Kaiser knew he had to act.

He reached out to his closest aid and personal friend, Heinrich Strasberg, with an idea. The Kaiser wanted to sue for peace. He had an all too clever idea of how to settle the war. An avid card player, he would play history's biggest bluff.

Kaiser Wilhelm II would make an offer to the Americans to pay one billion dollars in gold to halt the war, and have all sides retreat to their pre-1914 borders. Perhaps naïve, he hoped that President Wilson would effectively let him buy his way out.

The bluff was that the Kaiser did not have a billion dollars in gold. Germany had only $538 million in gold, in the German Reichsbank, but also had nearly $61 million in cash in a Swiss bank.

The Kaiser reasoned that, if the war was ended and some monies were transferred to the Americans, a public backlash would prevent Wilson from restarting the war simply for lack of full payment. He was fairly confident in this belief.

Regardless of how much gold and money Germany had, he was prepared to lose it all, if he could just save his realm.

Strasberg was assigned the task of approaching the Americans. He reached out to the American ambassador to Germany, James Gerrome, who in turn contacted the White House. Thinking this was probably a ruse or a ploy to delay the inevitable, the White House assigned the file to a young military officer named Wilbur Thomas.

Thomas and Strasberg met in Cairo two weeks later for direct talks. Both had agreed to come alone. Strasberg made his pitch to Wilbur, who agreed to take the offer back to Washington. Strasberg unknowingly brought falsified proof of there being over one billion in gold in the German Reichsbank, but had valid proof of $61 million in a Swiss bank account.

Wilbur suggested transferring the funds from one Swiss bank to another as a first step, and then Washington could take control of the gold when they were ready.

Wilbur told Strasberg that he could not make any promises, but he agreed to recommend the plan to President Wilson. The Allies were turning the tide in the war, so Wilson might prefer instead to finish the job on the battlefield. He wasn't sure.

Wilbur Thomas travelled home by ship and was back in Washington in twelve days. He went to the White House and met with an advisor to the president, who, upon hearing the story, took Wilbur in to see the president in the Oval Office.

President Wilson listened intently. The notion of America being paid off to end the war sounded promising but dishonourable. The idea of letting Germany off the hook for the destruction they had wrought seemed unacceptable. He would need some time to make a decision, and asked Wilbur to return the next day at four p.m.

The next day, the president agreed to the plan and instructed Wilbur to meet with Strasberg, to tell him that the US would accept an initial $50 million as a sign of good faith. Once that was received, they would open secret talks to end the war, contingent upon payment of the balance.

The next meeting was scheduled for Zurich on April 16, and Strasberg was pleased and grateful for the American's decision. He promised to deliver $50 million in bearer bonds, in US currency to the Americans within twenty-four hours. Bearer bonds were untraceable and would be used to facilitate the transfer.

Completely blindsiding the Americans, twenty-four-hours later, on April 17, 1918, the First Battle of Kemmel Ridge was launched as a massive German offensive.

Washington sent Thomas a message. It was simple: "Abandon your mission. Abort."

With the new German offensive underway, the sometimes-indecisive President Wilson had changed his mind, deciding that this offer to end the war was clearly a trick or a ploy. It was better to defeat the Hun bastards on the battlefield.

Heinrich Strasberg and Wilbur Thomas were about to meet that very morning, at eleven o'clock, in a Zurich town square called the Paradeplatz.

For a fourth time, Thomas reread the telegram, which he had received only moments before he was to meet his German counterpart. And in that moment, a good man went bad.

Against his orders, he would meet with Strasberg. He would help the war effort by keeping $50 million out of the hands of the Germans, and either be a hero to the Allies, or a rich man in the process. He hadn't yet decided which.

He met Strasberg at exactly eleven a.m., and Thomas accepted the bonds, which were carried in a heavy black leather satchel. Five hundred $100,000 bearer bonds. Under the original plan, Wilbur Thomas was to travel to Geneva, and deliver the satchel to the American Embassy.

He and Strasberg shook hands. Heinrich turned and walked away, never once looking back. Wilbur delayed a moment, pondering. As soon as Strasberg was out of sight, he knew he had done the wrong thing. He had to get rid of this money. He turned on his heel and walked straight into the nearest bank, right there on the Paradeplatz. The General Commercial Bank of Switzerland.

Wilbur knew immediately that he could not keep the funds for himself, but there was no reasonable way to return the money to the Germans, or to explain to the Americans that he had not followed orders. He quickly formulated an idea for the future, one he hoped would let him live with what he had done. He deposited the funds, wrote a letter of instructions to the bank on how to invest it, another letter to be opened in ninety years by the bank, and a last letter to be read in a hundred years. While writing the last letter, he was thinking about his brother Moses, whom he respected a great deal.

He left the bank, and began his return to the United States as though returning from an aborted mission. He resolved to not ever mention the matter to anyone, not a single word. He hoped no one would ever know of his crime.

Wilbur headed south to the Mediterranean to catch a ride aboard a British cargo ship, the *Matiana*. The ship would take him to the Atlantic, where he would switch to an American merchant ship back to the states. Due to heavier fighting in Europe, his trip home had to be more clandestine, and was much more dangerous that his previous junkets.

The *Matiana* headed south across the Mediterranean and into Tunisian waters. Also plying that same part of the sea was SM UC-27, a German Type UC II minelaying submarine U-boat. She had been launched on June 28, 1916, and was commissioned into the German Imperial Navy on July 25, 1916.

The *Matiana* was sighted, and a single torpedo was launched. The ship was steaming at 37°15–N 10°05–E when she was hit just below the waterline and sunk. Her entire crew survived, but their secret passenger was killed. History has never recorded the death of the man who was not supposed to have been on board. For all of time, Wilbur Thomas was simply lost and assumed dead.

Wilbur Thomas met eternity that day, and that same U-boat went on to sink fifty-six more ships by the end of the war.

Heinrich Strasberg returned to Germany, proudly believing he had begun the process to end the war. Now that the initial payment had been delivered, Strasberg reached out to the American Ambassador in Berlin to talk about the next steps in the process. When the Americans refused to acknowledge that any deal had been made, Strasberg was suspected of stealing the untraceable bonds for himself. He was arrested, questioned under torturous conditions, and summarily executed on direct order of his friend … the Kaiser.

Heinrich Strasberg's blood stains the incredible promise Wilbur's actions left for the future. Strasberg was an honourable man, who had to endure a dishonourable death.

And at the same time, the one-hundred-year countdown began to tick on the Thomas Protocol funds.

When the war ended, under the terms of the Treaty of Versailles Germany was assessed interim war reparations of five billion US dollars. In 1921, the London Schedule of Payments required Germany to pay final reparations of thirty-three billion US dollars.

The Kaiser's solution, if he'd really had the one billion in gold, and had the offer worked, would have saved his nation a fortune and changed the course of history.

CHAPTER 67

Back in Canada, I woke up in my bed in a gorgeous suite in the Fairmont Pacific Rim Hotel. We were now occupying the entire floor that we had been paying for since the beginning of my new life. We needed it for security, logistics, and convenience. We really didn't care much about the cost.

Later at the office, I sat in a meeting with the senior team, minus Jacob and Zach (whom we hoped would rejoin us in a few days).

Jack Dickinson chaired the meeting, which enabled me to fully engage in the discussions. With his senior team, he had worked through some planning and objectives. They showed me some of their recommendations, which were the result of a large group brainstorming session from a week earlier.

The first precept was that, other than the funds that we had already committed, we would try to keep project sizes below $10 billion each, allowing us a minimum of two thousand projects we could fund, and still have a few trillion left. We would look for small projects too. And we would welcome any opportunity to cost share a project with a government, business, or society to make our funds go even further.

There was another idea that was pretty amazing: We would take $500 billion and put it away for another hundred years, so that this process could be repeated every century. Even at a rate of return of 5 percent, it would be worth $65 trillion when it came due. What a gift to the future!

My own task was big enough, thanks! It was like winning a lottery so big that you could spend $3 billion every single day for the rest of your life, and still never run out of money. What would you do with that kind of money to make the world a better place?

"So, you guys have had your heads together now for a while. What are your top initiatives for us to consider?"

Jack flicked a switch, and the screen at the far end of the room displayed the top ten initiatives for my consideration:

1. Fund desalination plants in water-starved countries
2. Create portable solar power plants that can be airlifted and set up easily
3. Research carbon-reducing anti-pollution technology
4. Cure cancer
5. Cure HIV
6. Promote health and build hospitals around the world
7. Bring education to the uneducated
8. Promote human rights and equal rights through economics and prosperity
9. Feed the hungry
10. House the homeless

I was impressed. It was a pretty damn good start, but I wasn't sure they were thinking big enough. I added a few thoughts of my own, and asked the group to think in broader terms that could be adapted to individual needs but still maintain our mission to make the world a better place. I told them to work on it some more and call me when they were ready.

In my office, I called Jacob to see how things were going. He picked up the call quickly.

"Hi, Steve, nice of you to call."

"How are things going with you guys?"

"Things here are getting better. I have to admit, it's surprising how quickly death leaves the forefront of your mind. I need to get back to Vancouver. My mother is getting ready to start her new role. It will be pretty strange for her, moving into her father's office, but as you probably noticed, even while maintaining an elegant femininity, she is a formidable woman."

"She sure is. Any idea when you two are coming back to Vancouver?"

"Yes. Day after tomorrow, if that's okay with you."

"I don't want rush you guys, but I will be glad to see you back. I will tell Paige to give you a call to sort out the plane."

"No, Steve, I will call Paige. I assist you, remember, sir? You have better things to do. See you soon—oh, and Zach says hi!"

"Okay, okay, see you both soon."

I looked over some papers in my office, signed some documents, and read the electronic news clippings the communications department had sent me, with the reports about the Canadian National debt, which had now been paid off, and the imminent sending of the lump sum payments to US veterans. As hoped, all the press was positive. As it should be.

I wandered back to the boardroom, and found that the team had sharpened up the goals for our mission.

The extra time they had spent working on the list made a big difference. They said they had argued and haggled over every word, trying to keep it short but meaningful, obvious, but powerful.

The revised list became the following:

The Thomas Protocol Global Initiatives
1. Promote human rights and equal rights
2. Heal the sick and cure disease
3. Feed the hungry
4. Quench the world's thirst

5. House the homeless
6. Educate the uneducated
7. Clean energy
8. Reduce pollution
9. Reimagine infrastructure
10. Celebrate heroes

I loved it.

"Excellent work! Now, flesh it out, define every one of the ten initiatives, and then we can have Jack structure the organization around these items. We are off to the races, people. Awesome work. I am proud of you all! This will become our living document, which will no doubt morph and evolve over time, but it gives us an excellent starting point.

"Have it ready for tomorrow morning." I grinned. "There is no time to waste when you are doing noble work."

CHAPTER 68

With two bodyguards, provided through Guardian Security, Frau Ursula Van Vloten arrived at the bank in an armoured vehicle. Swiss bankers didn't usually need protection, but these were not usual times.

As she walked through the lobby, all of the staff stood up at their desks and politely nodded in her direction. It was both a sign of respect for her new role, and for the loss of her father.

Ursula was well respected at the bank. There was never any doubt that she was the daughter of the president of the bank; she had started in the mail room, worked her way through the bank's frontline positions, and on up into more and more senior roles, culminating two years earlier with her appointment as Senior Vice-President of International Accounts.

She was also feared. She had been ruthless with staff changes in her department, and did not accept half efforts or people "trying." She often said, "We are a world-class bank. We hire world-class employees, and we expect world-class performance." It was that simple.

When needed, she could be tough as nails. Unlike some of her male colleagues, though, you always knew that every difficult decision that she made was the right decision, and made for the right reason.

Ursula rode up in the elevator, buzzed through the glass barrier, and went into her new office. Her father's personal belongings had been boxed up and moved out, and her stuff had been moved in from her old office and set up so she could be instantly comfortable.

The three former assistants to Herr Altermatt, Jeffrey, Noah, and Julian, were now her assistants. They had all been at the bank for at least ten years, and worked at a very high level supporting the bank president. Personally close to Altermatt, they had been honorary pallbearers at the funeral as well.

As she came through the door of the office, her pace slowed by half. She could still smell her father in the room. She walked to her desk while eyeing the room, and spotted her belongings amongst the bank's historical pieces. She handed her bag to Jeffrey, while Noah helped her off with her coat and hung it in a small closet for her.

"Alright, gentlemen, I need to be brought up to speed in a number of areas that my father had been working on. I know that you were all intimately involved in his projects. I assume you are ready to brief me, but if not, when can you be ready?"

Noah spoke for the group. "Frau Van Vloten, we assumed today would be about making you feel comfortable, and that you might like to meet with senior staff to signal the continuity and resilience of the GCBS. We had tentatively scheduled a brief meeting with the executive team at eleven a.m., and a staff session for two p.m. today."

"Noah, cancel both meetings and reschedule them for tomorrow. Today, I want to be briefed, in detail, on the Thomas Accounts. I want to review the holdings, the origins, the track record and performance, and the original account documents. Everything we have on Wilbur Thomas.

"And for now, some coffee please, and some privacy."

The three men quickly left the office, with Noah closing the door behind them. Jeffrey returned a moment later with a cup of coffee and some biscuits. He placed them on the right side of her desk, and waited a second to see if she needed anything more.

"Thank you, Jeffrey," she said, and nodded her dismissal.

He bowed slightly, and then swiftly left the room.

CHAPTER 69

Paige had heard from Jacob. The new Boeing 737 was in the air, en route to Zurich to pick up Zachary and Jacob and bring them home to Vancouver. The plane would land, refuel, and be ready for departure at three p.m.

Arriving at the bank at about eleven in the morning, Jacob made his way to the fifth floor and went in to see his mother. Jeffrey alerted Ursula, and showed Jacob in.

Ursula rose from her desk and met him halfway across the room.

"Jacob, darling." She kissed each cheek and hugged him close. "Please, let's sit."

With a sweep of her arm she motioned toward the sofa and chairs by the fireplace. He sat in one corner of the sofa while she sat in the chair closest to him.

"How does it feel, Mama ... being in *this* office?"

"Strangely comforting. I can still smell his scent and almost feel his presence. Your opa was a magnificent man. I have big shoes to fill."

With that comment, she pointed to her size six and a half shoes, and laughed. "Not sure it's possible, but I will do my best ... Jacob, I do wish you would stay here and help me run the bank. I hope this will all be yours one day."

"Mama, this adventure with Steve is truly that—an adventure. Let's just let me work out my one-year secondment at this stage. I was dealing with grandfather every day on the file, the logistics, et cetera, so now I will be speaking to you every day.

"Working on all these positive projects is like living a dream, and Steve, considering he was previously a relatively small businessman, has grown about a foot in the last few weeks as his life has unravelled and then come together. He understands people, and leadership, and has a sense of toughness and compassion that is infectious. Both Zach and I want to stay and help him, but I am sure we will be back here one day soon."

She nodded, understanding but clearly unmoved. "I heard from your father yesterday. He says you have not called him in a month. I told him how busy you were."

"Mama, the *Schweinhund* didn't even come to the funeral."

"Jacob, he was in Iceland, and your grandfather always treated him like a pauper, so maybe it was for the best. We are separated after all."

"He is separated from you, Mama, not from me. I needed him this week."

"Fair point, dear. So how much longer will you be here with me?"

"Zach and I leave around three p.m."

"Which airline?"

"Oh, we are flying Thomas Protocol Private." Jacob grinned, and straightened his back to seem playfully important.

"My, oh my … what happened to my little boy? I am very proud of you, dear." She stood, signalling the meeting was over.

"Call your mama every day now." She kissed his cheeks again, gave him a squeeze, and then took him by the arm and ushered him to the door.

As he walked out, she closed the door behind him, leaned against it for support, and exhaled a long sigh.

CHAPTER 70

LARKMAN, WYOMING

The last of the six men arrived back at the bunker and were all catching up, describing their travel adventures to one another. All six men had taken different paths home, and only by coincidence had any of their paths crossed along the way.

Their payment had made its way into their Swiss bank account and would be distributed in the normal way, with 40 percent off the top for the team's funds and expenses, and the other 60 percent divided between the men who had done the job. The contract for Altermatt was five hundred thousand dollars. So, the split was two hundred thousand for the house, and fifty thousand per man for the hit. It was more money than each of them had earned in a year when they were in the service. There were usually four to six jobs a year, so they were all living quite comfortably.

They discussed in minute detail what had gone well and what they could do better next time. Looking at maps, they figured out how they could have exited the area quicker, and questioned whether there were faster routes home that were still safe. Each job provided a new learning experience. They all agreed that this last job had been flawless in its execution.

The communications officer looked at his watch. It was time to call in. He called the special number, and input his security code to receive new instructions. This was a weekly process. There was a recorded message. "Stand down. New instructions to follow within eight weeks."

"Looks like we have some time off, men. Eight weeks."

They left in their usual manner, one vehicle departing every thirty minutes in different directions. Until they would be needed again, they quietly vanished into the fabric of America.

CHAPTER 71

Back at the office, the team had fleshed out a more detailed set of initiatives for the Thomas Protocol. We discussed it as a group, and took a team vote to see if they felt we had nailed it. It was unanimous, but everyone agreed it needed to be a living document, changing as needs changed.

We set up a press conference for the next day. We were becoming a worldwide phenomenon with people, corporations, governments, and NGO's all lining up with ideas. We needed to focus our goals and announce them, so that submissions were also focused and aligned. We wanted to receive ideas and approaches, as well as directly seek out needs in the world that we could remedy.

The programs had fleshed out as follows:

The Thomas Protocol Global Initiatives

1. **Promote human rights and equal rights**
   - Eliminate discrimination
   - Support emerging democracies
2. **Heal the sick and cure disease**
   - Build medical facilities and hospitals worldwide
   - Research to cure disease
   - Cure cancer
   - Cure HIV

3. **Feed the hungry**
   - Provide food to eliminate immediate hunger issues
   - Teach food-growth initiatives

4. **Quench the world's thirst**
   - Create new water sources
   - Build water-delivery systems
   - Purify existing water sources

5. **House the homeless**
   - Build low-income housing around the world
   - Deal with homeless mental-health issues

6. **Educate the uneducated**
   - Build a Peace Corps of teachers
   - Build universities

7. **Clean energy**
   - Build solar, wind, tidal, and fusion-energy systems
   - Research non-fossil-fuel sources of energy

8. **Reduce pollution**
   - Research carbon-emissions solutions
   - Develop worldwide recycling programs
   - Clean the oceans
   - Protect aquifers

9. **Reimagine infrastructure**
   - Research, test, and build new systems
   - Reimagine water, sewage, power, sanitation systems
   - Develop future solutions for roads, mass transit, air travel

10. **Celebrate heroes**
    - Help military veterans worldwide

- Promote sports and recreation
- Support the Olympics and fairness in competition
- Recognize everyday heroes

And all initiatives would be judged on the most important criteria: "Will this make the world a better place?" Press kits were produced. We would really rev up our engines tomorrow, and launch our ambitious initiatives in a big way.

CHAPTER 72

In Zurich, Jacob and Zach were driven to the airport by a Guardian driver and vehicle. Soon, they rolled up next to the brand-new Boeing 737 Max BBJ ER emblazoned with "Thomas Protocol Private" across its upper side. Gorgeous. Its full description was a 737 Max Boeing Business Jet Extended Range.

The interior, while substantially smaller than the Dreamliner, was done up beautifully. This plane would be used to travel the world to search for and monitor projects. It was outfitted for a small team with long-term travel needs. In a combination of business-class seats, sofas, and tables, there was seating for eighteen. There were six small staterooms, two with queen-size beds, and four with singles. There were two washrooms at the front of the plane, and two more at the back that were larger and included showers. This plane could be used for both travel and accommodation for our teams.

The galley was much larger than usual, and was equipped to store prepared meals and allow crew to prepare meals from scratch as well.

At the top of the stairs, the two male flight attendants welcomed the boys aboard and gave them the grand tour. They also popped into the cockpit to meet the new captain and co-pilot who had just joined the team.

Jacob and Zachary asked for a couple of drinks: the usual, a European beer and a scotch.

An hour and a half into the flight, dinner was served. The boys invited the flight attendants to join them, and the four of them enjoyed dinner and a bottle of wine.

While it was way too early for bed, it had been a very stressful few days, and they had a long flight ahead. They decided to try to get some sleep.

Lying in bed together, they were finally alone.

Zachary rolled over to face Jacob.

"How are you doing, for real?"

"I don't know. I feel really empty and sad, like there is a hole in my stomach somewhere. And it isn't just that I lost a grandfather. I mean, I am not nine years old. It's two things really. I know he had a tough exterior, but he was one of my best friends. I could talk to him about almost anything. The other thing is the way he died. So horrible! My God, it's one thing to die in his sleep, but this … Jesus fucking Christ. So horrible. I just can't stop imagining what that must have been like for him."

"I know it has been awful, Jacob, but I want you to know how proud I am of you. You stood up to help your mother so well, you gave a beautiful eulogy, and your grandfather would have been so proud of your speech. In fact, so was I! I am not sure I knew you had that gift … of speaking so well, under such awful circumstances."

"Thanks. To be honest, I am looking forward to getting back to Vancouver. Paige said we are all living at the hotel now, so no more helicopter rides to the yacht. It will be nice to be a bit nearer the action of the city. Maybe we can get out to a club one of these nights, and blow off some steam."

Zach nodded and put his arms into the air, pretending he was dancing. Jacob giggled.

With that, Jacob rolled into Zachary's arms and immediately fell asleep. They were awake again in three hours.

Tomorrow, Steve would be making a big announcement.

CHAPTER 73

The press conference was held in the Star Sapphire Ballroom at our hotel, the Fairmont Pacific Rim. It was the largest ballroom in the hotel and seats were placed for a press retinue of up to two hundred reporters, plus cameras and equipment.

Mark Crombie, our head of communications, got the room under control, and then introduced me. I entered the room from the hallway, walked up onto the riser, and stood at the podium.

"Today is a day of both great excitement and anticipation, as well as a time of mourning. We grieve today for Wilhelm Altermatt, the former president of the GCBS in Zurich. Mr. Altermatt personally managed the Thomas Protocol funds for forty years, and like his predecessors before him, did a brilliant job of building a massive fund that we now get to offer and donate to the world.

"As you know, he was gunned down last week in a cowardly act, and we shall not rest until his murderers are captured and brought to justice.

"Mr. Altermatt has our heartfelt thanks, as it is his life's work that results in this press conference today. We would not be here without him, and our thoughts are with his family and his friends at this time."

The room was crammed with press from all over the world. From my vantage point, it was a sight to behold. Standing off to one side of the room, Jacob and Zachary both looked at the floor as I paid tribute to Wilhelm.

"Now I will move on to the good news. We are incredibly pleased to announce the Thomas Protocol Global Initiatives. Our team has worked hard to set out ten general initiative areas where we will seek out projects, accept proposals from others, and where we can fund work that will improve people's lives.

"I believe that the world equally distributes human potential, but it does not equally distribute education or opportunity. We believe that, with wonderful partnerships around the world, we can harness unused human potential, and through education and opportunity, improve lives. Truly making the world a better place, one life at a time. That is the void we want to fill.

"The words of St. Francis likely say it better: Where there is hatred, let me bring love; where there is despair, let me bring hope; where there is darkness, let me bring light; where there is sadness, let me bring joy.

"To make our contributions go even further, we would love to be involved in some projects where we cost share with other governments or philanthropists. We do not seek to own anything. We want to donate funds so that others may build, research, improve, invent, and reimagine the way things are today, so as to manifest the way they should be tomorrow. Our hope is that our contribution on any individual project will not exceed ten billion dollars, and that by limiting it to that amount, we will be able to do so many more things in so many more places.

"I want to thank the world's press. You have already helped us, and can help us even more by getting the word out, thereby helping us to notice areas that need the most help, and where we can have the largest impact. Our organization and our finances will be completely transparent. We will answer all your questions, and give interviews ... and we will thank you for helping us shine the light on the darkness that exists in our world.

"Our work will take a generation, and maybe more, but we will plant the seeds of progress as quickly as we can. I hope to see the fruits of our endeavours in my lifetime. We are a strange organization. We are one of the only private organizations in the world whose goal is to spend more than we take in and eventually run out of money. Until now, the only organizations doing that were governments!"

The press corps laughed at that.

"We would also be delighted, on each of our mission trips abroad, to embed a reporter or two within our team. We have applications for that, and you will be invited to come along, all expenses paid, so that you can see and report firsthand on what we are up to. Again, we want to be totally open and transparent in all we do.

"Our teams will soon be fanning out over the globe, seeking to do good and noble work. Soon enough, you will see a fleet of Thomas Protocol private jets. We have taken delivery of two large aircraft and two Gulfstream G650s, and we have eight more to come in the next short while to help us do our work. We also have a fleet of cargo jets that will assist in getting help to places in the world that need it as quickly as possible.

"This new role for me has quickly become a dream come true, and now that the preliminary work is out of the way, let the adventures begin!

"Now I would be happy to take your questions…"

CHAPTER 74

Mark Crombie came into my office as soon as the press conference ended.

"Great press conference, Steve! Well done! The place was abuzz with excitement. We have had seventy-five press applications picked up already, with reporters wanting to join us on a trip somewhere."

"Awesome. I felt good about it too. I mean seriously, it is not like we are trying to do something bad; we are trying to do nothing but good."

"Steve, we have had a request from Diane Wallace from *60 Minutes* for an interview as soon as you can make time available. What do you think?"

"Set it up. She's great. Love her."

I pressed a button on my phone, and Paige popped into the office.

"Paige, can you find Jacob and Zach for me?"

"Easy as pie, they are right out here talking to me!"

In came Jacob and Zach. I motioned them to the small conference table and we sat. Knowing what everyone drank, Paige was kind enough to get the boys a coffee, and for me, a Pepsi on ice.

"Thanks Paige, you are too kind."

"Well, boys, how was the trip back?"

"Well, let me just say the 737 is amazing," Jacob said. "Outfitted exactly as it should be. Functional, comfortable, with six little staterooms in the back section. Basically, a flying office and hotel for an away team. We got some sleep, and let's just say, that for the two of us, it was the best travel experience we have ever had as a couple."

I was grinning at them, knowing I would feel the same way.

"And your mom?"

"She is moving on. She is always very serious about work and is hard at it. I think she will be fine. I was always convinced she loved that bank more than she loved me anyway."

"And Zach, how about you?"

"Personally, I'm glad to be back. We had a chance to deal with our apartment and belongings in the couple of days we were there, so that was good. We brought a bunch of boxes and bags with us, so we can get settled here and set up our lives better. Other than that, I was just trying to be a good future-husband and son-in-law, and help out where I could. Not to be rude, but I confess that I never felt much warmth for, or from, Wilhelm …" He glanced at his partner and quickly added, "Although he was always perfectly civil with me, of course. But as such, I am not suffering the loss as Jacob is. Having said that, the manner of his death just reinforces our need for security for you and our key people. Someone is not happy that we have this money to spend."

"Jacob, do the police have any clues about your grandfather's killers yet? Have they stayed in touch at all?"

"We really only received one report. They said it was clearly a professional job, and that the killers escaped. There is some video footage from security cameras in the Paradeplatz area, but between hats and sunglasses, there was no way to identify anyone up close. No sightings of the snipers, but it looks like there were two or possibly three men at ground level as well. Other than that, there is not much to report yet."

"Would you be okay with me posting a worldwide reward for information leading to the capture of the killers? I was thinking we could arrange it through the Swiss Police and Interpol. I can probably call the prime minister here to see how to go about it."

"I am touched, and I am sure my mother will be very grateful. Thank you, Steve," Jacob said as he rose, came around the table, leaned over, and unexpectedly hugged me. I have to admit, I was touched by the action.

"Guys, the more I think of it, the more I realize it could be anyone, so we will have to keep our guard up. My idea of noble work won't be the same as what the Iranians or the Saudis might think, or the Russians, Chinese, or the Somalis for that matter. We will need to make sure that any nation we go to invites us in as guests. We cannot impose our views or values on nations that want no part of it. That will just be the fastest way to a quick death or kidnapping or something. We will have to protect our crew."

Everyone agreed.

"Now, we want to get rolling on our initiatives, so I want to send you, Jacob, on your first expedition. Let's meet in the morning after you have had a decent sleep, and we can go from there. And Zach, we need to check on the building plans for the house here, and see where things are at. That is your job, so you will need to get up to speed this afternoon on that one, okay?"

They left my office, and Crombie came back in. "Wallace is available day after tomorrow. Is that okay? About two p.m.?"

"Done." I smiled. Crombie zipped back to his own office.

CHAPTER 75

Ursula was having trouble sleeping. She had known it would be huge, but after her briefing on the Thomas Fund, she was staggered at just how essential the management fees earned from the fund were for driving the financial success of the bank. The fees for managing the account were massive, and constituted a large portion of both the bank's revenues and profits. Shareholders would not be amused by depleted dividends and reducing profits. The account generated about $7 billion a year in fees. Perhaps as the account shrank, they could increase the fees charged, and maintain their position. Smaller accounts generally were charged higher fee percentages. It might work.

She had suspected this was the case for a long time, but her father was very tight-lipped about the account and had it walled off from other executives. In a very strategic manner, she needed to slow down the liquidation of the portfolio. It would be even better if it just stopped completely, but that wouldn't happen.

She missed Jacob already. She could use his company at a time like this. She tossed and turned some more as she thought about her father. His death made her very sad, and she felt quite alone without his presence.

Even though they had been separated for a very long time, she also still missed her ex-husband, Rolf. Her father had been against the marriage from the beginning. On a vacation to Germany, she had met Rolf one morning at a café. Rolf worked in a printing shop, while Ursula was the daughter of a rich banker. Not exactly a natural fit. He was charming, handsome, and had a great sense of humour. It wasn't long before there were wedding bells, and a year and a half later, little feet were running around their flat. Jacob was a delight to them both. Rolf had moved to Switzerland and fit into the general community easily, but his ink-stained hands made him stand out from the rather snooty banking crowd that his wife moved with, and he struggled to feel like a strong German man, often feeling more like he was in his wife's shadow. They only had the one child and Ursula had returned to work quickly.

With her career taking up more and more time as she climbed the ladder of success, their marriage began to falter. Rolf eventually found solace and confidence in the arms of another woman and left his wife. Jacob was nineteen at the time. Rolf had not been a major part of his life ever since, and had returned to Germany shortly after the breakup.

Jacob usually saw him two or three times a year for a few days, but it was more like visiting a long-lost uncle than visiting his papa. Over time, the distance between them grew, and the visits became even less frequent. Jacob had not seen his father for a couple of years now, and was often annoyed at the lack of love from his father. His failure to show up for the funeral was, in many ways, the final straw for Jacob. Ursula was sorry that they were not closer.

As she lay in bed, she wondered what she had done wrong. Here she was, a very successful banker, still attractive, and all alone at her age. And now her husband and son were nowhere nearby, and her father was gone. She made a mental note to call Steve at the end of her day tomorrow, hopefully catching up with him before his day started. She needed to talk about fees. She tossed and turned much of the night, haunted by her father's murder. Morning came too soon.

CHAPTER 76

I woke up in the hotel room, and it was pouring rain outside. The wind was blowing and the raindrops were pelting the building. When you are in a nice warm bed on a cool night, the falling rain feels romantic, cozy, and relaxing. When you have to get up, get dressed, and head to the office, it is anything but. It is just wet.

Andrew, who had a passkey to my room, entered the suite and called out to me.

"Morning, sir, are you up yet?"

"Sure am ... I'm in the bedroom. Come on in."

Andrew entered and found me wearing my robe and checking personal emails on my iPad.

"Sir, since it is raining today I thought you might like to walk to the office. After all, it's only five blocks."

I pulled a face at him, and then said, "Careful or I might take you up on that, Mr. Smarty."

"Sir, it is six forty-five now, and we will have the cars ready for you at eight fifteen as usual, okay?"

"Yup, that's fine. Hey, can we chat a bit about my family?"

"Sure, what's up?"

"The day after we returned to Vancouver, do you remember that interview I had with Everett Copper, when I suddenly realized the impact all this would have on my family? I remember feeling pretty stupid that I hadn't said anything to any of them, but I confess, we are not all that close, and I was just a tad bit overwhelmed at that point."

"Yes, sir, I certainly do. As I recall, at the same time that you were making calls to each of your siblings, we were sending security teams in to protect them."

"Exactly. Andrew, I've decided that it's time for a family reunion. I am thinking this coming weekend. We will bring them all to the yacht, and have both a celebration and some serious chats about our new lives. We will make the various aircraft available to go and collect everyone. Is that something you can organize from a security standpoint?"

"I think that should be fine, sir. I get a security update from each security chief every day, so I know things are going well. I do think your family would appreciate an update though."

I climbed to my feet. "Thanks. I will get Jack and his team to take care of all the details for everything else, but you are the key to safety, so I wanted to run it by you first."

Andrew nodded. "Perhaps we can have a few round table sessions and make sure they understand both the benefits and risks of their new lives."

"Yup, that's just what they need. Family is always complicated. I have had several calls, some emails, and a bunch of texts from them, but I haven't done enough. They need information, and to know what to do and how to conduct themselves. I am going to send them a blanket email invitation, to let them know they will receive more info later today. Oh, and I will be ready for departure on time. Thanks, Andrew."

With that, Andrew withdrew, and headed off to make some calls of his own.

I have a brother and two sisters, and they all have kids and families. They were all pretty excited about this notion of being rich, but were horrified by the reality of the security issues faced by the super wealthy. It was important to fly under the radar and not attract attention, but the press descended on each of them, so they became instant celebrities in their communities.

I had set each of them up with a personal financial advisor from my office accounting division, had Andrew appoint three security chiefs to oversee the three siblings and their families, and of course, I gave them money. Lots of money. One and a half billion to each sibling, and they were to handle their own families from that. They would never run out of money. They were all pretty straightforward people, and I knew they'd be good with their money. All except one sister, of course, who was always too generous and liked to spend money when she had it. Still, I figured even she couldn't burn through $1.5 billion.

I hit the shower, dressed, ate some of the breakfast that had been delivered to the room, and headed out the door. The two agents who guarded the door to my room were chatting with my four-man escort. Joe was in charge of this group today, and we headed down to the cars and over the five blocks to the office, in the rain...

Jack Dickinson, Jacob, and Zachary were waiting in my office when I arrived.

Paige followed me into the office with a cup of tea.

"Good morning, everyone," I said, and was greeted with friendly replies.

"Jack, I copied you on an email to my brother and sisters. I want to gather the family here this weekend. We can use the planes to get them here. We will meet and stay on the yacht, and have some chats about what the future holds for everyone. Make sure everyone understands this is mandatory... although phrase that as diplomatically as possible."

"I already have the team on it, Steve. We also want to meet with you and Zach about the house construction this morning—now, if possible—and then we can all meet regarding the first expeditions for our 'away teams.'"

"Great."

"Now, Steve, I have a few updates on logistics. We have now taken delivery of all four of the Gulfstream Jets; we have received the other three 737 Max BBJs, in the same configuration as the first one, and the second Dreamliner has been delivered as well. It is a twin of Protocol 1. There are still two more 787s to come. We are almost going to need our own airport." Everyone laughed.

"We also have four of the twelve cargo jets."

"What type of aircraft are the cargo jets anyway?" I interjected.

"We needed aircraft that were good for big loads and could also land in small airports, so we have four 747 cargo jets, and eight 737 cargo jets. We have taken delivery of two of each and the balance will be delivered within sixty days. These were ordered several years ago, so they have been in production for a while."

"Wilhelm thought of everything, didn't he, Jacob?" I asked.

He nodded and smiled.

"Pilots?" I asked.

"Yes, sir—I mean, Steve. We have hired and trained a full team. We will have twenty-two aircraft in total, and our pilots are checked out on all four models. All former navy or air-force flyers. Some Canadian and some American, and a couple of Brits thrown in for good measure. To cover times at full capacity, we have hired thirty pilots, thirty co-pilots, four communications officers for the Dreamliner duties, and we have forty flight attendants. You are actually running a larger airline than some domestic carriers. Crazy, huh?"

"So, just out of curiosity, what is all this costing?"

"The total gross capital outlay was four point one billion dollars, but we negotiated that down to three point seven billion. Then you need a stock of ready parts and repair gear, et cetera, which cost another six hundred million dollars. The flight crews, cleaning crews, and mechanical maintenance staff will run about fifteen million a year. Fuel varies from aircraft to aircraft, but for quick math, plan on an average of six thousand dollars in fuel per hour. We expect to be flying a lot, so we calculate annual operating costs of about one hundred and fifty million dollars. These are huge numbers, but still tiny when compared to what we will be doing with the rest of the money."

"Wow, Jack, amazing numbers. Now just to be clear ... even with my plan to keep only one percent of this money for myself, I will cover all of these costs out of my end. The returns on my portion of the fund should be about twenty billion dollars a year, so I should be able to personally cover all of our operating costs, no problem. We're going to donate or reinvest the whole ninety-nine percent if we can. I feel good about that. Now, we need to put all these people and aircraft to work!

"Zachary, where are we on the house?"

"We are coming along nicely. I continued working on this project while in Zurich. The plans were completed in forty-eight hours. Since we started with some existing plans and made changes to suit your needs, it was easy. They put a team on it and reconfigured them quickly. The city approved the site plan, the house plans, and setbacks, and issued the building permit twenty-four hours later. They broke ground the next morning and your concrete footings were put in. The basement walls and the underground parking area has been poured, and they are pouring the concrete for the main floor today. The rest of the structure going up from there will be wood frame.

"The contractor has people off-site constructing all the woodwork and trim. All the cabinets and everything has been ordered, from flooring to lighting, et cetera. They are running a super-tight timeline. The longest period will be for the drywall and paint crews, and the electrical and plumbing installers. But in both cases, we have huge crews doing the work. Once framing is complete, the electrician and plumbers will each have twenty-four-man crews working in each of the three buildings, and should be done in two days. Drywall will be installed in one day with a massive crew. Drywall finishing and detailing will take four more days, followed by paint crews, flooring installers, and so on. Paying twice the normal price for everything has guaranteed exceptional service, and the city has an inspector on site every day to move things along. This house will be completed in thirty-five days, including landscaping. We are already on day six."

"None of that sounds even remotely possible," I mused.

"Wanna bet?" Zach asked.

"Sure, I will bet you one billion dollars, but you have to lay your money on the table now. Jack, can you hold our money?" We all cracked up at my joke (even me, I'm ashamed to say).

"Well, Zach, if you manage that, you will be a hero to me, and to Andrew! He would like to get us somewhere more private. So, between you and me ... take thirty-eight days."

Zach smiled again. "I didn't include decorating and furnishings, but we expect to have those basics all in place on days thirty-six through thirty-eight, and the balance of smaller stuff can be finished over the next few weeks."

"Thanks, Zach, I'm glad I gave you thirty-eight days then. Now, Jacob, I know you just got back, but are you ready to be my eyes and ears on some high-level meetings in Mexico?"

"Absolutely."

"Good. Let me tell you want I have in mind for Mexico..."

CHAPTER 77

Jacob, Jack Dickinson, and I were in my office.

"Jack, I know we have a larger overall plan, but I also know we can get some early wins with some easy donations to reliable groups that will truly make a difference around the world in a hurry."

"What have you got in mind, Steve?"

"When I was in business, I was involved in a few service clubs. When I was a young guy, I was a member of a Kiwanis Club. When I was a bit older, I became a Rotarian. These are service clubs. Basically, good people with good hearts who get together to have some fun and a few laughs while doing great work in their communities. So, it occurred to me that, if we gave every Rotary Club in the world three hundred thousand dollars, it would run us about ten billion, and we could task them with spending it within six months to make their community a better place. We could easily do something similar with other service organizations that are community focused. Think about it, the Thomas Protocol would literally be doing something immediately in almost every corner of the world."

Jack grinned. "I like it. I'll reach out to the folks at Rotary International. Let's see if we can get their president to come here for a visit."

"Good; those guys are on the road all the time, so find out where he is and send one of our planes to get him and bring him here. The sooner the better. Tell him that what we have in mind is a large donation.

"Now, on to you, Jacob. I want you to go to Mexico, meet with the president, and see what we can do to help his country. By and large, the Mexican people are lovely, kind, hard-working, family people. Sadly, their reputation gets tarnished by the bad apples running drugs and killing people in the border region. Let's see what we can do to create more opportunity for the Mexican people, create more wealth, try to diminish the drug trade, and reduce the need to flee to the US. It's an open-ended topic. What do you think?"

"If they have more opportunity at home, it sounds like a good way to reduce emigration and immigration issues by reducing the demand for a better life elsewhere."

"Exactly. So, Jacob, as my emissary, go with an open mind. Tell the president we want to help in a variety of ways, and see what he has to say. Later, if he wants to get together, we can meet here or in Mexico City, whatever works best for him."

Jacob looked a bit lost. "How exactly do I get a meeting with the president of Mexico?"

I smiled at him. "I am pretty sure we can get a meeting with just about anybody. Jack, can you make a call? If it is at all difficult, call the local Canadian Embassy or consulate in Mexico City."

Jack's cell phone vibrated in his pocket. His eyes widened a bit as he looked at the number and he got up suddenly to leave. "Steve, no worries, we are on it. Sorry, but I have to take this call."

I watched him leave the office, wondering about the sudden urgency. My curiosity was interrupted by Jacob, who asked, "How much money do we want to send to Mexico? What do I tell him when he asks?"

"You know, Jacob, you're a smart guy. Go figure it out. I trust you. By the way, your mother called this morning. We had a nice chat. She sounds like she is getting up to speed on her new role. She is an impressive person, but I am sure you know that."

"Impressive is one description. My mother is uh … pretty powerful. She is always very demanding and works really hard, but was absent a lot when I was growing up. I love her, but I wish we knew each other better. I was raised more by my nanny than my mother. To be perfectly honest, with just a look she can scare the hell out of me!"

"Hmm, I think I need to learn that look." And then I laughed, as did he. "Jacob, sit in with me, okay? We need to meet with Mark Crombie to prepare for the Diane Wallace interview tomorrow. I'd appreciate your thoughts."

Paige poked her head in the door and escorted Mark into the office. We sat in the sofa area while he ran through a list of probable questions. Until he felt I was ready, we role played a bit to get it right. We would use my office as the set for the interview, and we would answer every question she had. We needed a better interview than the one we had with Everett Copper. Diane was known to be a tough interviewer, but we would just be honest and transparent and tell the truth.

"Okay, boys," I said, "I am done for the day. I am heading back to the hotel for the night. See you all in the morning." They left and I buzzed for Andrew. They were always ready within five minutes for simple transport.

Then I remembered something that had been bothering me. "Andrew, sorry for the delay, but can you hold for a minute? Paige, can you come in and see me for a minute, please?"

Paige came in, looking a little bit nervous. I closed the door and told her to have a seat on the couch.

"Paige, I am struggling with some of the things you do around here." Paige immediately blushed and looked hurt.

"No, no, no … Paige, I am not explaining this well. I hate the appearance of chauvinism … of some guy having some girl get him coffee or a drink or lunch or running errands. I have always done that for myself. Now I have you and a couple of other people doing what I perceive as sort of menial tasks, and I feel guilty about it. So, I wanted you to know that that's how I feel, and I want you to know how much I appreciate what you have been doing for me. When you get tired of this stuff, just speak up and we will give you a new challenge, okay? You're a well-educated, smart young woman, and I want to make sure your career grows, so you don't just get stuck working with me as an assistant. Okay?"

"Uh, Steve... um... do you have any idea how jealous my friends are right now? I work with, and assist, the richest man in the world, who spends every day trying to make the world better. I get to fly around on a private jet and travel to cool places. I am twenty-three years old, and this is the best job in the world right now. Anything I can do to make your day run better is just my small way of helping you achieve those goals. Team effort! And it is not exactly like you can do this stuff yourself anymore. I doubt you will ever be able to wander out and pick up your dry cleaning or stop for milk at a corner store again. So, if this job gets on my nerves, I will tell you. Until then, don't you worry. There is nowhere I would rather be right now."

"Oh... well, okay then." I laughed. "You are amazing, Paige." I shook my head a bit. *Hell of kid.* "Okay, I am heading home."

"Night, sir—sorry, Steve, but you deserved a 'sir' there. That was very sweet and considerate. See you tomorrow."

"Tomorrow then." I nodded and opened the office door. "Okay, Andrew, let's go."

As we walked down the hall, we passed Jack standing in Jacob's office doorway. "Steve," he said, "we have a busy day tomorrow. Rotary International President Ian Ridgely will be here at ten a.m. He was in Winnipeg, of all places, so we are sending one of the 737s to pick him up."

"Awesome!"

"There's more! Tomorrow evening, President Enrique Peña Nieto is looking forward to welcoming Jacob to a casual dinner at the Presidential Residence, Los Pinos, at seven p.m."

"Jacob," I said, looking past Jack into his office, "you better organize a plane and a change of clothes! Those beds and shower on the plane might just come in handy. I know you will do well. Good luck." I looked over my shoulder at Andrew. "Sort out some security for him as well."

"Done. No problem, sir."

And with that, I got the hell out of there for the night. I was tired. Hell, I had been retired for nearly the past three years, and wasn't quite used to ratcheting back up to this pace. A quiet dinner, a little TV, and an early night would be good. Meeting the Rotary president tomorrow would be fun though!

CHAPTER 78

Rotary International President Ian Ridgely walked into my office at ten a.m. sharp and greeted me in his deep New Zealand accent. He was instantly warm and likeable. I showed him to a nearby chair at my meeting table, and he introduced me to his assistant. Jack joined the meeting and sat quietly while Ian and I shared old Rotary stories. He had fallen in love with the private jet, and of course, we had also sent an armoured SUV to pick him up. We gave him the royal treatment to be sure. This was all about building goodwill and better friendships, one of the key goals of Rotary.

"Ian, it has been a long time since I was a Rotarian, but I enjoyed the experience. I served as a club president, won a few awards, and made some good friends. I left with a great feeling about the organization."

He smiled. "We are certainly proud of what Rotary has become. One point two million members worldwide, and thirty-three thousand clubs. You may have noticed that my theme this year is a lot like your organization's goals. Ours is 'Rotary: Making A Difference.' And each club decides what that difference is."

"I had noticed that, actually." I grinned at him. "And the one thing I know about Rotarians is that we can trust them. I want to partner with you and get some projects going all over the world in a hurry. Why build an army of volunteers when Rotary already has one?"

"Exactly! What do you have in mind?"

"What would you think if we were to give you three hundred thousand dollars per club? About ten billion dollars total."

In his New Zealand accent, a shocked Ian mumbled under his breath, "Jesus H. Christ!"

I couldn't help but laugh a little, as he quietly apologized.

"Now, there are some small strings attached. We want each club to use the money to make a difference, as you would say, in their community. We want the projects to be theirs, be local, and be done in six months. This can really kick-start our efforts and make your organization into an even bigger hero all over the world. We don't want any credit; just get out there and make things better. How does that sound?"

"Bloody amazing! My word … this is huge for us, and such a great way to work together!"

I was nodding as he spoke, and Jack was sitting there, grinning at the reaction.

Ian gathered himself, suddenly looking thoughtful. "Steve, I would be remiss if I didn't make a small pitch for the Rotary Foundation as well. If there is any chance you might consider a donation there, we would be so honoured."

"Ian, take the ten billion first, get it spent in six months, and report back to us on all the initiatives. Just a quick paragraph for every project completed. That's all we want, and when you deliver that report to us, we will have a donation for the foundation as well. Jack will work with you from here and sort out the logistics. Now, if you don't mind, Jack will take you to his office, and I will hopefully see you again in six months or so!"

"You're a helluva guy, Steve! My God indeed! Gimme a hug, mate!"

I have to say he was a damn good hugger, and obviously a tremendously fine man. I was thrilled to have met him. He and Jack retreated to Jack's office.

It was now close to eleven thirty, and the CBS production team had arrived. I decided to go out for some lunch at the Terminal City Club, a nearby businesspersons' private club where I had been a member for many years. I invited Zachary to join me, and Dan, Joe, and four other agents accompanied us as we walked the three blocks. We were all getting braver about our security concerns.

We wandered into the club and headed to the 1812 Dining Room. The four extra agents stationed themselves by the door, and Joe and Dan agreed to join us for lunch. It was far more discreet to have them sitting at the table than standing a few feet away eyeing the other members and making them uncomfortable. We sat in a corner, and Joe and Dan had the seats that faced the room.

We had a good lunch, while Zach brought me up to speed on the latest developments about the house. A huge crew would be working twenty-four hours a day, and the framing would be completed within forty-eight hours. I told Zach I wanted to zip over for a tour in the next couple of days. Joe and Dan made a note of that as well.

At the club, I had never been very well known to the members. I just came and went as I pleased and entertained friends and business colleagues when I wanted to. Now it seemed everyone in the place knew who I was. As we were leaving, I heard a man mumble something about "that guy coming in here, bringing his goons."

I stopped dead in my tracks, turned, and walked back to his table.

Speaking deliberately a little too loudly, I said, "Excuse me, sir, I don't believe we've met. I'm Steve Thomas. I think I overheard you call my professional bodyguards, who are all former military veterans, 'goons.' Did I hear that correctly?"

"Well, um ... I, uh ... well, uh—"

"Sir, I imagine you have likely heard I recently came into a bunch of money. And these gentlemen have protected my life, and have already saved my life more than once. They are retired Special Forces officers who have served their country and protected freedom. Since my quest is to try to make the world a better place, perhaps we can start with the elimination of ignorance and rudeness, and you can do your part, right now. Apologize."

He squirmed in his seat, and finally choked out the words, "I am very sorry, gentlemen. I apologize."

"Thank you. I think you have just made the world a better place. Have a lovely day!"

With that, we turned to leave, and the stunned room of diners, who had been silently eavesdropping, burst into spontaneous applause, making the rude man turn completely purple. I smiled again, turned and bowed ever so slightly to the room, and said in a loud voice to the head waiter, "Put all their lunches on my account." Pointing at the purple-faced man, I said, "His too."

With that, we wandered out of the club. Zach could not stop laughing all the way back to the office. Every time he thought of the look on the man's face when he was confronted, he laughed again.

"I just hate bullies," I said. "I always have. And I have to admit, that was sort of fun… With the level of fear we have been dealing with, that guy was like a mosquito. Oh God, though … Zach. I think I may have just qualified as an ass back there. You were supposed to tell me when that happens."

Zach responded, holding his hands out in front of him like scales of justice, weighing each word he said next: "Ass, hero, ass, hero… hard to tell the difference, Steve. I'll let this one go."

Now we had to get ready for Diane Wallace. It was one p.m. when we arrived back in the office, and she was already there, reviewing notes and having makeup applied. They were using one of the smaller meeting rooms as a dressing-room/makeup room.

The door was open, but I knocked anyway to say hello.

"Ms. Wallace, hello. I'm Steve Thomas. Welcome to our office and thank you so much for coming today. I'm looking forward to taking your questions."

"Well, Mr. Thomas, not too many *60 Minutes* guests are excited to answer our questions. Most are trying to figure out how NOT to answer them."

"Well, that's not us. I will go and get ready."

The makeup artist asked if I could come back in ten minutes for a bit of a dusting.

I entered my office, forgetting that it was now a "studio." There were cords running everywhere, some furniture had been moved a bit, there were lights and bounce lights, microphones, and two cameras. This was going to be fun.

CHAPTER 79

Jacob left Vancouver at nine a.m. local time and was the first passenger aboard one of our new Gulfstream 650 jets. These aircraft were outfitted for up to fourteen passengers in our chosen configuration, with two fold-down sofa beds at the rear of the aircraft. They were in sofa configuration today, and Jacob and two agents were aboard the flight, along with one flight attendant and an extra pilot and co-pilot for the return trip. They planned to return late that evening. So, in total, today the plane was carrying eight people. Jacob settled into one of the business-class seats. His seat was in front of a table and had another similar seat opposite. The extra crew sat at the front of the plane, right behind the cockpit, and the agents were just behind them, so Jacob had the back of the plane all to himself.

To say he felt awkward would be an understatement. What the hell did he know about meeting the president of a country and holding talks about how we could help them? He knew his grandfather would be pretty proud of him right now, which made him feel a little better. He decided he would take his sage advice: "Just be your usual, well-mannered, charming self."

Basically, he knew what Steve's goals were, and he had the ten key objectives of the Thomas Protocol Global Initiative to rely on. He knew all that. He just didn't know what to say. His stomach was churning. He had never been so nervous. Ever.

The flight attendant brought him a small plate of fresh fruit and some cheese, and a cup of coffee. Jacob smiled at her and said thanks, and then reached into his bag and pulled out a bottle of Pepto-Bismol and took a healthy swig of it.

Dickinson had given him some briefing notes to prepare for his visit, including some general info on the president. He learned that the president was in his last year in office, and according to the notes, Mexican presidents could not seek a second term. He was divorced and had married his current wife in 2010, and had a total of five children from the two marriages. Strikingly handsome, from Jacob's perspective, he was shocked to see that Enrique Peña Nieto, with an approval rating near 12 percent, was the least popular president in Mexican history. In Jacob's mind, he should have got twenty-five points for looks alone!

He decided to watch a movie to pass the time and take his mind off his meeting. He found a selection of DVDs and asked if anyone had a favourite. They picked one they could all enjoy, and he and the two agents watched it together. The extra crew were catching a nap.

At a little past five hours and ten minutes into the flight, the pilots announced that they would begin their descent into the Mexico City International Airport, and land on Runway 05 right, to the northeast. The aircraft taxied to stall S7 and came to a full stop. Two black SUVs pulled up alongside as soon as the aircraft had shut down its engines. There were four agents in the rear vehicle, and a driver in the front vehicle. Jacob and the two agents climbed into the first SUV, with Jacob and one agent in the backseat. And then they were off for the twenty-five-minute drive to the Canadian Embassy for a courtesy call that had been arranged by the prime minister's office in Ottawa. Jean Claude Lamonde had been a career foreign-service worker in Canada before leaving for a lucrative business career, only to eventually return to the foreign service in 2015 as an ambassador to Mexico. A French Canadian in his late fifties, he was a big promoter of Canada in Mexico and was well regarded as an effective ambassador.

The embassy, located only about a mile or so from the presidential residence, was a large, brown block building of questionable design. It looked more like a detention centre than an embassy. It was very securely fenced and access was highly restricted. Toward the east-side rear of the building, on Schiller Street, was a security gate, where the SUVs pulled up and showed passes before being waved inside. The gate was immediately locked behind them.

Exiting the vehicle, only one agent escorted Jacob to the door of the secure building. He was ushered inside by an aide to the ambassador, cleared through security, and taken up to the top floor. The armed agents remained outside.

The aide, he learned, was a Canadian career foreign service worker on her third posting, and she escorted Jacob directly to the ambassador's office. She told Jacob she was from Regina, Saskatchewan. Jacob smiled and told her how nice that was, but he was really thinking, *Where the hell is Regina?*

Ambassador Lamonde was standing outside his office door, chatting with an office assistant.

"Buenos días, Jacob! Welcome to Mexico City," he said, with a pleasant French accent. "Please, come into my office."

The office was impressive, as befitting the office of the representative of a G7 country. The two men sat down to chat, and Jacob was offered a cold drink.

"Thank you for seeing me today, Your Excellency. It's very kind of you. I would be grateful for any advice you can give me on how best to speak to the president."

Lamonde started off by laughing. "Jacob, I had the same call about you from the president earlier today. I had very little advice for him, and I have very little advice for you. The president is a charming man, well mannered, gregarious, and polite. He cares deeply about his country and is frustrated by the Americans treating Mexicans like dirt. He's angry at the drug lords ravaging the northern part of the country, hates the crime and violence, and the kidnappings and violence toward tourists. This country is currently a powder keg. They need more economic opportunity, better ethics in business and government, and neighbours to the north who will treat them with courtesy and respect.

"If I was to give you one piece of advice, Jacob, it is that foreign relations and foreign affairs generally are about two things and two things only: power and interests."

"Can you expand on that for me, Mr. Ambassador?"

"Of course. Many people make the mistake of thinking that foreign affairs is about building relationships, and let's face it, a cordial relationship makes things easier, but countries do things to gain power, or preserve power, and they seek wins that will improve their own interests. They are not interested in helping you achieve your goals at their expense; they are only interested in achieving their own. If by some happy miracle, a win-win can be achieved, well… that is a tremendous advantage, but winning is paramount. Power and interests. Those are everything."

Jacob considered his words before speaking. "I am here to give away money. I guess we are losing right away. We don't even want anything back for it."

"Ah, but that is where you are wrong, Jacob. One of the first countries you are visiting is Mexico. In doing so, you are showing tremendous respect. You are here because you care about Mexico and the Mexican people. You want them to succeed and do better, and you want to help the president to have other opportunities than just relying on the Americans, who are currently treating him with such disrespect. So, you are actually in a tremendously powerful position today, and the respect you have to offer is the power the president can gain, not to mention the interests of his people for economic gains. It is a huge win for him. Just try not to make what you are doing feel like charity. Treat it like you are here to invest in a powerful growing nation and want to see it flourish."

Jacob wasn't sure he would remember much of this, but he would try.

The two of them spoke more about their backgrounds, their travels, and their jobs.

"Jacob, I agreed that I would accompany you and introduce you to the president. Once I have presented you, I will excuse myself and let you two meet and enjoy your evening. We should get going."

With that, they left the office, and Jacob was invited to join the ambassador in his car for the ride. Jacob's security vehicles followed along behind the ambassador's security vehicles.

The president's official residence and main workplace is called Los Pinos, which is located inside the Bosque de Chapultepec (Chapultepec Park). The entire area is fenced and secured, which allows tremendous freedom inside the gates for those who live and work there. The residence itself is a large, white, Spanish building with two storeys and a basement level, impressive without being overbearing.

The ambassador escorted Jacob inside, while again, the security team waited with the vehicles.

A Mexican security attendant invited them inside the residence, cleared them through security, and asked them to sit in a waiting area for a few minutes. It was 6:55, and at exactly 7:00 p.m., the president appeared with his electric smile. He was dressed stylishly in light cream linen slacks, loafers, an open-necked white shirt, and a black sports jacket.

Immediately impressive, he spoke in flawless English with a beautiful Spanish accent. Jacob was introduced and welcomed, and after a few pleasantries, the ambassador excused himself. The president and Jacob retired to a small formal dining room with a large table set for two. Peña Nieto sat at the head of the table, and Jacob sat near him to one side.

"Mr. President, I have to confess, you are the first president I have met, and this new role I have is still in its infancy. I hope you will forgive me if I break any sort of protocol." Jacob was always trying to please.

"Jacob, the doors are closed. Call me 'Enrique.' We are men. Let us sit and reason together and see how your Thomas Protocol can be of assistance to my people."

All Jacob could do was smile. This was an elegant, classy man, who was far more charming than the always-charming Jacob Van Vloten.

The president continued. "Just so you know, if you want to pay off our national debt, I can afford to get us a better bottle of wine." Hard to resist, he smiled that electric smile again.

"I am afraid that deal was only for Canada, no doubt a bit of favouritism shown by my employer. Now, Enrique, my understanding is that your gross domestic product is about one point three trillion dollars a year, and your national debt is about six hundred and seventy billion dollars. The kind of support we would like to offer is quite significant when thought of in those terms, and perhaps I can outline a few areas we have considered… but ultimately what we think doesn't matter. We really want to hear from you."

"Go on please, Jacob."

Jacob gave a quick overview of the ten areas the Thomas Protocol would initially focus on and then got specific.

"Mr. Thomas wants to offer funds to support your military veterans and your police-force veterans—those disabled and in need. To that end, he asked me to offer you the sum of twenty billion dollars to be used to fund pensions, buy better equipment for your police, and pay for the rehabilitation of the wounded or disabled."

"Impressive, Jacob, go on."

"He would like to do some other things as well, to help to create more opportunities for Mexicans within Mexico, so that they will want to stay in their beautiful country and build it for the future.

"We don't know what those initiatives should be though. Should it be education, factories, food production, energy production? We don't want to own anything ourselves; we want to help fund initiatives and then get out of the way. Can you offer some suggestions?"

The president thought for a moment and then nodded. "I have an idea that you might like. One of the issues we have to worry about in this country is corruption. Living in Mexico today, there are four reasonably young former Mexican presidents. The eldest one of those is about seventy-five. I will be joining them at the end of the year when my term ends. Perhaps we could have a past-presidential commission formed to oversee the expenditures and ensure the money gets to the people and the causes for which it is intended. That would be a really positive way of managing the distribution, I think. What do you think of that?"

Recognizing that the president was doing exactly what the ambassador had suggested, focusing on power and interests, Jacob knew he was on the right track.

"Mr. President, I think that sounds amazing. To be partnering with such impressive leaders would be fantastic for us and for your country. We could leave it to your presidential quintet to submit further proposals for funding. I think you can assume that we are prepared to offer up to one hundred billion dollars, but no more than ten billion on any one project. I will leave you the materials detailing the areas of support on which the Thomas Protocol Global Initiatives focuses."

Jacob sat back and took a deep breath, smiling at Enrique. "Thank you, Mr. President, this arrangement sounds like it could be perfect. I will convey this idea to Mr. Thomas as soon as I return!"

"Enrique, Jacob," the president corrected. "Please … now, some wine and food." He pressed a small button on the underside of the table, and immediately the doors opened and two male servants entered the room with silver trays, serving large dinner plates to the two men.

"Jacob, I would have arranged for Swiss food, but the only one we are familiar with is chocolate, and that seemed inappropriate. I hope you like steak. Now, eat … enjoy."

And with that, the two men shared small talk and enjoyed their meals, told a few harmless jokes, and chatted about the future for both of them. Soon it was time to leave.

"Mr. President, you have made my first assignment an absolute delight. Thank you so much for your kindness and courtesy. I am flying home this evening and will report to Mr. Thomas in the morning. I am sure he will be most favourable toward this arrangement."

"Jacob, I will contact each of my predecessors, and see if they will be interested in working together. I am certain they will. While we have differing political views, each of us love our country, and I believe they will wish to help. The card I gave you has my personal office number. If you are able, let's try to speak tomorrow afternoon. I should have spoken to my predecessors by then. Good night, Jacob, fly safe, and be well." This was followed by a firm handshake and a momentary grasp of Jacob's right shoulder.

The president left Jacob with a butler, who escorted him to the front door. When the door opened, the agents snapped to attention.

Motors were started and doors were opened. Soon, they were on their way back to the airport and Protocol 9.

The foundation had already named all the aircraft "Protocol" followed by a number. The four Dreamliners were 1, 2, 3, and 4, the four 737s were 5, 6, 7, and 8, and the four Gulfstreams were 9, 10, 11, and 12. The helicopters were 13 and 14, and the twelve cargo planes would be Protocol Cargo 1 through 12 starting with the four 747s. Oh, and of course, the yacht had its own MY designation, for "Motor Yacht" and was therefore *Protocol MY IV*.

As they roared down the runway, Jacob quietly said, "Buenas noches, Mexico," as the nose of the plane lifted up at the fifteen-second mark. They were airborne two seconds later. The powerful aircraft lifted off, climbed to five hundred feet as the landing gear stored itself, then banked slightly left to get some clean air, and clear the air space.

The second flight crew was in charge of the return flight home. They were enjoying flying the new aircraft. As they were passing over Arizona, they encountered some very serious turbulence. The plane was buffeted heavily. The pilot immediately radioed for permission to change his altitude, and the plane quickly ascended by two thousand feet, finding some calmer air.

Jacob, sitting mid cabin, was wiping Heineken beer, which had spilled during the first bounce, from his trousers. The flight attendant came back to see if he was okay. She returned with a few extra napkins and a fresh drink. Once he was breathing normally again, Jacob sat back to consider his first liaison with a country's leader.

It had been completely amazing. To think that, a month earlier, he had been escorting Steve Thomas to Altermatt's office for the first time, like a gofer, and now he was meeting with the president of Mexico and flying around on a private jet. He looked heavenward, toward the ceiling, and thanked his grandfather. He would try to follow Steve's lead in staying humble and being grateful for the opportunity.

They would be back in Vancouver at about one a.m. local time. In the meantime, he was able to make a satellite call to Zachary.

"Hi, I just wanted to call and tell you that I love you."

"Aw. That is so sweet, Jacob. I love you too. How did it go?"

"Amazing. The president is a great guy. We talked about ideas, and have come up with some good stuff. I will fill you in later. I plan to wake you up when I get to the hotel, so don't be shocked when a strange man crawls into bed with you."

"Oh? Who are you bringing along?" They both laughed. "See you soon, Jacob. Love you."

Jacob decided he had better get some rest, and then realized he'd better make a few notes from the meeting first, and then again, he decided he was just too tired. He reclined his seat and closed his eyes.

He could hardly wait to tell Steve the good news in the morning.

CHAPTER 80

While Jacob was jet-setting to Mexico and getting to have dinner with the president, I was preparing for what would likely be a tough interview with Diane Wallace.

We started with a walking tour around the office with a camera crew following us. I showed her around the various floors and departments we had set up, and the teams that we had organized to gather information, receive submissions, and decide on our projects. She asked for a tour of the yacht, and since it was now close by, docked in the harbour, we toured it as well. During this walking interview, she asked how we had so many things set up in just a month, and I explained what the bank had done in advance for us, including purchasing the yacht. She was as amazed as I had been.

In my office, at about four p.m., we sat down for the formal interview.

"Mr. Thomas, it was not long ago that you were a quiet, retired business person, living your life and relaxing. Here we are, several weeks later, and you are the richest man on the planet, and already the world's greatest philanthropist. You're surrounded by security like a world leader, running a major organization, and have survived a brutal assassination attempt at the airport. How are you managing to handle all that and still seem pretty normal?"

"Well, I guess I am pretty normal. I was raised as a middle-class kid here in Vancouver, did okay in business, and was able to retire young. This last few weeks has been bewildering for sure, but I was a bit bored anyway, so this has given me something to do with my spare time." I raised a single eyebrow and laughed a little.

"Tell us about learning about the amount of money involved."

"Let me start by saying I knew nothing about this matter at all. I had never heard of the relative who left the money, and when I was approached about receiving this money, I thought it was probably a scam. As we all know now, it wasn't a scam. Then I thought maybe it would be a few thousand dollars, or maybe a couple of million, but I was staggered by the actual amount. I could barely breathe when I saw how much money was involved."

"And this long-lost uncle who left the funds, he had some instructions for you?"

"He did. There was a brief letter saying I should keep ten percent for myself, and donate the rest to make the world a better place. Keeping in mind this money was deposited at the end of the First World War, the idea of doing something to improve the world was probably on everyone's mind."

"Can we see the letter?"

"Diane, I am ashamed to admit that in all the craziness of the last few weeks, and all the travel, I have mislaid it somewhere. When I find it, I'll happily show it to you."

"Mr. Thomas, you have indicated you will only keep one percent of the funds. What made you decide to keep less for yourself and donate even more?"

"One percent is still about two hundred and seventy billion dollars. I am going to keep that aside, live my life and help my family, and when I die, leave everything that's left to charity, so in truth, I will be donating nearly all of it, which I just think is the right thing to do."

"How is your family holding up?"

"I am a single man, so I don't have a wife or children of my own, so I am easy to take care of. I have given money to each of my siblings, so that they can each fund their own family's lives and protect themselves. I've yet to discuss the possibilities of them joining us in this project, although that will likely be a main point of discussion at our next gathering. Whether they want to be involved or not, though, they are my family. Good people, thrust into a spotlight they never asked for. As such, I've made sure they are very well taken care of. In direct answer to your question, they are holding up fine, but truthfully, I think they would rather have their old lives back."

"And what about you, Mr. Thomas, what gets you through the days and nights?"

"You know, Diane, when all this started, it made me think of a quote from Shakespeare's *Twelfth Night*. So... I wrote it down, edited and modernized it a bit for my own purposes, and I read it to myself every morning. I have it right here if you don't mind me reading it. It sounds a bit arrogant at first, but..."

I cleared my throat and began. "'Some are born great, some achieve greatness, and some have greatness thrust upon them. Accept it in body and spirit. Get used to the life you'll be leading. Show eagerness for the life that's awaiting you. Argue like a nobleman. Talk about politics and affairs of state, and act freely and independently. A happy new life is there if you want it. Who's not brave enough to grab the happiness before him? Stay humble and be grateful.'"

I had gotten emotional and wiped a tear from my right eye. Diane leaned in, showing her compassion.

"Mr. Thomas, the burden and the gift that has been given to you is enormous. I am not sure I could cope."

"I hope I am coping fine. I just don't want anyone to believe that I think I'm special, simply because someone has left me money. That's why I say that I've had greatness, or wealth in this case, thrust upon me. I had nothing to do with it. So now, instead of that quiet life, I have this crazy busy life that I will embrace and find happiness in, and do my best every day to do good work. Really, when you think about it, what an amazing opportunity! Do you think I should complain? Never!"

Diane smiled back at me.

"There's actually another quote I love," I offered. "It's from George Bernard Shaw, that one Bobby Kennedy loved so much: 'Some men see things as they are, and wonder why, I dream things that never were, and say why not?' Quotes like these inspire me. I have the financial ability to truly live that now, and to spend every day I have left on this earth trying to change things for the better."

Diane was listening carefully, and her smile seemed genuine, but she was also a professional and had certain questions that needed to be asked.

"Mr. Thomas, there may be those around the world, be they democratic governments, dictators, warlords, religious leaders, and so on, who may not take kindly to your view of what constitutes making the world a better place. Have you thought about that?"

"I certainly have, and have instructed my team accordingly. We know we need to be invited to a country. We want to help with the things they want help with, so long as those projects fit within our overall protocol. If we are not invited, or welcomed, we will stay away. It's that simple. We are not here to force our ideas or values on anyone.

"We just committed a ten-billion-dollar donation to Rotary International. That will put three hundred thousand dollars into the hands of every Rotary club in the world, to do whatever they decide to do with it in their own communities to help improve things. No direction from us whatsoever. All we asked was that they get it spent within six months, and let us know how it turns out. We want to see immediate action. We know we can count on them and trust them to do it right, and make the best use of the funds that they can. We will look for other groups like that.

"As you are aware, we also gave a massive donation to the Canadian Government to pay off the national debt. That was very much a special circumstance for my own country, and while the payment included some small conditions, we were transparent and open about those, and the matter passed parliament unanimously. And in opinion polls, ninety-seven percent of Canadians are in favour of what we did. My only question is ... who are the three percent who thought it was a bad idea?"

Diane smiled broadly and laughed a little at that.

"What drove your decision to support military veterans?"

"Diane, I have never served a day in the military, and frankly am not sure I would be brave enough to complete basic training, let alone serve in combat. Anyone who does is incredibly dedicated and courageous, and they have my respect and admiration. It truly pains me to see homeless vets, disabled vets, impoverished vets ... all left behind instead of being celebrated as heroes and treated as such. We approached the US Government with some ideas. They agreed to help us with distributing lump-sum payments to disabled vets. We are also working with hospitals and home builders to help remedy the issues of homelessness and insufficient medical care. We are close to making more formal announcements on both of these issues, and appreciate the US Government and the acting secretary of Veterans Affairs for letting us be part of a solution. We are very grateful. We will be providing similar help to veterans here in Canada, and are also working with Mexico on some initiatives. We hope to have more to report on that very soon."

"Mr. Thomas, are there any areas you will make sure to avoid?"

"Yes, politics. We don't want to impact any nation's political balance in a good or bad direction. We don't care who gets the credit for our work, and we don't want the credit for our efforts. We don't want a single thing to stand in the way of helping people. We don't need to be praised; we don't need awards or thank-you cards. We just want to see the lives of people everywhere improving, be that in terms of education, opportunities, health, equality, food, housing... whatever form it takes. If it proves to be the best way to move forward, I could see us partnering with the United Nations for some of their programs.

"We want to avoid corrupt governments, but some of those corrupt countries have people who are the most in need. So, if there are ways to help solve their problems, and in doing so move them into less corrupt ways of governing, perhaps everyone wins."

"And how long until you will be done... out of money?"

"We have already set aside five hundred billion dollars to begin a new hundred-year fund, so we may never run out of money. As for our current quest, I think it will take about twenty-five years to finish, but I hope we will have the bulk spent in ten years. We will be mostly monitoring successes and failures after that, and fine tuning for the future."

"I wonder if we can talk about Wilbur Thomas and who he was. What do you know about him?"

"Diane, I don't know a thing. I don't know when he was born or died. He was probably dead well before I was even born. I barely knew my own grandfather. I think I was five or six when he died, and Wilbur was supposedly one of his brothers. I say supposedly because I don't even know who my grandfather's brothers and sisters were. From my memory and stories from my dad, his father came from a family of about ten or eleven kids. And that is truly all I know. I never heard of Wilbur Thomas before all of this happened, although I know how strange that must sound."

"What about the money? Any idea where it came from?"

"Not to be evasive, Diane, but I have been told nothing. All I know is that in April of 1918, he deposited fifty million dollars into a Swiss bank account. It was the war, so who knows where it came from. I doubt it was in his piggy bank, or that he made it selling pencils in the street. All I know is that, wherever it came from, good or bad, we will use it to do nothing but good work in this century. It is a mystery, and in time, I am sure we will learn more. Swiss banks are very tight-lipped about their accounts, though, so I am not sure they will tell any of us anything. Your guess is as good as mine."

"Are you at least curious about its origin?"

"Yes, sure, but I want to be grateful for the role I have now, regardless where it came from. I have something so much more important to focus on, and that's where I think my energy should be focused. I am sure there will be lots of mystery hunters, members of the media, and perhaps others who will do some digging to find out the truth. Maybe one day we will know. And hey, let me know if you find out anything!"

"Alright, so … last question, Mr. Thomas: Why you? How did Wilbur divine, one hundred years ago, that you should be the one to do this job?"

"It's all pretty strange, Diane. Wilbur left the money to the second son of the first son of his brother, my grandfather. I think my grandfather was born around the late 1880s. He could have been married and had his children by say 1910, and his first son could have had his second son in say 1930. In other words, I could have already been dead of old age. Just another weird coincidence that my grandfather married around 1928, had his first son in 1929, and I was born in 1963. My theory is that Wilbur just made up a riddle in a bit of a hurry. But, what do I know?"

I smiled, Diane Wallace smiled back, and the interview was over.

"Good interview, Steve. I think we have enough here to piece together a good story. You seem like a very good man, and I wish you the best. And unless I find out something in my other research, you can count on this being a good news story, not a hit job like Everett pulled on you. I suspect he is a bit embarrassed in hindsight."

With the cameras and microphones being packed up, I asked, "Diane, it is really important for us that our story gets told. I know that people in the media hear things and see situations where help is needed. Please tell your colleagues that if they know of any areas where we can help, they should let us know. We are genuinely serious about doing good work, and making the world a better place!"

"I will, Steve. I will. I didn't ask about Mexico, but what are you up to down there?"

"Not sure yet. One of my key people is there now and meeting with the president for dinner. I will know more tomorrow. Would you like me to let you know?"

"That would be great. Might be a story there too. Thanks again, Steve, and best of luck with all this." She shook my hand and gave me that winning smile.

With that, she slung her bag over her shoulder and headed to the door. She was a very classy lady and an excellent reporter. She was probably bored with a puff piece like this, but I sure appreciated having someone of her calibre help tell our story.

CHAPTER 81

Ursula Van Vloten was at her office at the bank at nine a.m. Noah had finally pulled together the entire original file documents from the Thomas account. They had been stored in her father's private safe in his office for the past ten years.

She was alone as she looked over the documents, some of which he had printed from scans that had been made of the original documents. Today, everything was done in an electronic format. The ancient files had been scanned and digitized about fifteen years earlier and the original paper documents eventually destroyed.

She reviewed the original signature card, the original application for an account, and the faint carbon copy of the original and only deposit slip. There were no photocopiers in those days, so notes were made about the identification that was offered by Wilbur at the time. He had shown a military identification and a US diplomatic passport. It was noted that the deposit of $50 million was in the form of bearer bonds.

Ursula re-read the documents. *US diplomatic passport? Why would a military man have that?* At least in this day and age, a diplomatic passport was only issued to a Foreign Service Officer, or to a person having diplomatic status because he or she is travelling abroad to carry out diplomatic duties. Was he a government representative or agent?

And bearer bonds? *Nice.* Convenient and completely untraceable. She knew this money had to have been stolen from somewhere, or perhaps was the product of espionage, but from the bank's view, this was all just a nice man with $50 million in bearer bonds who wanted to open an account. The bank was likely ecstatic to get the funds, regardless of where the money came from. No human being or entity had that kind of cash money in 1918. *Except governments,* she thought.

Everything was legal and in order though. There was no obligation on the part of the bank to verify the origin of the funds. The bearer bonds were legal tender, the account was set up perfectly, the identification verified. Nothing was technically or legally wrong.

So, an American citizen walked into the bank with $50 million in bearer bonds, filled out all the forms correctly, provided the correct identification, wrote three letters of instructions for the bank, and left.

Wilbur Thomas, though, was never seen or heard from again. One letter was for a descendant—in this case, Steve Thomas—to be opened in a hundred years, one letter was to be opened by the bank in ninety years to prepare for the other, and the last was a general letter of what to do with his account and investments and instructions to watch for his heir to appear in the future. There was a copy of the instruction letter, and a copy of the ninety-year letter, but no copy of the one-hundred-year letter. She would have liked to have seen a copy of that one, too.

And even though the account had had no account activity for a hundred years, it was not considered an inactive account, because of the letter of instructions.

Ursula saw no technical or legal way to void the account. That scratched another possible solution off the list. She might just have to rely on Steve's generosity, and that did not leave her feeling very strong or powerful. It made her feel like she might have to beg, and Ursula never begged, or relented. Just ask her ex-husband, Rolf.

CHAPTER 82

It was midnight in Vancouver, and I couldn't sleep. I got up and put on my robe. I needed to take care of something, and needed to do it now.

I went to my briefcase and removed the item that had been keeping me awake.

It was a cool night out but not raining. In the living room of my suite, there was an open-flame gas fireplace. Barefoot, I entered the room, flipping on the fireplace.

Sitting down, I slid the letter out of the envelope and read it again. There was that one section that bothered me...

I cannot say that this money came easily, nor did it come completely honestly, but as soon as I had it I knew that I could not keep it. But I thought perhaps, if left for a while, it could lose its dirty stench and do some good one day.

Yup, this had to go. I reread the full letter twice, smelled the paper one last time, and then reached over and carefully let the flames lick the paper. I held the corner until the whole page had burned, and then tossed it into the fire as the flames singed my fingers. I watched as it broke up into ashes. The envelope followed in exactly the same way. I turned off the fireplace and let it cool. I then picked out the larger ash pieces and put them in a coffee cup. I gently blew the rest of the ashes off the fake logs and then, with a damp cloth wiped up the dust that had billowed out onto the marble floors.

In the washroom, I flushed the ashes, rinsed the cloth several times, washed it with soap, and even washed the coffee cup.

I was all alone. No witnesses. All I had done was burn a letter that belonged to me. It was better to be the only person alive who knew what it really said. Just in case. No crime here, but I felt like a criminal nonetheless.

Back in bed, I felt better. It took an hour more, but I finally fell asleep.

CHAPTER 83

First thing in the morning, the motorcade took Zachary and me over to the house construction site. We pulled up to the site and tried to park on the street, but there were construction vehicles everywhere up and down the street. Eventually, we briefly double parked and got out with our agents, and the motorcade started circling the block in the area, waiting for us to call to get picked up again.

There were people working everywhere. Today was framing day, and the studs were being put up fast and furious. All three buildings were being built at the same time, and it was moving at breakneck speed. It was just too busy though to see much of anything, so I promised to stay the hell away for a couple of weeks. I knew I was just in the way.

"Andrew, call the cars back."

We hopped back in, and I had another idea.

"Have you guys eaten yet today? I missed breakfast. Let's go to Denny's"

Andrew did a slow turn from the front passenger seat. "Denny's … Seriously, sir?"

"Yes, do we really think a killer has been waiting in a random Denny's to assassinate me for eating too many hash browns? Come on, breakfast for the whole crew! My treat. There is one up on Broadway, just past Granville."

Andrew spoke into his sleeve, and the three black SUVs whisked us a couple of miles to Denny's. We pulled in, found parking, and walked into the restaurant together. We caused a bit of a buzz, but I was just thrilled to be somewhere normal.

"Table for ten, please?" I knew they didn't have tables for ten.

The middle-aged supervisor said, "How about two fours and a two top?"

"Perfect." It was mid-morning, so there was lots of room. We got three tables almost right next to each other. Every head in the place turned. It was apparent many people knew who I was. Camera phones came out, videos were taken, and selfies were snapped with us in the background. Someone was even live on Instagram, broadcasting our breakfast.

I ordered mine. "Moons Over My Hammy and a large milk." With that, I took a nervous breath and got up.

Andrew rose "Sir, what are you up to?"

"Just saying hello. Come on, Andrew, real people. *Normal* people. I used to be one of them and sometimes still wish I was." He motioned for the other agents to remain seated and followed about six feet behind me. I went around to every table that had a phone out and said hello, shook hands, took pictures, and enjoyed mixing with real people again. It felt so good. I asked folks what we could do to help, what did they think of our donation to the city, did they think the federal tax decrease would help their families, and what did they think the three biggest issues were that we could work on.

Real people. Good ideas. Some silly comments, some jokes, one marriage proposal, and one guy who told me to go fuck myself. There's always one in every crowd.

I quietly told the supervisor to bring me everyone's checks. We were buying them breakfast.

I walked back to the kitchen and said hello to the staff. They were all smiles. I thanked them in advance for breakfast and went back to my table.

Zachary looked at me, smiling. "You running for office?"

"Don't have time, I'm afraid. But this is fun. Great to hear what they think. And to be clear, I actually like Denny's breakfasts. Wait until you taste it!"

Zach had never been to a Denny's. Guess they didn't have them in Zurich. His loss!

Zach could not believe the size of the meal he received. I had ordered for him: the Lumberjack Slam. Two eggs, two bacon, two sausages, ham, hash browns, toast, and two pancakes. Just a normal breakfast, right? It came on two plates. In Zurich, he would have had yogurt, fresh fruit, and maybe some bread. Welcome to North America! He only ate about a third of it, shaking his head and smiling at its sheer enormity.

And then, we were done. I paid the bill for the whole restaurant, left a five-hundred-dollar tip to be shared among the staff, and we headed out. Just as we were preparing to drive out of the parking lot, a news crew was arriving. Someone must have tipped them off.

"Boys, let's not give them a reason to hate us."

I jumped out of the SUV, with Andrew and Dan on my heels. The local reporter and cameraperson were coming our way.

"Mr. Thomas, what are you doing here today?"

"We were just out looking at a project, and I convinced all these guys to join me for breakfast. Just helping out the local economy! And all those nice people in there were kind enough to let us join them. Great to be with good, hard-working people. They were full of great ideas for us. Thanks for saying hello, but we have to get going. Have a great day!"

We turned and got back in the cars and left. The reporter went into the Denny's and interviewed a bunch of the people. Even the grouchy guy got interviewed and said he was happy to have gotten a free breakfast, and that he was a big fan. He was probably lying, but that was okay.

In ten minutes, we were back downtown at the office.

"We need to do stuff like that more often."

"No, sir, actually we don't. But I am glad you had some fun," Andrew said.

"Party pooper."

CHAPTER 84

Fifty-one-year-old Mexican President Enrique Peña Nieto was a man of his word. First thing in the morning, he had contacted all of the former presidents of Mexico still living. Fifty-five-year-old President Felipe Calderon, seventy-five-year-old President Vicente Fox, sixty-six-year-old President Ernesto Zedillo, seventy-year-old President Carlos Salinas de Gortari, and unexpectedly, ninety-two-year-old President Luis Echeverría all agreed to serve on a committee to oversee the Thomas Protocol funds in Mexico.

After individual calls to each in the morning, he managed to get them all on a conference call at one thirty p.m. Still the active president, Peña Nieto indicated he would not join the committee until after his term was over, but would work hard to seek funding. They discussed who should chair the group and everyone was comfortable with Vicente Fox taking the role for the first year and that they would rotate the job after that. President Echeverría, being ninety-two, said he would pass on the chair role, but would otherwise love to contribute.

The distribution of these funds would give each man a moment in the political sunshine again, and allow them to do positive work for their country and their people. It felt good, and even better to have a national purpose again. Nothing ever replaces the prestige of being in power.

They set a meeting date for one week later to begin their discussions on how best to help Mexico and Mexicans. They hoped they could meet with Steve Thomas soon.

Jacob was at his desk in his office when the phone rang, and he was asked to hold for the president of Mexico. Jacob, out of innate respect for the caller, automatically stood up at his desk.

"Jacob, it's Enrique. How are you today?"

"Mr. President, I am well, sir, and how are you today?"

"I am very well. I promised I would call you today to let you know about my efforts, and I can confirm that all five of the living former presidents of Mexico want to participate. I won't be able to participate in this private committee, but I will act as a liaison, and will join them at the end of my term. President Fox will chair the group for the first year. They are all very excited, and will meet soon to put some proposals together. They were hoping to meet with Mr. Thomas, perhaps even next week. Is that possible, Jacob?

"I will check with him, and get back to you, Mr. President. I will call you by morning, sir."

"Jacob, it's Enrique, remember?"

"No, Mr. President, that was at a private dinner. You are Mr. President again today."

Peña Nieto laughed at the young man's formality.

"And Mr. President, thank you so much for dinner and the fascinating conversation last night. I enjoyed it immensely, sir."

"You are most welcome, Jacob. I will speak to you tomorrow then. Good day, my friend."

And with that, the phone call ended. Jacob stood there holding the receiver for a moment longer.

How unreal, he thought. *I just got a call from the president of Mexico, my new pal. What a crazy job this is going to be.*

With that he put down the phone and dashed to Steve's office.

CHAPTER 85

EIGHT YEARS EARLIER, 2010, PULLACH, GERMANY

Rolf Van Vloten arrived at work. It was about a twenty-five-minute drive from his flat in Munich, south to the BND campus in Pullach. The BND (Bundesnachrichtendienst) is Foreign Intelligence Agency of Germany.

The BND was located on about two square kilometres of land overlooking a nearby river, the Isarwerkkanal. Similar to CIA Headquarters being called "Langley," the BND property was known as Camp Nikolaus. From the air, it appeared to be a large campus or university, but on the ground, it was the centre of thousands of Germans working in large and small buildings on a variety of espionage goals.

The BND was founded during the Cold War in 1956 and had an intimate relationship with the CIA. Very often, the BND was the source for the western world's only spies and informants within Eastern Bloc countries.

When the cold war ended, the BND had to reinvent itself. The Iron Curtain didn't exist anymore, the Soviet Union was defunct, and the Warsaw Pact had been disbanded. Communism had seemingly disappeared overnight. But as in any vacuum, those threats were quickly replaced by others.

The threats now were terrorism, weapons of mass destruction, human trafficking, organized crime, the international sale of weapons and drugs, money laundering, and information warfare. As a result of these new threats, the BND became leaders in wiretapping, computer hacking, and electronic surveillance of international communications.

And like the CIA, the BND's mandate specified no espionage activities within Germany, no subversive operations abroad, and strict political control of the organization by a parliamentary committee. Everyone knew, though, that the committee would only be told what the committee needed to be told.

Rolf worked most of his career on crimes related to money laundering through Swiss Banks. He had been an agent of the BND since he was twenty-four years old, which was about twenty-six years ago. When he started with the BND, he had a cover as a local printer, and his paycheques came from the print shop, but he didn't actually work there. He applied some ink to his hands a couple of times a week, and then washed it off, leaving stains to prove his occupation to anyone who might ask.

He had been with the BND for a few years when he met Ursula and fell in love. When he reported to his superiors of his intention to marry and they found out who his father-in-law would be, they made him a field agent, and agreed to relocate him to Zurich. Just prior to leaving his wife, Ursula, in 2009, he had learned of some strange activities that old Wilhelm had been involved with, setting up companies and buying assets in Canada. He reported this to the BND in his regular communications. It did not take long, through a combination of hacking, wiretapping, and electronic surveillance, for the story to begin to unfold. They learned of a massive account controlled by Wilhelm Altermatt and the GCBS, but were unable to determine who the account ultimately belonged to.

It was still early days for computer security, and while the Swiss had the best security, they were still no match for the Bundesnachrichtendienst. It took thousands of attempts, through millions of computer pathways, but they were eventually able to access the scanned and stored account details, which included the original account application, signature card, instruction letter to the bank, and file notes. There was a reference to two more letters, but these had not been scanned.

Rolf's employers were applying tremendous pressure on him to try to convince his wife to join the BND, so they could access more information. Rolf resisted, but told Ursula who he really worked for, and eventually, left his wife to protect his family. He created a story of having found another woman, and that (to be with her), he was returning to Germany. It broke his heart, but he knew he had to do this to make a clean break and protect Ursula and his son, Jacob.

His superiors were furious with Rolf for leaving his wife and jeopardizing their investigation. He was removed from the case for a few months, as punishment, but eventually it was reassigned to him.

Sometime in the mid-1960s, the BND had been able to determine that a US military officer named Wilbur Thomas had opened an account with $50 million in bearer bonds on April 17, 1918. They also knew that, at that time, the account had grown to a value in the multiple billions of dollars.

They also knew that, on April 17, 1918, $50 million in bearer bonds had left the German treasury in the company of an agent of the Kaiser, Heinrich Strasberg, and that those funds were never seen again.

From extensive and detailed German records, they knew exactly how Wilbur Thomas had died. The Kaiser and his people knew, within a few days of the initial payment being made, that they had been swindled, either by Strasberg himself or by Wilbur. After executing Strasberg, the Kaiser ordered the assassination of Wilbur as well. When Wilbur had fled south from Zurich, his scent was picked up by German spies, just before he boarded the British merchant ship *Matiana*.

A German submarine in the area, SM UC-27 trailed the boat until it reached Tunisian waters, at which time they surfaced and pulled alongside and boarded the *Matiana* by force. The captain of the ship begged for his life and gave up Wilbur in return, who was hiding in a crate in the hold of the ship. The Germans found Wilbur, verified his identity, futilely searched the ship for the stolen bonds, and began their interrogation.

Wilber knew he was a dead man, whether he talked or not, so he decided not to talk. Fuck the Kaiser. He had kept $50 million out of German hands, and he was damn proud of it. Finally, one of their blows landed in the wrong place, and he lost consciousness. They couldn't rouse him, so they sealed the crate with nails and ropes and left him alive inside. They ordered the captain and his crew to abandon ship, and to start rowing toward shore, six miles away. It was then that the submarine pulled away a few hundred yards, launched a torpedo, and sunk the *Matiana*, sending it to the bottom of the sea, along with one man trapped alive but unconscious in a crate in the hold. The crew of the *Matiana*, cowards that they had been, swore to each other never to tell the true story of their sinking. Their story never rang true though, because it was so rare for the crew of an unarmed merchant ship to survive a sinking.

So, the Germans knew almost from the beginning who stole the money, and how the thief had died. While it took decades to figure out where Wilbur had hidden it, they also knew they had no way to prove that those untraceable bearer bonds were originally German property. That was the whole point of the bonds being untraceable in the first place.

Who knows though, if they had not been tricked out of it, that extra $50 million might have turned the tide in the war for the Germans.

Suffice it to say that they had wanted their money back... with interest.

And maybe a pound or two of flesh as well.

CHAPTER 86

Jacob walked through the open door to Steve's office. "Great news!"

"Jacob, what's up? How was Mexico?"

"The president was fantastic. He is thrilled with the twenty billion dollars for the military veterans and retired police officers. He also had this amazing idea to be able to distribute more help to Mexico by creating a committee of former Mexican presidents to oversee it."

"Wow, that is awesome!"

"It gets better. He just called to say he has spoken to each of the five former presidents and they are all on board, including one guy who is ninety-two! I briefed Jack while you were out. If possible, they want to get together next week to meet with you."

"Jacob, great work. Really, great work. Hang on a sec."

I buzzed Jack in his office and asked him to join us.

"Jack, can you come into my office, please?"

He was there in under sixty seconds. "Jack, on this Mexico thing, we need to find a day next week that is open, and then let's fly the five of them up here aboard Protocol 2. We will host them for an afternoon meeting, followed by dinner on the yacht. They can stay aboard for the night, and then we'll send them home the next morning. If Peña Nieto feels he can join in, invite him along too."

Everyone scattered to put the balls in the air to make this happen. Moments later, Jack was back, and he had a man with him.

"Steve, we need to have a chat."

"Sure, come on back in, what can I do for you?" Something about his tone seemed a bit weird, so I got up from my desk and walked over to meet this new person.

"Hi, I'm Steve Thomas."

"Good morning, Mr. Thomas. My name is Dan Charbonneau, and I am an inspector with the Royal Canadian Mounted Police."

I am sure I raised my eyebrows in response. "Great, have a seat. What can I do for you?"

Jack spoke first. "Steve, on the day you first came to the office, you may recall I wasn't here to greet you and missed most of that day. I know that was unprofessional, but I was involved in something that I had to keep discreet."

"Uh … okay. Go on."

Jack looked very nervous. "I was approached by … well, a member of the mafia, I guess. He was trying to coerce me into helping defraud you of millions of dollars."

Dan spoke up. "Mr. Thomas, the suspect is a gentleman named Marco Monganonzo, from Detroit. He contacted Jack with a scheme to make Jack a rich man. Jack took the call, agreed to meet with this man, and then immediately called the police. We tapped Jack's cell phone, and followed him to his meeting. We asked Jack not to tell you anything. We didn't know who else in the organization could be a target, or maybe was in on it, and we wanted to keep the list of those who knew anything as small as possible."

Jack added, "I reported it to our internal counsel the moment I got off the call with the RCMP, so we had an internal record of my involvement and activities. Here is a report from our lawyer documenting it all."

I interjected, "Obviously the guy wanted money, but what was his scheme?"

Jack replied, "It was like an old mafia shakedown. He didn't want much, just a 'piece of the action.' A small rake-off for him and his friends and he would provide us with certain protections from criminal elements. He actually used the phrase, 'I just want to wet my beak,' and I confess that, while I was scared meeting him, that one almost made me laugh. It was right out of a cheap mob movie."

It was Daniel's turn next. "What these types of shakedowns involve is usually the creation of fake invoices that get paid as part of an overall project. The important thing, Mr. Thomas, is that we have this guy in custody, and he is being charged with extortion and uttering threats. We could not determine if others were involved. He appeared to be a lone wolf."

"Steve, I feel like I have been lying to you, which I haven't been exactly, but I have been withholding this from you. It's been quite stressful actually."

"Well, Jack, I have to admit I was starting to wonder if it was me. I thought maybe you just didn't like my jokes." I grinned at him, feeling quite relieved to have the matter cleared up.

"I'm sorry about that. I hated all the secrecy; I just didn't think you needed the added stress of this on top of everything else going on, but I promise … I handled the situation as properly and cautiously as I could, all the way down the line."

As relieved as I was, my mind was spinning a bit. I had been worried about personal security since the start of this, but never thought of all the little extortion methods that could be employed by bad people to "get a little piece" for themselves.

"Okay, gentlemen, thank you. Jack, thanks for being the honest man I hoped you were. You did look uncomfortable around me a few times, and my 'spidey sense' was tingling, but I had no idea this was happening. Dan, thank you and the RCMP for your efforts. Is there anything you two need from me at this point?"

"Not a thing, but we'll be sure to keep you in the loop from here on out."

"Thank you, I'd appreciate that."

They stood, hands were shaken all around, and they left.

I sat back in my chair, leaned back, let out a deep sigh, and thought, *Jesus Christ, what's next?*

CHAPTER 87

Jacob was in his office when his cell rang. Looking at his call display, he was shocked to see who was on the line.

"Oh … hi, Papa. I am surprised to hear from you." Jacob sat in his chair and leaned back, tipping back his chair and running his hand through his hair as though in exasperation. He didn't want this call.

"Hi, Jacob. It's good to speak to you. I hear you are working with the Thomas Protocol for the next year. Good for you, Jacob. I am sorry I wasn't at the funeral. I just couldn't get away."

"Papa, you never even called. No word, text, email, flowers, nothing. I couldn't believe it. How could you do that to us?"

"As I said, I couldn't get away. I uh …"

Jacob rolled his eyes. "Yeah, uh … I confess, uh … look, I have given up on you, Papa. I don't think I want to see you or talk to you anymore. It's just too painful. I can't believe that you would be so hurtful to Mama and me at a time of terrible family tragedy. No excuse is really good enough, so … please don't call me again. I need to move on. Good luck with your life."

"Jacob, I am sorry, I know I could have done better. I … Jacob? Jacob? Are you there?"

Jacob listened to his father's seemingly meaningless words and pleas, and then hung up without another word. With tears in his eyes, he walked down the hall to the washroom. He needed to splash some cold water on his face.

Jacob had told himself for a while that it would be better to cut the cord, rather than somehow continue to believe that his father loved, cared, or even gave a shit about him. He kept hoping they would be closer, but his father made no effort whatsoever anymore, so why should he? Jacob would focus on his work, and on Zachary.

Hell, Steve had been more of a friend and father figure in the last several weeks than his father had been in the past nine years.

CHAPTER 88

One week later, Protocol 2 was in the air and flying to Vancouver with the current president of Mexico, his security team, the five former presidents, and a Guardian security team. The thirty-two seats in the rear of the aircraft were full. There was also a couple of executive assistants along for the ride. The eldest president, nine-two-year-old Luis Echeverría, was given the large stateroom, and was having a nap. The rest were seated in the forward salon, enjoying some drinks and food and swapping stories from their years in office.

Vicente Fox was retelling the story of saying, in an interview on American television, "We are not paying for Tripplehorn's fucking border wall." They all laughed. No one could believe it got through the sensors and went out live on CNN.

Felipe Calderon asked Enrique how much money he felt they could expect to have to manage. There were so many things they could do to help Mexico improve economically and socially.

"I have been told we could expect a total of one hundred billion dollars, with an initial twenty billion of that to support our military veterans, the disabled vets, disabled police, and to fund their pensions."

Calderon let out a low whistle, amazed by the sum.

It was a big number; there was little doubt. The entire annual budget for Mexico was about $300 billion, so comparatively, this was an enormous sum.

Ernesto Zedillo had reviewed the Thomas Protocol Global Initiative list of categories, and could see several that would work.

"In my view, education, healthcare, and economic opportunities are the best areas. If our people are smarter, healthier and wealthier, we will automatically have less crime, and be able to create a better society." No one disagreed.

These men had rarely spent this much time together, and they were surprised that they got along so well. They were a rare breed of men who had held the same office, faced similar challenges, and knew both the highs and lows, the hectic pace, sleepless nights, and the loneliness of office.

Truly, they loved their country and their people, and all had hoped to accomplish more during their tenures as president, but it was an uphill battle to build a thriving, united country out of a challenging indebted nation.

The flight attendant offered another round of drinks. She advised that the two small staterooms had beds if anyone wanted to rest. They would land in about two hours.

When Protocol 2 touched down in Vancouver and had taxied to its berth, the motorcade swung into position. In order to make everyone's life easier, the six special guests would divide into two groups of three presidents, accompanied by three of Peña Nieto's security men in each group, and would be flown in two groups to the yacht, by our helicopters. The balance of the passengers on the flight would be driven to the harbour in the motorcade.

Once airborne, the presidents had a wonderful view of the beautiful city of Vancouver, the harbour, the mountains, the ocean, and the Gulf Islands off to the west. Within eleven minutes, the two helicopters, in perfect unison, were settling down on the aft deck and the foredeck of *Protocol MY IV*. The yacht was gleaming! It was an impressive sight.

Andrew had the docks and yacht fully secured, and our three patrol boats were in the water. Because of the high-security level of the guests we were entertaining, the RCMP also had two patrol boats to assist us, and the Coast Guard was nearby.

Once the balance of the teams in the motorcade arrived, the yacht would set sail for a cruise through the harbour and up Indian Arm to where the boat had been anchored during our first days aboard her. It would be a classic three-hour cruise, but hopefully with a better ending than on *Gilligan's Island.*

As they climbed out of the helicopters and were escorted inside, Jacob and I were there to greet them.

For Enrique, it was suddenly like a reunion. "Jacob, my old friend! So good to see you again!" He hugged Jacob.

I was pretty sure a blushing Jacob had a small man-crush going on, and I couldn't help smirking at him.

I introduced myself to each of the presidents and asked that, for tonight, we would just be normal men and use our first names. Vicente Fox was the first to say, "Fuck, of course, Steve."

We served champagne and several local cheeses, and made sure each man was comfortable. The yacht's captain took three men at a time for a tour of the yacht, and assigned them to their cabins. I had given my cabin to Peña Nieto. It seemed the right thing to do, and I would be just fine in a normal cabin. They were all made very comfortable.

Twenty minutes after the helicopters had landed, the motorcade arrived, bringing the remaining assistants, security, and luggage aboard.

Since eight staterooms would be used by myself, Jacob, and the six presidents, there were seven more staterooms that the security detail could share in groups of two. We would allow fourteen security guards on the boat. The rest would stay at the hotel, and everyone would be well protected by our patrol boats, the police boats, and the coast guard.

When we pulled away from the dock, it was quite a flotilla heading down the harbour. Coast Guard in front and rear, the yacht second, RCMP on each rear flank, and our own patrol boats flanking us and keeping other boats at a distance.

These fine gentlemen were enjoying themselves, and wandered the decks to take in the sun dropping in the west.

Our chef called for our attention to indicate that dinner would be served in about twenty minutes, and requested each person's preference, from rare to well done, for their main course, which was filet mignon.

Vicente, clearly the comedian of the group, pretended to appear aghast. "What? No tacos?"

I found myself really liking these men.

I proposed a toast: "Let us raise our glasses to celebrate working together across party lines and national borders, to create an even greater Mexico for all the Mexican people."

Peña Nieto added, "And here is to new and old friends!"

I spoke up. "I would like to say a few words. Since I sent Jacob to Mexico last week, my idea has grown a bit. We would like to give Mexico the equivalent of thirty of our maximum donations. That will be three hundred billion dollars. But we will want to see a minimum of thirty different areas supported by that. We want the money to be mostly spent within five years, and we want to sign off on your overall plans before we deliver the funds.

"We also want to make sure that there is no corruption, real or perceived, so it is important that none of you benefit financially from any of the projects, and that the Thomas Protocol does not eventually own any of the assets you will build. The state or country should be the owner of any assets. We don't want any credit. You can say who funded the project, if you like, but from there, give the credit to the Mexican people.

"And lastly, I want you all to be paid for your work. Create a board of directors, and we will fund a payment of two hundred and fifty thousand dollars per year, for the next ten years, for each president who sits on the board."

The six of them burst into some Mexican song of celebration. It was in Spanish. I have no idea what it was, but they enjoyed it, so I just smiled while they sang. When they were done, we all drank our champagne. It was a night to celebrate.

After dinner, anchored at the far end of Indian Arm, we sat outside on the deck and enjoyed the cool evening air. Everyone was so happy. I was so happy. Old Luis seemed happiest of all. He kissed me on each cheek and hugged me before he retired to his cabin for the night. The rest of us were up until about one a.m., chatting, drinking, and discussing ideas for the future of a renewed Mexico.

I could not have been prouder to have helped bring this together. Jacob, who did the real work, was with us and had been quiet most of the evening. He was sitting there listening, smiling, and nodding. It might have been the booze, but I was pretty sure one of those seven deadly sins was showing itself again. Pride. It was always pride it seemed. He was so proud of all this. And he should be. His family's work had made it all possible.

Little did I know at that time, that much of his silence was because he had cut ties with his own father earlier that day. But there he was, surrounded by six selfless leaders, working together, laughing, and trying to change the world. Jacob later told me that he had realized that evening what real fathers were like: They were like these men. Selfless and supportive, happy, and maybe even a little drunk once in a while. He said he'd felt taller being among them.

It was a wonderful evening all around. Oh … and if anyone asks, Vicente says "fuck" a lot. Crazy bastard. You couldn't help but love the guy!

CHAPTER 89

I had helicoptered to the office early, and my first call in the morning was from Ursula. After the usual pleasantries, she got down to business.

"Steve, I have a problem that you can solve for me, but it will take some very serious consideration on your part."

"How can I help, Ursula?"

"Just to give you a sense of our normal fee structure, to manage funds and investments for a client we normally charge a rate somewhere between point two five and one point two five percent of a fund's annual value. With the Thomas Funds, and the nature of the 'buy and hold' investment strategy, the workload was relatively small, considering that the fund's size was so massive. But even so, we actually have a staff of forty-seven people who work on nothing but monitoring and growing the Thomas fund. When the total annual fee on your account reached seven billion dollars a year, my father capped the fees at that amount. That was a few decades ago. Even at point two five percent, our normal fee last year would have been nearly ten times that amount.

"So, what I am asking is this: Because we flat-rated the fees on the period of growth, I want to ask that we flat-rate the fees on the liquidation years as well, and on the growth of the new fund you have established. Anything less for the bank and we will be in some serious financial difficulty in terms of revenue, dividends, and perhaps even solvency. We have come to rely too heavily on the Thomas Funds, but suffice it to say … that is where we are at."

I was shocked. I hadn't really considered how all of this change had to be impacting their bottom line. "Ursula, there is so much money involved here, why would I want to do anything to damage the GCBS? That would be both arrogant and ungrateful. Let's leave the fees at the flat rate and keep it there indefinitely. Fair enough?"

"Oh, my goodness … thank you, Herr Thomas. That will work well for us, and my first crisis as president of the bank has been averted. You made that all too easy."

"Other than people trying to kill me, the bank has made it pretty easy for me too!"

After an almost imperceptible pause, she chuckled a bit uncomfortably at my somewhat tasteless joke, which I had regretted the instant it left my mouth. *Her father was just killed at the bank, you moron!* I was about to apologize when her professionalism shone through once more and she carried on.

"Yes well … thank you again, Steve. Now, I will let you get back to work. Please tell Jacob to call his mother, okay?

CHAPTER 90

It was the end of the workday in Zurich, and Ursula signed onto her computer, keyed in some special codes designed to make the connection untraceable, and then keyed in a series of codes to take her into a special section of the internet.

Opening a specific page, she deleted the earlier message and posted a new one. Then she launched the page and closed out of the account.

She picked up her phone and called a special number. When the line beeped, she punched in her security code. A recorded voice on the line told her it was prepared to record her message.

"Check the dark web for instructions, new orders loaded."

With that, she hung up her phone, and called her assistants back into her office, and relayed the good news about the Thomas Funds and the new fee agreement. Then she clapped her hands together briskly and got down to business.

They had some banking to do.

CHAPTER 91

LARKMAN, WYOMING

The men had started to assemble. Only three men this time. They would map out a strategy, gather their information, and then two of them would set out on this mission. Small, fast, and efficient.

They had called in for instructions at eight o'clock that morning, and heard, "Check the dark web for instructions, new orders loaded."

Once they accessed the dark web, there were far more detailed instructions ending with "Be prepared to act within fourteen days. Immediate Go Order."

The instructions on the dark web gave all the details they needed. A name, home address, vehicle driven, and photograph. Based on their normal code, they knew the hit was scheduled for five days from now.

Their target was a person of importance, and this death would either cause some sort of international incident or would be quietly covered up. They would be airborne within twelve hours. Another long flight to Europe.

Their travel plans were to drive to Bozeman and catch a flight to Chicago. They would then catch a separate flight to Frankfurt, Germany. Next, they would drive from Frankfurt to Nuremberg, where they would switch vehicles and pick up a small black SUV and weapons, provided to them by a contact in that city. They would then drive to their final location where they would have two days to track and monitor their target.

As morning came, the two men grabbed their gear, said goodbye to the colonel, and began their journey.

CHAPTER 92

We had been through a few busy days. The Mexican leaders had returned home two days earlier, and had made an announcement upon their return. President Peña Nieto got some good press for a change, and spoke about a brighter future for all Mexicans. His popularity had risen to 31 percent. While his speech was going on and on, I imagined Vicente mumbling "fuck," and even though I was just imagining it, it made me laugh. I really liked all those guys. Such decent men. They had tried so hard but had left their terms in office feeling like there was so much left undone.

Today, I was to receive a presentation on African initiatives. Jack had created teams for each continent, and he and the African team were in the boardroom, with a full presentation to give on their initial findings about a continent filled with so many complications.

The presentation was to be made by the team leader of the African team. Clearly a bit nervous, Kabeera Kamau, who was from Nairobi, Kenya, was standing at the head of the board table. Her team surrounded the table, and was joined by Jacob, Jack, and myself. She had the awkward habit of looking only at me as she began her presentation and ignoring the rest of the room. It was clear she was trying very hard to make both a good impression and a good presentation. She was only about a minute into her presentation when I was reminded that I had never even met most of the people in the room.

I stood up. "Kabeera, please forgive me for interrupting."

She stopped and stood motionless. Jack looked at me a bit strangely, as I got up and walked to the front of the room.

"Kabeera, it occurs to me that I have never even shaken your hand or met you before. That makes me feel like a bit of a jerk. Please accept my apology and let me say how good it is to be working with you."

She immediately accepted the apology. "No, that's fine, no problem, you are a very busy man."

"Not too busy to point out that we are all in this together. Every single person in this room wants to help Africa to improve, to end starvation, provide water, and help the people in their daily lives. But let's start by getting to know everyone in this room just a bit, first. I think when you take a group of people and turn them into a group of friends, you can accomplish a lot together. So, if you don't mind, let's go around the table. Tell us who you are, where you are from originally, and why you wanted to join this team.

"I will start. I'm Steve Thomas. Up until a couple of months ago, I was a mild-mannered retired guy enjoying a quiet existence. Now they call me the world's richest man, and the world's greatest phi-lanthropist. I guess we will see about that. I only came to work here because Jack told me I had to."

Everyone laughed and looked at Jack, who smiled and shrugged.

"But I want to be part of this team, because together, we have a once-in-a-century chance to truly make a difference in the hearts, minds, and lives of people everywhere, and without fine people like all of you, I could accomplish very little. I want you to know that I remind myself every morning to stay humble, and be grateful for this opportunity I have been given. So … everyone, that's me. Kabeera, you're next."

She smiled and joined in. "My name is Kabeera Kamau, and I grew up in Nairobi. I was one of the lucky Africans who came from a family who had some money, a good home, and an education. I am on this team because I want to make the world a better place, and in particular, to help the African people, many of whom are some of the poorest on the planet."

She pointed to the person next to her, and we went around the table. Twenty-five members of the team, and then Jacob, Jack, and back to me.

The atmosphere in the room had totally changed.

"Okay, Kabeera, let's restart that presentation from the top. Take it away!"

Kabeera was almost glowing. Now she was comfortable, animated, funny, and in the zone.

She quoted research from an organization in Africa, and added in some general goals from the African Union. Their research asked nearly sixty thousand African citizens from thirty-two countries about their top issues. Its findings meshed tremendously well with our initiatives.

In order of priority, education was number one. Not surprisingly, healthcare was the next major area where Africans wanted to see more spending. Agriculture was third, and this included everything from land, to water, and to having enough food.

Infrastructure was big too, and it was seen not just as better roads and bridges but as a vehicle for food distribution and economic opportunity. If you can't move people and goods, you can't succeed, or feed your people.

Energy concerns were a priority throughout the continent. Access to consistent, reliable, and especially renewable energy was something developing countries needed.

Unemployment was naturally an issue. Even if employed, many people earned very little money. The average unemployment rate across countries surveyed was 23 percent.

I would have guessed, as an outsider, that access to clean water would have been the number one issue. However, while clean water was certainly a concern among Africans, it depended a great deal on the region.

Shockingly to me, poverty ranked well down the priority list. Food security, food shortages, and famine concerns varied greatly across the continent.

"What can we learn from studies like this one?" Kabeera asked us rhetorically, before giving us the answer. "It's all about listening and responding on a micro level. We see that the importance of listening at a local level before making decisions cannot be understated. Delivering a water solution to a country that didn't have a water problem, or food to a nation with effective food distribution is just foolish, and confirms to Africans that outside countries think they know better. We need to listen to the people we want to help.

"Governments, non-governmental organizations, and world leaders know that many factors matter when considering how to help Africa. Success for the Thomas Protocol will start by listening to the concerns of African citizens. Young people want jobs and education, older people want healthcare and agricultural development. We have to listen.

"This is just our preliminary presentation, Steve, and we know we still have to drill down within each country to see what the biggest concerns are for that nation, and then come back with recommendations for approval. Finally, I want to thank my colleagues for their work on this. Now … does anyone have any questions?"

Everyone applauded. Questions were asked and answered, and then the room grew silent again.

Jack spoke up. "Well done, Kabeera, and well done to the team. I think this is a great start. Now, please tell Steve what you have in mind for the next step."

Kabeera looked mildly nervous again. "Steve, we would like to suggest that we take you on a fact-finding and listening tour of several African countries, getting our feet on the ground. You can meet with government and business leaders, while we fan out into communities to see the real problems first hand. We would like to leave in seventeen days. Oh, and uh … we already have all the plans made, and uh … we heard that you like to travel."

I sat quietly for a minute, trying to suppress a grin, and looked around the table at the faces of the team who were looking so hopefully at me.

"Kabeera, do you work for me, or do I work for you?"

Before she could begin to answer, I held up my hand and turned away a bit, "No, don't answer that. I already know the answer. Apparently, I work for you!" Both Kabeera and the team broke up laughing. "Tell me when we leave and I will be ready. Well done Kabeera, and to all of you. Fantastic initiative. I am proud of you."

I stood up to leave, "Let's go to Africa and make a difference. Jacob will coordinate everything with you from here. Thanks, team. Well done."

The room erupted in applause again and everyone was smiling as Jacob and I left the room, waving goodbye as we went. What a team. These people were amazing.

I wondered if I would get to ride an elephant. I really wanted to ride an elephant. I wondered if they even allowed that anymore. Yeah, okay … I'm still a kid at heart. Sorry.

CHAPTER 93

The flight from Chicago had been long, boring, and cramped in economy. The men had sat separately and tried to sleep so as to not have to engage in conversation with their seat mates, nodding and grunting occasionally to ward off conversation. The two hit men landed at the massive Frankfurt Airport. Frankfurt is a major international hub airport, and nearly every plane at the gates was either a 747 or an Airbus A380. Massive jet after massive jet. They weren't in Larkman anymore.

They cleared through customs and immigration, using not-quite-so-fake passports. These had been issued to them through the CIA two years before, so they were legitimate government issued passports, just not in their real names.

Using a driver's licence and credit card with a fake name, they rented a car and began the drive to Nuremberg. It was about a two-and-a-half-hour drive. Using the GPS on one of their phones, they found the house they were looking for. They parked the rental car down the block, walked to the house, and went to the rear door as instructed. The door opened as they approached. The man inside had been watching for them.

They were welcomed inside. The house had a small garage that exited onto the street in front. Inside the small black SUV were two handguns, and one fully automatic M-16 rifle with a twenty-round clip and three additional clips. These were all the weapons they had requested. There were also two balaclava ski masks, and black surgical gloves.

There was a significant payment that would be deposited into this man's Swiss bank account for supplying the vehicle and weapons.

Once inside the vehicle, the garage door was opened. Trying hard not to attract any attention, the hit men quietly exited onto the street and drove away. The whole process had taken less than four minutes.

Their next and last destination was about one hour and forty-five minutes away. They would rent a hotel room for one night and change hotels the next night. In the meantime, they would begin to track their target.

After two days of tracking and determining the target's patterns, the hit team was ready. The target's car was parked in the street in front of the target's home.

A small black SUV had managed to park directly in front of the car during the night. At 6:33 a.m., the target exited the home. After settling into the driver's seat and clicking the seat belt into its lock, his eyes were drawn to the opening up of the back-window gate of the SUV parked in front of him. For an instant, he saw a man in a black balaclava, and then a torrent of bullets fired. The full clip of twenty bullets ripped through the windshield of the car. Ten of them slammed into the target's body, mainly in his upper chest. Four bullets shattered his skull, and six more destroyed his neck and throat, nearly severing his head.

The black SUV pulled away at moderate speed, and drove down the street. The execution had taken less than three seconds. The SUV was gone before anyone could even look out their window.

Running on adrenaline, the hit men from Larkman had elevated heart rates for the next ten minutes. They muttered "nice job" to each other, and then drove on in silence, heading for Nuremberg, where they would switch cars and return to the Frankfurt airport.

Once on the highway, the man in the passenger seat called the special number and punched in his security code.

"Report?"

"Target eliminated."

The line went dead.

Back on a quiet street in Munich, slumped backward over the broken front bucket seat of his car, was the ripped and torn body of Rolf Van Vloten. Jacob's father was dead.

CHAPTER 94

Ursula was in her office at the GCBS when Noah came in at five fifteen p.m.

"Frau Van Vloten, we have two men from the Federal Intelligence Service in the outer office, and they would like to see you."

"What do they want?"

"I have no idea, Frau."

"All right, Noah, please show them in."

Noah returned quickly to the outer office, and within seconds was showing the two gentlemen into her office. After they showed Ursula their official identification, she motioned for them to be seated at the board table.

"Now, how can I be of service to you, gentlemen?"

"Frau Van Vloten, we have some very bad news."

Ursula placed a hand on her upper chest, "Oh my God, not Jacob I hope?"

"Jacob? Uh, no, Frau Van Vloten, we are here about your ex-husband. We heard from our counterparts in the German BND, and well … they have advised us that Herr Rolf Van Vloten was found shot to death in his vehicle earlier today. We are very sorry."

"OH MY GOD!" Ursula shrieked. She stood, then sat, then stood again and paced back and forth, one hand on her hip and another on her forehead.

"Do they know who did it, or why?"

"So, you were obviously aware your ex-husband worked for the BND?"

"Yes, yes, I have known for many years. I know he shouldn't have told me, but he did."

She sat again. "Oh my God, this is horrible." She had both hands on her forehead now as she looked down at the tabletop for a few moments.

"Would there have been anyone from your circle that would have had a reason to want Rolf dead? With the recent death of your father, this all seems more than coincidental."

"I can't imagine."

Ursula realized she had not cried yet. She rose, went to her desk and got some tissue, and facing away from the officers, pretended to sob slightly, blowing her nose, and wiping her eyes.

CHAPTER 95

Jacob was in my office at about eight forty-five a.m. We were chatting about the upcoming Africa trip when Andrew burst into my office along with Dan and Joe.

"SIR! Oh my God … Jacob, you are in here. Thank goodness."

"Andrew, what's going on? What do you need Jacob for?"

Jacob was sitting across my desk in an armchair. Andrew did something rare. He sat down. Sitting in the chair next to Jacob, he turned to face him and leaned forward in his chair.

"Jacob, I have some bad news for you. I just heard from the Guardian Security office in Munich that your father was killed early this morning."

"What? Jesus Christ … What?" Jacob turned pale and he looked like he might faint.

I got up and got some water and a couple of aspirin. "Jacob, take these and drink."

He took the pills, and then sat forward in his chair with his elbows resting in his lap and his upper body bent way over. His shoulders started to shake. There was no sound. Then he reared back and we saw his face, contorted in a mask of tears. The silence was broken as a huge burst of pain and rage and sorrow roared from his lungs.

He sobbed, and then he sobbed some more. None of us knew where to let our eyes come to rest. Joe and Dan left the office and stood outside the door. I buzzed Paige and asked her to find Zachary, fast. I went around my desk and knelt beside Jacob's chair, putting an arm around his shoulders. He leaned into me and continued to shake, racked by more quiet sobs.

"Oh, Steve ... oh my God ... Why? What the fuck is going on in this fucking world?"

Still sobbing, he turned to Andrew. "Oh my God, is ... is my mother okay?"

"Yes Jacob, our Zurich office has been protecting her since the death of your grandfather, remember? We have increased the size of her detail until we know what the hell is going on. We are going to protect you too. It's going to be okay."

"Going to be okay? Seriously? Oh my God ..."

Zach burst through the door. Dan had informed him in the hallway of what had happened. He rushed to Jacob's side and took over my role. He just kept holding a crushed Jacob. After a few minutes, Jacob regained much of his composure and turned to address Andrew.

"Andrew, what do we know about this? How did he die? Don't hold back; I want to know."

"We can talk about that later, Jacob."

"NO I want to know NOW!" he shouted. "Please, Andrew."

I spoke up. "Okay, let's everyone go and sit on the sofas." I opened a cabinet in one corner of the room and poured everyone a cognac. Yeah, it was morning, but it was appropriate.

Jacob and Zach were sitting next to each other now. Jacob looked like a little boy. Hands in his lap, red-eyed and red-faced. Zachary sat tight to him with a hand on his knee.

Andrew gave his report. "Jacob, I don't know how much of this you are aware of, but your father was an employee of the German Foreign Intelligence Service, known as the BND. He has worked for them his whole adult life. At this point, we don't know why your dad was killed. It could have been for any number of reasons, or for enemies he has made in his work, but he was assassinated this morning in a professional killing, right in front of his flat. They shot him in his car. That's about all we have for now, but we will stay in touch with my contacts in the BND. I will keep you posted."

"Hold it... My papa was a spy? What the fuck? Huh? Is my mother in danger? I mean, my grandfather was killed and now my papa... Is Mama next... or me?"

"Jacob, as we told you, your mom has protection in Zurich, and you have protection here. You are both safe. As for your dad, I have not been told much. They acknowledged that he's been an agent since he was twenty-four. That's all I know. Until we know more, you will have round-the-clock protection."

Andrew looked at me for approval, and I gave him a vigorous nod of affirmation.

I took over. "Jacob, no one can ever replace a man's father, but we are all here to support you, and if there is anything I can do for you, you just have to ask. Zachary is here; we all are. I think maybe we should get you back to the hotel or to the yacht where you can rest and grieve in a more private setting. Is there anything I can do for you right now?"

He sniffled, and appeared completely empty. Looking at the ground, he shook his head.

Zachary took him by the hand. "Come on, let's go back to the hotel. Andrew, how should we get there?"

Andrew spoke into his sleeve, and the office door opened. Six men were ready to escort them downstairs to the vehicles and get them back to the hotel and into their suite.

After they left, I looked at Andrew. "What the fuck is going on? This is weird shit, my friend."

"You've got that right, sir. I have no explanation. I have no idea if this is related or unrelated to the Altermatt killing. I am putting some extra security on you again. Consider us back to SECPRO 1 for the next while."

"Roger that. You know what's also weird, Andrew? Somehow... I've moved past fear. I'm not the least bit scared or even intimidated right now. I am just pissed off that this kind of shit seems to be following this money. Let's do what we can to help get the killer."

I walked Andrew to my office door. And patted him on the back as he left.

"Paige, call the transport group; we'll be heading to Munich in the morning."

CHAPTER 96

Ursula met with the chairman of the board of the General Commercial Bank of Switzerland in his office. She advised him of Rolf's death, and the news that would likely come out that he was with the German spy agency. This meant that the current president of the GCBS was still technically married to a German spy, and that the last president of the bank had been the father-in-law of a German spy. The media would go crazy.

She knew this could cause reverberations within the bank and damage the confidence of their clients and shareholders, but she was certain she could weather the storm. Out of professional courtesy, she offered her resignation, and to her utter shock, Grohmann actually accepted it—immediately and without hesitation.

He asked her to wait, while he called security, explained the situation, and had them "assist" her off the premises. She was not allowed to return to her office. The guards retrieved her coat and purse, demanded she turn over keys, passes, and security codes, and she was escorted to the lobby door. Six Guardian Security men were waiting outside to drive her home.

Helmut Grohmann, the chairman, contacted Noah, and asked him to bring Jeffrey and Julian to his office.

While they were on their way, he contacted the head of compliance and ordered him to have their stock trading halted on both stock markets where it traded, which were the London FTSE and the NYSE, until an announcement was made.

He then contacted the head of internal security and ordered Ursula's office door sealed and the authorities notified. He had no idea if there was anything to be concerned about in that office, but they had to follow protocol, and if Ursula had been involved in any way with her husband's activities, they needed to make certain that evidence was preserved.

Noah, Jeffrey, and Julian were now standing in front of his desk.

"Gentlemen, first I must ask you to keep what I'm about to tell you in the strictest of confidence. I have just accepted Frau Van Vloten's resignation."

Clearly shocked, the three assistants looked at one another and shuffled a bit.

"Apparently, her husband was a German spy. We have no idea yet if this involves the bank. We have sealed her office, contacted the authorities, and halted trading on our stock. Because you worked so closely with her, I am quite sure the authorities will have questions for each of you. For now, I want all three of you to go home and stay there until we contact you. Tell no one anything about this. It will legally complicate your lives if you do. Do each of you understand?"

The three young men all nodded.

"Once we have met with the authorities, we will ask them to meet with you and take your statements. Then you may return to work. Don't worry about your pay; you will be on paid leave for now, and we will look forward to your speedy return. Thank you in advance for your complete cooperation in this matter. Go now, and again, don't even speak to one another about this. Speak to no one. I cannot emphasize it any stronger. Understood?"

All three nodded, and said, "Yes, Herr Grohmann."

With their minds reeling, the three young men headed for the exits, and as true Swiss banking professionals, they did not speak a word. As instructed, they collected their coats and left the building silently.

Grohmann then issued a communication to the board of directors advising them of what had happened. He followed that up with a statement to the staff, informing them of the immediate resignation of Frau Ursula Van Vloten, and indicated that he would be the acting president on an interim basis.

Grohmann knew this was going to be a very long night.

CHAPTER 97

Back at the hotel, Jacob had taken a long shower, thinking the whole time that the very last memory his father would have formed was of his only son severing all ties with him. The guilt he was feeling weighed on him like a ton of bricks.

Just in case he needed anything, Zachary monitored him closely, and sat quietly in the bathroom while Jacob showered. Jacob dried off and moved into the living room, curling up on the couch. Zach brought him a cup of hot chocolate. Jacob was silent, looking off into some middle distance, seeming to not focus on anything. Zach turned on the television to provide a distraction and tuned in to a home improvement show that Jacob liked.

Steve had Paige call his personal doctor to stop by the hotel. She examined Jacob, and could see he was suffering from some mental shock and likely a deep depression brought on by the obvious. These were natural human emotions. Dr. Leisa Withers left Zach with a dozen lorazepam tablets (Ativan), with instructions on their use, and advised that the tiny tablets would not only calm Jacob but also help him sleep. She believed Jacob would be fine in a day or two, but she would come back in the morning to check on him.

Jacob put two of the tiny pills under his tongue as instructed and within minutes was feeling much calmer.

As Jacob relaxed more, he began to cry a little. Although he would continue to carry a deep sadness and guilt for several days, after a few hours, he was regaining his normal composure.

"Oh my God, Zachary, I didn't even call my mother! Where is my phone?"

Zachary got through to Ursula on her cell phone, expressed his condolences, and handed the phone to Jacob.

"Mama, this is terrible."

"Jacob, I am so glad to hear from you. I tried to call but your phone must have been off."

Zachary had turned the ringer off the night before when they went to bed.

"Mama, a spy? Papa was a spy? What the fuck?"

"I know, dear. It is very shocking. Shocking indeed."

"Did you know about him being a spy, Mama?"

"Today was the first I ever heard of it, dear. I guess he was good at his job. By the way, you will find out soon that I tendered my resignation at the bank today. This whole matter with the German BND would have brought great damage to the bank's reputation."

"Surely they didn't accept your resignation—"

"Jacob, lambs have to be sacrificed. They accepted my resignation in a heartbeat, although I confess I was completely shocked by that. I was escorted off the property within minutes. They made me feel like a criminal."

"Those fuckers! You have virtually given your life to that bank, and Opa *actually* gave his life for that bank!"

"Now, dear, this is life. I will be fine. I never need to work again, but I would have rather left under better circumstances."

"What is happening with Papa's body, and the funeral and stuff?"

"I am not sure yet, Jacob. I will call as soon as I know anything. I love you, dear. Come home soon."

Jacob ended the call on his cell phone.

Zachary asked, "How did she sound?"

For the first time, Jacob realized she had seemed remarkably calm, not emotional at all… no sobs, not choked up… "She must be in shock. It was like she had ice water in her veins. Such a strong woman. Not like the emotional mush of a son she gave birth to."

Zachary couldn't help rolling his eyes. "She has *always* had ice water in her veins." He immediately regretted saying anything.

Jacob looked at him a bit harshly for a second, and then deliberately leaned over sideways on the couch, laying his head in Zachary's lap and closing his eyes. The Ativan had done the trick, and he drifted off to sleep within minutes.

Meanwhile in Zurich, Ursula was cursing herself. She had just told Jacob she knew nothing about Rolf being a spy, while earlier she had told the foreign intelligence officer she had known about it for years. Such a small, simple lie, but she had tripped up.

CHAPTER 98

Sitting in a locked interview chamber at the *Polizeiinspektion Nürnberg*, the Nuremberg Police Station, were the two killers from Larkman. Both were handcuffed, leg shackled, and not happy.

When they had arrived at the house to drop off the SUV, they found the garage door open, and pulled inside as they had been instructed. They were to leave the guns in the vehicle for disposal, and exit through the back door of the house, leaving the same way they had entered. As they came through the door from the garage into the house, they walked into a trap. Eight men in black fatigues, with raised weapons, started yelling at them to get down on the ground.

The hit men were unarmed and complied immediately.

The authorities had been monitoring the house for weeks. They had eavesdropping equipment in place, and hidden cameras inside as well as out front. A team had trailed them from Nuremberg to Munich, and followed their every move. The SUV had listening devices and tracking devices. Overly confident, the Larkman boys had not even noticed.

The men refused to answer any questions, and demanded both a lawyer and access to the American embassy. Both requests were denied. This was not a standard police investigation. This involved espionage, and as such, the rules were different. They had just murdered an official of the German government. They were now officially classified as foreign terrorists and subject to a different set of laws.

Their interrogation would be handled by senior members of the BND, who were not known for their considerate and kind interview techniques.

A special armoured vehicle for transporting prisoners arrived at the Polizeiinspektion Nürnberg, and the two prisoners were loaded into the vehicle for transport to Camp Nikolas in Pullach, about two and a half hours away. They would be held there at the BND compound for interrogation. The vehicle left Nuremberg with the two men locked in the back, and drove south with a police escort. These terrorists were considered extremely high-value targets, and would be held secretly until their silence had been broken. The BND had them dead to rights anyway. The idiots had been dumb enough to use their own cell phones for a GPS routing to the house in Nuremberg, to the house in Munich, and then back again. The two killers were like terrorist versions of Hansel and Gretel, leaving a trail of electronic breadcrumbs behind them.

They would talk. Camp Nikolaus had a way of making people talk.

No one found out if they ever revealed anything or not. They simply vanished. The hit men from Larkman, Wyoming were never seen again, and the BND never admitted or acknowledged that they ever had the two men in custody.

CHAPTER 99

Morning came to Zurich, and the GCBS was filled with people. The chairman wanted to make sure that there were no problems or issues created by Ursula's conduct or associations, and the best way to achieve that was through a deep investigation and total transparency.

Inside Ursula's unsealed office, her communications for the last thirty-six months were being reviewed. Every phone call, both incoming and outgoing, were analyzed and compared against phone numbers of interest to authorities. These were all easily traceable through the bank's systems, which kept complete records. The calls were not recorded, but certain patterns would emerge if there was trouble. The Federal Intelligence Service coordinated with other allies on all potential bank fraud or crimes. They took a data dump of Ursula's communications, and another dump of Altermatt's, and ran them through one of their private contractor sites.

There were no matches on Altermatt's data. He was clean.

On Ursula's call records, there were six matches, all to the same number in the US. The number, the NSA said, was connected through a series of security measures to an operational group of domestic terrorists, who also acted as guns for hire, and were located somewhere in Wyoming.

Ursula's computer was even more fruitful. The hackers given the job to dig into her computer activities quickly found pathways that had been used to enter the dark web, and were even able to locate specific web pages. They could also determine, through keystroke recordings, that her computer was used to enter messages onto a web page used by the same American domestic terrorist group that was connected with Ursula's calls.

What they found were four kill orders on Steve Thomas, the last two of which would also have killed her son, although she was likely unaware that he was with the group at the time. There was also one kill order on Wilhelm Altermatt, and the last one on Rolf Van Vloten.

They also found that she had syphoned off $47 million from the Thomas funds in the last several days, and stashed it in a numbered account in Bermuda.

The analysts were able to report all of this after only about eight hours of work, and reported it to both the Federal Intelligence Service and to GCBS Chairman Grohmann. Ursula thought she was much smarter than she proved to be. Her tracks were everywhere.

The local police were contacted and an arrest warrant issued for Frau Ursula Van Vloten. The charges were bank fraud, theft, two counts of murder, and multiple counts of conspiracy to commit murder. And that was just for starters. The attack in Vancouver would fall under Canadian law, so they could not charge her for that one, but they would have her in custody within the hour.

CHAPTER 100

After we waited behind eight other aircraft for our turn, Protocol 1 was wheels up from Vancouver International Airport at 8:17 a.m.

I had to get Jacob back to Europe. We were heading to Munich to see about his father's remains and burial.

The regular passengers on board were Jacob, Zachary, Paige, and me. For security, Andrew led two security details of eight men each.

Jacob was feeling quite a bit better today, and while quiet and clearly saddened, he seemed normal. He had brought along a couple of books to try to take his mind off things. He was lying on the couch in one of the smaller staterooms, reading and drinking a morning beer.

The rest of us were in the forward salon. Andrew was briefing us on what was going to be done in Zurich that day with the routine computer and communications audit being conducted on Ursula. He felt it was unlikely it would turn up anything.

His contacts at the BND advised they had no leads on Rolf's killers, and were unsure if they would ever be found. It was described as a very professional job, and it looked like they had made a clean getaway.

As for the body, it had been analyzed and autopsied. Because of its condition, the BND had already had the remains cremated. The ashes would be available to them by tomorrow. If Jacob and Ursula didn't want them, they would be buried in a gravesite on the property of Camp Nikolaus, where other fallen agents were buried. It was considered a place of honour. Jacob could decide on that in the next twenty-four hours.

Rolf's flat, which he had occupied alone, had been sealed, and we would not be allowed in anytime soon. While Rolf had told everyone he had another woman in his life, that turned out to be a deception or part of a cover. Call it what you want, but it seemed like most of what Rolf had said or done was based on lies, deceit, and false claims.

Andrew was alerted that there was a satellite phone call for him, and it was put through to a nearby phone in the main salon.

Zach and I were sitting there, wondering what lay ahead for the next couple of days; regardless, we just wanted to support Jacob. He and Zach were becoming like sons to me, and for a guy who never had kids, that was saying something. They were fine young men, and I enjoyed their company and loved seeing them succeed so well in their tasks. It was really hard to see Jacob suffering, as it is to see anyone you care about in that state.

Andrew hung up the phone and turned toward us. He had a look of shock on his face. He slumped into a nearby chair and appeared distraught.

CHAPTER 101

Ursula was sitting in an interview room at the *Stadtpolizei Zürich, Regionalwache City* (the Zurich Police Station). The room was locked and a guard was at the door. A female officer was in the room with her. She had her rights explained, and her lawyer had been called. Ursula sat quietly. She knew not to say a word.

Less than an hour earlier, police had arrived at her home with a warrant for her arrest. Her Guardian Security detail had followed police direction, and had stepped aside so they could arrest her.

Her lawyer arrived, and when he read through the charges, he advised her that he was unable to represent her. He wanted no part of this case, and based on the charges, he wanted nothing to do with Ursula Van Vloten either. He was a business lawyer. He had never done any criminal work in his life. He left her with a couple of names and excused himself.

Ursula sat there, thinking to herself about the other choices that could have been made. Her father had told her about the fund a few weeks before contacting Steve Thomas. If only her father had listened to her pleas. The loss of those funds might have destroyed the bank. Steve Thomas knew nothing of the fund. He would not even have known the accounts existed, if they had just kept quiet.

They could have placed the matter in the hands of the court, and it would have been tied up for decades. She knew for years that Rolf had been sniffing around about the bank's holdings. It was only in hindsight that she realized he knew something about the origins of the money. If the BND was interested in it, they must have believed it was German money. Her father suspected as much, but had no proof. By getting rid of both these men, and hopefully Steve Thomas too, she could have contained the matter and saved the bank's future, as well as her own.

As she had said to Jacob, lambs must be sacrificed.

The female officer asked Ursula if she would like to make a statement. Ursula declined. They placed her in a private cell. It was nine feet long, and six feet wide. It had a single bed, thirty-inches wide, a thin mattress, sheets, a blanket, and a pillow. There was a stainless-steel sink and toilet attached to the wall. Some toilet paper, a bar of soap, and a hand towel rounded out the so-called amenities. There was a window fairly high up, and it had bars on it.

Surveying all the items in the room, she knew what she needed to do, and that she needed to do it fast. Lambs must be sacrificed.

CHAPTER 102

The colonel had not heard from his two men. They had missed two check-in calls. The payment for the job had not been received either. They were either dead or arrested. Either way, the Larkman bunker was shutting down shop, and everyone was going to ground. There would be no help for them if they had failed in their mission. He locked the door to the bunker, then chained and locked the security gate across the opening.

Inside his truck, he started the engine and quietly backed the vehicle out from under the camouflage netting covering the parking area. Then he headed down the dirt road. At the entrance, he closed the gate and chained and locked it shut, checked to make sure the no-trespassing signs were in place, and drove off. He might never be back. Then again, when the heat died down, maybe they would re-emerge ... here or somewhere else.

CHAPTER 103

Back aboard Protocol 1, and flying somewhere over the Northwest Territories in Canada, Andrew was telling us what he had heard from his contacts in the BND and from the GCBS in Zurich.

"Ursula has been arrested. They believe that she ordered the killings of her father and Jacob's father, and that she ordered four hits against you, sir, all of which failed. They said one attack was to blow up this aircraft we are riding in now... on the first night we flew it out of Zurich. Jacob was on that plane, and so was Zach. It seems she wanted the bank to keep all the money. I suppose she was angry at her father for letting the money go so easily."

"When did they arrest her?" I asked.

"She has been in custody for a couple of hours or so, and is waiting for a criminal lawyer to be located. It took some time to put the pieces together and to call me with the details."

Zach literally had his mouth open, and was shaking his head from side to side.

"How could she do all those things? We tried to love her! That fucking bitch... She was going to kill us all? What are we supposed to say to Jacob?"

I have to admit my heart was pounding, hearing all of this. I handle stress pretty well, but this was brutal.

I looked at Zachary. "I think the three of us need to talk to him together. Let's go back there, and Zach, you need to sit down with him and hold him as we tell him. He is going to take this hard."

"He has me to lean on," Zach said forcefully.

"That he does."

Then Zach muttered again, "That fucking bitch … unbelievable …"

CHAPTER 104

Ursula had been alone in the room for some time by the time the police had managed to round up a criminal defence lawyer to represent her before the Federal Court. When they came to get Ursula and opened the door, there was yet another horror. Ursula was dangling from a rope.

Ursula had torn the bed sheets into strips, fashioned a rope out of it, and hung herself from the bars on the windows. Likely she had stood on the bed, tied the rope around her neck, and then swung her feet to the right and hung there as the blood turned her face purple, and her body was deprived of air. It would not have been an easy death.

The guards rushed in, one lifted her by the waist to take the pressure off her neck while the other tried to cut her down. They shouted for someone to call an ambulance, but it was all too much effort, and far too late. She had been dead for at least an hour.

Capital punishment had been forbidden in Switzerland since it was abolished in 1942, but if a crime or set of crimes called for death, Ursula's crimes certainly did. She had ordered her father and husband executed, and had tried several times to have Steve killed. She had stolen $47 million of funds that would have been used for charity. She defrauded her bank and her employer. And almost worst of all, she betrayed her only son. If convicted, she would have been in prison every single day for the rest of her life.

Death was actually the easy way out, and Ursula knew it. The humiliation she would have felt would have killed her anyway. She could not go to prison. She would not go to prison. It would not have been survivable. The only thing she had to live for was Jacob, and she could never face him again after killing his father and his beloved grandfather. Now she wouldn't have to face him or anyone else. It may be the coward's way out, but it took more than a coward's courage to take her own life.

CHAPTER 105

Andrew was being beckoned by the flight attendant. There was another call, this time in the cockpit.

"I will be right back, sir. Just give me a minute."

Andrew returned within a couple of minutes.

"If it is possible, sir, it just got worse. Ursula Van Vloten was found dead in her cell about fifteen minutes ago. It appears she hanged herself."

"Jesus Christ…" I muttered.

"Good, it'll save me from strangling the fucking bitch myself," Zachary growled.

"Okay, guys, we need to speak to Jacob. Zach, I need you to be at your best. Be calm, loving, and supportive, got it?"

He took a deep breath, nodded, and the three of us headed to the small stateroom.

When we got there, Jacob was lying on the sofa with his feet up, his head propped up on a couple of pillows, and was reading a book. He was struggling to concentrate, and had read each of the last pages about six times, but still wasn't sure he had comprehended anything.

Zach lifted Jacob's feet, sat on the couch, and then lowered Jacob's legs into his lap.

"So, why the delegation?" Jacob looked at us and knew we were not there to deliver good news. "Oh my God, what the hell has happened now?"

Andrew spoke up and began to relay the whole story to Jacob. I sat on the arm of the couch and had my hand on Jacob's shoulder.

It took a few minutes, and by the time Andrew reached the conclusion, he seemed to have aged ten years. "They found your mother deceased in her cell about twenty minutes ago. It appears she had been dead about an hour. She hanged herself, Jacob. I am so very sorry."

Jacob had no tears. He looked at Zachary, and then at me. He had no emotion left. He felt empty and very alone. His whole family was now deceased, and apparently his mother had been a killer and his father had been a German espionage agent.

"Andrew ... so, you're saying that she ordered this very airplane, this one we are on right now, to be shot out of the sky, with all of us on board, including Zachary and me?"

"That's what I am saying. Maybe ... is it possible she didn't know you were on board?"

After a silent moment, Jacob looked at me and spoke in a soft but shockingly clear voice. "No, she wouldn't have known. I didn't tell her I was going with you guys." He didn't seem to take any comfort in that. "But she knew that other people were on board. Lots of people ...

"Steve, can we just turn this plane around? I want to go home, and by home, I mean Vancouver. I don't need to go to Munich or Zurich. There is nothing there for me. At least not today. I feel betrayed. I *am* betrayed ... and that's not something I'm going to get over easily. I probably never will ... While I honestly cannot believe any of this, I somehow know it's all true ... and we've got better things to do, right? Let's go home. Fuck the funerals. I am done."

I looked at Andrew. "Let's turn this bird around." He nodded and headed for the cockpit. Moments later, Protocol 1 banked to the right, kept turning sharply, and finally headed back the way it had come.

We headed home.

EPILOGUE

During the investigation into the deaths of Ursula and Rolf, it came out that, in all likelihood, Wilbur's original money had originated in Germany... and I felt compelled to attempt to make that right. Using the Thomas Funds, I paid the full cost of the new BND Headquarters being built in Berlin, which would open in the fall of 2018. The cost was $1.3 billion. I also paid for a new state-of-the-art football stadium, "Stadium Van Vloten," to be built in Munich, at a cost of another $600 million. Circumstantial evidence aside, the BND knew that there was no way they could definitively prove that the original bearer bonds had come from Germany, so we all shook hands and agreed the debt had been repaid.

With all this money going to Germany, I felt it was an important time to donate $5 billion to Holocaust survivors and Jewish causes. My money didn't originate from the Second World War, when the Holocaust occurred, but you cannot begin to repair flaws in the world without addressing some of its greatest atrocities. The Nation of Kumar was furious at me, and a fatwa was ordered for my execution. I shrugged it off, thinking, *Whatever*...

Contrary to my initial concerns, the American government hadn't been involved in any manner with the awful things that had transpired. They were simply the second beneficiary in a will and had missed out. The US Government was thrilled with the massive investments being made in veterans' causes, and I also promised to build a new and modern public airport on the grounds of Andrews

Air Force Base in Maryland. The "President John D. Tripplehorn International Airport," due to open in 2021, would be the biggest, most modern airport in all of the United States. The president was ecstatic to have it named after himself. As a joke, I asked Vicente Fox for twenty dollars the next time I saw him. He gave it to me, and asked what it was for, and I told him that he had just helped pay for a piece of "the fucking wall" in the Tripplehorn Airport. I thought he would never stop laughing.

I promoted Andrew to CEO of Guardian Security International. I would miss seeing him on a daily basis, but he was a security genius, had kept me alive, and deserved a more settled existence. I told him he could come along on a few of our future adventures, but only as an advisor. He had to promise to leave his gun at home. Joe Mortlock is now head of my personal security detail.

Helmut Grohmann has remained as both chairman and president of the GCBS, and focuses a vast amount of his time on the Thomas Fund. He is worth $800 million in his own right, so I feel confident that he won't feel the need to steal. So far, so good.

I hired Altermatt's three former assistants from the GCBS, Noah, Julian and Jeffrey, and they are a big help to me as the organization grows (Jeffrey still makes one hell of a good cup of tea). These sorts of brilliant young people are the ones we have been waiting for... to step up and help lead the world.

Paige is now my senior executive assistant in the office. She doesn't travel with us much anymore. She has fallen for her damn boyfriend, Angus, and wants to stay closer to home. They are getting married soon. Very soon. She seems to be putting on weight in her midsection. I haven't asked, but I am pretty sure she's eating for two. I couldn't be happier for her. Paige once said her mother would kill her if she moved in with her boyfriend. Her mom is really going to love this! Paige will be a great mom, but selfishly, I hope she returns to work quickly.

Jack Dickinson is one hell of an executive. He runs the business side brilliantly. He leaves me all the time I want to travel the world, looking for new opportunities and waving the flag for the Thomas Protocol Global Initiative. He will be here until the day he wants to retire. I have my eye on his replacement. When Jacob is ready, I will know what to do.

Kabeera Kamau is really growing in her role. Africa will soon be a better place, even though it is so damn dangerous it scares the hell out of most of us. We have to take extreme security measures there, and the "chatter" on the internet and dark web shows us every day that there are people just as anxious to kill us as to take our money. It's not just about poverty and power; it's also about religion. As I said from the beginning, you would be amazed how tough it can be to give away money.

Zachary got my house built and furnished in seventy-one days. He was way off his thirty-eight-day estimate, but it was still done in record time. He technically owes me a billion dollars for that bet we made. I told him he can owe me. He and Jacob are getting married in Vancouver soon. We will send the plane to bring all their friends over from Europe, and lend them the yacht for a great honeymoon.

And Jacob? His strength of character has served him well. I sent him to a grief therapist. It is hard to imagine losing your grandfather and both parents within weeks of each other. He quit the bank and works full time for me now. I am glad he is by my side, helping me every day. Rolf had left a letter to Jacob in his safe deposit box. After reading it, Jacob listened to his better angels and had Rolf's ashes shipped to Vancouver. We took the yacht out, as the sun was setting, and sprinkled Rolf's remains into the Pacific Ocean. With a great bottle of champagne, Jacob and Zachary proposed toasts, and shed a few tears for what might have been. Fittingly, Ursula was buried in a prison grave. Oh, and with the wedding coming up, Jacob gave me the greatest honour that the richest man in the world could be given. He asked me, Steve Thomas, if I would give him away at his wedding. I have to admit, I got very choked up when he asked. That day, I will think of his grandfather, Wilhelm Altermatt, and how proud he would have been to fulfill that role himself, and how happy he would be for the boys.

We have the money, the team, and the commitment to make the world a better place. There is so much more to do, and we are just beginning. I can hardly wait to get at it. And I won't forget to remind myself to stay humble and be grateful.

I have to head to the airport now. With everything that happened, our trip to Africa and the Middle East was delayed by a couple of months, but we leave today.

Protocol 1 is wheels up in eighty-four minutes.

Coming Spring 2019

Coming Fall 2019

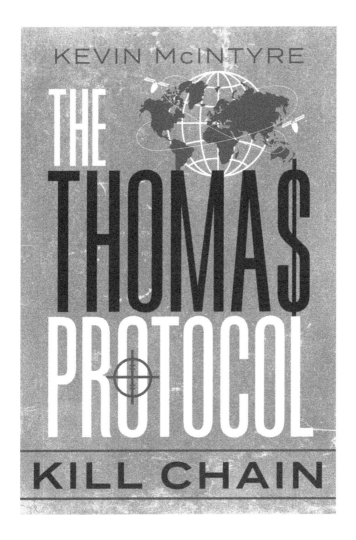

CPSIA information can be obtained
at www.ICGtesting.com
Printed in the USA
FSHW010405080119
54880FS